'Never has a character with a personality
disorder been more appealing'
Marie Claire

'You won't have to shop around to
find a more winning protagonist'
Ireland on Sunday

'Hilarious'
OK!

'Expect to laugh. A lot'
Company

'I almost cried with laughter'
Daily Mail

'A sure-fire, laugh-out-loud hit'
Sun

'High-octane,
laugh-a-minute entertainment'
Woman & Home

The Shopaholic Series

Starring the unforgettable Becky Bloomwood,
shopper extraordinaire . . .

The Secret Dreamworld of a Shopaholic
(also published as *Confessions of a Shopaholic*)

Meet Becky – a journalist who spends all her time
telling people how to manage money, and all her leisure
time spending it. But the letters from her bank manager
are getting harder to ignore. Can she ever escape this
dream world, find true love . . . and regain the use of
her credit card?

Shopaholic Abroad
Becky's life is peachy. Her balance is in the black –
well, nearly – and now her boyfriend has asked her
to move to New York with him. Can Becky keep the
man *and* the clothes when there's so much temptation
around every corner?

Shopaholic Ties the Knot
Becky finally has the perfect job, the perfect man and, at
last, the perfect wedding. Or rather, *weddings* . . . How
has Becky ended up with not one, but two big days?

Shopaholic & Sister
Becky has received some incredible news. She has a
long-lost sister! But how will she cope when she realizes
her sister is not a shopper . . . but a skinflint?

Shopaholic & Baby

Becky is pregnant! But being Becky, she decides to shop around – for a new, more expensive obstetrician – and unwittingly ends up employing Luke's ex-girlfriend! How will Becky make it through the longest nine months of her life?

Mini Shopaholic

Times are hard, so Becky's Cutting Back. She has the perfect idea: throw a budget-busting birthday party. But her daughter Minnie can turn the simplest event into chaos. Whose turn will it be to sit on the naughty step?

Shopaholic to the Stars

Becky is in Hollywood and her heart is set on a new career – she's going to be a stylist to the stars! But in between choosing clutch bags and chasing celebrities, Becky gets caught up in the whirlwind of Tinseltown. Has Becky gone too far this time?

Shopaholic to the Rescue

Becky is on a major rescue mission! Hollywood was full of surprises, and now she's on a road trip to Las Vegas to find out why her dad has mysteriously disappeared, help her best friend Suze and maybe even bond with Alicia Bitch Long-legs. She comes up with her biggest, boldest, most brilliant plan yet – can she save the day?

Other Books

Sophie Kinsella's hilarious, heart-warming
standalone novels:

Can You Keep a Secret?

Emma blurts out her deepest, darkest secrets to the sexy
stranger sitting next to her on the plane. After all, she'll
never see him again . . . will she?

The *Undomestic* Goddess

Samantha runs away from her workaholic life and
becomes a housekeeper in a country house. But what
will happen when her past catches up with her?

Remember Me?

What if you woke up and your life was perfect? Lexi's life
has fast-forwarded three years, and she has everything
she's ever wanted – and no idea how she got there.
Can she cope when she finds out the truth?

Twenties Girl

Lara has always had an overactive imagination. But when
the ghost of her great aunt Sadie shows up, asking for her
help, Lara wonders if she's losing her mind . . .

I've Got Your Number

After losing her engagement ring and her mobile phone,
Poppy takes a mobile she finds in a bin. Little knowing
that she's picked up another man in the process . . .

Wedding Night

Lottie is determined to get married. And Ben seems perfect – they'll iron out their little differences later. But their families have different plans . . .

My *Not So* Perfect Life

When Katie's ex-boss from hell books a glamping holiday at her family's farm, Katie plans to get her revenge on the woman with the perfect life. But does Demeter really have it so good? And what's wrong with not-so-perfect anyway?

Surprise Me

Sylvie and Dan have a happy marriage and are totally in sync. But when they introduce surprises into their relationship to keep things fresh, they begin to wonder if they know each other after all . . .

I Owe You *One*

When a handsome stranger asks Fixie to watch his laptop for a moment, she ends up saving it from certain disaster. To thank her, he scribbles her an IOU. Soon, small favours became life-changing.

For Young Adults

FINDING AUDREY

Audrey can't leave the house. She can't even take off her dark glasses inside. But then Linus stumbles into her life. And with him on her side, Audrey can do things she'd thought were too scary. Suddenly, finding her way back to the real world seems achievable . . .

For Younger Readers

The Mummy Fairy and Me Series

Ella's family have a big secret . . . her mummy is a fairy! She can do amazing spells with her Computawand to make delicious cupcakes, create the perfect birthday party and cause chaos at the supermarket. But sometimes the spells go a bit wrong and that's when Ella comes to the rescue!

Prepare for magic and mayhem in this sweet and funny new series for young readers.

sophie kinsella

Shopaholic
Abroad

BLACK
SWAN

TRANSWORLD PUBLISHERS
61–63 Uxbridge Road, London W5 5SA
www.penguin.co.uk

Transworld is part of the Penguin Random House group of companies
whose addresses can be found at global.penguinrandomhouse.com

Penguin
Random House
UK

First published in Great Britain in 2001 by Black Swan
an imprint of Transworld Publishers
Black Swan edition reissued 2012

A CIP catalogue record for this book
is available from the British Library.

ISBN
9780552778336 (B format)
9780552773478 (A format)

Set in 11/13pt Melior by Kestrel Data, Exeter, Devon.
Printed and bound in Great Britain by Clays Ltd, Elcograf S.p.A.

Penguin Random House is committed to a sustainable
future for our business, our readers and our planet. This book
is made from Forest Stewardship Council® certified paper.

For Gemma, who has always known the importance
to a girl of a Denny and George scarf.

ACKNOWLEDGEMENTS

Hugest thanks to Linda Evans, Patrick Plonkington-Smythe and all the fabulous Transworld team; and as always to Araminta Whitley, Celia Hayley, Mark Lucas, Nicki Kennedy, Kim Witherspoon and David Forrer.

Special thanks to Susan Kamil, Nita Taublib and all at The Dial Press, who made me so incredibly welcome in New York – and especially Zoe Rice, for a wonderful afternoon of research (shopping and eating chocolate). Also David Stefanou for the Gimlets and Sharyn Soleimani at Barneys who was so kind, and to all the people who have given me ideas, advice and inspiration along the way, in particular Athena Malpas, Lola Bubbosh, Mark Malley, Ana-Maria Mosley, Harrie Evans and all my family. And of course Henry, who has all the best ideas.

Endwich Bank
FULHAM BRANCH
3 Fulham Road
London SW6 9JH

Ms Rebecca Bloomwood
Flat 2
4 Burney Rd
London SW6 8FD

Dear Miss Bloomwood

Thank you for your letter of 15 July. I am pleased to hear that you have now been with Endwich Bank for nearly five years.

Unfortunately we do not offer a 'Five Year Bonus' as you suggest, nor a 'Clean Slate – Start Again' overdraft amnesty. I agree that both are good ideas.

I am instead prepared to extend your overdraft limit by another £500, taking it up to £4,000, and suggest that we meet before too long to discuss your ongoing financial needs.

Yours sincerely

Derek Smeath
Manager

ENDWICH – BECAUSE WE CARE

Endwich Bank
FULHAM BRANCH
3 Fulham Road
London SW6 9JH

Ms Rebecca Bloomwood
Flat 2
4 Burney Rd
London SW6 8FD

Dear Miss Bloomwood

I am glad that my letter of 18 July proved helpful.

I should however be grateful if you would refrain from referring to me personally on your television show as 'Sweetie Smeathie' and 'the best bank manager in the world'.

Although naturally I am pleased you feel this way, my superiors are a little anxious at the image of Endwich Bank which is being presented, and have asked that I write to you on the matter.

With all best wishes

Derek Smeath
Manager

ENDWICH – BECAUSE WE CARE

Endwich Bank
FULHAM BRANCH
3 Fulham Road
London SW6 9JH

Ms Rebecca Bloomwood
Flat 2
4 Burney Rd
London SW6 8FD

Dear Miss Bloomwood

Thank you for your letter of 18 August.

I was sorry to hear that keeping within your new overdraft limit is proving so difficult. I understand that the Pied à Terre summer sale does not happen every week, and I can certainly increase your limit by £63.50, if, as you say, this would 'make all the difference'.

However, I would also recommend that you come into the branch for a more comprehensive review of your financial situation. My assistant, Erica Parnell, will be pleased to set up an appointment.

Yours sincerely

Derek Smeath
Manager

ENDWICH – BECAUSE WE CARE

One

OK, don't panic. Don't *panic*. It's simply a question of being organized and staying calm and deciding what exactly I need to take. And then fitting it all neatly into my suitcase. I mean, just how hard can that be?

I step back from my cluttered bed and close my eyes, half hoping that if I wish hard enough, my clothes might magically arrange themselves into a series of neat folded piles. Like in those magazine articles on packing, which tell you how to go on holiday with one cheap sarong and cleverly turn it into six different outfits. (Which I always think is a complete con, because, OK, the sarong costs ten quid, but then they add loads of clothes which cost hundreds, and we're not supposed to notice.)

But when I open my eyes again, the clutter is all still there. In fact, there seems to be even more of it, as if while my eyes were shut, my clothes have been secretly jumping out of the drawers and running around on my bed. Everywhere I look, all around my room, there are huge great tangled piles of . . . well . . . *stuff*. Shoes, boots, T-shirts, magazines . . . a Body Shop gift basket that was on sale . . . a Linguaphone Italian course which I *must* start . . . a facial sauna thingy . . . And, sitting proudly on my dressing table, a fencing mask and sword which I bought yesterday. Only forty quid from a charity shop!

I pick up the sword and experimentally give a little

13

lunge towards my reflection in the mirror. It was a real coincidence, because I've been meaning to take up fencing for ages, ever since I read this article about it in the *Daily World*. Did you know that fencers have better legs than any other sports people? Plus if you're an expert you can become a stunt double in a film and earn loads of money! So what I'm planning to do is find some fencing lessons nearby, and get really good, which I should think I'll do quite quickly.

And then – this is my secret little plan – when I've got my gold badge, or whatever it is, I'll write to Catherine Zeta Jones. Because she must need a stunt double, mustn't she? And why shouldn't it be me? In fact she'd probably *prefer* someone British. Maybe she'll phone back and say she always watches my television appearances on cable, and she's always wanted to meet me! God, yes. Wouldn't that be great? We'll probably really hit it off, and turn out to have the same sense of humour and everything. And then I'll fly out to her luxury home, and get to meet Michael Douglas and play with the baby. We'll be all relaxed together like old friends, and some magazine will do a feature on celebrity best friends and have us in it, and maybe they'll even ask me to be . . .

'Hi Bex!' With a jolt, the happy pictures of me laughing with Michael and Catherine vanish from my head, and my brain snaps into focus. Suze my flatmate is wandering into my room, wearing a pair of ancient paisley pyjamas. 'What are you doing?' she asks curiously.

'Nothing!' I say, hastily putting the fencing sword back. 'Just . . . you know. Keep fit.'

'Oh right,' she says vaguely. 'So – how's the packing going?' She wanders over to my mantelpiece, picks up a lipstick and begins to apply it. Suze always does this in my room – just wanders about picking things up and looking at them and putting them down again. She says she loves the way you never know what you might find, like in a junk shop. Which I'm fairly sure she means in a nice way.

'It's going really well,' I say. 'I'm just deciding which suitcase to take.'

'Ooh,' says Suze turning round, her mouth half bright pink. 'What about that little cream one? Or your red holdhall?'

'I thought maybe this one,' I say, hauling my new acid green shell case out from under the bed. I bought it at the weekend, and it's absolutely gorgeous.

'Wow!' says Suze, her eyes widening. 'Bex! That's fab! Where did you get it?'

'Fenwicks,' I say, grinning broadly. 'Isn't it amazing?'

'It's the coolest case I've ever seen!' says Suze, running her fingers admiringly over it. 'So . . . how many suitcases have you got now?' She glances up at my wardrobe, on which are teetering a brown leather case, a lacquered trunk and three vanity cases.

'Oh, you know,' I say, shrugging a little defensively. 'The normal amount.'

I suppose I have been buying quite a bit of luggage recently. But the thing is, for ages I didn't have any, just one battered old canvas bag. Then, a few months ago I had an incredible revelation in the middle of Harrods, a bit like St Paul on the road to Mandalay. *Luggage*. And since then, I've been making up for all the lean years.

Besides which, everyone knows good luggage is an investment.

'I'm just making a cup of tea,' says Suze. 'D'you want one?'

'Ooh, yes please!' I say. 'And a KitKat?' Suze grins.

'Definitely a KitKat.'

Recently, we had this friend of Suze's to stay on our sofa – and when he left he gave us this huge box full of a hundred KitKats. Which is such a great thank-you present, but it means all we eat, all day long, is KitKats. Still, as Suze pointed out last night, the quicker we eat them, the quicker they'll be gone – so in a way, it's more healthy just to stuff in as many as possible.

Suze ambles out of the room and I turn to my case. Right. Concentrate. Packing. This really shouldn't take long. All I need is a very basic, pared-down capsule wardrobe for a mini-break in Somerset. I've even written out a list, which should make things nice and simple.

Jeans: two pairs. Easy. Scruffy and not quite so scruffy.

T-shirts:

Actually, make that three pairs of jeans. I've *got* to take my new Diesel ones, they're just so cool, even if they are a bit tight. I'll just wear them for a few hours in the evening or something.

T-shirts:

Oh, and my embroidered cutoffs from Oasis, because I haven't worn them yet. But they don't really count because they're practically shorts. And anyway, jeans hardly take up any room, do they?

OK, that's probably enough jeans. I can always add some more if I need to.

T-shirts: selection. So let's see. Plain white, obviously. Grey, ditto. Black cropped, black vest (Calvin Klein), other black vest (Warehouse but actually looks nicer), pink sleeveless, pink sparkly, pink—

I stop, halfway through transferring folded T-shirts into my case. This is stupid. How am I supposed to predict which T-shirts I'm going to want to wear? The whole point about T-shirts is you choose them in the morning according to your mood, like crystals, or aromatherapy oils. Imagine if I woke up in the mood for my 'Elvis is Groovy' T-shirt and I didn't have it with me?

You know, I think I'll just take them all. I mean, a few T-shirts aren't going to take up much room, are they? I'll hardly even notice them.

I tip them all into my case and add a couple of cropped bra-tops for luck.

Excellent. This capsule approach is working really well. OK, what's next?

Ten minutes later, Suze wanders back into the room, holding two mugs of tea and three KitKats to share. (We've come to agree that four sticks, frankly, doesn't do it.)

'Here you are,' she says – then gives me a closer look. 'Bex, are you OK?'

'I'm fine,' I say, rather pink in the face. 'I'm just trying to fold up this gilet a bit smaller.'

I've already packed a denim jacket and a leather jacket, but you just can't count on September weather, can you? I mean, at the moment it's hot and sunny, but it might well start snowing tomorrow. And what happens if Luke and I go for a really rustic country walk? Besides which, I've had this gorgeous Patagonia gilet for ages, and I've only worn it once. I try to fold it again, but it slithers out of my hands and onto the floor. God, this reminds me of camping trips with the Brownies, and trying to get my sleeping bag back into its tube.

'How long are you going for, again?' asks Suze.

'Three days.' I give up trying to squash the gilet into the size of a matchbox, and it springs jauntily back to shape. Feeling slightly discomfited, I sink onto the bed and take a sip of tea. What I don't understand is, how do other people manage to pack so lightly? You see businesspeople all the time, striding onto planes with only a tiny shoe-box suitcase on wheels and a smug expression. How do they do it? Do they have magic shrinking clothes? Is there some secret way to fold everything up so it fits into a matchbox?

'Why don't you take your holdall as well?' suggests Suze.

'D'you think?' I look uncertainly at my overflowing suitcase. Come to think of it, maybe I don't need three pairs of boots. Or a fur stole.

Then it occurs to me that Suze goes away nearly every weekend, and she only ever takes a tiny squashy bag. 'Suze, how do *you* pack? Do you have a system?'

'I dunno,' she says vaguely. 'I suppose I still do what they taught us at Miss Burton's. You work out an outfit for each occasion – and stick to that.' She begins to tick off on her fingers. 'Like . . . journey down, dinner, sitting by the pool, game of tennis . . .' She looks up. 'Oh yes, and each garment should be used at least three times.'

God, Suze is a genius. She knows all this kind of stuff. Her parents sent her to Miss Burton's Academy when she was eighteen, which is some posh place in London where they teach you things like how to talk to a bishop and get out of a sports car in a miniskirt. She knows how to make a rabbit out of chicken wire, too.

Quickly I start to jot some broad headings on a piece of paper. This is much more like it. Much better than randomly stuffing things into a case. This way, I won't have any superfluous clothes, just the bare minimum.

Outfit 1: Sitting by pool (sunny)
Outfit 2: Sitting by pool (cloudy)
Outfit 3: Sitting by pool (bottom looks huge in morning)
Outfit 4: Sitting by pool (someone else has same swimsuit)
Outfit 5:

In the hall the phone rings, but I barely look up. I can hear Suze talking excitedly – then a moment later she appears in the doorway, her face all pink and pleased.

'Guess what?' she says. 'Guess what?'

'What?'

'Box Beautiful have sold out of my frames! They just phoned up to order some more!'

'Oh Suze! That's fantastic!' I shriek.

'I know!' She comes running over, and we have a big hug, and sort of dance about, before she realizes she's holding a cigarette and is about to burn my hair.

The amazing thing is, Suze only started making frames a few months ago – but already, she's supplying four shops in London, and they're doing really well! She's been in loads of magazines, and everything. Which isn't surprising, because her frames are *so* cool. Her latest range is in purple tweed, and they come in these gorgeous grey sparkly boxes, all wrapped in bright turquoise tissue paper. (I helped choose the exact colour, by the way.) She's so successful, she doesn't even make them all herself any more, but sends off her designs to a little workshop in Kent, and they come back, all made up.

'So, have you finished working your wardrobe out?' she says, taking a drag on her cigarette.

'Yes,' I say, brandishing my sheet of paper at her. 'I've got it all sorted out. Down to every last pair of socks.'

'Well done!'

'And the *only* thing I need to buy,' I add casually, 'is a pair of lilac sandals.'

'Lilac sandals?'

'Mmm?' I look up innocently. 'Yes. I need some. You know, just a nice cheap little pair to pull a couple of outfits together . . .'

'Oh right,' says Suze, and pauses, frowning slightly.

19

'Bex . . . weren't you talking about a pair of lilac sandals last week? Really expensive, from LK Bennett?'

'Was I?' I feel myself flush a little. 'I . . . I don't remember. Maybe. Anyway—'

'Bex.' Suze gives me a suddenly suspicious look. 'Now tell me the truth. Do you really *need* a pair of lilac sandals? Or do you just want them?'

'No!' I say defensively. 'I really need them! Look!'

I take out my clothes plan, unfold it, and show it to Suze. I have to say, I'm rather proud of it. It's quite a complicated flow chart, all boxes and arrows and red asterisks.

'Wow!' says Suze. 'Where did you learn how to do that?'

'At university,' I say modestly. I read Business and Accounting for my degree – and it's amazing how often it comes in handy.

'What's this box?' she asks, pointing at the page.

'That's . . .' I squint at it, trying to remember. 'I think that's if we go out to some really smart restaurant and I've already worn my Whistles dress the night before.'

'And this one?'

'That's if we go rock-climbing. And this – ' I point to an empty box – 'is where I need a pair of lilac sandals. If I don't have them, then this outfit won't work, and neither will this one . . . and the whole thing will disintegrate. I might as well not bother going.'

Suze is silent for a while, perusing my clothes plan while I bite my lip anxiously and cross my fingers behind my back.

I know this may seem a little unusual. I know most people don't run every single purchase past their flat-mate. But the fact is, a while ago I kind of made Suze a little promise, which was that I'd let her keep tabs on my shopping. You know. Just keep an eye on things.

Don't get the wrong idea here. It's not like I have a shopping problem, or anything. It's just that a few

20

months ago, I did get into a . . . Well. A very slight money scrape. It was really just a tiny blip – nothing to worry about. But Suze got really freaked out when she found out about it, and said that for my own good, she'd vet all my spending from now on.

And she's been as good as her word. She's very strict, actually. Sometimes I'm really quite scared she might say no.

'I see what you mean,' she says at last. 'You haven't really got a choice, have you?'

'Exactly,' I say in relief. I take the plan from her, fold it up and put it into my bag.

'Hey Bex, is that new?' says Suze suddenly. She pulls my wardrobe door open and I feel a twinge of nerves. She's frowning at my lovely new honey-coloured coat, which I smuggled into the flat the other day when she was in the bath.

I mean, obviously I was planning to tell her about it. I just never got around to it.

Please don't look at the price tag, I think feverishly. Please don't look at the price tag.

'Erm . . . yes,' I say. 'Yes, it is new. But the thing is . . . I need a good coat, in case I get asked to do an outside broadcast for *Morning Coffee*.'

'Is that likely?' asks Suze, puzzled. 'I mean, I thought your job was just sitting in the studio, giving financial advice.'

'Well . . . you never know. It's always best to be prepared.'

'I suppose so . . .' says Suze doubtfully. 'And what about this top?' She pulls at a hanger. 'That's new, too!'

'That's to wear on the show,' I reply promptly.

'And this skirt?'

'For the show.'

'And these new trousers?'

'For the—'

21

'Bex.' Suze looks at me with narrowed eyes. 'How many outfits have you got to wear on the show?'

'Well – you know,' I say defensively. 'I need a few back-ups. I mean, Suze, this is my career we're talking about. My *career*.'

'Yes,' says Suze eventually. 'Yes, I suppose it is.' She reaches for my new red silk jacket. 'This is nice.'

'I know,' I beam. 'I bought it to wear on my January special!'

'Have you got a January special?' says Suze. 'Ooh, what's it about?'

'It's going to be called Becky's Fundamental Financial Principles,' I say, reaching for my lip gloss. 'It should be really good. Five ten-minute slots, just me!'

'So – what *are* your fundamental financial principles?' asks Suze interestedly.

'Erm . . . well, I haven't really got any yet,' I say, carefully painting my lips. 'But you know. I'll make them up a bit nearer the time.' I snap my lip gloss shut and reach for my jacket. 'See you later.'

'OK,' says Suze. 'And remember. Just one pair of shoes!'

'All right! I promise!'

It's really sweet of Suze to be so concerned about me. But she doesn't need to be. To be honest, she doesn't really understand what a changed person I am. OK, I did have a very slight financial crisis earlier this year. In fact, at one point I was in debt by . . . Well. Really quite a lot.

But then I landed my job on *Morning Coffee*, and everything changed. I turned my life around completely, worked really hard – and paid off all my debts. Yes, I paid them all off! I wrote out cheque after cheque – and cleared every single outstanding credit card, every store card, every scribbled IOU to Suze. (She couldn't believe it when I presented her with a cheque for several hundred pounds. At first she didn't want to take it, but then she changed her mind and went out and bought this most amazing sheepskin coat.)

Honestly, paying off those debts was the most wonderful, exhilarating feeling in the world. It was a few months ago now – but I still feel high as I think about it. There's really nothing to beat being completely and utterly financially solvent, is there?

And just look at me now. I'm a completely different person from the old Becky. I'm a reformed character. I haven't even got an overdraft!

Two

Well, OK. I have got a bit of an overdraft. But the only reason is, I've been taking the long view recently, and investing quite heavily in my career. Luke, my boyfriend, is an entrepreneur. He's got his own financial PR company and everything. And he said something a few weeks ago which really made sense to me: 'People who want to make a million borrow a million first.'

Honestly, I must have a naturally entrepreneurial mind, because as soon as he said it, I felt this weird chord of recognition. I even found myself murmuring it aloud. He's so right. How can you expect to make any money if you don't spend it first?

So I've invested in quite a few outfits to wear on the television – plus a few good haircuts, and quite a few manicures and facials. And a couple of massages. Because everyone knows you can't perform well if you're all stressed, can you?

I've also invested in a new computer, which cost £2,000 – but is an essential item because guess what? I'm writing a self-help book! Just after I'd become a regular on *Morning Coffee*, I met these really nice publishers, who took me out to lunch and said I was an inspiration to financially challenged people everywhere. Wasn't that nice? They paid me £1,000 before I'd even written a word – and I get a lot more when it's actually published. The book's going to be called Becky

Bloomwood's Guide to Money. Or possibly Manage Money the Becky Bloomwood Way.

I haven't quite had time to start writing it yet, but I really think the most important thing is to get the title right, and then the rest will just fall into place. And it's not like I've been doing nothing. I've already jotted down *loads* of ideas about what to wear in the photograph.

So basically, it's no surprise that I'm a little overdrawn at the moment. But the point is, all that money is out there, working for me. And luckily my bank manager, Derek Smeath, is very sympathetic. He's a real sweetie, actually. For a long time we didn't get on at all – which I think was more a communications problem than anything else. But now, I really think he understands where I'm coming from. And the truth is, of course, I'm a lot more sensible than I used to be.

For example, I have a completely different attitude to shopping. My new motto is 'Buy Only What You Need'. I know, it sounds almost *too* simple – but it really does work. Before each purchase, I ask myself one question: 'Do I *need* this?' And only if the answer is 'yes' do I make the purchase. It's all just a matter of self-discipline.

So for example, when I get to LK Bennett, I'm incredibly focused and direct. As I walk in, a pair of red boots with high heels catches my eye – but I quickly look away, and head straight for the display of sandals. This is how I shop these days: no pausing, no browsing, no eyeing up other items. Not even that gorgeous new range of sequined pumps over there. I simply go straight to the sandals I want, take them from the rack and say to the assistant,

'I'd like to have these in a six, please.'

Direct, and to the point. Just buy what you need and nothing else. This is the key to controlled shopping. I'm not even going to *glance* at those cool pink stilettos, even though they'd match my new Jigsaw cardigan perfectly.

Nor those slingbacks with the glittery heels.

They are nice though, aren't they? I wonder what they look like on.

Oh God. This is really hard.

What *is* it about shoes? I mean, I like most kinds of clothes, but a fabulous pair of shoes can just reduce me to jelly. Sometimes, when no-one else is at home, I open my wardrobe and just stare at all my pairs of shoes, like some mad collector. And once I lined them all up on my bed and took a photograph of them. Which might seem a bit weird – but I thought, I've got loads of photos of people I don't really like, so why not take one of something I love?

'Here you are!'

Thank goodness, the assistant is back with my lilac sandals in a box – and as I see them, my heart gives a little leap. Oh, these are gorgeous. *Gorgeous*. All delicate and strappy, with a tiny little blackberry by the toe. I fell in love with them as soon as I saw them. They're a bit expensive – but then, everyone knows you should never skimp on shoes, because you'll hurt your feet.

I slip my feet into them with a *frisson* of delight – and oh God, they're fantastic. My feet suddenly look elegant, and my legs look longer . . . and OK, it's a tiny bit difficult to walk in them, but that's probably because the shop floor is all slippery.

'I'll take them, please,' I say, and beam happily at the assistant.

You see, this is the reward for taking such a controlled approach to shopping. When you buy something, you really feel as though you've *earned* it.

We head towards the checkout, and I keep my eyes carefully away from the rack of accessories. In fact, I barely even notice that purple bag with the jet beading.

26

And I'm just reaching into my bag for my purse, congratulating myself on being so single-minded, when the assistant says conversationally, 'You know, we've got these sandals in clementine, as well.'

Clementine?

'Oh . . . right,' I say after a pause.

I'm not interested. I've got what I came in to buy – and that's the end of the story. Lilac sandals. Not clementine ones.

'They've just come in,' she adds, rooting around on the floor. 'I think they're going to be even more popular than the lilac.'

'Really?' I say, trying to sound as indifferent as I can. 'Well, I'll just take these, I think . . .'

'Here it is!' she exclaims. 'I knew there was one around here somewhere.'

And I freeze, as she puts the most exquisite sandal I've ever seen onto the counter. It's a pale, creamy orange colour, with the same strappy shape as the lilac one – but instead of the blackberry, there's a tiny clementine by the toe.

It's instant love. I can't move my eyes away.

'Would you like to try it?' says the girl, and I feel a lurch of desire, right to the pit of my stomach.

Just look at it. It's delicious. It's the most darling shoe I've ever seen. Oh God.

But I don't need a pair of clementine shoes, do I? I don't need them.

Come on, Becky. Just. Say. No.

'Actually . . .' I swallow hard, trying to get control of my voice. 'Actually . . .' God, I can hardly say it. 'I'll just take the lilac ones today,' I manage eventually. 'Thank you.'

'OK . . .' The girl punches a code into the till. 'That'll be £89, then. How would you like to pay?'

'Er . . . Visa card, please,' I say. I sign the slip, take my bag, and leave the shop, feeling slightly numb.

27

I did it! I did it! I controlled my desires! I only needed one pair of shoes – and I only bought one. In and out of the shop, completely according to plan. You see, this is what I can do when I really want to. This is the new Becky Bloomwood.

Having been so good, I deserve a little reward, so I go to a coffee shop and sit down outside in the sun with a cappuccino.

I want those clementine shoes, pops into my head as I take the first sip.

Stop. Stop it. Think about . . . something else. Luke. The holiday. Our first ever holiday together. God, I can't wait.

I've been wanting to suggest a holiday ever since Luke and I started to go out, but he works so hard, it would be like asking the Prime Minister to give up running the country for a bit. (Except come to think of it, he does that every summer, doesn't he? So how come Luke can't?)

Luke's so busy, he hasn't even met my parents yet, which I'm a bit upset about. They asked him over for Sunday lunch, a few weeks ago, and Mum spent ages cooking – or at least, she bought apricot-stuffed loin of pork from Sainsbury's and a really posh chocolate meringue pudding. But at the last minute he had to cancel because there was a crisis with one of his clients in the Sunday papers. So I had to go on my own – and it was all rather miserable, to be honest. You could tell Mum was really disappointed, but she kept saying brightly, 'Oh well, it was only a casual arrangement' – which it wasn't. He sent her a huge bouquet of flowers the next day to apologize (or at least, Mel, his assistant, did), but it's not the same, is it?

The worst bit was that our next-door neighbours, Janice and Martin, popped in for a glass of sherry and 'to meet the famous Luke', as they put it, and when they found out he wasn't there, they kept giving me all these pitying looks tinged with smugness, because their son Tom is getting married to his girlfriend Lucy next week. And I have a horrible suspicion that they think I have a crush on him. (Which I don't – in fact, quite the reverse. But once people believe something like that, it's completely impossible to convince them otherwise. Oh God. Hideous.)

When I got upset with Luke, he pointed out that I've never met his parents, either. But that's not quite true. I have briefly spoken to his dad and step-mum in a restaurant once, even if it wasn't my most glittering moment. And anyway, they live in Devon, and Luke's real mum lives in New York. So I mean, they're not exactly handy, are they?

Still, we made up – and at least he's making the effort to come on this little holiday. It was Mel, actually, who suggested the weekend idea. She told me Luke hadn't had a proper holiday for three years, and maybe he had to be weaned gently on to the idea. So I stopped talking about holidays and started talking about weekends away – and that did the trick! All of a sudden Luke told me to set aside this weekend. He booked the hotel himself and everything. I'm *so* looking forward to it. We'll just do nothing but relax and take it easy – and spend some time with each other for a change. Lovely.

I want those clementine shoes.

Stop it. Stop thinking about them.

I take another sip of coffee, lean back and force myself to survey the bustling street. People are striding along, holding bags and chatting, and there's a girl crossing the road with nice trousers on, which I think come from Nicole Farhi and . . . Oh God.

A middle-aged man in a dark suit is coming along the road towards me, and I recognize him. It's Derek Smeath, my bank manager.

Oh, and I think he's seen me.

OK, don't panic, I instruct myself firmly. There's no need to panic. Maybe once upon a time I would have been thrown by seeing him. I might have tried to hide behind a menu, or perhaps even run away. But that's all in the past. These days, Sweetie Smeathie and I have a very honest and amicable relationship.

Still, I find myself shifting my chair slightly further away from my LK Bennett bag, as though it hasn't got anything to do with me.

'Hello, Mr Smeath!' I say brightly as he approaches. 'How are you?'

'Very well,' says Derek Smeath, smiling. 'And you?'

'Oh, I'm fine, thanks. Would you . . . would you like a coffee?' I add politely, gesturing to the empty chair opposite me. I'm not really expecting him to say yes, but to my astonishment he sits down and picks up a menu.

How civilized is this? I'm having coffee with my bank manager at a pavement café! You know, maybe I'll find a way to work this into my *Morning Coffee* slot. 'I myself prefer the informal approach to personal finance,' I'll say, smiling warmly into the camera. 'My own bank manager and I often share a friendly cappuccino as we discuss my current financial strategies . . .'

'As it happens, Rebecca, I've just written a letter to you,' says Derek Smeath, as a waitress puts an espresso down in front of him. Suddenly his voice is more serious and I feel a small lurch of alarm. Oh God, what have I done now? 'You and all my customers,' he adds. 'To tell you that I'm leaving.'

'What?' I put my coffee cup down with a little crash. 'What do you mean, leaving?'

'I'm leaving Endwich Bank. I've decided to take early retirement.'

'But . . .'

I stare at him, appalled. Derek Smeath can't leave

Endwich Bank. He can't leave me in the lurch, just as everything was going so well. I mean, I know we haven't always exactly seen eye to eye – but recently we've developed a really good rapport. He understands me. He understands my overdraft. What am I going to do without him?

'Aren't you too young to retire?' I say, aware of the dismay in my voice. 'Won't you get bored?' He leans back in his chair and takes a sip of espresso.

'I'm not planning to give up work altogether. But I think there's a little more to life than looking after people's bank accounts, don't you? Fascinating though some of them have been.'

'Well . . . yes. Yes of course. And I'm glad for you, honestly.' I shrug, a little embarrassed. 'But I'll . . . miss you.'

'Believe it or not,' he says, smiling slightly, 'I think I'll miss you too, Rebecca. Yours has certainly been one of the most . . . interesting accounts I've dealt with.'

He gives me a penetrating look and I feel myself flush slightly. Why does he have to remind me of the past? The point is, that's all over. I'm a different person now. Surely people should be allowed to turn over new leaves and start again in life?

'Your career in television seems to be going well,' he says.

'I know! It's so great, isn't it? And it pays really well,' I add, a little pointedly.

'Your income has certainly gone up in recent months,' he says and puts down his coffee cup. My heart sinks slightly. 'However . . .'

I knew it. *Why* does there always have to be a 'however'? Why can't he just be pleased for me?

'However,' repeats Derek Smeath. 'Your outgoings have also risen. Substantially. In fact, your overdraft is now higher than it was at the height of your . . . shall we say, your excesses.'

Excesses? That is so mean.

'You really must make more effort to keep within your overdraft limit,' he's saying now. 'Or, even better, pay it off.'

'I know,' I say vaguely. 'I'm planning to.'

I've just spotted a girl on the other side of the road, with an LK Bennett bag. She's holding a great big bag – with *two* shoe boxes in it.

If she's allowed to buy two pairs of shoes, then why aren't I? What's the rule that says you can only buy one pair of shoes at a time? I mean, it's so arbitrary.

'What about your other finances?' Derek Smeath is asking. 'Do you have any store card bills, for example?'

'No,' I say with a tinge of smugness. 'I paid them all off months ago.'

'And you haven't spent anything since?'

'Only bits and pieces. Hardly anything.'

Anyway what's ninety quid, really? In the greater scheme of things?

'The reason I'm asking these questions,' says Derek Smeath, 'is that I feel I should warn you. The bank is restructuring somewhat, and my successor, John Gavin, may not take quite the same relaxed approach as I have towards your account. I'm not sure you're aware quite how lenient I have been with you.'

'Really?' I say, not really listening.

I mean, suppose I took up smoking. I'd easily spend ninety quid on cigarettes without even thinking about it, wouldn't I?

In fact, think of all the money I've saved by *not* smoking. Easily enough to afford one little pair of shoes.

'He's a very capable man,' Derek Smeath is saying. 'But also very . . . rigorous. Not particularly known for his flexibility.'

'Right,' I say, nodding absently.

'I would certainly recommend that you address your

overdraft without delay.' He takes a sip of coffee. 'And tell me, have you done anything about taking out a pension?'

'Erm . . . I went to visit that independent adviser you recommended.'

'And did you fill in any of the forms?'

Unwillingly, I drag my attention back to him.

'Well, I'm just considering my options,' I say, and put on my wise, financial-expert look. 'There's nothing worse than rushing into the wrong investment, you know. Particularly when it comes to something as important as a pension.'

'Very true,' says Derek Smeath. 'But don't spend too long considering, will you? Your money won't save itself.'

'I know!' I say and take a sip of cappuccino.

Oh God, now I feel a bit uncomfortable. Maybe he's right. Maybe I should put £90 into a pension fund instead of buying another pair of shoes.

But on the other hand – what good is a pension fund of £90? That's not exactly going to keep me in my old age, is it? Ninety measly quid. And by the time I'm old, the world will probably have blown up, or something.

Whereas a pair of shoes is tangible, it's there in your hand . . .

Oh, sod it. I'm going to get them.

'Mr Smeath, I have to go,' I say abruptly, putting down my cup. 'There's something I have to . . . do.'

Now I've decided, I *have* to get back there as quickly as possible. I pick up my carrier bag and drop a fiver on the table. 'Lovely to see you. And good luck in your retirement.'

'Best of luck to you too, Rebecca,' says Derek Smeath, smiling kindly at me. 'But do remember what I've said. John Gavin won't indulge you in the way that I have. So just . . . watch your step, won't you?'

'I will!' I say brightly.

And without quite running, I'm off down the street, as quick as I can, back to LK Bennett.

OK, so perhaps strictly speaking I didn't need to buy a pair of clementine shoes. They weren't exactly essential. But what occurred to me while I was trying them on was, I haven't actually broken my new rule. Because the point is, I *will* need them.

After all, I will need new shoes *at some point*, won't I? Everyone needs shoes. And surely it's far more prudent to stock up now in a style I really like than to wait until my last pair wears out and then find nothing nice in the shops. It's only sensible. It's like . . . hedging my future position in the shoe market.

As I come out of LK Bennett, happily grasping my two shiny new bags, there's a warm, happy glow all around me. I'm not in the mood for going home, so I decide to pop across the street to Gifts and Goodies. This is one of the shops that stocks Suze's frames and I have a little habit of going in whenever I pass, just to see if anyone's buying one.

I push the door open with a ping, and smile at the assistant, who looks up. This is such a lovely shop. It's warm and scented, and full of gorgeous things like chrome wire racks and glass etched coasters. I sidle past a shelf of pale mauve leather notebooks, and look up – and there they are! Three purple tweed photo frames, made by Suze! I still get a thrill, every time I see them.

Oh my God! I feel a zing of excitement. There's a customer standing there – and she's holding one. She's actually holding one!

To be perfectly honest, I've never actually seen anyone buying one of Suze's frames. I mean, I know people must buy them, because they keep selling out – but I've never seen it happen. God, this is exciting!

I walk quietly forward just as the customer turns the

frame over. She frowns at the price, and my heart gives a little flurry.

'That's a really beautiful photo frame,' I say casually. 'Really unusual.'

'Yes,' she says, and puts it back down on the shelf.

No! I think in dismay. Pick it up again!

'It's so difficult to find a nice frame these days,' I say conversationally. 'Don't you think? When you find one, you should just . . . buy it! Before someone else gets it.'

'I suppose so,' says the customer, picking up a paper-weight and frowning at that, too.

Now she's walking away. What can I do?

'Well, I think I'll get one,' I say distinctly, and pick it up. 'It'll make a perfect present. For a man, or a woman . . . I mean, everyone needs photograph frames, don't they?'

The customer doesn't seem to be taking any notice. But never mind, when she sees *me* buying it, maybe she'll rethink.

I hurry to the checkout, and the woman behind the till smiles at me. I think she's the shop owner, because I've seen her interviewing staff and talking to suppliers. (Not that I come in here very often, it's just coincidence or something.)

'Hello again,' she says. 'You really like these frames, don't you?'

'Yes,' I say loudly. 'And such *fantastic* value!' But the customer's looking at a glass decanter, and not even listening.

'How many of them have you bought, now? It must be about . . . twenty?'

What? My attention snaps back to the shop owner. What's she saying?

'Or even thirty?'

I stare at her in shock. Has she been monitoring me, every time I've been in here? Isn't that against the law?

'Quite a collection!' she adds pleasantly, as she wraps it up in tissue paper.

I've got to say something, or she'll get the idea that it's me buying all Suze's frames instead of the general public. Which is ridiculous. I ask you, thirty! I've only bought about . . . four. Five, maybe.

'I haven't got that many!' I say hurriedly. 'I should think you've been mixing me up with . . . other people. And I didn't just come in to buy a frame!' I laugh gaily to show what a ludicrous idea that is. 'I actually wanted some of . . . these, too.' I grab randomly at some big carved wooden letters in a nearby basket, and hand them to her. She smiles, and starts laying them out on tissue paper one by one.

'P . . . T . . . R . . . R.'

She stops, and looks at the letters puzzledly. 'Were you trying to make "Peter"?'

Oh for God's sake. Does there always have to be a *reason* to buy things?

'Erm . . . yes,' I say. 'For my . . . my godson. He's three.'

'Lovely! Here we are then. Two Es, and take away the R . . .'

She's looking at me kindly, as if I'm a complete halfwit. Which I suppose is fair enough, since I can't spell 'Peter' and it's the name of my own godson.

'That'll be . . . £48,' she says, as I reach for my purse. 'You know, if you spend £50, you get a free scented candle.'

'Really?' I look up with interest. I could do with a nice scented candle. And for the sake of two pounds . . .

'I'm sure I could find something . . .' I say, looking vaguely round the shop.

'Spell out the rest of your godson's name in wooden letters,' suggests the shop owner helpfully. 'What's his surname?'

'Um, Wilson,' I say without thinking.

'Wilson.' And to my horror, she begins to root around in the basket. 'W . . . L . . . here's an O . . .'

'Actually,' I say quickly, 'actually, better not. Because . . . because . . . his parents are divorcing and he might be going to change his surname.'

'Really?' says the shop owner, and pulls a sympathetic face as she drops the letters back in. 'How awful. Is it an acrimonious split, then?'

'Yes,' I say, looking around the shop for something else to buy. 'Very. His . . . his mother ran off with the gardener.'

'Are you serious?' The shop owner's staring at me, and I suddenly notice a couple nearby listening as well. 'She ran off with the *gardener*?'

'He was . . . very hunky,' I improvise, picking up a jewellery box and seeing that it costs £75. 'She couldn't keep her hands off him. The husband found them together in the tool shed. Anyway—'

'Goodness me!' says the shop owner. 'That sounds incredible!'

'It's completely true,' chimes in a voice from across the shop.

What?

My head whips round – and the woman who was looking at Suze's frames is walking towards me. 'I assume you're talking about Jane and Tim?' she says. 'Such a terrible scandal, wasn't it? But I thought the little boy was called Toby.'

I stare at her, unable to speak.

'Maybe Peter is his baptismal name,' suggests the shop owner, and gestures to me. 'This is his godmother.'

'Oh you're the godmother!' exclaims the woman. 'Yes, I've heard all about you.'

This isn't happening. This can't be happening.

'Now, perhaps *you* can tell me.' The woman comes

forward and lowers her voice confidentially. 'Did Tim accept Maud's offer?'

I look around the silent shop. Everyone is waiting for my answer.

'Yes he did,' I say carefully. 'He did accept.'

'And did it work out?' she asks, staring at me agog.

'Um . . . no. He and Maud actually . . . they . . . they had a fight.'

'Really?' The woman lifts a hand to her mouth. 'A *fight*? What about?'

'Oh, you know,' I say desperately. 'This and that . . . the washing up . . . erm, actually, I think I'll pay by cash.' I fumble in my purse, and plonk £50 on the counter. 'Keep the change.'

'What about your scented candle?' says the shop owner. 'You can choose from vanilla, sandalwood—'

'Never mind,' I say, hurrying towards the door.

'Wait!' calls the woman urgently. 'What happened to Ivan?'

'He . . . emigrated to Australia,' I say, and slam the door behind me.

God, that was a bit close. I think I'd better go home.

As I reach the corner of our road, I pause, and do a little rearranging of my bags. Which is to say, I put them all in one LK Bennett carrier, and push them down until you can't see them.

It's not that I'm hiding them or anything. It's just . . . I prefer to arrive home with only one shopping bag in my hand.

I'm kind of hoping I'll be able to scuttle into my room without Suze seeing me, but when I open the front door she's sitting on the floor of the hall, parcelling something up.

'Hi!' she says. 'Did you get the shoes?'

'Yes,' I say brightly. 'Absolutely. Right size, and everything.'

'Let's have a look, then!'

'I'll just . . . unpack them,' I say casually, and head towards my room, trying to keep relaxed. But I know I look guilty. I'm even *walking* guiltily.

'Bex,' she says suddenly. 'What else is in the bag? That's not just one pair of shoes.'

'Bag?' I turn as though in surprise. 'Oh, *this* bag. Erm . . . just a few bits and pieces. You know . . . odds and ends . . .'

I tail away guiltily as Suze folds her arms, looking as stern as she can.

'Show me.'

'OK, listen,' I say in a rush. 'I know I said only one pair. But before you get angry, just look.' I reach into my second LK Bennett bag, slip open the box, and slowly pull out one of the clementine sandals. 'Just . . . look at that.'

'Oh my God,' breathes Suze, staring at it. 'That's absolutely . . . stunning.' She takes it from me and strokes the soft leather gently – then her stern expression returns. 'But did you *need* them?'

'Yes!' I say defensively. 'Or at least . . . I was just stocking up for the future. You know, like a kind of . . . investment.'

'An investment?'

'Yes. And in a way, it's *saving* money – because now I've got these, I won't need to spend any money on shoes next year. None!'

'Really?' says Suze suspiciously. 'None at all?'

'Absolutely! Honestly, Suze, I'm going to live in these shoes. I won't need to buy any more for at least a year. Probably two!'

Suze is silent and I bite my lip, waiting for her to tell me to take them back to the shop. But she's looking down at the sandal again, and touching the little clementine.

'Put them on,' she says suddenly. 'Let me see!'

With a small thrill I pull out the other sandal and slip them on – and they're just perfect. My perfect clementine slippers, just like Cinderella.

'Oh Bex,' says Suze – and she doesn't have to say anything else. It's all there in her softened eyes.

Honestly, sometimes I wish I could marry Suze.

After I've paraded back and forth a few times, Suze gives a contented sigh, then reaches inside the big carrier for the Gifts and Goodies bag. 'So – what did you get from here?' she says interestedly. The wooden letters spill out, and she begins to arrange them on the carpet.

'P-E-T-E-R. Who's Peter?'

'I don't know,' I say vaguely, grabbing for the Gifts and Goodies bag before she can spot her own frame in there. (She once caught me buying one in Fancy Free and got all cross, and said she would always make me one if I wanted it.) 'Do you know anyone called Peter?'

'No,' says Suze. 'I don't think so . . . But we could get a cat and call it Peter, maybe!'

'Yes,' I say doubtfully. 'Maybe . . . Anyway – I'd better go and get ready for tomorrow.'

'Ooh, that reminds me,' says Suze, reaching for a piece of paper. 'Luke rang for you.'

'Really?' I say, trying to hide my delight. It's always a nice surprise when Luke rings, because to be honest, he doesn't do it that much. I mean, he phones to arrange times of meeting and that kind of stuff – but he doesn't often phone for a chat. Sometimes he sends me e-mails, but they're not what you'd call chatty, more . . . Well, put it like this, the first time I got one, I was quite shocked. (But I sort of look forward to them, now.)

'He said, he'll pick you up from the studio tomorrow at twelve. And the Mercedes has had to go into the garage, so you'll be going down in the MGF.'

'Really?' I say. 'That's so cool!'

'I know,' says Suze, beaming back at me. 'Isn't it

great? Oh, and he also said can you pack light, because the boot isn't very big.'

I stare at her, my smile fading.

'What did you say?'

'Pack light,' repeats Suze. 'You know: not much luggage, maybe one small bag or holdall . . .'

'I know what "pack light" means!' I say, my voice shrill with alarm. 'But . . . I can't!'

'Of course you can.'

'Suze, have you *seen* how much stuff I've got?' I say, going to my bedroom door and flinging it open. 'I mean, just look at that.'

Suze follows my gaze uncertainly, and we both stare at my bed. My big acid green suitcase is full. Another pile of clothes is sitting beside it. And I haven't even *got* to makeup and stuff yet.

'I can't do it, Suze,' I wail. 'What am I going to do?'

'Phone Luke and tell him?' suggests Suze. 'And say he'll have to hire a car with a bigger boot?'

For a moment I'm silent. I'm trying to imagine Luke's face if I tell him he has to hire a bigger car to hold my clothes.

'The thing is,' I say at last, 'I'm not sure he'd *completely* understand . . .'

The doorbell rings and Suze gets up.

'That'll be Special Express for my parcel,' she says. 'Listen Bex, it'll be fine. Just . . . prune away a few things.' She goes to answer the door and leaves me staring at my jumbled bed.

Prune away? But prune away what, exactly? It's not as though I've packed a load of stuff I don't need. If I just start removing things at random my whole system will collapse.

OK, come on. Think laterally. There *must* be a solution.

Maybe I could . . . secretly fix a trailer onto the car when Luke isn't looking?

Or maybe I could *wear* all my clothes, on top of each other, and say I'm feeling a bit chilly . . .

Oh, this is hopeless. What am I going to do?

Distractedly, I wander out of my room and into the hall, where Suze is handing a padded envelope to a man in uniform.

'That's great,' he says. 'If you could just sign there . . . Hello!' he adds cheerfully to me, and I nod back, staring blankly at his badge, which reads: *Anything, anywhere, by tomorrow morning.*

'Here's your receipt,' says the man to Suze, and turns to leave. He's halfway out of the door when the words on his badge start jumping about in my mind.

Anything.

Anywhere.

By tomorrow—

'Hey wait!' I call, just as the door's about to slam. 'Could you just hold on one sec . . .'

Paradigm Self-Help Books Ltd
695 Soho Square
London W1 5AS

Ms Rebecca Bloomwood
Flat 2
4 Burney Rd
London SW6 8FD

Dear Becky

Thanks so much for your voice-mail. I'm really glad to hear that the book is going well!

You may remember, when we spoke two weeks ago, you assured me the first draft would be with me within days. I'm sure it's on its way – or has it possibly got lost in the post? Maybe you could send me another copy?

As far as the author photograph goes, just wear whatever you feel comfortable with. An Agnès B top sounds fine, as do the earrings you described.

I look forward to seeing the manuscript – and again, let me say how thrilled and delighted we are that you're writing for us.

With all best wishes

Pippa Brady
Editor

PARADIGM BOOKS: HELPING YOU TO HELP YOURSELF

COMING SOON! *Jungle Survival* by Brig. Roger Flintwood

Three

At five to twelve the next day I'm still sitting under the bright lights of the *Morning Coffee* set, wondering how much longer we'll be. Normally my financial advice slot is over by 11.40, but they got so engrossed with the psychic who reckons she's the reincarnated spirit of Mary Queen of Scots, that everything's overrun since then. And Luke will be here any minute, and I've still got to change out of this stuffy suit . . .

'Becky?' says Emma, who's one of the presenters of *Morning Coffee* and is sitting opposite me on a blue sofa. 'This sounds quite a problem.'

'Absolutely,' I say, dragging my mind back to the present. I glance down at the sheet in front of me, then smile sympathetically at the camera. 'So, to recap, Judy, you and your husband Bill have inherited some money. You'd like to invest some of it in the stock market – but he's refusing.'

'It's like talking to a brick wall!' comes Judy's indignant voice. 'He says I'll lose it all, and it's his money too, and if all I want to do is gamble it away, then I can go to . . .'

'Yes,' interrupts Emma smoothly. 'Well. This does sound difficult, Becky. Two partners disagreeing about what to do with their money.'

'I just don't understand him!' exclaims Judy. 'This is our one chance to make a serious investment. It's a fantastic opportunity! Why can't he *see* that?'

She breaks off, and there's an expectant silence around the studio. Everyone's waiting for my answer.

'Judy . . .' I pause thoughtfully. 'May I ask a question? What outfit is Bill wearing today?'

'A suit,' says Judy, sounding taken aback. 'A grey suit for work.'

'What kind of tie? Plain or patterned?'

'Plain,' says Judy at once. 'All his ties are plain.'

'Would he ever wear, say . . . a cartoon tie?'

'Never!'

'I see.' I raise my eyebrows. 'Judy, would it be fair to say Bill is generally quite an unadventurous person? That he doesn't like taking risks?'

'Well . . . yes,' says Judy. 'Now you say it, I suppose he is.'

'Ah!' says Rory suddenly, on the opposite side of the sofa. Rory is the other presenter of *Morning Coffee*. He's very chiselled-looking and is great at flirting with film stars, but he's not exactly the Brain of Britain. 'I think I see where you're going here, Becky.'

'Yes, thanks Rory,' says Emma, rolling her eyes at me. 'I think we all do. So Becky, if Bill doesn't like risk, are you saying he's right to avoid the stock market?'

'No,' I reply. 'I'm not saying that at all. Because maybe what Bill isn't quite seeing is that there's more than one kind of risk. If you invest in the stock market, yes, you risk losing money in the short term. But if you simply tuck it away in the bank for years and years, an even greater risk is that this inheritance will be eroded over time by inflation.'

'Aha,' puts in Rory wisely. 'Inflation.'

'In twenty years' time, it could well be worth very little – compared to what it would probably have achieved on the stock market. So if Bill is only in his thirties and wants to make a long-term investment, although it seems risky it's in many ways *safer* to choose a balanced stock-market portfolio.'

'I see,' says Emma, and gives me an admiring look. 'I would never have looked at it like that.'

'Successful investment is often simply a question of thinking laterally,' I say, smiling modestly.

God, I *love* it when I get the answer right and everyone looks impressed.

'Does that help you, Judy?' says Emma.

'Yes,' says Judy. 'Yes it does! I've videotaped this call, so I'll show it to Bill tonight.'

'Oh, right!' I say. 'Well – check what kind of tie he's wearing, first.'

Everyone laughs, and I join in after a pause – even though I wasn't actually joking.

'Time for one more quick call,' says Emma. 'We have Enid from Northampton, who wants to know if she's got enough money to retire on. Enid, is that right?'

'Yes, that's right,' comes Enid's voice down the line. 'My husband Tony's recently retired, and I was on holiday last week – just at home with him, cooking and so forth. And he . . . we got to thinking . . . how about I retire early, too? But I wasn't sure I had enough saved up, so I thought I'd call in.'

'What kind of financial provision have you made for retirement, Enid?' I ask.

'I've a pension which I've contributed to all my life,' says Enid hesitantly, 'and I've a couple of savings plans . . . and I've a recent inheritance which should see off the mortgage . . .'

'Well!' says Emma brightly. 'Even *I* can see that you're pretty well set up, Enid. I'd say, happy retirement!'

'Right,' says Enid. 'I see. So – there's no reason for me not to retire. It's just as Tony said.' There's silence apart from her breathing unsteadily down the line, and Emma gives me a quick glance. I know the producer Barry must be yelling into her earpiece to fill the space.

'So good luck, Enid!' she says brightly. 'Becky, on the subject of retirement planning—'

'Just . . . hold on a moment,' I say, frowning slightly. 'Enid – there's no obvious financial reason for you not to retire. But . . . what about the most important reason of all? Do you actually *want* to retire?'

'Well.' Enid's voice falters slightly. 'I'm in my fifties now. I mean, you have to move on, don't you? And as Tony said, it'll give us a chance to spend more time together.'

'Do you enjoy your job?'

There's another silence.

'I do. Yes. It's a good crowd, at work. I'm older than most of them, of course. But somehow that doesn't seem to matter when we're having a laugh . . .'

'Well, I'm afraid that's all we've got time for,' cuts in Emma, who has been listening intently to her earpiece. She smiles at the camera. 'Good luck in your retirement, Enid . . .'

'Wait!' I say quickly. 'Enid, please stay on the line if you'd like to talk about this a bit more. OK?'

'Yes,' says Enid after a pause. 'Yes, I'd like that.'

'We're going to go to weather now,' says Rory, who always perks up as the finance slot comes to an end. 'But a final word, Becky?'

'Same as always,' I say, smiling at the camera. 'Look after your money . . .'

'. . . and your money will look after you!' chime in Rory and Emma. After a frozen pause, everyone relaxes and Zelda, the assistant producer, strides onto the set.

'Well done!' she says. 'Great stuff. Now, Becky, we've still got Enid on line 4. But we can get rid of her if you like . . .'

'No,' I say in surprise. 'I want to talk to her. You know, I reckon she doesn't want to retire at all!'

'Whatever,' says Zelda, ticking something on her clipboard. 'Oh, and Luke's waiting for you at reception.'

'Already?' I look at my watch. 'Oh God . . . OK – can you tell him I won't be long?'

I honestly don't intend to spend that long on the phone. But once I get talking to Enid, it all comes out – about how she's dreading retiring, and how her husband just wants her at home to cook for him. How she really loves her job and she was thinking about doing a computer course but her husband says it's a waste of money . . . By the end I'm completely outraged. I've said exactly what I think, several times over, and am in the middle of asking Enid if she considers herself a feminist, when Zelda taps me on the shoulder and I suddenly remember where I am.

It takes me another five minutes to apologize to Enid and say I've got to go, then for her to apologize to me – and for us both to say 'goodbye' and 'thank you' and 'don't mention it' about twenty times. Then, as quickly as possible, I head to my dressing room and change out of my *Morning Coffee* outfit into my driving down outfit.

I'm quite pleased with my appearance as I look at myself in the mirror. I'm wearing a Pucci-esque multi-coloured top, frayed denim cutoffs, my new sandals, Gucci shades (Harvey Nichols sale – half price!) and my treasured pale blue Denny and George scarf.

Luke's got a real thing about my Denny and George scarf. When people ask us how we met, he always says, 'Our eyes met across a Denny and George scarf' – which is actually kind of true. He lent me some of the money I needed to buy it, and he still maintains I never paid him back so it's partly his. (Which is *so* not true. I paid him back straight away.)

Anyway, I tend to wear it quite a lot when we go out together. Also when we stay in together. In fact, I'll tell you a small secret – sometimes we even . . .

Actually, no. You don't need to know that. Forget I mentioned it.

As I finally hurry into reception I glance at my watch – and oh God, I'm forty minutes late. And there's Luke sitting on a squashy chair, looking all tall and gorgeous in the polo shirt I bought him in the Ralph Lauren sale.

'I'm really sorry,' I say. 'I was just . . .'

'I know,' says Luke, closing his paper and standing up. 'You were talking to Enid.' He gives me a kiss and squeezes my arm. 'I saw the last couple of calls. Good for you.'

'You just won't believe what her husband's like,' I say as we go through the swing doors and out into the car park. 'No wonder she wants to keep working!'

'I can imagine.'

'He just thinks she's there to give him an easy life.' I shake my head fiercely. 'God, you know, I'm never going to just stay at home and cook your supper. Never in a million years.'

There's a short silence, and I look up to see a tiny smile on Luke's lips.

'Or . . . you know,' I add hastily, 'anyone's supper.'

'I'm glad to hear it,' says Luke mildly. 'I'm especially glad you're never going to cook me Moroccan couscous surprise.'

'You know what I mean,' I say, flushing slightly. 'And you promised you weren't going to talk about that any more.'

My famous Moroccan evening was quite soon after we started going out. I really wanted to show Luke that I could cook – and I'd seen this programme about Moroccan cooking which made it look really easy and impressive. Plus there was some gorgeous Moroccan tableware on sale in Debenhams, so it should have all been perfect.

But oh God. That soggy couscous. It was the most revolting stuff I've ever seen in my life. Even after I

49

tried Suze's suggestion of stir-frying it with mango chutney. And there was so *much* of it, all swelling up in bowls everywhere . . .

Anyway. Never mind. We had quite a nice pizza in the end.

We're approaching Luke's convertible in the corner of the car park, and he bleeps it open.

'You got my message, did you?' he says. 'About luggage?'

'Yes, I did. Here it is.'

Smugly, I hand him the dinkiest little suitcase in the world, which I got from a children's gift shop in Guildford. It's white canvas with red hearts stencilled round it, and I use it as a vanity case.

'Is that it?' says Luke, looking astonished, and I stifle a giggle. Ha! This'll show him who can pack light.

I am *so* pleased with myself. All I've got in this case is my makeup and shampoo – but Luke doesn't need to know that, does he?

'Yes that's it,' I say, raising my eyebrows slightly. 'You did say, "pack light".'

'So I did,' says Luke. 'But this—' He gestures to the case. 'I'm impressed.'

As he opens the boot, I get into the driving seat and adjust the seat forwards so I can reach the pedals. I've always wanted to drive a convertible!

The boot slams, and Luke comes round, a quizzical look on his face.

'You're driving, are you?'

'Part of the way, I thought,' I say carelessly. 'Just to take the pressure off you. You know, it's very dangerous to drive for too long.'

'You can drive, can you, in those shoes?' He's looking down at my clementine sandals – and I have to admit, the heel is a bit high for pedalling. But I'm not going to admit that to him. 'They're new, aren't they?' he adds, looking more closely at them.

I'm about to say 'yes', when I remember that the last time I saw him I had new shoes on – and the time before that, too. Which is really weird and must be one of those random cluster things.

'No!' I reply instead. 'I've had them for ages. Actually . . .' I clear my throat. 'They're my driving shoes.'

'Your driving shoes,' echoes Luke sceptically.

'Yes,' I say, and start the engine before he can say any more. God, this car is amazing! It makes a fantastic roaring sound, and a kind of screech as I move it into gear.

'Becky—'

'I'm fine!' I say, and slowly move off across the car park towards the street. Oh this is such a fantastic moment. I wonder if anybody's watching me. I wonder if Emma and Rory are looking out of the window. And that sound guy who thinks he's so cool with his motorbike. Ha! He hasn't got a convertible, has he? Accidentally on purpose, I lean on the horn, and as the sound echoes round the car park I see at least three people turning to look. Ha! Look at me! Hahaha . . .

'My petal,' says Luke beside me. 'You're causing a traffic jam.'

I glance into my rear mirror – and there are three cars creeping along behind me. Which is ridiculous, because I'm not going *that* slowly.

'Try moving it up a notch,' suggests Luke. 'Ten miles an hour, say?'

'I *am*,' I say crossly. 'You can't expect me just to whiz off at a million miles an hour! There is a speed limit, you know.'

I reach the exit, smile nonchalantly at the porter at the gate, who gives me a surprised look, and pull out into the road. I signal left and take a last glance back to check if anyone I know has just come out and is watching me admiringly. Then, as a car behind me starts to beep, I carefully pull in at the pavement.

'There we are,' I say. 'Your turn.'

'My turn?' Luke stares at me. 'Already?'

'I have to do my nails now,' I explain. 'And anyway, I know you think I can't drive. I don't want to have you pulling faces at me, all the way down to Somerset.'

'I do not think you can't drive,' protests Luke, half laughing. 'When have I ever said that?'

'You don't need to say it. I can see it coming out of your head in a thought bubble: "Becky Bloomwood cannot drive".'

'Well that's where you're wrong,' retorts Luke. 'The bubble actually reads "Becky Bloomwood cannot drive in her new orange shoes because the heels are too high and pointy".'

He raises his eyebrows, and I feel myself flush slightly.

'They're my driving shoes,' I mutter, shifting over to the passenger seat. 'And I've had them for years.'

As I reach into my bag for my nail file, Luke gets into the driver's seat, leans over and gives me a kiss.

'Thank you for doing that stint, anyway,' he says. 'I'm sure it'll lessen my risk of fatigue on the motorway.'

'Well, good!' I say, starting on my nails. 'You need to conserve your energy for all those long country walks we're going to go on tomorrow.'

There's silence, and after a while I look up.

'Yes,' says Luke – and he isn't smiling any more. 'Becky . . . I was going to talk to you about tomorrow.' He pauses and I stare at him, feeling my own smile fade slightly.

'What is it?' I say, trying not to sound anxious.

There's silence – then Luke exhales sharply.

'Here's the thing. A business opportunity has arisen which I really would like to . . . to take advantage of. And there are some people over from the States who I need to talk to. Urgently.'

'Oh,' I say, uncertainly. 'Well – that's OK. If you've got your phone with you . . .'

'Not by phone.' He looks straight at me. 'I've scheduled in a meeting for tomorrow.'

'Tomorrow?' I echo, and give a little laugh. 'But you can't have a meeting. We'll be at the hotel.'

'So will the people I need to talk to,' says Luke. 'I've invited them down.'

I stare at him in shock.

'You've invited business people down on our holiday?'

'Purely for the meeting,' says Luke. 'The rest of the time it'll just be the two of us.'

'And how long will the meeting go on?' I exclaim. 'Don't tell me! All day.'

I just can't believe it. After waiting all this time, after getting all excited, after all my packing . . .

'Becky, it won't be as bad as that . . .'

'You *promised* me you'd take time off! You said we'd have a lovely romantic time.'

'We will have a lovely romantic time.'

'With all your business friends. With all your horrible contacts, networking away like . . . like maggots!'

'They won't be networking with us,' says Luke with a grin. 'Becky—' He reaches for my hand, but I pull it away.

'To be honest, I don't see any point in me coming if it's just you doing business,' I say miserably. 'I might as well just stay at home. In fact—' I open the car door. 'In fact, I think I'll go home right now. I'll call a taxi from the studio.'

I slam the car door and begin to stride off along the street, my clementine sandals making a click-clack sound against the hot pavement. I've almost got to the studio gate before I hear his voice, raised so loud that several people turn to look.

'Becky! Wait there!'

I stop and slowly turn on the spot – to see him standing up in the car, dialling a number on his mobile phone.

'What are you doing?' I call suspiciously.

'I'm phoning my horrible business contact,' says Luke. 'To put him off. To cancel.'

I fold my arms and stare at him with narrowed eyes.

'Hello?' he says. 'Room 301, please. Michael Ellis. Thanks. I guess I'll just have to fly out and see him in Washington,' he adds to me in deadpan tones. 'Or wait until the next time he and his associates are all together in Britain. Which could be a while, bearing in mind their completely crazy schedules. Still, it's only business, after all. Only a deal. It's only the deal I've been wanting to make for—'

'Oh . . . stop it!' I say furiously. 'Stop it. Have your stupid meeting.'

'Are you sure?' says Luke, putting a hand over the receiver. 'Absolutely sure?'

'Quite sure,' I say, giving a morose shrug. 'If it's *that* important . . .'

'It's pretty important,' says Luke, and meets my eyes, suddenly serious. 'Believe me, I wouldn't be doing it otherwise.'

I walk slowly back to the car as Luke puts away his mobile phone.

'Thanks, Becky,' he says as I get in. 'I mean it.' He touches my cheek gently, then reaches for the keys and starts the engine.

As we drive off towards a set of traffic lights, I glance at him, and then at his mobile phone, still sticking out of his pocket.

'Were you *really* phoning your business contact?' I say.

'Were you really going home?' he replies, without moving his head.

This is what's so annoying about going out with Luke. You can't get away with anything.

We drive for about an hour into the countryside, stop for lunch in a village pub, then drive for another hour and a half down to Somerset. By the time we reach Blakeley Hall, I feel like a different person. It's so good to get out of London – and I'm already incredibly energized and refreshed by all this wonderful country air. I step out of the car, do a few stretches – and honestly, I already feel fitter and more toned. I reckon if I came to the country every week, I'd lose half a stone, if not more.

'Do you want any more of these?' says Luke, reaching down and picking up the nearly-empty packet of Maltesers which I've been snacking on. (I have to eat in the car, otherwise I get carsick.) 'And what about these magazines?' He picks up the stack of glossies which have been at my feet, then makes a grab as they start slithering out of his hands.

'I'm not going to read magazines here,' I say in surprise. 'This is the country!'

Honestly. Doesn't Luke know anything about rural life?

As he's getting the bags out of the boot I wander over to a fence and gaze peacefully at a field full of browny-yellow stuff. You know, I reckon I have a natural affinity with the countryside. It's like I've got this whole nurturing, earth-mother side, which has been gradually creeping up on me almost without me noticing. For example the other day I found myself buying a Fair Isle jersey from French Connection. And I've recently started gardening! Or at least, I've bought some sweet ceramic flowerpots from the Pier, marked 'basil' and 'coriander' and stuff – and I'm definitely going to get some of those little plants from the supermarket and have a whole row of them on the windowsill. (I mean, they're only about 50p, so if they die you can just buy another one.)

'Ready?' says Luke.

'Absolutely!' I say, and teeter back towards him, slightly cursing the mud.

We crunch over the gravel to the hotel – and I have to say, I'm impressed. It's a great big old-fashioned country house, with beautiful gardens, and modern sculptures in the gardens and its own cinema, according to the brochure. Luke's been here quite a few times before, and he says it's his favourite hotel. And lots of celebrities come here too! Like Madonna. (Or was it Sporty Spice? Someone, anyway.) But apparently they're always very discreet and usually stay in some separate coach-housey bit, and the staff never let on.

Still, as we go into the reception hall I have a good look around, just in case. There are lots of cool people in trendy spectacles and denim, and there's a blonde girl who sort of looks famous-ish, and standing over there . . .

Oh my God. I feel myself freeze in excitement. It's him, isn't it? It's Elton John! Elton John himself is standing right there, only a few—

Then he turns round – and it's just a dumpy guy in an anorak and spectacles. Damn. Still, it was *nearly* Elton John.

We've reached the reception desk by now, and a concierge in a trendy Nehru jacket smiles at us. 'Good afternoon Mr Brandon,' he says. 'And Miss Bloomwood. Welcome to Blakeley Hall.'

He knew our names! We didn't even have to tell him! No wonder celebrities come here.

'I've put you in room 9,' he says, as Luke starts to fill in a form. 'Overlooking the rose garden.'

'Great,' says Luke. 'Becky, which paper would you like in the morning?'

'The *Financial Times*,' I say smoothly.

'Of course,' says Luke, writing. 'So that's one *FT* and a *Daily World* for me.'

I give him a suspicious look, but his face is completely blank.

'Would you like tea in the morning?' says the concierge, tapping at his computer. 'Or coffee?'

'Coffee, please,' says Luke. 'For both of us, I think.' He looks at me questioningly, and I nod.

'You'll find a complimentary bottle of champagne in your room,' says the concierge, 'and room service is available twenty-four hours.'

This really is a top-class place. They know your face immediately, they give you champagne – and they haven't even mentioned my Special Express parcel yet. Obviously they realize it's a matter of discretion. They realize that a girl doesn't necessarily want her boyfriend knowing about every single package that is delivered to her – and are going to wait until Luke is out of earshot before they tell me about it. Talk about personal service! *This* is why it's worth coming to a good hotel.

'If there's anything else you require, Miss Bloomwood,' says the concierge, looking at me meaningfully, 'please don't hesitate to let me know.'

You see? Coded messages and everything.

'I will, don't worry,' I say, and give him a knowing smile. 'In just a moment.' I flick my eyes meaningfully towards Luke, and the concierge gives me a blank stare, exactly as though he's got no idea what I'm talking about. God, these people are good!

Eventually, Luke finishes the forms and hands them back. The concierge hands him a big, old-fashioned room key, and summons a porter.

'I don't think we need any help,' says Luke, with a smile, and lifts up my dinky suitcase. 'I'm not exactly overburdened.'

'You go on up,' I say. 'I just want to . . . check

57

something. For tomorrow.' I smile at Luke and after a moment, to my relief, he heads off towards the staircase.

As soon as he's out of earshot I swivel back to the desk.

'I'll take it now,' I murmur to the concierge, who has turned away and is looking in a drawer. He raises his head and looks at me in surprise.

'I'm sorry, Miss Bloomwood?'

'It's OK,' I say more meaningfully. 'You can give it to me now. While Luke's gone.'

A flicker of apprehension passes over the concierge's face.

'What exactly—'

'You can give me my package.' I lower my voice. 'And thanks for not letting on.'

'Your . . . package?'

'My Special Express.'

'What Special Express?'

I stare at him, feeling a few misgivings.

'The parcel with all my clothes in it! The one you weren't mentioning. The one . . .'

I tail away at the sight of his face. He doesn't have a clue what I'm talking about, does he? OK. Don't panic. Someone else will know where it is.

'I should have a parcel waiting for me,' I explain. 'About this big . . . It should have arrived this morning . . .'

The concierge is shaking his head.

'I'm sorry, Miss Bloomwood. There aren't any packages for you.'

Suddenly I feel a little hollow.

'But . . . there has to be a package. I sent it by Special Express, yesterday. To Blakeley Hall.'

The concierge frowns.

'Charlotte?' he says, calling into a back room. 'Has a parcel arrived for Rebecca Bloomwood?'

'No,' says Charlotte, coming out. 'When was it supposed to arrive?'

'This morning,' I say, trying to hide my agitation. '"Anything, anywhere, by tomorrow morning"! I mean, this is anywhere, isn't it?'

'I'm sorry,' says Charlotte, 'but nothing's come. Was it very important?'

'Rebecca?' comes a voice from the stairs – and I turn, to see Luke peering down at me. 'Is something wrong?'

Oh God.

'No!' I say brightly. 'Of course not! What on earth could be wrong?' Quickly I swivel away from the desk and, before Charlotte or the concierge can say anything, hurry towards the stairs.

'Everything all right?' he says as I reach him, and smiles at me.

'Absolutely!' I say, my voice two notches higher than usual. 'Everything's absolutely fine!'

This cannot be happening. I have no clothes.

I'm on holiday with Luke, in a smart hotel – and I have no clothes. What am I going to do?

I can't admit the truth to him. I just *can't* admit that my dinky suitcase was only the tip of the clothes-berg. Not after having been so smug about it. I'll just have to . . . improvise, I think wildly, as we turn a corner and start walking down another plushy corridor. Wear *his* clothes, like Annie Hall or . . . or rip down the curtains and find some sewing stuff . . . and quickly learn how to sew . . .

'All right?' asks Luke, and I grin weakly back.

Calm down, I tell myself firmly. Just . . . calm down. The parcel is bound to arrive tomorrow morning, so I've only got to last one night. And at least I've got my makeup with me . . .

'Here we are,' says Luke, stopping at a door and opening it. 'What do you think?'

Oh wow. For a moment my worries are swept away as I gaze around the enormous airy room. Now I can see why Luke likes this hotel so much. It's gorgeous – exactly like his flat, all huge white bed with an enormous waffle duvet, and a state-of-the-art music system and two suede sofas.

'Take a look at the bathroom,' says Luke. I follow him through – and it's stunning. A huge great sunken mosaic Jacuzzi with the hugest shower I've ever seen above, and a whole rack of gorgeous-looking aromatherapy oils.

Maybe I could just spend the whole weekend in the bath.

'So,' he says, turning back into the room. 'I don't know what you'd like to do . . .' He walks over to his suitcase and clicks it open – and I can see serried rows of shirts, all ironed by his housekeeper. 'I suppose we should unpack first . . .'

'Unpack! Absolutely,' I say brightly. I walk over to my own little suitcase and finger the clasp, without opening it. 'Or else . . .' I say, as though the idea's just occurring to me – 'why don't we go and have a drink – and unpack later!'

Genius. We'll go downstairs and get really pissed, and then tomorrow morning I'll just pretend to be really sleepy and stay in bed until my package comes. Thank God. For a moment there I was starting to—

'Excellent idea,' says Luke. 'I'll just get changed.' He reaches into his case and pulls out a pair of trousers and a crisp blue shirt.

'Changed?' I say after a pause. 'Is there . . . a strict dress code?'

'Oh no, not strict,' says Luke. 'You just wouldn't go down in . . . say, in what you're wearing at the moment.' He gestures to my denim cutoffs with a grin.

'Of course not!' I say, laughing as though the idea's

ridiculous. 'Right. Well. I'll just . . . choose an outfit, then.'

I turn to my case again, snap it open, lift the lid and look at my sponge bag.

What am I going to do? Luke's unbuttoning his shirt. He's calmly reaching for the blue one. In a minute he's going to look up and say, Are you ready?

OK, I need a radical plan of action here.

'Luke – I've changed my mind,' I say, and close the lid of my case. 'Let's not go down to the bar.' Luke looks up in surprise, and I give him the most seductive smile I can muster. 'Let's stay up here and order room service, and . . .' I take a few steps towards him, loosening my wrap top '. . . and see where the night leads us.'

Luke stares at me, his hands still halfway up the buttons of his blue shirt.

'Take that off,' I say huskily. 'What's the point of dressing up when all we want to do is undress each other?'

A slow smile spreads across Luke's face, and his eyes begin to gleam.

'You're so right,' he says, and walks towards me, unbuttoning his shirt and letting it fall to the floor. 'I don't know what I was thinking of.'

Thank God! I think in relief, as he reaches for my wrap top and gently starts to untie it. This is perfect. This is exactly what I—

Ooh. Mmmmm.

Actually, this *is* pretty bloody perfect.

Four

By 8.30 the next morning, I still haven't got up. I don't want to move an inch. I want to stay in this lovely comfortable bed, wrapped in this gorgeous white waffle duvet.

'Are you staying there all day?' says Luke, smiling down at me – and I snuggle down in the pillows, pretending I can't hear him. I just don't want to get up. I'm so cosy and warm and happy here.

Plus – just a very small point – I still don't have any clothes.

I've already secretly rung down to reception three times about my Special Express. (Once while Luke was in the shower, once while I was in the shower – from the posh bathroom phone – and once very quickly when I sent Luke into the corridor because I said I heard a cat meowing.)

And it still hasn't arrived. I have nil clothes. Nada.

Which hasn't mattered up until now, because I've just been lounging around in bed. But I can't possibly eat any more croissants or drink any more coffee, nor can I have another shower, and Luke's half-dressed already.

Oh God, there's nothing for it – I'm just going to have to put on yesterday's clothes again. Which is really hideous, but what else can I do? I'll just pretend I'm sentimental about them, or maybe hope I can slip them on and Luke won't even realize. I mean, do men really *notice* what you . . .

Hang on.

Hang-on-a-minute. Where *are* yesterday's clothes? I'm sure I dropped them just there on the floor . . .

'Luke?' I say, as casually as possible. 'Have you seen the clothes I was wearing yesterday?'

'Oh yes,' he says, glancing up from his suitcase. 'I sent them to the laundry this morning, along with my stuff.'

I stare at him, unable to breathe.

My only clothes in the whole world have *gone to the laundry*?

'When . . . when will they be back?' I say at last.

'Tomorrow morning.' Luke turns to look at me. 'Sorry, I should have said. But it's not a problem, is it? I mean, I don't think you have to worry. They do an excellent job.'

'Oh no!' I say in a high, brittle voice. 'No, I'm not worried!'

'Good,' he says, and smiles.

'Good,' I say, and smile back.

Oh God. What am I going to do?

'Oh, and there's plenty of room in the wardrobe,' says Luke, 'if you want me to hang anything up?' He reaches towards my little case and in a panic I hear myself crying 'Nooo!' before I can stop myself. 'It's all right,' I add, as he looks at me in surprise. 'My clothes are mostly . . . knitwear.'

Oh God. Oh God. Now he's putting on his shoes. *What am I going to do?*

OK, come on Becky, I think frantically. Clothes. Something to wear. Doesn't matter what.

One of Luke's suits?

No. He'll just think it's too weird, and anyway, his suits all cost about a thousand pounds so I won't be able to roll the sleeves up.

My hotel robe? Pretend robes and waffle slippers are the latest fashion? Oh, but I can't walk around in a dressing gown as if I think I'm in a spa. Everyone will laugh at me.

Come on, there *must* be clothes in a hotel. What about . . . the chambermaids' uniforms! Yes, that's more like it! They must keep a rack of them somewhere, mustn't they? Neat little dresses with matching hats. I could tell Luke they're the latest thing from Prada – and just hope no-one asks me to clear out their room . . .

'By the way,' says Luke, reaching into his case, 'you left this behind at my flat.'

I look up, startled, and he chucks something across the room at me. It's soft, it's fabric . . . as I catch it, I want to weep with relief. It's clothes! A single over-sized Calvin Klein T-shirt, to be precise. I have never been so glad to see a plain washed-out grey T-shirt in my life.

'Thanks!' I say, and I force myself to count to ten before I add casually, 'Actually – maybe I'll wear this today.'

'That?' says Luke, giving me a strange look. 'I thought it was a nightshirt.'

'It is! It's a nightshirt . . . stroke . . . dress,' I say, popping it over my head – and thank God, it comes halfway down my thighs. It could easily be a dress. And ha! I've got a stretchy black headband in my makeup bag, which just about fits me as a belt . . .

'Very nice,' says Luke quizzically, watching me wriggle into it. 'A *little* on the short side . . .'

'It's a mini-dress,' I say firmly, and turn to look at my reflection. And . . . oh God, it is a bit short. But it's too late to do anything about that now. I step into my clementine sandals and shake back my hair, not allowing myself to think about all the great outfits I had planned for this morning.

'Here,' says Luke. He reaches for my Denny and

George scarf and winds it slowly round my neck. 'Denny and George scarf, no knickers. Just the way I like it.'

'I'm going to wear knickers!' I say indignantly.

Which is true. I'll wait until Luke's gone, then pinch a pair of his boxer shorts.

'So – what's your deal about,' I ask hurriedly, to change the subject. 'Something exciting?'

'It's . . . pretty big,' says Luke after a pause. He holds up a pair of silk ties. 'Which one will bring me luck?'

'The red one,' I say after a little consideration. I watch as he ties it round his neck, with brisk, efficient movements. 'So come on – tell me. Is it a big new client?'

Luke smiles and shakes his head.

'Is it NatWest? I know, Lloyds Bank!'

'Let's just say . . . it's something I want very much,' Luke says eventually. 'Something I've always wanted. Now – what are you going to do today?' he asks, in a different tone. 'Will you be all right?'

Now *he's* changing the subject. I don't know why he has to get so bloody cagey about work. I mean, doesn't he trust me?

'Have you heard the pool is closed this morning?' he says.

'I know,' I say, reaching for my blusher. 'But that doesn't matter. I'll easily amuse myself.'

There's silence and I look up, to see Luke surveying me doubtfully.

'Would you like me to order you a taxi to take you to the shops? Bath is quite near here—'

'No,' I say indignantly. 'I don't want to go shopping!'

Which is true. When Suze found out how much those clementine sandals were, she got worried that she hadn't been strict enough with me, and made me promise not to do any shopping this weekend. She made me cross my heart and swear on – well, on my clementine sandals, actually. And I'm going to make a real effort to keep to it.

I mean, she's completely right. If she can last a whole week without going to the shops, I should be able to last forty-eight hours.

'I'm going to do all lovely rural things,' I say, snapping my blusher closed.

'Like . . .'

'Like look at the scenery . . . and maybe go to a farm and watch them milking the cows, or something . . .'

'I see.' A tiny smile is twitching at his mouth.

'What?' I say suspiciously. 'What's that supposed to mean?'

'You're just going to pitch up at a farm, are you, and ask if you can milk the cows?'

'I didn't say *I* was going to milk the cows,' I say with dignity. 'I said I was going to *watch* the cows. And anyway, I might not go to a farm, I might go and look at some local attractions.' I reach for a pile of leaflets on the dressing table. 'Like . . . this tractor exhibition. Or . . . St Winifred's Convent with its famous Bevington Triptych.'

'A convent,' echoes Luke after a pause.

'Yes, a convent!' I give him an indignant look. 'Why shouldn't I visit a convent? I'm actually a very spiritual person.'

'I'm sure you are, my darling,' says Luke, giving me a quizzical look. 'You *might* want to put on more than a T-shirt before you go . . .'

'It's a dress,' I say, pulling the T-shirt down over my bum. 'Anyway, spirituality has nothing to do with clothes. "Consider the lilies of the field." ' I shoot him a satisfied glance.

'Fair enough.' Luke grins. 'Well, enjoy yourself.' He gives me a kiss. 'And I really am sorry about all this.'

'Yeah well,' I say, and give him a little poke in the

chest. 'You just make sure this mysterious deal is worth it.'

I'm expecting Luke to laugh, or at least smile – but he gives me a tiny nod, picks up his briefcase and heads for the door. God, he takes business seriously, sometimes.

Still, I don't actually mind having this morning to myself, because I've always secretly wanted to see what it's like inside a convent. I mean, I know I don't exactly make it to church every week, but it seems obvious to me that there's a greater force out there at work than us mere mortals – which is why I always read my horoscope in the *Daily World*. Plus I love that plainchant they play in yoga classes, and all the lovely candles and incense. And Audrey Hepburn in *The Nun's Story*.

To tell you the truth, a part of me has always been attracted to the simplicity of a nun's life. No worries, no decisions, no having to work. Just singing and walking around all day. I mean, wouldn't that be great?

So when I've done my makeup and watched a bit of *Trisha*, I go down to reception – and after asking fruitlessly again about my package (honestly, I'm going to sue), I order a taxi to St Winifred's. As we trundle along the country lanes, I look out at all the lovely scenery, and find myself wondering what Luke's deal can be about. What on earth is this mysterious 'something he's always wanted'? New client? New office? Expanding the company, maybe?

I screw up my face, trying to recall if I've overheard anything recently – then, with a jolt, remember hearing him on the phone, a few weeks ago. He was talking about an advertising agency, and even at the time, I wondered why.

Advertising. Maybe that's it. Maybe he's always secretly wanted to be an ad director or something.

God, yes. It's obvious, now I think about it. That's

what this deal is all about. He's going to branch out from PR and start making adverts.

And I could be in them! Yes!

I'm so excited at this thought, I almost swallow my chewing gum. I can be in an ad! Oh, this is going to be *so* cool. Maybe I'll be in one of those Barcardi ads where they're all on a boat, laughing and waterskiing and having a great time. I mean, I know it's usually fashion models – but I could easily be somewhere in the background, couldn't I? Or I could be the one driving the boat. God, it'll be so fantastic. We'll fly out to Barbados or somewhere, and it'll be all hot and sunny and glamorous, with loads of free Barcardi, and we'll stay in a really amazing hotel . . . I'll have to buy a new bikini, of course . . . or maybe two . . . and some new flip-flops . . .

'St Winifred's,' says the taxi driver – and with a start I come to. I'm not in Barbados, am I? I'm in the middle of bloody nowhere, in Somerset.

We've stopped outside an old honey-coloured building, and I peer through the window curiously. So this is a convent. It doesn't look that special – just like a school, or a big country house. I'm wondering whether I should even bother getting out, when I see something that makes me stiffen slightly. A real live nun. Walking past, in black robes, and a wimple and everything! A real nun, in her real habitat. And she's completely natural. She hasn't even *looked* at the taxi. This is like being on safari!

I get out and pay the driver, and as I walk towards the heavy front door I feel prickles of intrigue. There's an elderly woman going in at the same time who seems to know the way – so I follow her along a corridor towards the chapel. When we walk in, I feel this amazing, holy, almost euphoric sensation coming over me. Maybe it's the gorgeous smell in the air or the organ music, but I'm definitely getting something.

'Thank you, Sister,' says the elderly woman to the nun, and she starts walking off to the front of the chapel. But I stand still, slightly transfixed.

Sister. Wow.

Sister Rebecca.

And one of those lovely flowing black habits, and a fantastic clear nun-complexion all the time.

Sister Rebecca of the Holy . . .

'You look a little lost, my dear,' a nun says behind me, and I jump. 'Were you interested in seeing the Bevington Triptych?'

'Oh,' I say. 'Erm . . . yes. Absolutely.'

'Up there,' she points, and I walk tentatively towards the front of the chapel, hoping it will become obvious what the Bevington Triptych is. A statue, maybe? Or a . . . a piece of tapestry?

But as I reach the elderly lady, I see that she's staring up at a whole wall of stained glass windows. I have to admit, they're pretty amazing. I mean look at that huge blue one in the middle. It's fantastic!

'The Bevington Triptych,' says the elderly woman. 'It simply has no parallel, does it?'

'Wow,' I breathe reverentially, staring up with her. 'It's beautiful.'

It really is stunning. God, it just shows, there's no mistaking a real work of art, is there? When you come across real genius, it just leaps out at you. And I'm not even an expert.

'Wonderful colours,' I murmur.

'The detail,' says the woman, clasping her hands, 'is absolutely incomparable.'

'Incomparable,' I echo.

I'm just about to point out the rainbow, which I think is a really nice touch – when I suddenly notice that the elderly woman and I aren't looking at the same thing. She's looking at some painted wooden thing which I hadn't even noticed.

As inconspicuously as possible, I shift my gaze – and feel a pang of disappointment. Is *this* the Bevington triptych? But it isn't even pretty!

'Whereas this Victorian rubbish,' the woman suddenly adds savagely, 'is absolutely criminal! That rainbow! Doesn't it make you feel sick?' She gestures to my big blue window, and I gulp.

'I know,' I say. 'It's shocking, isn't it? Absolutely . . . You know – I think I'll just go for a little wander . . .'

Hastily I back away, before she can say any more. I'm sidling back down the side of the pews, wondering vaguely what to do next, when I notice a little side chapel in the corner.

Spiritual retreat, reads a notice outside. *A place to sit quietly, pray, and discover more about the Catholic faith.*

Cautiously I poke my head into the side chapel – and there's an old nun, sitting on a chair, doing embroidery. She smiles at me, and nervously I smile back and walk inside.

I sit down on a dark wooden pew, trying not to make any creaking sounds, and for a while I'm too awe-struck to say anything. This is just amazing. The atmosphere is fantastic, all quiet and still – and I feel incredibly cleansed and holy just from being here. I smile again at the nun, shyly, and she puts down her embroidery and looks at me as though waiting for me to speak.

'I really like your candles,' I say in a quiet, reverent voice. 'Are they from Habitat?'

'No,' says the nun, looking a bit startled. 'I don't believe so.'

'Oh right.'

I give a tiny yawn – because I'm still sleepy from all this country air – and as I do so, notice that one of my nails has chipped. So very quietly, I unzip my bag, get out my nail file, and start to buff it. The nun looks up, and I give her a rueful smile and point to my nail (silently, because I don't want to ruin the spiritual atmosphere). Then, when I've finished, the edge is looking a bit ragged – so I take out my Mabelline express dry polish and very quickly touch it up.

All the while, the nun is watching me with a perplexed expression, and as I'm finishing, she says, 'My dear, are you a Catholic?'

'No, I'm not, actually,' I say.

'Was there anything you wanted to talk about?'

'Um . . . not really.' I run my hand fondly over the pew I'm sitting on, and give her a friendly smile. 'This carving is really nice, isn't it? Is all your furniture as nice as this?'

'This is the chapel,' says the nun, giving me a strange look.

'Oh, I know! But you know, loads of people have pews in their houses, too, these days. They're quite trendy, actually. I saw this article in *Harpers*—'

'My child . . .' The nun lifts a hand to interrupt me. 'My child, this is a place of spiritual retreat. Of quietness.'

'I know!' I say in surprise. 'That's why I came in. For quietness.'

'Good,' says the nun, and we lapse into silence again.

In the distance, a bell starts tolling, and I notice the nun begins murmuring very quietly under her breath. I wonder what she's saying. She reminds me of when my granny used to knit things, and mutter the pattern to herself. Maybe she's lost track of her embroidery.

'Your sewing's going really well,' I say encouragingly. 'What's it going to be?' She gives a tiny start, and puts down her embroidery.

'My dear . . .' she says, and exhales sharply. Then she gives me a warm smile. 'My dear we have some quite famous lavender fields. Would you like to go and see them?'

'No, it's all right.' I beam at her. 'I'm just happy, sitting here with you.' The nun's smile wavers slightly.

'What about the crypt?' she says. 'Would you be interested in that?'

'Not particularly. But honestly, don't worry. I'm not bored! It's just so lovely here. So . . . tranquil. Just like *The Sound of Music*.'

She stares at me as though I'm speaking gibberish, and I realize she's probably been in the convent so long, she doesn't know what *The Sound of Music* is.

'There was this film . . .' I start to explain. Then it occurs to me, maybe she doesn't know what a film is, even. 'It's like, moving pictures,' I say carefully. 'You watch it on a screen. And there was this nun called Maria . . .'

'We have a shop,' interrupts the nun urgently. 'A shop. What about that?'

A shop! For a moment I feel all excited, and want to ask what they sell. But then I remember the promise I made to Suze.

'I can't,' I say regretfully. 'I told my flatmate I wouldn't go shopping today.'

'Your flatmate?' says the nun. 'What does she have to do with it?'

'She just gets really worried about me spending money—'

'Does your flatmate run your life?'

'Well, it's just I made her this quite serious promise a while ago. You know, a bit like a vow, I suppose . . .'

'She'll never know!' says the nun. 'Not if you don't tell her.'

I stare at her, a bit taken aback.

'But I'd feel really bad, breaking my promise! No, I'll just stay here with you for a bit longer, if that's OK.' I pick up a little statue of Mary which has caught my eye. 'This is nice. Where did you get it?'

The nun stares at me, her eyes narrowing.

'Don't think of it as shopping,' she says at last. 'Think of it as making a donation.' She leans forward. 'You donate the money – and we give you a little something in return. You couldn't really count it as shopping at all. More . . . an act of charity.'

I'm silent for a few moments, letting this idea sink in. The truth is, I do always mean to do more for charity – and maybe this is my chance.

'So – it'll be like . . . doing a good deed?' I say, just to be sure.

'Exactly the same. And Jesus and all His angels will bless you for it.' She takes hold of my arm, quite firmly. 'Now, you go along and have a browse. Come on, I'll show you the way . . .'

As we leave the side chapel the nun shuts the door and takes down the *Spiritual retreat* notice.

'Aren't you coming back?' I say.

'Not today, no,' she says, and gives me an odd look. 'I think I'll leave it for today.'

You know, it's just like they say – virtue is its own reward. As I arrive back at the hotel later that afternoon, I'm glowing with happiness at all the good I've done. I must have donated at least £50 in that shop, if not more! In fact, not to show off or anything – but I'm obviously naturally very altruistic. Because once I started donating, I couldn't stop! Each time I parted with a bit more money, I felt a real high. And although it's a completely incidental point – I ended up with some really nice stuff in return. Lots of lavender honey, and lavender essential oil, and some lavender tea, which I'm sure will be delicious – and a lavender pillow to help me sleep.

The amazing thing is, I'd never really given lavender much thought before. I just thought of it as a plant in people's gardens. But that young nun behind the table was quite right – it has such vital, life-enhancing properties that it should be part of everyone's life. Plus St Winifred's lavender is completely organic, she explained – so it's vastly superior to other varieties, but the prices are much lower than many competing mail-order catalogues. She was the one who persuaded me to buy the lavender pillow, actually, and to put my name down on the mailing list. She was really quite persistent, for a nun.

When I get back to Blakeley Hall, the minicab driver offers to help me lug it all in, because the box of lavender honey is quite heavy. I'm standing at the reception desk, giving him a hefty tip and thinking I might go and have a nice bath with my new lavender bath essence . . . when the front door into reception swings open. Into the hotel strides a girl with blond hair, a Louis Vuitton bag and long tanned legs.

I stare at her in disbelief. It's Alicia Billington. Or, as I call her, Alicia Bitch Long-legs. What's *she* doing here?

Alicia is one of the account executives in Brandon Communications – which is Luke's PR company – and we've never exactly got along. In fact, between you and me, she's a bit of a cow and secretly, I wish Luke would fire her. A few months ago, she nearly did get fired – and it was kind of to do with me. (I was a financial journalist then, and I wrote this piece . . . oh, it's a bit of a long story.) But in the end she just got a stiff warning, and since then she's really pulled her socks up.

I know all this because I have little chats every now and then with Luke's assistant, Mel, who's a real sweetie and keeps me up with all the gossip. She was telling me only the other day that she reckons Alicia's really changed. She isn't any *nicer* – but she certainly works harder. She badgers journalists until they put her clients into their stories, and often stays really late at the office, tapping at her computer. Only the other day she told Mel she wanted a full list of all the company's clients, with contact names, so she could familiarize herself with them. Mel added gloomily that she reckons Alicia wants a promotion – and I think she could be right. The trouble with Luke is, he only looks at how hard a person works and what results they get – and not at what a completely horrible cow they are. So the chances are, she probably will get a promotion and become even more unbearable.

As I watch her come in, half of me wants to run away and half of me wants to know what she's doing here. But before I can decide, she spots me, and raises her eyebrows slightly. And oh God, suddenly I realize what I must look like – in a grotty old grey T-shirt that, to be honest, looks nothing like a dress, and my hair a mess, and my face all red from lugging carrier bags full of lavender honey. And she's in an immaculate white suit.

'Rebecca!' she says, and puts her hand over her mouth in mock dismay. 'You're not supposed to know I'm here! Just pretend you haven't seen me.'

'What . . . what do you mean?' I say, trying not to sound as disconcerted as I feel. 'What *are* you doing here?'

'I've just popped in for a quick introductory meeting with the new associates,' says Alicia. 'You know my parents only live five miles away? So it made sense.'

'Oh right,' I say. 'No, I didn't.'

'But Luke's given us all *strict* instructions,' says Alicia. 'We're not allowed to bother you. After all, this is your holiday!'

There's something about the way she says it that makes me feel like a child.

'Oh, I don't mind,' I say robustly. 'When something as . . . as important as this is going on. In fact, Luke and I were talking about it earlier on. Over breakfast.'

OK, so I only mentioned breakfast to remind her that Luke and I are going out together. Which I *know* is really pathetic. But, whenever I'm talking to Alicia, I feel we're in some secret little competition, and if I don't fight back, she'll think she's won.

'Really?' says Alicia. 'How sweet.' Her eyes narrow slightly. 'So – what do you think of this whole enterprise? You must have a view.'

'I think it's great,' I say after a pause. 'Really great.'

'You don't mind?' Her eyes are probing my face.

'Well . . . not really.' I shrug. 'I mean, it was supposed to be a holiday, but if it's that important—'

'I don't mean the meetings,' says Alicia, laughing a little. 'I mean – this whole deal. The whole New York thing.'

I open my mouth to reply – then feebly close it again. What New York thing?

Like a buzzard sensing weakness, she leans forward, a tiny, malicious smile at her lips. 'You do *know*, don't you, Rebecca, that Luke's going to move to New York?'

I can't move for shock. Luke's moving to New York. That's what he's so excited about. He's moving to New York. But . . . but why hasn't he told me?

My face feels rather hot and there's a horrible thickening in my chest. Luke's going to New York and he hasn't even told me.

'Rebecca?'

My head jerks up, and I quickly force a smile onto my face. I can't let Alicia realize this is all news to me. I just *can't*.

'Of course I know about it,' I say huskily, and clear my throat. 'I know all about it. But I . . . I never discuss business in public. Much better to be discreet, don't you think?'

'Oh absolutely,' she answers – and the way she looks at me makes me think she isn't convinced for a minute. 'So will you be going out there too?'

I stare back, my lips trembling, unable to think of an

answer, my face growing pinker and pinker – when suddenly, thank God, a voice behind me says,

'Rebecca Bloomwood. Parcel for a Miss Rebecca Bloomwood.'

My head jerks round in astonishment, and . . . I don't believe it. A man in uniform is approaching the desk, holding my huge, battered Special Express parcel, which I'd honestly given up for lost. All my things, at last. All my carefully chosen outfits. I can wear anything I like tonight!

But somehow . . . I don't really care any more. I just want to go off somewhere and be on my own and think for a bit.

'That's me,' I say, managing a smile. 'I'm Rebecca Bloomwood.'

'Oh right!' says the man. 'That's nice and easy then. If you could just sign here . . .'

'Well, I mustn't keep you!' exclaims Alicia, eyeing my parcel amusedly. 'Enjoy the rest of your stay, won't you?'

'Thanks,' I reply. 'I will.' And, feeling slightly numb, I walk away, clutching my clothes tightly to me.

Endwich Bank
FULHAM BRANCH
3 Fulham Road
London SW6 9JH

Ms Rebecca Bloomwood
Flat 2
4 Burney Rd
London SW6 8FD

Dear Miss Bloomwood

Thank you for your letter of 4 September, addressed to Sweetie Smeathie, in which you ask him to rush through an extension of your overdraft 'before the new guy arrives'.

I am the new guy.

I am currently reviewing all customer files and will be in touch regarding your request.

Yours sincerely

John Gavin
Overdraft Facilities Director

ENDWICH – BECAUSE WE CARE

Five

We arrive back in London the next day – and Luke still hasn't mentioned his deal, or New York, or anything. And I know I should just ask him outright. I know I should casually say, 'What's this I hear about New York, Luke?' and wait and see what he says. But somehow . . . I can't bring myself to do it.

I mean, for a start, he's made it plain enough that he doesn't want to talk about his deal. If I start mentioning New York, he might think I've been trying to find out stuff behind his back. And for another start, Alicia might have got it wrong – or even be making it up. (She's quite capable of it, believe me. When I was a financial journalist she once sent me to completely the wrong room for a press conference – and I'm sure it was deliberate.) So until I'm absolutely certain of my facts, there's no point saying anything.

At least, this is what I tell myself. But I suppose if I'm really honest, the reason is that I just can't bear the idea of Luke turning to me and giving me a kind look and saying, 'Rebecca, we've had a lot of fun, but . . .'

So I end up saying nothing, and smiling a lot – even though inside, I feel more and more tense and miserable. As we arrive back outside my flat, I want to turn to him and wail, 'Are you going to New York? Are you?'

But instead I give him a kiss, and say lightly, 'You will be OK for Saturday, won't you?'

It turns out Luke's got to fly off to Zurich tomorrow and have lots of meetings with finance people. Which of course is very important and I completely understand that. But Saturday is Tom and Lucy's wedding at home – and that's even more important. He just *has* to be there.

'I'll make it,' he says. 'I promise.' He squeezes my hand and I get out of the car and he says he has to shoot off. And then he's gone.

Disconsolately, I open the door to our flat, and a moment later Suze comes out of her room, dragging a full black bin liner along the ground.

'Hi!' she says. 'You're back.'

'Yes!' I reply, trying to sound cheerful. 'I'm back!'

Suze disappears out of our door, and I hear her lugging her black bag down the stairs and out of the main front door – then bounding up to our flat again.

'So, how was it?' she says breathlessly, closing the door behind her.

'It was fine,' I say, walking into my bedroom. 'It was . . . nice.'

'Nice?' Suze's eyes narrow and she follows me in. 'Only nice?'

'It was . . . good.'

'*Good?* Bex, what's wrong? Didn't you have a lovely time?'

I wasn't really planning to say anything to Suze, because after all, I don't know the facts yet. Plus I read in a magazine recently that couples should try to sort their problems out alone, without recourse to others. But as I look at her warm, friendly face, I just can't help it. I hear myself blurting out,

'Luke's moving to New York.'

'Really?' says Suze, missing the point. 'Fantastic! God, I love New York. I went there three years ago, and—'

'Suze, he's moving to New York – but he hasn't told me.'

'Oh,' says Suze, looking taken aback. 'Oh, right.'

'And I don't want to bring it up, because I'm not supposed to know, but I keep thinking, why hasn't he told me? Is he just going to . . . *go*?' My voice is rising in distress. 'Will I just get a postcard from the Empire State Building saying "Hi I live in New York now, love Luke"?'

'No!' says Suze at once. 'Of course not! He wouldn't do that.'

'Wouldn't he?'

'No. Definitely not.' Suze folds her arms and thinks for a few moments – then looks up. 'Are you absolutely sure he hasn't told you? Like, maybe when you were half asleep or daydreaming or something?'

She looks at me expectantly and for a few moments I think hard, wondering if she could be right. Maybe he told me in the car and I just wasn't listening. Or last night, while I was eyeing up that girl's Lulu Guinness handbag in the bar . . . But then I shake my head.

'No I'm sure I'd remember if he'd mentioned New York.' I sink miserably onto the bed. 'He's just not telling me because he's going to chuck me.'

'No he's not!' retorts Suze. 'Honestly, Bex, men never mention things. That's just what they're like.' She picks her way over a pile of CDs and sits cross-legged on the bed beside me. 'My brother never mentioned when he got done for drugs. We had to find it out from the paper! And my father once bought a whole island without telling my mother.'

'Really?'

'Oh yes! And then he forgot about it, too. And he only remembered when he got this letter out of the blue inviting him to roll the pig in the barrel.'

'To do *what*?'

'Oh, this ancient ceremony thing,' says Suze vaguely.

'My dad gets to roll the first pig, because he owns the island.' Her eyes brighten. 'In fact, he's always looking for people to do it instead of him. I don't suppose you fancy doing it this year, do you? You get to wear this funny hat, and you have to learn a poem in Gaelic but it's quite easy . . .'

'Suze—'

'Maybe not,' says Suze hurriedly. 'Sorry.' She leans back on my pillow and chews a fingernail thoughtfully. Then suddenly she looks up. 'Hang on a minute. Who told you about New York? If it wasn't Luke?'

'Alicia,' I say gloomily. 'She knew all about it.'

'Alicia?' Suze stares at me. 'Alicia Bitch Long-legs? Oh for goodness' sake. She's probably making it up. Honestly Bex, I'm surprised you even listened!'

She sounds so sure that I feel my heart giving a joyful leap. Of course. That must be the answer. Didn't I suspect it myself? Didn't I tell you what Alicia was like?

The only thing – tiny niggle – is I'm not sure Suze is completely one hundred per cent unbiased here. There's a bit of history between Suze and Alicia, which is that they both started working at Brandon Communications at the same time – but Suze got the sack after three weeks and Alicia went on to have a high-flying career. Not that Suze really wanted to be a PR girl, but still.

'I don't know,' I say doubtfully. 'Would Alicia really do that?'

'Of course she would!' says Suze. 'She's just trying to wind you up. Come on, Bex, who do you trust more? Alicia or Luke?'

'Luke,' I say after a pause. 'Luke, of course.'

'Well then!'

'You're right,' I say, feeling more cheerful. 'You're right! I should just trust Luke, shouldn't I? I shouldn't listen to gossip and rumours.'

'Exactly.'

Suze reaches for a bundle of envelopes. 'Here are your letters, by the way. And your messages.'

'Ooh thanks!' I take the bundle with a pang of hope. Because you never know, do you, what might have happened while you're away? Maybe one of these envelopes is a letter from a long-lost friend, or a wonderful job offer, or news that I've won a holiday!

But of course, they aren't. It's just one boring old bill after another. I leaf through them dismissively before dropping the whole lot to the floor without even opening them.

You know, this always happens. Whenever I go away, I always think I'll come back to mountains of thrilling post, with parcels and telegrams and letters full of scintillating news – and I'm always disappointed. In fact, I really think someone should set up a company called holidaypost.com which you would pay to write you loads of exciting letters, just so you had *something* to look forward to when you got home.

I turn to my phone messages. Suze has written them down really conscientiously:

Your mum – what are you wearing to Tom and Lucy's wedding?
Your mum – don't wear violet as it will clash with her hat.
Your mum – Luke does know it's morning dress?
Your mum – Luke *is* definitely coming, isn't he?
David Barrow – please could you ring him.
Your mum –

Hang on. David Barrow. Who's that?

'Hey, Suze!' I yell. 'Did David Barrow say who he was?'

'No,' says Suze, appearing in the hall. 'He just said could you ring him.'

'Oh, right.' I look again at the message. 'What did he sound like?'

Suze screws up her nose.

'Oh, you know. Quite posh. Quite . . . smooth.'

I feel intrigued as I dial the number. David Barrow. It sounds almost familiar. Maybe he's a film producer or something!

'David Barrow,' comes his voice – and Suze is right, he is quite posh.

'Hello!' I say. 'This is Rebecca Bloomwood. I had a message to call you?'

'Ah, Miss Bloomwood. I'm the special customer manager of La Rosa.'

'Oh.' I screw up my face, puzzled. La Rosa? What on earth's—

Oh yes. That trendy boutique in Hampstead. But I've only been in there about once, and that was ages ago. So why is he calling me?

'May I say first what an honour it is to have a television personality of your calibre as one of our customers?'

'Oh! Well – thank you,' I say, beaming at the phone. 'It's a pleasure, actually.'

This is great. I know exactly why he's calling. They're going to give me some free clothes, aren't they? Or maybe . . . yes! They want me to design a new range for them! God, yes. I'll be a designer. They'll call it the Becky Bloomwood collection. Simple, stylish, wearable garments, with maybe one or two evening dresses . . .

'This is simply a courtesy call,' says David Barrow, interrupting my thoughts. 'I just want to ensure that you are completely happy with our service and ask if you have any other needs we can help you with.'

'Well – thanks!' I say. 'I'm very happy, thanks. I mean, I'm not exactly a regular customer but—'

'Also to mention the small matter of your out-standing La Rosa Card account,' adds David Barrow as though I haven't spoken. 'And to inform you that if payment is not received within seven days, further action will have to be taken.'

I stare at the phone, feeling my smile fade. This isn't a courtesy call at all, is it? He doesn't want me to design a collection of clothes. He's phoning about money!

I feel slightly outraged. Surely people aren't just allowed to telephone you in your own home and demand money with no warning? I mean, *obviously* I'm going to pay them. Just because I don't send a cheque off the moment the bill comes through the letterbox . . .

'It has been three months now since your first bill,' David Barrow is saying. 'And I must inform you that our policy after the three-month period is to hand over all outstanding accounts to—'

'Yes, well,' I interrupt coolly. 'My . . . accountants are dealing with all my bills at the moment. I'll speak to them.'

'I'm so glad to hear it. Of course, we look forward to seeing you again in La Rosa very soon!'

'Yeah well,' I say grumpily. 'Maybe.'

I put the phone down as Suze comes past the door again, dragging another black bin bag. 'Suze, what *are* you doing?' I say, staring at her.

'I'm decluttering!' she says. 'It's brilliant. So cleansing! You should try it. So – who was David Barrow?'

'Just some stupid bill I hadn't paid,' I say. 'Honestly! Phoning me at home!'

'Ooh, that reminds me. Hang on . . .'

She disappears for a moment, then appears again, holding a bundle of envelopes.

'I found these under my bed when I was tidying up, and this other lot were on my dressing table . . . I think you must have left them in my room.' She pulls a face. 'I think they're all bills, too.'

'Oh, thanks,' I say, and throw them onto the bed.

'Maybe . . .' says Suze hesitantly, 'maybe you should pay some of them off? You know. Just one or two.'

'But I have paid them off!' I say in surprise. 'I paid them all off in June. Don't you remember?'

'Oh yes!' says Suze. 'Yes, of course I do.' She bites her lip. 'But the thing is, Bex . . .'

'What?'

'Well . . . that was a while ago, wasn't it? And maybe you've built up a few debts since then.'

'Since *June*?' I give a little laugh. 'But that was only about five minutes ago! Honestly, Suze, you don't need to worry. I mean . . . take this one.' I reach randomly for an envelope. 'I mean what have I bought in M&S recently? Nothing!'

'Oh right,' says Suze, looking relieved. 'So this bill will just be for . . . zero, will it?'

'Absolutely,' I say ripping it open. 'Zero! Or, you know, ten quid. You know, for the odd pair of knickers—'

I pull out the account and look at it. For a moment I can't speak.

'How much is it?' says Suze in alarm.

'It's . . . it's wrong,' I say, trying to stuff it back in the envelope. 'It has to be wrong. I'll write them a letter . . .'

'Let me see.' Suze grabs the bill and her eyes widen. '£365? Bex—'

'It has to be wrong,' I say – but my voice is holding less conviction. Suddenly I'm remembering those leather trousers I bought in the Marble Arch sale. And that dressing gown. And that phase I went through of eating M&S sushi every day.

Suze stares at me for a few minutes, her face creased anxiously.

'Bex – d'you think all of these other bills are as high as that?'

Silently I reach for the envelope from Selfridges, and tear it open. Even as I do so, I'm remembering that chrome juicer, the one I saw and *had* to have . . . I've never even used it. And that fur-trimmed dress. Where did that go?

'How much is it?'

'It's . . . it's enough,' I reply, pushing it quickly back inside, before she can see that it's well over £400.

I turn away, trying to keep calm. But I feel alarmed and slightly angry. This is all wrong. The whole point is, I paid off my cards. I *paid them off.* I mean – what's the point of paying off all your credit cards if they all just go and sprout huge new debts again? What is the point? We all may as well just give up right now.

'Look, Bex, don't worry,' says Suze. 'You'll be OK! I just won't cash your rent cheque this month.'

'No!' I exclaim. 'Don't be silly. You've been good enough to me already. I don't want to owe you anything. I'd rather owe M&S.' I look round and see her anxious face. 'Suze, don't *worry*! I can easily put this lot off for a bit.' I hit the letter. 'And meanwhile, I'll get a bigger overdraft or something. In fact, I've just asked the bank for an extension – so I can easily ask for a bit more. I'll phone them right now!'

'What, this minute?'

'Why not?'

I pick up the phone again, reach for an old bank statement and briskly dial the Endwich number.

'You see, there really isn't a problem,' I say reassuringly. 'One little phone call is all it'll take.'

'Your call is being transferred to the Central Endwich Call Centre,' comes a tinny voice down the line. 'Kindly memorize the following number for future use: 0800 . . .'

'What's going on?' says Suze.

'I'm being transferred to some central system,' I say, as *The Four Seasons* starts to play. 'They'll probably be really quick and efficient. This is great, isn't it? Doing it all over the phone.'

'Welcome to Endwich Bank!' says a new woman's voice in my ear. 'Please key in your account number.'

What's my account number? Shit! I've got no idea—

Oh yes. On my bank statement.

'Thank you!' says a voice as I finish pressing the numbers. 'Now please key in your personal identification number.'

What?

Personal identification number? I didn't know I had a personal identification number. Honestly! They never told me—

Actually . . . maybe that does ring a slight bell.

Oh God. What was it again? 73-something? 37-something?

'Please key in your personal identification number,' repeats the voice pleasantly.

'But I don't *know* my bloody personal identification number!' I say. 'Quick, Suze, if you were me, what would you choose as a personal identification number?'

'Ooh!' says Suze. 'Um . . . I'd choose . . . um . . . 1234?'

'Please key in your personal identification number,' says the voice, with a definite edge to it this time.

God, this is really stressful.

'Try my number for my bicycle lock,' suggests Suze. 'It's 435.'

'Suze – I need *my* number. Not yours.'

'You might have chosen the same. You never know!'

'Please key in—'

'All right!' I yell, and punch in 435.

'I'm sorry,' intones the voice. 'This password is invalid.'

'I knew it wouldn't work!'

'It might have done,' says Suze defensively.

'It should be four digits, anyway,' I say, having a sudden flash of memory. 'I had to phone up and register it . . . and I was standing in the kitchen . . . and . . . yes! Yes! I'd just got my new Karen Millen shoes, and I was looking at the price tag . . . and that was the number I used!'

'How much were they?' says Suze in excitement.

'They were . . . 120 reduced to . . . 84.99!'

'Punch it in! 8499!'

Excitedly I punch in 8499 – and to my disbelief, the voice says, 'Thank you! You are through to the Endwich Banking Corporation. Endwich – because we care. For debt control, press 1. For mortgage arrears, press 2. For overdrafts and bank charges, press 3. For . . .'

'Right! I'm through.' I exhale sharply, feeling a bit like James Bond breaking the code to save the world. 'Am I debt control? Or overdrafts and bank charges?'

'Overdrafts and bank charges,' says Suze knowledgeably.

'OK.' I press 3 and a moment later a cheerful singsong voice greets me.

'Hello! Welcome to the Endwich Central Call Centre. I'm Dawna, how can I help you Miss Bloomwood?'

'Oh, hi!' I say, taken aback. 'Are you real?'

'Yes!' says Dawna, and laughs. 'I'm real. Can I help you?'

'Erm . . . yes. I'm phoning because I need an extension to my overdraft. A few hundred pounds if that's all right. Or, you know, more, if you've got it . . .'

'I see,' says Dawna pleasantly. 'Was there a specific reason? Or just a general need?'

She sounds so nice and friendly, I feel myself start to relax.

'Well, the thing is, I've had to invest quite a bit in my

career recently, and a few bills have come in, and kind of . . . taken me by surprise.'

'Oh right,' says Dawna sympathetically.

'I mean, it's not as if I'm in *trouble*. It's just a temporary thing.'

'A temporary thing,' she echoes, and I hear her typing in the background.

'I suppose I have been letting things mount up a bit. But the thing was, I paid everything off. I thought I'd be able to relax for a bit!'

'Oh right.'

'So you understand?' I give a relieved beam at Suze, who offers me thumbs-up in return. God, this is more like it. Just one quick and easy call, exactly like in the adverts. No nasty letters, no tricky questions . . .

'I completely understand,' Dawna's saying. 'It happens to us all, doesn't it?'

'So – can I have the overdraft?' I say joyfully.

'Oh, I'm not authorized to extend your overdraft by more than £50,' says Dawna. 'You'll have to get in touch with your branch Overdraft Facilities Director. Who is a . . . let me see . . . Fulham . . . a Mr John Gavin.'

I stare at the phone in dismay.

'But I've already written to him!'

'Well, that's all right then, isn't it? Now, is there anything else I can help you with?'

'No,' I say. 'No, I don't think so. Thanks anyway.'

I put down the phone disconsolately.

'Stupid bank. Stupid call centre.'

'So are they going to give you the money?' asks Suze.

'I don't know. It all depends on this John Gavin bloke.' I look up and see Suze's anxious face. 'But I'm sure he'll say yes,' I add hastily. 'He's just got to review my file. It'll be fine!'

'I suppose if you just don't spend anything for a while, you'll easily get back on track, won't you?' she says hopefully. 'I mean, you're making loads of money from the telly, aren't you?'

'Yes,' I say after a pause, not liking to tell her that after rent, taxi fares, meals out and outfits for the show, it doesn't actually amount to that much.

'And there's your book, too . . .'

'My book?'

For a moment I stare at her blankly. Then suddenly, with a lift of the heart, I remember. Of course! My self-help book! I've been meaning to do something about that.

Well, thank God. This is the answer. All I have to do is write my book really quickly and get a nice big cheque – and then I'll pay all these cards off and everything will be happy again. Ha. I don't need any stupid overdraft. I'll start straight away. This evening!

The truth is, I'm rather looking forward to getting down to my book. I have so many important themes I want to address in it, like poverty and wealth, comparative religion . . . philosophy maybe . . . I mean, I know the publishers have just asked for a simple self-help book, but there's no reason why I can't encompass broader questions too, is there?

In fact, if it does really well, I might give lectures. God that would be great, wouldn't it? I could become a kind of lifestyle guru and tour the world, and people would flock to see me, and ask my advice on all sorts of issues—

'How's it going?' says Suze, appearing at my door in a towel, and I jump guiltily. I've been sitting at my computer for quite a while now but I haven't actually turned it on.

'I'm just thinking,' I say, hastily reaching to the back of the computer and flipping the switch. 'You know, focusing my thoughts . . . and letting the creative juices meld into a coherent pattern.'

'Wow,' says Suze, and looks at me in slight awe. 'That's amazing. Is it hard?'

'Not really,' I say, after a bit of thought. 'It's quite easy, actually.'

The computer bursts into a riot of sound and colour, and we both stare at it, mesmerized.

'Wow!' says Suze again. 'Did you do that?'

'Erm . . . yes,' I say. Which is true. I mean, I did switch it on.

'God, you're so clever, Bex,' breathes Suze. 'When do you think you'll finish it?'

'Oh, quite soon I expect,' I say breezily. 'You know. Once I get going.'

'Well, I'll leave you to get on with it, then,' says Suze. 'I just wanted to borrow a dress for tonight.'

'Oh right,' I say, with interest. 'Where are you going?'

'Venetia's party,' says Suze. 'D'you want to come too? Oh go on, come! Everyone's going!'

For a moment I'm tempted. I've met Venetia a few times, and I know she gives amazing parties at her parents' house in Kensington.

'No,' I say at last. 'I'd better not. I've got work to do.'

'Oh well.' Suze's face droops briefly. 'But I can borrow a dress, can I?'

'Of course.' I screw up my face for a moment, thinking hard. 'Why don't you wear my new Tocca dress with your red shoes and my English Eccentrics wrap.'

'Excellent!' says Suze, going to my wardrobe. 'Thanks, Bex. And . . . could I borrow some knickers?' she adds casually. 'And some tights and makeup?'

I turn in my chair and give her a close look.

'Suze – when you decluttered your room, did you keep *anything*?'

'Of course I did!' she says, a little defensively. 'You know. A few things.' She meets my gaze. 'OK, perhaps I went a bit too far.'

'Do you have *any* underwear left?'

'Well . . . no. But you know, I feel so good, and kind of positive about my life – it doesn't matter! It's feng shui. You should try it.'

I watch as Suze gathers up the dress and underwear and rifles through my makeup bag. Then she leaves the room and I stretch my arms out in front of me, flexing my fingers. Right. To work. The book.

I open a file, type 'Chapter One', and stare at it proudly. Chapter One! This is so cool! I've actually started! Now all I have to do is come up with a really memorable, striking opening sentence.

I sit quite still for a while, concentrating on the empty screen in front of me, then type briskly,

Finance is the

I stop, and take a sip of Diet Coke. Obviously the right sentence takes a bit of honing. You can't just expect it to land straight in your head.

Finance is the most

God, I wish I was writing a book about clothes. Or makeup. Becky Bloomwood's Guide to Lipstick.

Anyway, I'm not. So concentrate.

Finance is something which

You know, my chair's quite uncomfortable. I'm sure it can't be healthy, sitting on a squashy chair like this for hours on end. I'll get repetitive strain injury, or something. Really, if I'm going to be a writer, I should invest in one of those ergonomic ones that swivel round and go up and down.

Finance is very

Maybe they sell chairs like that on the Internet. Maybe I should just have a quick little look. Since the computer's on, and everything.

In fact – surely it would be irresponsible of me if I didn't. I mean, you have to look after yourself, don't you? 'Mens sana in healthy sana', or whatever it is.

I reach for my mouse, quickly click onto the Internet icon and search for 'office chairs' – and soon I'm coasting happily through the list. I've already noted down a few good possibilities when all of a sudden I land on this incredible website which I've never seen before, all full of office supplies. Not just boring white envelopes, but really amazing hi-tech stuff. Like smart chrome filing cabinets, and cool pen holders and really nice personalized name-plates to put on your door.

I scroll through all the photographs, utterly mesmerized. I mean, I know I'm not supposed to be spending money at the moment – but this is different. This is investment in my career. After all, this is my office, isn't it? It should be well equipped. It *needs* to be well equipped. In fact, I can't believe how short-sighted I've been. How on earth was I expecting to write a book without the necessary equipment? It would be like climbing Everest without a tent.

I'm so dazzled by the array of stuff that I almost can't decide what to get. But there are a few essentials which I absolutely must buy.

So I click on an ergonomic swivel chair upholstered in purple to match my iMac, plus a Dictaphone which translates stuff straight into your computer. And then I find myself adding a really cool steel claw which holds up notes while you're typing, a set of laminated presentation folders – which are bound to come in useful – and a mini paper shredder. Which is a complete essential because I don't want the whole world seeing my first drafts, do I? I'm toying with the idea of some modular reception furniture – except I don't really have a reception area in my bedroom – when Suze comes back into the room.

'Hi! How's it going?'

I jump guiltily, quickly click on SEND without even bothering to check what the final amount was, click off the Internet – and look up just as my Chapter One reappears on the screen.

'You're working really hard,' says Suze, shaking her head. 'You should take a break. How much have you done?'

'Oh . . . quite a lot.'

'Can I read it?' And to my horror she starts coming towards me.

'No!' I exclaim. 'I mean – it's a work in progress. It's . . . sensitive material.' Hastily I close the document and stand up. 'You look really great, Suze. Fantastic!'

'Thanks!' She beams at me and as she twirls around in my dress the doorbell rings. 'Ooh! That'll be Fenny.'

Fenella is one of Suze's weird posh cousins from Scotland. Except to be fair, she's not actually that weird any more. She used to be as peculiar as her brother Tarquin and spend the whole time riding horses and shooting fish, or whatever they do. But recently she's moved to London and got a job in an art gallery, and now she just goes to parties instead. Suze opens the front door and I can hear Fenella's high-pitched voice – and a whole gaggle of girls' voices following her. Fenny can't move three feet without a huge cloud of shrieking people around her. She's like some socialite version of a rain god.

'Hi!' she says, bursting into my room. She's wearing a really nice pink velvet skirt from Whistles, which I've also got – but she's teamed it with a disastrous brown Lurex polo neck. 'Hi Becky! Are you coming tonight?'

'Not tonight,' I say. 'I've got to work.'

'Oh well.' Fenella's face droops just like Suze's did –

then brightens. 'Then can I borrow your Jimmy Choos? We've got the same size feet, haven't we?'

'OK,' I say. 'They're in the wardrobe.' I hesitate, trying to be tactful. 'And do you want to borrow a top? It's just I've actually got the top that goes with your skirt. Pink cashmere with little beads. Really nice.'

'Have you?' says Fenny. 'Ooh yes! I shoved on this polo neck without really thinking.' As she peels it off, a blonde girl in a black shift comes in and beams at me.

'Hi, er . . . Milla,' I say, remembering her name just in time. 'How are you?'

'I'm fine,' she says, and gives me a hopeful look. 'Fenny said I could borrow your English Eccentrics wrap.'

'I'm lending it to Suze,' I say, pulling a regretful face. 'But what about . . . a purple shawl with sequins?'

'Yes please! And Binky says, have you still got that black wrap-around skirt?'

'I have,' I say thoughtfully. 'But actually, I've got another skirt I think would look even better on her . . .'

It's about half an hour before everyone has borrowed what they want. Eventually they pile out of my room, shrieking to me that they'll return it all in the morning, and Suze comes in, looking completely stunning with her hair piled up on her head and hanging down in blond tendrils.

'Bex, are you sure you don't want to come?' she says. 'Tarquin's going to be there, and I know he'd like to see you.'

'Oh right,' I say, trying not to look too appalled at the idea. 'Is he in London, then?'

'Just for a few days.' Suze looks at me, a little sorrowfully. 'You know, Bex, if it weren't for Luke . . . I reckon Tarkie still likes you.'

'I'm sure he doesn't,' I say quickly. 'That was ages ago now. Ages!'

My one and only date with Tarquin is an event I am trying very hard never to remember again, ever.

'Oh well,' says Suze, shrugging. 'See you later. And don't work too hard!'

'I won't,' I reply, and give a world-weary sigh. 'Or at least, I'll try not to.'

I wait until the front door bangs behind her, and the taxis waiting outside have roared off. Then I take a sip of tea and turn back to my first chapter.

Chapter One

Finance is very

Actually, I'm not really in the mood for this any more. Suze is right. I should have a break. I mean, if I sit here hour after hour I'll get all jaded, and lose the creative flow. And the point is, I've made a good start.

I stand up and stretch, then wander into the sitting room and pick up a copy of *Tatler*. It's *EastEnders* in a minute, and then it might be *Changing Rooms* or something, or that documentary about the vets. I'll just watch that – and then I'll go back to work. I mean, I've got a whole evening ahead, haven't I? I need to pace myself.

Idly, I flick open the magazine and am scanning the contents page for something interesting when suddenly my eye stops in surprise. It's a little picture of Luke, with the caption *Best of Brandon, page 74*! Why on earth didn't he tell me he was going to be in *Tatler*?

The photograph is his new official one, the one I helped him choose an outfit for (blue shirt, dark blue Fendi tie). He's staring at the camera, looking all serious and businesslike – but if you look closely at his eyes, there's a tiny smile in there. As I stare at his familiar face I feel a tug of affection and realize Suze is right. I should just trust him, shouldn't I? I mean, what does Alicia Bitchy-pants know about anything?

I turn to page 74, and it's an article on Britain's Top Movers and Shakers. I scan down the page . . . and I can't help noticing that some of the Movers and Shakers are pictured with their partners. Maybe there'll be a picture of me, with Luke! After all, somebody might have taken a picture of us together at a party or something, mightn't they? Come to think of it, we were once snapped by the *Evening Standard* at a launch for some new magazine, although it never actually got into the paper.

Ooh! Here he is, number 34! And it's just him, in that same official photo, with not a glimpse of me. Still, I feel a twinge of pride as I see his picture (much bigger than some of the others, ha!) and a caption reading: *Brandon's ruthless pursuit of success has knocked lesser competitors off the starting blocks.* Then the piece starts: 'Luke Brandon, dynamic owner and founder of Brandon Communications, the blah-di blah-di . . .'

I skim over the text, feeling a pleasant anticipation as I reach the section labelled 'Vital Statistics'. This is the bit where I'll be mentioned! 'Currently dating TV personality Rebecca Bloomwood'. Or maybe, 'Partner of well-known finance expert Rebecca Bloomwood'. Or else—

Luke James Brandon
Age: 34
Education: Cambridge
Current status: Single

Single?

Luke told them he was *single*?

A hurt anger begins to rise through me as I stare at Luke's confident, arrogant gaze. Suddenly I've had enough of all this. I've had enough of being made to

98

feel insecure and paranoid and wondering what's going on. Hands trembling, I pick up the phone and jab in Luke's number.

'Yes,' I say, as soon as the message has finished. 'Yes, well. If you're single, Luke, then I'm single too. OK? And if you're going to New York, then I'm going to . . . to Outer Mongolia. And if you're . . .'

Suddenly my mind goes blank. Shit, and it was going so well.

'. . . if you're too cowardly to tell me these things yourself, then maybe it's better for both of us if we simply . . .'

I'm really struggling here. I should have written it all down before I began.

'. . . if we just call it a day. Or perhaps that's what you think you've already done,' I finish, breathing hard.

'Becky?' Suddenly Luke's deep voice is in my ear, and I jump with fright.

'Yes?' I say, trying to sound dignified.

'What *is* all this gibberish you're spouting on my machine?' he asks calmly.

'It's not gibberish!' I reply indignantly. 'It's the truth!'

' "If you're single, then I'm single?" What's that supposed to be? Lyrics to a pop song?'

'I was talking about you! And the fact that you've told the whole world you're single.'

'I've done what?' says Luke, sounding amused. 'When did I do that?'

'It's in *Tatler*!' I say furiously. 'This month!' I grab for the magazine and flip it open. ' "Britain's Top Movers and Shakers. Number 34, Luke Brandon." '

'Oh, for God's sake,' says Luke. 'That thing.'

'Yes, that thing!' I exclaim. 'That thing! And it says you're single. How do you think it felt for me to see you'd said you were single?'

'It quotes me, does it?'

'Well . . . no,' I say after a pause. 'It doesn't exactly quote you. But I mean, they must have phoned you up and asked you—'

'They did phone me up and ask me,' he says. 'And I said no comment.'

'Oh.' I'm silenced for a moment, trying to think clearly. OK, so maybe he didn't say he was single – but I'm not sure I like 'no comment'. Isn't that what people say when things are going really badly?

'Why did you say no comment?' I say at last. 'Why didn't you say you were going out with me?'

'My darling,' says Luke, sounding a little weary, 'think about it. Do you *want* our private life splashed all over the media?'

'Of course not.' I twist my hands into a complicated knot. 'Of course not. But you . . .' I stop.

'What?'

'You told the media when you were going out with Sacha,' I say in a small voice.

Sacha is Luke's ex-girlfriend.

I can't quite believe I just said that.

Luke sighs.

'Becky, *Sacha* told the media about us. She would have had *Hello!* photographing us in the bath if they'd been interested. That's the kind of girl she was.'

'Oh,' I say, winding the telephone cord round my finger.

'I'm not interested in that kind of thing. My clients can do what they like, but personally, I can't think of anything worse. Hence the no comment.' He pauses. 'But you're right. I should have thought. I should have warned you. I'm sorry.'

'That's all right,' I say awkwardly. 'I suppose I shouldn't have jumped to conclusions.'

'So are we OK?' says Luke, and there's a warm, teasing note in his voice. 'Are we back on course?'

'What about New York?' I say, hating myself. 'Is that all a mistake, too?'

There's a long, horrible silence.

'What have you heard about New York?' says Luke at last – and to my horror, he sounds businesslike and distant.

Oh God. *Why* couldn't I keep my mouth closed?

'Nothing really,' I stammer. 'I . . . I don't know. I just . . .'

I tail off feebly, and for what seems like hours, neither of us says anything. My heart is pounding hard and I'm clutching the receiver so hard, my ear's starting to hurt.

'Becky, I need to talk to you about a few things,' says Luke finally. 'But now is not the time.'

'Right,' I say, feeling a pang of fright. 'What . . . sort of things?'

'Not now. We'll talk when I get back, OK? Saturday. At the wedding.'

'Right,' I say again, talking brightly to hide the nerves in my voice. 'OK! Well I'll . . . I'll see you then, then . . .'

But before I can say any more, he's gone.

MANAGING YOUR MONEY

A COMPREHENSIVE GUIDE TO PERSONAL FINANCE

BY REBECCA BLOOMWOOD

FIRST EDITION (UK)

(FIRST DRAFT)

PART ONE

CHAPTER ONE

Finance is very

Endwich Bank
FULHAM BRANCH
3 Fulham Road
London SW6 9JH

Ms Rebecca Bloomwood
Flat 2
4 Burney Rd
London SW6 8FD

Dear Miss Bloomwood

Further to my letter of 8 September, I have conducted a thorough examination of your account. Your current overdraft limit vastly exceeds the bank's approved ratios. I cannot see any need for this excessive level of debt, nor that any genuine attempts have been made to reduce it. The situation is little short of a disgrace.

Whatever special status you have enjoyed in the past will not be continuing in the future. I will certainly not be increasing your overdraft limit as you request, and would ask as a matter of urgency that you make an appointment with me to discuss your position.

Yours sincerely

John Gavin
Overdraft Facilities Director

ENDWICH – BECAUSE WE CARE

Six

I arrive at my parent's house at ten o'clock on Saturday, to find the street full of festivity. There are balloons tied to every tree, our drive is full of cars, and a billowing marquee is just visible from next door's garden. I get out of my car, reach for my overnight bag – then stand still for a few moments, staring at the Websters' house. God, this is strange. Tom Webster getting married. I can hardly believe it. To be honest – and this may sound a bit mean – I can hardly believe that anyone would *want* to marry Tom Webster. He has smartened up his act recently, admittedly. He's got a few new clothes, and a better hairstyle. But his hands are still all huge and clammy – and frankly, he's not Brad Pitt, is he?

Still, that's the point of love, I think, closing my car door with a bang. You love people despite their flaws. Lucy obviously doesn't mind that Tom's got clammy hands – and he obviously doesn't mind that her hair's all flat and boring. It's quite romantic, I suppose.

As I'm standing there, gazing at the house, a girl in jeans and a circlet of flowers in her hair appears at the Websters' front door. She gives me an odd, almost aggressive look – then disappears inside the house again. One of Lucy's bridesmaids, obviously. I expect she's a bit nervous about being seen in her jeans.

Lucy's probably in there too, it occurs to me – and instinctively I turn away. I know she's the bride and everything, but to be honest, I'm not desperately looking forward to seeing Lucy again. I've only met her a couple of times and we've never gelled. Probably because she had the idea I was in love with Tom. Oh God. Still, at least when Luke arrives I'll finally be able to prove them all wrong.

At the thought of Luke, a flurry of nerves goes through me, and I take a deep, slow breath to calm myself. I'm determined I'm not going to put the cart before the horse this time. I'm going to keep an open mind, and see what he says today. And if he does tell me he's moving away to New York then I'll just . . . deal with it. Somehow.

Anyway. Don't think about it now. Briskly I head for the front door and let myself in. In the kitchen I find my dad drinking coffee in his waistcoat, while Mum, dressed in a nylon cape with her hair in curlers, is buttering a round of sandwiches.

'I just don't think it's right,' she's saying as I walk in. 'It's not right. They're supposed to be leading our country, and look at them. They're a mess! Dowdy jackets, dreadful ties . . .'

'You really think the ability to govern is affected by what you wear, do you?'

'Hi, Mum,' I say, dumping my bag on the floor. 'Hi, Dad.'

'It's the principle of the thing!' says Mum. 'If they're not prepared to make an effort with their dress, then why should they make any effort with the economy?'

'It's hardly the same thing!'

'It's exactly the same thing. Becky, *you* think Gordon Brown should dress more smartly, don't you? All this lounge suit nonsense.'

'I don't know,' I say vaguely. 'Maybe.'

'You see? Becky agrees with me. Now, let me have a look at you, darling.' She puts down her knife and surveys me properly, and I feel myself glowing a little, because I know I look good. I'm wearing a shocking pink dress and jacket, a Philip Treacy feathered hat, and the most beautiful black satin shoes, each decorated with a single gossamer butterfly. 'Oh, Becky,' says Mum at last. 'You look lovely. You'll upstage the bride!' She reaches for my hat and looks at it. 'This is very unusual! How much did it cost?'

'Erm . . . I can't remember,' I say vaguely. 'Maybe fifty quid?'

This is not quite true. It was actually more like . . . Well anyway, quite a lot. Still, it was worth it.

'So, where's Luke?' says Mum, popping my hat back on my head. 'Parking the car?'

'Yes, where's Luke?' says my father, looking up, and gives a jocular laugh. 'We've been looking forward to meeting this young man of yours at last.'

'Luke's coming separately,' I say – and flinch slightly as I see their faces fall.

'Separately?' says Mum at last. 'Why's that?'

'He's flying back from Zurich this morning,' I explain. 'He had to go there for business. But he'll be here, I promise.'

'He does know the service starts at twelve?' says Mum anxiously. 'And you've told him where the church is?'

'Yes!' I say. 'Honestly, he'll be here.'

I'm aware that I sound slightly snappy, but I can't help it. To be honest, I'm a bit stressed out myself about where Luke's got to. He was supposed to be ringing me when he landed at the airport – and that was supposed to be half an hour ago. But so far I haven't heard anything.

Still. He said he'd be here.

'Can I do anything to help?' I ask, to change the subject.

'Be a darling, and take these upstairs for me,' says

Mum, cutting the sandwiches briskly into triangles. 'I've got to pack away the patio cushions.'

'Who's upstairs?' I say, picking up the plate.

'Maureen's come over to blow-dry Janice's hair,' says Mum. 'They wanted to keep out of Lucy's way. You know, while she's getting ready.'

'Have you seen her yet?' I ask interestedly. 'Has she got a nice dress?'

'I haven't seen it,' says Mum, and lowers her voice. 'But apparently it cost *three thousand pounds*. And that's not including the veil!'

'Wow,' I say, impressed. For a second I feel ever so slightly envious. I mean, I can't think of anything worse than marrying Tom Webster – but still. A £3,000 dress. And a party . . . and loads of presents . . . I mean, people who get married have it all, don't they?

Upstairs I hear the sound of blow-drying coming from Mum and Dad's bedroom, and as I go in, I see Janice sitting on the dressing-room stool, wearing a dressing gown, holding a sherry glass, and dabbing at her eyes with a hanky. Maureen, who's been doing Mum's and Janice's hair for years now, is brandishing a hair-drier at her, and a woman I don't recognize with a mahogany tan, dyed blond curly hair and a silk lilac suit is sitting on the window seat and smoking a cigarette.

'Hello, Janice,' I say, going over and giving her a hug. 'How are you feeling?'

'I'm fine, dear,' she says, and gives a sniff. 'A little wobbly. You know. To think of Tom getting married!'

'I know,' I say sympathetically. 'It doesn't seem like yesterday that we were kids, riding our bikes together!'

'Have another sherry, Janice,' says Maureen comfortably, and slooshes a deep brown liquid into her glass. 'It'll help you relax.'

'Oh Becky,' says Janice, and squeezes my hand. 'This must be a hard day for you, too.'

I knew it. She does still think I fancy Tom, doesn't she? *Why* do all mothers think their sons are irresistible?

'Not really!' I say, as brightly as I can. 'I mean, I'm just pleased for Tom. And Lucy, of course . . .'

'Becky?' The woman on the window seat turns towards me, eyes narrowed suspiciously. 'This is Becky?'

There's not an ounce of friendliness in her face. Oh God, don't say *she* thinks I'm after Tom, too.

'Er . . . yes.' I smile at her. 'I'm Rebecca Bloomwood. And you must be Lucy's mother?'

'Yes,' says the woman, still staring at me. 'I'm Angela Harrison. Mother of the bride,' she adds, emphasizing 'the bride', as though I don't understand English or something.

'You must be very excited,' I say politely. 'Your daughter getting married.'

'Yes well, of course, Tom is devoted to Lucy,' she says aggressively. 'Utterly devoted. Never *looks* in any other direction.' She gives me a sharp glance and I smile feebly back.

Honestly, what am I supposed to do? Throw up all over Tom or something? Tell him he's the ugliest man I've ever known? They'd all still just say I was jealous, wouldn't they? They'd say I was in denial.

'Is . . . Luke here, Becky?' says Janice, and gives me a hopeful smile. And suddenly – which is rather bizzare – everyone in the room is completely still, waiting for my answer.

'Not yet, I'm afraid,' I say. 'I think he must have been held up.'

There's silence, and I'm aware of glances flying around the room.

'Held up,' echoes Angela, and there's a tone to her voice which I don't much like. 'Is that right? Well, there's a surprise.'

What's that supposed to mean?

'He's coming back from Zurich,' I explain. 'I should think the flight's been delayed or something.' I look at Janice and, to my surprise, she flushes.

'Zurich,' she says, nodding a little too emphatically. 'I see. Of course. Zurich.' And she shoots me an embarrassed, almost sympathetic look.

What's wrong with her?

'This *is* Luke Brandon, we're talking about here,' says Angela, taking a puff on her cigarette. 'The famous entrepreneur.'

'Well – yes,' I say, a bit surprised. I mean, I don't *know* any other Lukes.

'And he's your boyfriend.'

'Yes.'

There's a slightly awkward silence, and even Maureen seems to be gazing at me curiously. Suddenly, I see a copy of this month's *Tatler* lying on the floor by Janice's chair. Oh God.

'That article in *Tatler*, by the way,' I say hastily, 'is all wrong. He didn't say he was single. He said no comment.'

'Article?' says Janice unconvincingly. 'I don't know what you're talking about, dear.'

'I . . . I don't read magazines,' says Maureen, blushes bright red and looks away.

'We just look foward to meeting him,' says Angela, and blows out a cloud of smoke. 'Don't we, Janice?'

I stare at her in confusion – then turn to Janice, who will barely meet my eye, and Maureen, who's pretending to root about in a beauty case.

Hang on a minute.

They surely don't think—

'Janice,' I say, trying to keep my voice steady. 'You know Luke's coming. He even wrote you a reply!'

'Of course he did, Becky!' says Janice, staring at the floor. 'Well – as Angela says, we're all looking forward to meeting him.'

Oh my God. She doesn't believe me.

I feel a swoosh of humiliated colour fill my cheeks. What does she think? That I've just *made up* that I'm going out with Luke?

'Well, enjoy your sandwiches, won't you?' I say, trying not to sound as flustered as I feel. 'I'll just . . . see if Mum needs me.'

When I find Mum, she's on the top-floor landing, packing patio cushions into transparent plastic bags, then suctioning all the air out with the nozzle of her vacuum cleaner.

'I've some of these bags on order for you, by the way,' she shouts over the noise of the vacuum. 'From Country Ways. Plus some turkey foil, a casserole dish, a microwave egg poacher . . .'

'I don't want any turkey foil!' I yell.

'It's not for you!' says Mum, turning off the vacuum. 'They had a special offer – introduce a friend and receive a set of earthenware pots. So I nominated you as the friend. It's a very good catalogue, actually. I'll give it to you to have a browse.'

'Mum—'

'Lovely duvet covers. I'm sure you could do with a new—'

'Mum, listen!' I say agitatedly. 'Listen. You do believe I'm going out with Luke, don't you?'

There's a slightly too long pause.

'Of course I do,' she says eventually.

I stare at her in horror.

'You don't, do you? You all think I've just made it up!'

'No!' says Mum firmly. She puts down her hoover and looks me straight in the eye. 'Becky, you've told us you're going out with Luke Brandon – and as far as Dad and I are concerned, that's enough.'

'But Janice and Martin. Do they think I've made it up?'

Mum gazes at me – then sighs, and reaches for another patio cushion.

'Oh, Becky. The thing is, love, you have to remember, they once believed you had a stalker. And that turned out to be . . . well. Not quite true. Didn't it?'

A cold dismay creeps over me. OK, maybe I did once kind of pretend I had a stalker. Which I shouldn't have done. But I mean, just because you invent one tiny stalker, that doesn't make you a complete nutcase, does it?

'And the trouble is, we've never actually . . . well, *seen* him with you, have we, love?' Mum continues, as she stuffs the cushion into its transparent bag. 'Not in the flesh. And then there was that piece in the paper saying he was single . . .'

'He didn't say single!' My voice is shrill with frustration. 'He said no comment! Mum, have Janice and Martin told you they don't believe me?'

'No.' Mum lifts her chin defiantly. 'They wouldn't dare say a thing like that to me.'

'But you know that's what they're saying behind our backs.'

We stare at each other, and I see the strain in Mum's face, hidden behind her bright façade. She must have been *so* hoping we'd pull up together in Luke's flash car, I suddenly realize. She must have been so wanting to prove Janice wrong. And instead, here I am, on my own again . . .

'He'll be here,' I say, almost to reassure myself. 'He'll be here any minute.'

'Of course he will!' exclaims Mum brightly. 'And as soon as he turns up – well, then everyone will have to eat their words, won't they?'

111

The doorbell rings and we both stiffen, staring at each other.

'I'll get that, shall I?' I say, trying to sound casual.

'Why don't you?' agrees Mum, and I can see a tiny shine of hope in her eyes.

Trying not to run, I hurry down the stairs and, with a light heart, fling the front door open. And it's . . . not Luke.

It's a man laden with flowers. Baskets of flowers, a bouquet of flowers, and several flat boxes at his feet.

'Wedding flowers,' he says. 'Where do you want them?'

'Oh,' I say, trying to hide my disappointment. 'Actually, you've got the wrong house, I'm afraid. They need to go next door. Number 41.'

'Really?' The man frowns. 'Let me just look at my list . . . Hold that, would you?'

He thrusts the bridal bouquet at me and starts rooting around in his pocket.

'Honestly,' I say, 'they need to go next door. Look, I'll just get my—'

I turn round, holding Lucy's bouquet with both hands, because it's quite heavy. And to my horror, Angela Harrison is just arriving at the foot of the stairs. She stares at me, and for a moment I almost think she's going to kill me.

'What are you doing?' she snaps. 'Give me that!' She wrenches the bouquet out of my hands and brings her face so close to mine I can smell the gin on her breath. 'Listen, young lady,' she hisses. 'I'm not fooled by the smiles. I know what you're up to. And you can just forget it, all right? I'm not having my daughter's wedding wrecked by some deranged little psychopath.'

'I'm not deranged!' I exclaim furiously. 'And I'm not going to wreck anything! I don't fancy Tom! I've got a boyfriend!'

'Oh yes,' she says, folding her arms. 'The famous boyfriend. Is he here yet?'

'No, he isn't,' I say, and flinch at the expression on her face. 'But he . . . he just called.'

'He just called,' echoes Angela with a little sneer. 'To say he can't make it?'

Why won't these people believe that Luke's coming?

'Actually . . . he's half an hour away,' I hear myself saying defiantly.

'Good,' says Angela Harrison, and gives me a nasty smile. 'Well – we'll see him very soon then, won't we?'

Oh shit.

By twelve o'clock, Luke still hasn't arrived, and I'm beside myself. This is a complete nightmare. Where *is* he? I loiter outside the church until the very last minute, desperately dialling his number, hoping against hope I'm going to see him running up the road. But the bridesmaids have arrived, and another Rolls-Royce has just pulled up – and he's still not here. As I see the car door open and a glimpse of wedding dress, I hastily retreat into the church before anyone can think I'm waiting outside to disrupt the bridal procession.

I creep in, trying not to disturb the organ music. Angela Harrison darts me an evil look, and there's a rippling and whispering from Lucy's side of the church. I sit down near the back, trying to keep composed and tranquil – but I'm well aware that all Lucy's friends are shooting surreptitious glances at me. What the hell has she been telling everyone?

For a second I feel like getting up and walking out. I never wanted to come to this stupid wedding anyhow. I only said yes because I didn't want to offend Janice and Martin. But it's too late, the bridal march is starting, and Lucy's walking in. And I have to hand it to her, she's wearing the most drop-dead gorgeous dress

113

I've ever seen. I stare wistfully after it, trying not to imagine what I would look like in a dress like that.

The music stops and the vicar starts talking. I'm aware that people on Lucy's side of the church are still darting me little looks – but I adjust my hat and lift my chin and ignore them.

'. . . to join together this man and this woman in holy matrimony,' intones the vicar. 'Which is an honourable estate . . .'

The bridesmaids have got really nice shoes, I notice. I wonder where they're from?

Shame about the dresses, though.

'Therefore if any person can show any just cause why they may not lawfully be joined together, let him speak now or else hereafter for ever hold his peace.'

I always love this moment in weddings. Everyone sitting on their hands as though they're afraid they might suddenly bid for the Van Gogh by mistake. I look up to see if anyone's going to say anything – and to my horror, Angela Harrison has turned round in her pew and is giving me the evil eye. What's wrong with her?

Now a load of people on the other side are looking at me, as well – and even a woman in front, wearing a big blue hat, is turning round to have a good stare!

'What?' I whisper angrily to her. '*What?*'

'What?' says the vicar, putting his hand behind his ear. 'Did someone say something?'

'Yes!' says the woman in the blue hat, and points to me. 'She did!'

What?

Oh my God. No. Please, no. The entire church is slowly turning to look at me. I don't believe this is happening. Now Tom's staring at me too and shaking his head, with this awful expression of pity.

'I didn't . . . I didn't . . .' I stutter. 'I just meant . . .'

'Would you mind standing up?' calls the vicar. 'I'm a little deaf, so if you have something to say . . .'

114

'Really, I—'

'Stand up!' says the woman next to me, and prods me hard with her service sheet.

Very slowly I rise to my feet, feeling two hundred pairs of eyes on me like torches. I can't look anywhere near Tom and Lucy. I can't look at Mum or Dad. I have never been so embarrassed in all my life.

'I don't have anything to say! Honestly! I was just . . .' Helplessly, I hold up my phone. 'It was . . . my mobile phone. I thought it . . . Sorry. Carry on.'

I sit back down with trembling legs and there's silence. Gradually the congregation begins to turn back and settle itself, and the vicar clears his throat and begins the vows.

The rest of the service goes by in a blur. After it's all over, Lucy and Tom process out, studiously ignoring me as they do so – and everyone gathers around them in the churchyard to throw confetti and take photos. I slip away without anyone noticing, and hurry feverishly up the road to the Websters' house. Because Luke must be there by now. He *must*. He must have arrived late, and decided not to come to the church, but go straight to the reception. It's obvious, when you think about it. It's what any sensible person would do.

I hurry through the Websters' house, which is full of caterers and waitresses – and head straight for the marquee. Already there's a joyful smile on my face at the thought of seeing him, and telling him about that hideous moment in the church, and seeing his face crease up in laughter—

But the marquee's empty. Completely empty.

I stand there, bewildered, for a few moments – then quickly head out again and hurry towards my parents' house. Because maybe Luke went there instead, it suddenly occurs to me. Maybe he got the time wrong,

115

or maybe he had to get changed into his wedding outfit. Or maybe—

But he's not there either. Not in the kitchen, not upstairs. And when I dial his mobile number, it clicks straight on to messages.

Slowly, I walk into my bedroom and sink down onto the bed, trying not to let myself think all the bad thoughts which are creeping into my mind.

He's coming, I tell myself again and again. He's just . . . on his way.

Through the window I can see Tom and Lucy and all the guests starting to arrive in next door's garden. There are lots of hats and morning suits, and waitresses handing round champagne. In fact, it all looks rather jolly. I know I should be down there with them – but I just can't face it. Not without Luke, not all on my own.

But after sitting there for a while, it occurs to me that by staying up here, I'll just be fuelling the intrigue. They'll all think I can't face the happy couple and that I'm off slitting my wrists somewhere. It'll confirm all their suspicions for ever. I *have* to go and show my face, even if it's just for half an hour.

I force myself to stand up, take a deep breath and put some fresh lipstick on. Then I walk out of the house and round to the Websters'. I slip inconspicuously into the marquee through a side flap and stand watching for a moment. People are milling about and the hubbub is huge, and no-one even notices me. Near the entrance there's a formal line-up with Tom and Lucy and their parents, but no way am I going near that. So instead I sidle off to an empty table and sit down, and after a bit a waitress comes and gives me a glass of champagne.

For a while I just sit there, sipping my drink and watching people and feeling myself start to relax. Then there's a rustling sound. I look up – and my heart sinks. Lucy is standing right in front of me in her beautiful wedding dress, with a large bridesmaid in a really unflattering shade of green. (Which I think says quite a lot about Lucy.)

'Hello, Rebecca,' says Lucy pleasantly – and I can just tell she's congratulating herself on being so polite to the loony girl who nearly wrecked her wedding.

'Hi,' I say. 'Listen, I'm really sorry about the service. I honestly didn't mean to . . .'

'That doesn't matter,' says Lucy, and gives me a tight smile. 'After all, Tom and I are married. That's the main thing.' She gives her wedding-ringed hand a satisfied glance.

'Absolutely!' I say. 'Congratulations. Are you going on—'

'We were just wondering,' interrupts Lucy pleasantly. 'Is Luke here yet?'

My heart sinks.

'Oh,' I say, playing for time. 'Well . . .'

'It's only that Mummy said you told her he was half an hour away. But no sign of him! Which seems a bit strange, don't you think?' She raises her eyebrows innocently, and her bridesmaid gives a half-snort of laughter. I glance over Lucy's shoulder and see Angela Harrison standing with Tom, a few yards away, watching with gimlet, triumphant eyes. God, they're enjoying this, aren't they?

'After all, that was oh, a good two hours ago now,' Lucy's saying. 'At least! So if he *isn't* here, it does seem a teeny bit peculiar.' She gives me a mock-concerned look. 'Or maybe he's had an accident? Maybe he's got held up in . . . Zurich, was it?'

I stare at her smug, mocking face, and something violent rushes to my head.

'He's here,' I say before I can stop myself.

There's a stunned silence. Lucy and her bridesmaid glance at each other, while I take a deep gulp of champagne

117

'He's *here*?' says Lucy at last. 'You mean . . . here at the wedding?'

'Absolutely!' I say. 'He's . . . he's been here a while, actually.'

'But where? Where is he?'

'Well, he was just here a few moments ago . . .' I gesture to the chair next to me. 'Didn't you see him?'

'No!' says Lucy, with wide eyes. 'Where is he now?' And she starts to look around the marquee.

'Just there,' I say, pointing vaguely through the crowd. 'He's wearing a morning coat . . .'

'And? What else?'

'And he's . . . he's holding a glass of champagne . . .' Thank *God* men all look alike at weddings.

'Which one?' says Lucy impatiently.

'The dark one,' I say, and take another gulp of champagne. 'Look, he's waving at me.' I lift my hand and give a little wave. 'Hi, Luke!'

'*Where?*' exclaims Lucy, peering into the crowd. 'Kate, can you see him?'

'No,' says the bridesmaid hopelessly. 'What does he look like?'

'He's . . . actually, he's just disappeared,' I say. 'He must be getting me a drink or something.'

Lucy turns to me again, her eyes narrowed.

'So – how come he wasn't at the service?'

'He didn't want to interrupt,' I say after a pause, and force myself to smile naturally. 'Well – I won't keep you. You must want to mingle with your guests.'

'Yes,' says Lucy after a pause. 'Yes, I will.'

Giving me another suspicious look, she rustles off towards her mother, and they all start hobnobbing in a little group, shooting glances at me every so often. One of the bridesmaids rushes off to another group of guests, and they all start giving me glances, too. And then one runs off to *another* group. It's like seeing a bush fire begin.

118

A few moments later, Janice comes up, all flushed and teary looking, with a flowery hat perched lop-sidedly on her head.

'Becky!' she says. 'Becky, we've just heard that Luke's here!'

My heart plummets. Oh God. Putting down the bride from hell was one thing. But I can't bring myself to tell Janice that Luke's here. I just can't do it. So I quickly take a gulp of champagne, and wave my glass at her in a vague manner that could mean anything.

'Oh Becky . . .' Janice clasps her hands. 'Becky, I feel absolutely . . . Have your parents met him yet? I know your mother will be over the moon!'

Oh fuck.

Suddenly I feel a bit sick. My parents. I didn't think of that.

'Janice, I've just got to go and . . . and powder my nose,' I say, and get hastily to my feet. 'See you later.'

'And Luke!' she says.

'And Luke, of course!' I say, and give a shrill little laugh.

I hurry to the portaloos without meeting anyone's eye, lock myself in a cubicle, and sit, swigging the last warm dregs of my champagne. OK, let's not panic about this. Let's just . . . think clearly, and go over my options.

Option One: Tell everybody that Luke isn't really here, I made a mistake.

Not unless I want to be stoned to death with cham-pagne glasses and never show my face in Oxshott again.

Option Two: Tell Mum and Dad in private that Luke isn't really here.

But they'll be so disappointed. They'll be mortified, and they won't enjoy the day and it'll be all my fault.

Option Three: Bluff it out – and tell Mum and Dad

119

the truth at the end of the day. Yes. That could work. It has to work. I can easily convince everyone Luke's here for about an hour or so – and then I'll say he's got a migraine, and has gone off to lie down quietly.

Right, this is what I'm going to do. OK – let's go.

And you know, it's easier than I thought. Before long, everyone seems to be taking it for granted that Luke is around somewhere. Tom's granny even tells me she's already spotted him, and isn't he handsome and will it be my turn next? I've told countless people that he was here just a minute ago, have collected two plates of food from the buffet – one for me, one for Luke (tipped one into the flowerbed) and have even borrowed some stranger's morning coat and put it on the chair next to me, as though it's his. The great thing is, no-one can prove he's not here! There are so many people milling about, it's impossible to keep track of who's here and who isn't. God, I should have done this ages ago.

'Group photograph in a minute,' says Lucy, bustling up to me. 'We all have to line up. Where's Luke?'

'Talking to some guy about property prices,' I reply without hesitation. 'They were over by the drinks table.'

'Well, make sure you introduce me,' says Lucy. 'I still haven't met him!'

'OK,' I say, and give her a bright smile. 'As soon as I track him down!' I take a swig of champagne, look up – and there's Mum in her lime green wedding outfit, heading towards me.

Oh God. So far, I've managed to avoid her and Dad completely, basically by running away whenever they've come close. It's really bad of me – but I just know I won't be able to lie to Mum. Quickly I slip out of the marquee into the garden and head for the shrubbery, dodging the photographer's assistant, who's rounding up all the children. I sit down behind a tree and finish my glass of champagne, staring up blankly at the blue afternoon sky.

I stay there for what seems like hours, until my legs are starting to ache and the breeze is making me shiver. Then at last, I slowly wander back, and slip inconspicuously into the tent. I won't hang around much longer. Just long enough to have a piece of wedding cake, maybe, and some more champagne . . .

'There she is!' comes a voice behind me.

I freeze for an instant – then slowly turn round. To my utter horror, all the guests are standing in neat rows in the centre of the marquee, while a photographer adjusts a tripod.

'Becky, where's Luke?' says Lucy sharply. 'We're trying to get everybody in.'

Shit. *Shit.*

'Erm . . .' I swallow, trying to stay nonchalant. 'Maybe he's in the house?'

'No, he's not,' says Kate the bridesmaid. 'I've just been looking in there.'

'Well, he must be . . . in the garden then.'

'But you were in the garden,' says Lucy, narrowing her eyes. 'Didn't you see him?'

'Erm . . . I'm not sure.' I look around the marquee hurriedly, wondering if I could pretend to spot him in the distance. But it's different when there are no milling crowds. Why did they have to stop milling?

'He must be somewhere!' says a cheerful woman. 'Who saw him last?'

There's a deathly silence. Two hundred people are staring at me. I catch Mum's anxious eye, and quickly look away again.

'Actually . . .' I clear my throat. 'Now I remember, he was saying he had a bit of a headache! So maybe he went to—'

'Who's seen him *at all*?' cuts in Lucy, ignoring me.

She looks around the assembled guests. 'Who here can say they've actually seen Luke Brandon in the flesh? Anyone?'

'I've seen him!' comes a wavering voice from the back. 'Such a good-looking young man . . .'

'Apart from Tom's gran,' says Lucy, rolling her eyes. 'Anyone?'

There's another awful silence.

'I've seen his morning coat,' ventures Janice timidly. 'But not his actual . . . body,' she whispers.

'I knew it. I knew it!' Lucy's voice is loud and triumphant. 'He never was here, was he?'

'Of course he was,' I say, trying to sound confident. 'I expect he's just in the—'

'You're not going out with Luke Brandon at all, are you?' Her voice lashes across the marquee. 'You just made the whole thing up! You're just living in your own sad little fantasy-land!'

'I'm not!' To my horror, my voice is thickening, and I can feel tears pricking at my eyes. 'I'm not! Luke and I are a couple!'

But as I look at all the faces gazing at me – some hostile, some astonished, some amused – I don't even feel so sure of that any more. I mean, if we were a couple, he'd be here, wouldn't he? He'd be here with me.

'I'll just . . .' I say in a trembling voice. 'I'll just check if he's . . .'

And without looking anyone in the eye, I back out of the marquee.

'She's a bloody fruit loop!' I hear Lucy saying. 'Honestly, Tom, she could be dangerous!'

'*You're* dangerous, young lady!' I hear Mum retorting, her voice shaking a little. 'Janice, I don't know how you could let your daughter-in-law be so rude! Becky's been a good friend to you, over the years. And to you, Tom, standing there, pretending this is nothing to do with you. And this is the way you treat her. Come on, Graham. We're going.'

A moment later, I see Mum stalking out of the marquee, Dad in tow, her lime-green hat quivering on her head. They head towards the front drive, and I know they're going back to our house for a nice, calming cup of tea.

But I don't follow them. I can't bring myself to see them – or anyone. Right now, I have to be on my own.

I walk quickly, stumbling slightly, towards the other end of the garden. Then, when I'm far enough away, I sink down onto the grass. I bury my head in my hands – and, for the first time today, feel tears oozing out of my eyes.

This should have been such a good day. It should have been such a wonderful, happy occasion. Seeing Tom get married, introducing Luke to my parents and all our friends, dancing together into the night . . . and instead, it's been spoiled for everyone. Mum, Dad, Janice, Martin . . . I even feel sorry for Lucy and Tom. I mean, they didn't want all this disruption at their wedding, did they?

I sit without moving, staring down at the ground. From the marquee I can hear the sounds of a band starting up, and Lucy's voice bossing somebody about. Children are playing with a bean bag in the garden and occasionally it lands near me. But I don't flicker. I wish I could just sit here for ever, without having to see any of them ever again.

And then I hear my name, low across the grass.

At first I think Lucy's right, and I'm hearing imaginary voices. But as I look up, my heart gives an almighty flip and I feel something hard blocking my throat. I don't believe it.

It's him.

It's Luke, walking across the grass, towards me, like a dream. He's wearing morning dress and holding two glasses of champagne, and I've never seen him looking more handsome.

'I'm sorry,' he says as he reaches me. 'I'm beyond sorry. Four hours late is . . . well, it's unforgivable.' He shakes his head.

I stare up at him dazedly. I'd almost started to believe that Lucy was right, and he only existed in my imagination.

'Were you . . . held up?' I say at last.

'A guy had a heart attack. The plane was diverted . . .' He frowns. 'But I left a message on your phone as soon as I could. Didn't you get it?'

I grab for my phone, realizing with a sickening thud that I haven't checked it for a good while. And sure enough, the message icon is blinking merrily.

'No, I didn't get it,' I say, staring at it blankly. 'I didn't. I thought . . .'

I break off and shake my head. I don't know what I thought any more. Did I really believe he wasn't planning to come at all?

'Are you all right?' says Luke, sitting down beside me and handing me a glass of champagne. He runs a finger gently down my face and I flinch.

'No,' I say, rubbing my cheek. 'Since you ask, I'm not all right. You promised you'd be here. You *promised*, Luke.'

'I am here.'

'You know what I mean.' I hunch my arms miserably round my knees. 'I wanted you to be there at the service, not arrive when it's all nearly over. I wanted everyone to meet you, and see us together . . .' My voice starts to wobble. 'It's just been . . . awful! They all thought I was after the bridegroom—'

'The bridegroom?' says Luke incredulously. 'You mean the pale-faced nonentity called Tom?'

'Yes, him.' I look up and give a reluctant half-giggle as I see Luke's expression. 'Did you meet him, then?'

'I met him just now. And his very unlovely wife. Quite a pair.' He takes a sip of champagne and leans back on his elbows. 'By the way – she looked rather taken aback to meet me. Almost . . . gobsmacked, one might say. As did most of the guests.' He gives me a quizzical look. 'Anything I should know, Becky?'

'Erm . . .' I clear my throat. 'Erm . . . not really. Nothing important.'

'I thought as much,' says Luke. 'So the bridesmaid who cried out, "Oh my God, he exists!" when I walked in. She's presumably . . .'

'Barking,' I say without moving my head.

'Right.' He nods. 'Just checking.'

He reaches for my hand, and I let him take it. For a while we sit in silence. A bird is wheeling round and round overhead, and in the distance I can hear the band playing 'Lady in Red'.

'Becky, I'm sorry I was late.' His voice is suddenly serious. 'There was really nothing I could do.'

'I know.' I exhale sharply. 'I know. You couldn't help it. Just one of those things.'

For a while longer we're both silent.

'Good champagne,' says Luke at last, and takes a sip.

'Yes,' I say. 'It's . . . very nice. Nice and . . . dry . . .' I break off and rub my face, trying to hide how nervous I am.

There's a part of me that wants to sit here, making small talk for as long as we can. But another part is thinking, what's the point of putting it off any longer? There's only one thing I want to know. I feel a spasm of nerves in my stomach, but somehow force myself to take a deep breath and turn to him.

'So. How did your meetings in Zurich go? How's the . . . the new deal coming along?'

I'm trying to stay calm and collected, but I can feel

my lips starting to tremble, and my hands are twisting themselves into knots.

'Becky . . .' says Luke. He stares into his glass for a moment, then puts it down and looks at me. 'There's something I need to tell you. I'm moving to New York.'

I feel cold and heavy. So this is the end to a completely disastrous day. Luke's leaving me. It's the end. It's all over.

'Right,' I manage, and give a careless shrug. 'I see. Well – OK.'

'And I'm really, *really* hoping . . .' Luke takes both my hands and squeezes them tight, '. . . that you'll come with me.'

REGAL AIRLINES
Head Office
Preston House
354 Kingsway
London WC2 4TH

Ms Rebecca Bloomwood
Flat 2
4 Burney Rd
London SW6 8FD

Dear Rebecca Bloomwood

Thank you for your letter of 15 September.

I am glad that you are looking forward to flying with us and have already recommended us highly to all your friends. I agree that word-of-mouth business is invaluable for a company such as ours.

Unfortunately this does not, as you suggest, qualify you for 'a special thank you' regarding luggage. Regal Airlines is unable to increase your luggage allowance beyond the standard 20 kg. Any excess weight will be subject to a charge; I enclose an explanatory leaflet.

Please enjoy your flight.

Mary Stevens
Customer Care Manager

PGNI First Bank Visa
7 Camel Square
Liverpool L1 5NP

Ms Rebecca Bloomwood
Flat 2
4 Burney Rd
London SW6 8FD

GOOD NEWS!
YOUR NEW CREDIT LIMIT IS £10,000

Dear Ms Bloomwood

We are delighted to announce that you have been given an increase to your credit limit. Your new credit limit of £10,000 is available for you to spend immediately and will be shown on your next statement.

You can use your new credit limit to do many things. Pay for a holiday, a car, even transfer balances from other cards!

However, we realize that some customers do not wish to take advantage of increased credit limits. If you would prefer your credit limit to remain at its original level, please call one of our Customer Satisfaction Representatives, or return the form below.

Yours sincerely

Michael Hunt
Customer Satisfaction Manager

....

Name: REBECCA BLOOMWOOD   Account Number: 0003 4572 0990 2765

I would/would not like to take up the offer of my new £10,000 credit limit.

Please delete as appropriate

Seven

New York! I'm going to New York! *New York!*

Everything is transformed. Everything has fallen into place. *This* is why Luke has been so secretive. We had a lovely long chat at the wedding, and Luke explained everything to me, and suddenly it all made sense. It turns out he's opening up a new office of Brandon Communications in New York, in partnership with some advertising person based in Washington. And he's going to go over there and head it up. He said he's been wanting to ask me all along to come with him – but he knew I wouldn't want to give up my career just to trail along with him. So – this is the best bit – he's been speaking to some contacts in television, and he reckons I'll be able to get a job as a financial expert on an American TV show! In fact, he says I'll get 'snapped up' because Americans love British accents. Apparently one producer has already practically offered me a job just from seeing a tape Luke showed him. Isn't that great?

The reason he didn't say anything before was he didn't want to raise my hopes before things started looking definite. But now, it seems, all the investors are on board, and everyone's really positive, and they're hoping to finalize the deal as soon as possible. There are already loads of potential clients out there, he says, and that's before he's even started.

And guess what? We're going over there in three

days' time! Hooray! Luke's going to have meetings with some of his backers – and I'm going to have interviews with TV people, and explore the city. God, it's exciting. In just seventy-two hours, I'll be there. In the Big Apple. The city that never sleeps. The—

'Becky?'

Oh shit. I snap to attention and hastily give a bright smile. I'm sitting on the set of *Morning Coffee*, doing my usual phone-in, and Jane from Lincoln has been explaining over the line that she wants to buy a property but doesn't know which kind of mortgage to take out.

Oh for God's sake. How many times have I explained the difference between repayment plans and endowment policies? You know, sometimes this job can be so interesting, hearing about people and their problems and trying to help them. But other times it's just as boring as writing for *Successful Saving* ever was. I mean, mortgages *again*? I feel like yelling, 'Didn't you watch last week's show?'

'Well, Jane,' I say, stifling a yawn. 'The question of mortgages is very tricky.'

As I speak, my mind begins to drift again towards New York. Just think. We'll have an apartment in Manhattan. In some amazing Upper East Side condo – or maybe somewhere really cool in Greenwich Village. God yes! It's just going to be perfect.

To be honest, I hadn't thought of Luke and me living together for . . . well, for ages. I reckon if we'd stayed in London, perhaps we wouldn't have. I mean, it's quite a big step, isn't it? But the point is, this is different. As Luke said, this is the chance of a lifetime for both of us. It's a whole new beginning. It's yellow taxi cabs and skyscrapers, and Woody Allen and *Breakfast at Tiffany's*.

The really weird thing is that although I've never actually been to New York, I already feel an affinity with it. Like for example, I adore sushi – and that was invented in New York, wasn't it? And I always watch *Friends*, unless I'm going out that night. And *Cheers*. (Except now I come to think of it, that's Boston, isn't it? Still, it's the same thing, really.)

'So really, Jane, whatever you're buying,' I say dreamily, 'be it a . . . a Fifth Avenue duplex . . . or an East Village walk-up . . . you must maximize the potential of your dollar. Which means . . .'

I stop as I see both Emma and Rory staring at me strangely.

'Becky, Jane is planning to buy a semi-detached house in Skegness,' says Emma.

'And surely it's pounds?' says Rory, looking around, as though for support. 'Isn't it?'

'Yes, well,' I say hurriedly. 'Obviously, I was just using those as examples. The principles apply wherever you're buying. London, New York, Skegness . . .'

'And on that international note, I'm afraid we'll have to finish,' says Emma. 'Hope that helped you, Jane, and thanks once again to Becky Bloomwood, our financial expert . . . do you have time for a last word, Becky?'

'The same message as ever,' I say, smiling warmly into the camera. 'Look after your money . . .'

'And your money will look after you,' everyone choruses dutifully.

'And that brings us to the end of the show,' says Emma. 'Join us tomorrow, when we'll be making over a trio of teachers from Teddington . . .'

'. . . talking to the man who became a circus performer at sixty-five . . .' says Rory.

'. . . and giving away £5,000 in Go On – Have A Guess! Goodbye!'

There's a frozen pause – then everyone relaxes as the signature music starts blaring out of the loud-speakers.

'So, Becky – are you going to New York or some-thing?' says Rory.

'Yes,' I say, beaming back at him. 'For two weeks!'

'How nice!' says Emma. 'What brought this on?'

'Oh, I don't know . . .' I shrug vaguely. 'Just a sudden whim.'

I'm not telling anyone at *Morning Coffee* yet about moving to New York. It was Luke's advice, actually. Just in case.

'Becky, I wanted a quick word,' says Zelda, the assistant producer, bustling onto the set with some papers in her hand. 'Your new contract is ready to be signed, but I'll need to go through it with you. There's a new clause about representing the image of the station.' She lowers her voice. 'After all that business with Professor Jamie.'

'Oh right,' I say, and pull a sympathetic face. Pro-fessor Jamie is the education expert on *Morning Coffee*. Or at least he was, until the *Daily World* ran an exposé on him last month in their series 'Are They What They Seem?' revealing that he isn't a real professor at all. In fact, he hasn't even got a degree, except the fake one he bought from the 'University of Oxbridge'. All the tabloids picked up the story, and kept showing photo-graphs of him in the dunce's hat he wore for last year's telethon. I felt really sorry for him, because he used to give really good advice.

And I was a bit surprised at the *Daily World* being so vicious. I've actually written for the *Daily World* myself, once or twice, and I'd always thought they were quite reasonable, for a tabloid.

'It won't take five minutes,' says Zelda. 'We could go into my office—'

'Well . . .' I say, and hesitate. Because I don't really want to sign anything at the moment, do I? Not if I'm planning a switch in jobs. 'I'm in a bit of a hurry, actually.' Which is true, because I've got to get to Luke's office by twelve, and then start getting my stuff ready for New York. (Ha! Haha!) 'Can it wait till I come back?'

'OK,' says Zelda. 'No problem.' She puts the contract back in its brown envelope and grins at me. 'Have a great time. Hey, you know, you must do some shopping while you're there.'

'Shopping?' I say, as though it hadn't occurred to me. 'Yes, I suppose I could.'

'Ooh yes!' says Emma. 'You can't go to New York without shopping! Although I suppose Becky would tell us we should put our money into a savings plan instead.'

She laughs merrily and Zelda joins in. I smile back, feeling a bit uncomfortable. Somehow, all the people at *Morning Coffee* have got the idea I'm incredibly organized with my money – and, without quite meaning to, I've gone along with it. Still, I don't suppose it really matters.

'A savings plan is a good idea, of course . . .' I hear myself saying. 'But as I always say, there's no harm going shopping once in a while as long as you stick to a budget.'

'Is that what you're going to do, then?' asks Emma interestedly. 'Give yourself a budget?'

'Oh, absolutely,' I say wisely. 'It's the only way.'

Which is completely true. I mean, obviously I'm planning to give myself a New York shopping budget. I'll set realistic limits and I'll stick to them. It's really very simple.

Although what I'll probably do is make the limits fairly broad and flexible. Because it's always a good idea to allow some extra leeway for emergencies or one-offs.

'You're so virtuous!' says Emma, shaking her head. 'Still, that's why you're the financial expert and I'm not.' She looks up as the sandwich man approaches us

133

with a tray. 'Ooh lovely, I'm starving! I'll have . . . bacon and avocado.'

'And I'll have tuna and sweetcorn,' says Zelda. 'What do you want, Becky?'

'Pastrami on rye,' I say casually. 'Hold the mayo.'

'I don't think they do that,' says Zelda, wrinkling her brow. 'They've got ham salad . . .'

'Then a bagel. Cream cheese and lox. And a soda.'

'Soda water, do you mean?' says Zelda.

'What's lox?' says Emma, puzzled – and I pretend I haven't heard. I'm not actually sure what lox is – but they eat it in New York, so it's got to be delicious, hasn't it?

'Whatever it is,' says the sandwich man, 'I 'aven't got it. You can 'ave cheese and tomato and a nice packet of Hula Hoops.'

'OK,' I say reluctantly, and reach for my purse. As I do so, a pile of post that I picked up this morning falls out of my bag, onto the floor. Shit. Hastily, I gather all the letters up, and shove them into my Conran Shop carrier bag, hoping no-one spotted them. But bloody Rory was looking straight at me.

'Hey, Becky,' he says, giving a guffaw. 'Was that a red bill I saw there?'

'No!' I say at once. 'Of course not. It's a . . . a birthday card. A joke birthday card. For my accountant. Anyway, I must run. Ciao!'

OK, so that wasn't quite true. It was a red bill. To be honest, there have been quite a few red bills arriving for me over the last few days, which I'm completely intending to get round to paying off when I've got the cash. But I just can't get worked up about them. I mean, I've got more important things happening in my life than a few crappy final demands. In a few months' time I'll be living on the other side of the Atlantic! I'm going to be an American television star!

Luke says I'll probably earn twice in the States what I do here. If not more! So a few crummy bills won't exactly matter then, will they? A few outstanding pounds won't exactly ruin my sleep when I'm a household name and living in a Park Avenue penthouse, will they?

God, and that'll completely suss that horrible John Gavin. That'll completely floor him. Just imagine his face when I march in and tell him I'm going to be the new anchorwoman on CNN, on a salary six times what he earns. That'll teach him to be so nasty. I finally got round to opening his latest letter this morning, and it actually quite upset me. What does he mean, 'excessive level of debt'? What does he mean, 'special status'? You know, Derek Smeath would never have been so rude to me, not in a million years.

Luke's having a meeting when I arrive, but that's OK, because I don't mind hanging around. I love visiting the Brandon Communications offices – in fact, I pop in there quite a lot, just for the atmosphere. It's such a cool place – all blondwood floors and spotlights and trendy sofas, and everyone rushes around being really busy and dynamic. Everyone stays really late at night, even though they don't have to – and at about seven o'clock someone always opens a bottle of wine and passes it around.

I've got a present to give his assistant Mel for her birthday, which was yesterday. I'm quite pleased with it, actually – it's a gorgeous pair of cushions from the Conran Shop – and as I hand over the carrier bag, I hear her gasp,

'Oh Becky! You shouldn't have!'

'I wanted to!' I beam, and perch companionably on her desk as she admires them. 'So – what's the latest?'

Ooh, you can't beat a good gossip. Mel puts down the carrier bag and gets out a box of toffees, and we have a

135

lovely old natter. I hear all about her terrible date with an awful guy her mother's been trying to set her up with, and she hears all about Tom's wedding. And then she lowers her voice and starts filling me in on the office gossip.

She tells me about the two receptionists who haven't been speaking ever since they came to work in the same Next jacket and both refused to take it off – and the girl in Accounts who has just come back from maternity leave and is throwing up every morning but won't admit anything.

'And here's a really juicy one!' she says, handing me the bag of toffees. 'I reckon Alicia's having an affair in the office.'

'No!' I stare at her in amazement. 'Really? With who?'

'With Ben Bridges.'

I screw up my face, trying to place the name.

'That new guy who used to be at Coupland Foster Bright?'

'Him?' I stare at Mel. 'Really?'

I have to say I'm surprised. He's very sweet, but quite short and thrusting and almost wide-boyish. Not what I would have said was Alicia's type.

'I keep seeing them together, kind of whispering. And the other day Alicia said she was going to the dentist – but I went into Ratchetts and there they were, having a secret lunch—'

She breaks off as Luke appears at the door of his office, ushering out a man in a purple shirt.

'Mel, order a taxi for Mr Mallory, would you, please?'

'Of course, Luke,' says Mel, switching into her efficient, secretary voice. She picks up the phone and we grin at each other, then I walk into Luke's office.

God, his office is smart. I always forget how grand he is. He's got a sweeping maple desk which was designed by some award-winning Danish designer, and on the shelves in the alcove behind it are lots of PR awards that he's won over the years.

'Here you are,' he says, handing me a sheaf of papers. On top is a letter from someone called 'Howski and Forlano, US Immigration Lawyers', and as I see the words, 'your proposed relocation to the United States', I feel a tingle of excitement.

'This is really happening, isn't it?' I say, walking over to his floor-length window and gazing down at the busy street. 'We're really going to New York.'

'The flights are booked,' he says, grinning at me.

'You know what I mean.'

'I do know just what you mean,' he confirms, and wraps me in his arms. 'And it's very exciting.'

For a while we just stand there, the two of us, looking at the busy London street below. I can hardly believe I'm planning to leave all this to live in a foreign country. It's exciting and wonderful – but just a little scary.

'Do you really think I'll get a job out there?' I say, as I have every time I've seen him in the past week. 'Do you honestly think I will?'

'Of course you will.' He sounds so assured and confident, I feel myself relax into his arms. 'They'll love you. No question at all.' He kisses me and holds me tight for a moment. Then he moves away to his desk, frowns absently and opens a huge file labelled NEW YORK. No wonder it's so huge. He told me the other day that he's been wanting to pull off a New York deal for three years. Three years!

'I can't believe you've been planning this for so long and never told me,' I say, watching him scribble something on a Post-It.

'Mm,' says Luke. I clench the papers in my hands slightly harder and take a deep breath. There's something I've been wanting to say for a while – and now is as good a moment as any.

'Luke, what would you have done if I hadn't wanted to go to New York?'

There's silence apart from the hum of the computer.

'I knew you'd want to go,' says Luke at last. 'It's the next obvious step for you.'

'But . . . what if I hadn't?' I bite my lip. 'Would you still have gone?' Luke sighs.

'Becky – you do want to go to New York, don't you?'

'Yes! You know I do!'

'So, what's the point of asking what-if questions? The point is, you want to go, I want to go . . . it's all perfect.' He smiles at me and puts down his pen. 'How are your parents doing?'

'They're . . . OK,' I say hesitantly. 'They're kind of getting used to the idea.'

Which is sort of true. They were fairly shocked when I told them, I have to admit. In hindsight, maybe I should have broken it to them more gently. Like, perhaps I should have introduced Luke to them *before* making the announcement. Because how it happened was, I hurried into the house where they were still sitting in their wedding gear, drinking tea in front of *Countdown* – and I switched off the telly and said joyfully, 'Mum, Dad, I'm moving to New York with Luke!'

Whereupon Mum just looked at Dad and said, 'Oh, Graham. She's gone.'

She said afterwards she didn't mean it like that – but I'm not so sure.

Then they actually met Luke, and he told them about his plans, and explained about all the opportunities in American TV for me, and I could see Mum's smile fading. Her face seemed to get smaller and smaller, and sort of closed in on itself. She went off to make some tea in the kitchen, and I followed her – and I could see she was upset. But she refused to show it. She just made the tea, with slightly shaking hands, and put out some biscuits – then she turned to me and smiled brightly, and said, 'I've always thought you would suit New York, Becky. It's the perfect place for you.'

I stared at her, suddenly realizing what I was talking about. Going and living hundreds of miles away from home, and my parents, and . . . my whole life, apart from Luke.

'You'll . . . you'll come and visit lots?' I said, my voice trembling slightly.

'Of course we will, darling! All the time!'

She squeezed my hand and looked away – and then we went out into the sitting room, and didn't say much more about it.

But the next morning, when we came down for breakfast, she and Dad were poring over an ad in the *Sunday Times* for holiday properties in Florida, which they claimed they had been thinking about anyway. As we left that afternoon, they were arguing vigorously over whether DisneyWorld in Florida was better than Disneyland in California, even though I happen to know neither of them has ever set foot near either of them in their lives.

'Becky, I have to get on,' says Luke, interrupting my thoughts. He picks up the phone and dials a number. 'I'll see you this evening, OK?'

'OK,' I say, still loitering by the window. Then, suddenly remembering, I turn round. 'Hey, have you heard about Alicia?'

'What about her?' Luke frowns at the receiver and puts it down.

'Mel reckons she's having an affair. With Ben Bridges! Can you believe it?'

'No, frankly,' says Luke, tapping at his keyboard. 'I can't.'

'So what do you think's going on?' I perch on his desk and look excitedly at him.

'My sweet,' says Luke patiently. 'I really do have to get on.'

'Aren't you *interested*?'

'No. As long as they're doing their jobs.'

'People are more than just their jobs,' I say reprovingly. But Luke isn't even listening. He's got that faraway, cut-off look which comes over him when he's concentrating.

'Oh well,' I say, and roll my eyes. 'See you later.'

When I come out, Mel is not at her desk. Alicia is standing at it in a smart black suit, staring at some papers. Her face seems more flushed than usual, and I wonder with an inward giggle if she's just been canoodling with Ben.

'Hi, Alicia,' I say politely. 'How are you?'

Alicia jumps, and quickly gathers up whatever it is she's reading – then looks at me with a strange expression, as though she's never seen me before.

'Becky,' she says slowly. 'Well I never. The financial expert herself. The money guru!'

What *is* it about Alicia? Why does everything she says sound like she's playing some stupid game?

'Yes,' I say. 'It's me. Where's Mel gone?'

As I approach Mel's desk, I feel sure I left something on it. But I can't quite think what. A scarf? Did I have an umbrella?

'She's gone to lunch,' says Alicia. 'She showed me the present you bought her. Very stylish.'

'Thanks,' I say shortly.

'So.' She gives me a faint smile. 'I gather you're tagging along with Luke to New York. Must be nice to have a rich boyfriend.'

God, she's a cow. She'd never say that in front of Luke.

'I'm not just "tagging along", actually,' I retort pleasantly. 'I've got lots of meetings with television

140

executives. It's a completely independent trip.'

'But . . .' Alicia frowns thoughtfully. 'Your flight's on the company, is it?'

'No! I paid for it myself!'

'Just wondering.' Alicia lifts her hands apologetically. 'Well, have a great time, won't you?' She gathers up some folders and pops them into her briefcase, then snaps it shut. 'Bye, now!'

'See you later,' I say, and watch as she walks briskly off to the lifts.

I stand there by Mel's desk for a few seconds longer, still wondering what on earth it was that I put down. But whatever it is, I can't remember. Oh, I don't suppose it can be important.

I get home to find Suze in the hall, talking on the phone. Her face is all red and shiny and her voice is trembling, and at once I'm seized by terror that something awful has happened. Fearfully, I raise my eyebrows at her – and she nods frantically back, in between saying, 'Yes', and 'I see', and 'When would that be?'

I sink onto a chair, feeling weak with worry. What's she talking about? A funeral? A brain operation? Oh God. As soon as I decide to go away – this happens.

'Guess what's happened?' she says shakily as she puts down the phone, and I leap up.

'Suze, I won't go to New York,' I say, and impulsively take her hands. 'I'll stay here and help you get through whatever it is. Has someone . . . died?'

'No,' says Suze dazedly, and I swallow hard.

'Are you ill?'

'No. No, Bex, this is *good* news! I just . . . don't quite believe it.'

'Well – what, then? Suze, what is it?'

'I've been offered my own line of home accessories in Hadleys. You know, the department store?' She shakes her head disbelievingly. 'They want me to design a whole range! Frames, vases, stationery . . . whatever I want, basically.'

'Oh my God!' I clap a hand over my mouth. 'That's *fantastic*!'

'This guy just rang up, out of the blue, and said his scouts have been monitoring sales of my frames. Apparently they've never seen anything like it.'

'Oh Suze!'

'I had no idea things were going so well.' Suze still looks shellshocked. 'This guy said it was a phenomenon! Everyone in the industry is talking about it. Apparently the only shop that hasn't done so well is that one which is miles away. Finchley or somewhere.'

'Oh, that's right,' I say vaguely. 'I don't think I've ever been to that one.'

'But he said that had to be a blip – because sales in all the other ones, in Fulham and Notting Hill and Chelsea, have all soared.' She gives an embarrassed smile. 'Apparently in Gifts and Goodies, around the corner, I'm the number one best-seller!'

'Well, I'm not surprised!' I exclaim. 'Your frames are easily the best thing in that shop. *Easily* the best.' I throw my arms around her. 'I'm so proud of you, Suze. I always knew you were going to be a star.'

'Well, I never would have done it if it weren't for you! I mean, it was you who got me started making frames in the first place . . .' Suddenly Suze looks almost tearful. 'Oh, Bex – I'm really going to miss you.'

'I know,' I say, biting my lip. 'Me too.'

For a while, we're both silent, and I honestly think I might start crying any second. But instead I take a deep breath and look up. 'Well, there's nothing for it. You'll just have to launch a New York branch.'

'Yes!' says Suze, brightening. 'Yes, I could do that, couldn't I?'

'Of course you could. You'll be all over the world,

soon.' I give her a hug. 'Hey, let's go out tonight and celebrate.'

'Oh Bex, I'd love to,' says Suze, 'but I can't. I'm going up to Scotland. In fact – ' she looks at her watch, and pulls a face – 'oh God, I didn't realize how late it was. Tarquin'll be here any moment.'

'Tarquin's coming here?' I say in shock. 'Now?'

Somehow, I've managed to avoid Suze's cousin Tarquin ever since that awful evening we spent together. Even the memory of it makes me feel uncomfortable. Basically, the date was going fine (at least, fine, given that I didn't fancy him or have anything in common with him) – until Tarquin caught me looking through his chequebook. Or at least, I think he did. I'm still not sure what he saw, and to be honest, I'm not keen to find out.

'I'm driving him up to my aunt's house for this dreary family party thing,' says Suze. 'We're going to be the only ones there under ninety.'

As she hurries off to her room, the doorbell rings and she calls over her shoulder, 'Could you get that, Bex? It's probably him.'

Oh God. Oh God. I *really* don't feel prepared for this.

Trying to assume an air of confident detachment I swing open the front door and say brightly,

'Tarquin!'

'Becky,' he says, staring at me as though I'm the lost treasure of Tutankhamun.

Oh God, he's looking as bony and strange as ever, with an odd green hand-knitted jersey stuffed under a tweed waistcoat, and a huge old fob watch dangling from his pocket. I'm sorry, but surely the fifteenth-richest man in England, or whatever he is, should be able to run to a nice new Timex?

'Well – come on in,' I say over-heartily, throwing my hand out like an Italian restaurant owner.

'Great,' says Tarquin, and follows me into the sitting

room. There's an awkward pause while I wait for him to sit down; in fact, I start to feel quite impatient as he hovers uncertainly in the middle of the room. Then suddenly I realize he's waiting for *me* to sit down, and hastily sink down onto the sofa.

'Would you like a titchy?' I ask politely.

'Bit early,' says Tarquin, with a nervous laugh.

('Titchy' is Tarquin-speak for drink, by the way. And trousers are 'tregs' and . . . you get the picture.)

We lapse into another dreadful silence. I just can't stop remembering awful details from our date – like when he tried to kiss me and I moved sharply away. Oh God. Forget. Forget.

'I . . . I heard you were moving to New York,' Tarquin says, staring at the floor. 'Is that true?'

'Yes,' I say, unable to stop myself smiling. 'Yes, that's the plan.'

'I went to New York once myself,' Tarquin says. 'Didn't really get on with it.'

'No,' I say consideringly. 'No, I can believe that. It's a bit different from Scotland, isn't it? Much more . . . frantic.'

'Absolutely!' he exclaims, as if I've said something very insightful. 'That was just it. Too frantic. And the people are absolutely extraordinary. Quite mad, in my opinion.'

Compared to what? I want to retort. At least they don't call water 'Ho' and sing Wagner in public.

But that wouldn't be kind. So I say nothing, and he says nothing – and when the door opens, we both look up gratefully.

'Hi!' says Suze. 'Tarkie, you're here! Listen, I've just got to get the car, because I had to park a few streets away the other night. I'll beep when I get back, and we can whiz off. OK?'

'OK,' says Tarquin, nodding. 'I'll just wait here with Becky.'

'Lovely!' I say, trying to smile brightly.

Suze disappears, I shift awkwardly in my seat, and Tarquin stretches his feet out and stares at them. Oh, this is excruciating. The very sight of him is niggling me more and more – and suddenly I know I *have* to say something now, otherwise I'll disappear off to New York and the chance will be lost.

'Tarquin,' I say, and exhale sharply. 'There's something I . . . I really want to say to you. I've been wanting to say it for a while, actually.'

'Yes?' he says, his head jerking up. 'What . . . what is it?' He meets my eyes anxiously, and I feel a slight pang of nerves. But now I've started, I've got to carry on. I've got to tell him the truth. I push my hair back, and take a deep breath.

'That jumper,' I say. 'It *really* doesn't go with that waistcoat.'

'Oh,' says Tarquin, looking taken aback. 'Really?'

'Yes!' I say, feeling a huge relief at having got it off my chest. 'In fact . . . it's frightful.'

'Should I take it off?'

'Yes. In fact, take the waistcoat off, too.'

Obediently he peels off the waistcoat and the jumper – and it's amazing how much better he looks when he's just in a plain blue shirt. Almost . . . normal! Then I have a sudden inspiration.

'Wait here!'

I hurry to my room and seize one of the carrier bags sitting on my chair. There's a jumper inside which I bought a few days ago for Luke's birthday, but I've discovered he's already got exactly the same one, so I was planning to take it back.

'Here!' I say, arriving back in the sitting room. 'Put this on. It's Paul Smith.'

Tarquin slips the plain black jumper over his head and pulls it down – and what a difference! He's actually starting to look quite distinguished.

'Your hair,' I say, staring critically at him. 'We need to do something with that.'

Ten minutes later I've wetted it, blow-dried it and sleeked it back with a bit of serum. And . . . I can't tell you. It's a transformation.

'Tarquin, you look wonderful!' I say – and I really mean it. He's still got that thin, bony look, but suddenly he doesn't look geeky any more, he looks kind of . . . interesting.

'Really?' says Tarquin, staring down at himself. He looks a little shell-shocked – and maybe I did slightly force him into this. But the point is, he'll thank me in the long run.

A car horn sounds from outside, and we both jump.

'Well, have a good time,' I say, suddenly like his mother. 'Tomorrow morning, just wet your hair again and push your fingers through it, and it should look OK.'

'Right,' says Tarquin, looking as though I've just given him a long mathematical formula to memorize. 'I'll try to remember. And the jersey? Shall I return it by post?'

'Don't return it!' I say in horror. 'It's yours to keep, and *wear*. A gift.'

'Thank you,' says Tarquin. 'I'm . . . very grateful, Becky.' He comes forward and pecks me on the cheek, and I pat him awkwardly on the hand. As he disappears out of the door, I find myself hoping that he'll get lucky at this party, and find someone. He really does deserve it.

Suze's car drives away and I wander into the kitchen to make a cup of tea, wondering what to do for the rest of the afternoon. I was half planning to do some more work on my self-help book. But my alternative is to watch *Manhattan*, which Suze videoed last night and would be really useful research for my trip. Because after all, I need to be well prepared, don't I?

And I can always work on the book when I get back from New York. Exactly.

I'm just happily putting the video into the machine when the phone rings.

'Oh, hello,' says a girl's voice. 'Sorry to disturb you. Is that Becky Bloomwood, by any chance?'

'Yes,' I say, reaching for the remote control.

'This is your um, travel agent,' says the girl, and clears her throat. 'We just wanted to confirm again which hotel you're staying at in New York.'

'Erm . . . the Four Seasons.'

'And that's with a Mr . . . Luke Brandon?'

'That's right.'

'For how many nights?'

'Erm . . . thirteen? Fourteen? I'm not sure.' I'm squinting at the telly, wondering if I've gone too far back. Surely they don't show that Walker's crisps ad any more?

'And are you staying in a room or a suite?'

'I think it's a suite.'

'And what's the cost per night?'

'Actually . . . I don't know,' I say. 'I could find out . . .'

'No, don't worry,' says the girl pleasantly. 'Well, I won't trouble you any more. Enjoy your trip.'

'Thanks!' I say, just as I find the start of the film. 'I'm sure we will.'

The phone goes dead, and I walk over to the sofa, frowning slightly. Surely the travel agent should have known how much the room was? I mean – surely that's her job?

I sit down, and take a sip of tea, waiting for the film to start. Now I come to think of it, that was quite a weird phone call. Why would someone phone up just to ask a load of really basic questions?

Unless – maybe she's new? Or just checking up, or something . . .

But then the whole thing is swept from my mind, as Gershwin's *Rhapsody in Blue* crashes through the air, and the screen is filled with pictures of Manhattan. I stare at the television, utterly gripped, feeling a tingle of excitement. This is where we're going! In three days' time we'll be there! I just cannot, cannot wait!

Endwich Bank
FULHAM BRANCH
3 Fulham Road
London SW6 9JH

Ms Rebecca Bloomwood
Flat 2
4 Burney Rd
London SW6 8FD

Dear Miss Bloomwood

Thank you for your letter of 19 September.

You have not broken your leg. Kindly contact my office without delay in order to arrange a meeting regarding your overdraft status.

You have been charged £20 for this letter.

Yours sincerely

John Gavin
Overdraft Facilities Director

ENDWICH – BECAUSE WE CARE

REGAL AIRLINES
Head Office
Preston House
354 Kingsway
London WC2 4TH

Ms Rebecca Bloomwood
Flat 2
4 Burney Rd
London SW6 8FD

Dear Rebecca Bloomwood

Thank you for your letter of 18 September, and I was sorry to hear that our luggage policy has been giving you sleepless nights and anxiety attacks.

I accept that you may well weigh considerably less than, as you put it, 'a fat business man from Antwerp, stuffing his face full of doughnuts'. Unfortunately Regal Airlines is still unable to increase your luggage allowance beyond the standard 20 kg.

You are welcome to start a petition and to write to Cherie Blair. However, our policy will remain the same.

Please enjoy your flight.

Mary Stevens
Customer Care Manager

Eight

OK, this is it. This is where I belong. I was *made* to live in America.

We've only been here since last night, but already I'm completely in love with the place. For a start, our hotel is fantastic – all limestone and marble and amazing high ceilings. We're staying in an enormous room overlooking Central Park, with a panelled dressing room, and the most incredible bath that fills up in about five seconds. Everything is so huge, and luxurious, and kind of . . . *more*. Like last night, after we arrived, Luke suggested a quick nightcap downstairs – and honestly, the Martini they brought me was the hugest drink I've ever seen. In fact, I nearly couldn't finish it. (But I managed it in the end. And then I had another one, just because it would have been churlish to refuse.)

Plus, everyone is so nice all the time. The hotel staff smile whenever they see you – and when you say 'thank you', they reply 'you're welcome', which they would *never* do in Britain, just kind of grunt. To my amazement, I've already been sent a lovely bouquet of flowers and an invitation to lunch from Luke's mother Elinor, who lives in New York, and another bouquet from the TV people I'm meeting on Wednesday, and a basket of fruit from someone I've never heard of but is apparently 'desperate' to meet me!

I mean, when did Zelda from *Morning Coffee* last send me a basket of fruit? Exactly.

I take a sip of coffee, and smile blissfully at Luke. We're sitting in the restaurant finishing breakfast before he whizzes off for a meeting, and I'm just deciding what to do with my day. I haven't got any interviews for a couple of days, so it's completely up to me whether I take in a few museums, or stroll in Central Park . . . or . . . pop into a shop or two . . .

'Would you like a refill?' comes a voice at my ear – and I look up to see a smiling waiter offering me a coffee pot. You see what I mean? They've been offering us endless coffee since we sat down, and when I asked for an orange juice they brought me a huge glass, all garnished with frosted orange peel. And as for those scrummy pancakes I've just polished off . . . I mean, pancakes for breakfast. It's pure genius, isn't it?

'So – I guess you'll be going to the gym?' says Luke, as he folds up his copy of the *Daily Telegraph*. He reads all the papers every day, American and British. Which is quite good, because it means I can still read my *Daily World* horoscope.

'The gym?' I say, puzzled.

'I thought that was going to be your routine,' he says, reaching for the *FT*. 'A workout every morning.'

I'm about to say, 'Don't be ridiculous!' when it occurs to me that I might have rashly announced something along those lines last night. After that second Martini.

Still – that's OK. I can go to the gym. In fact, it would be *good* to go to the gym. And then I could . . . well, I could always take in a few sights, I suppose. Maybe look at a few famous buildings.

You know, I'm sure I read somewhere that Bloomingdale's is quite an admired piece of architecture.

'And then what will you do?'

'I don't know,' I say vaguely, watching as a waiter puts a plate of French toast down on the table next to ours. God, that looks delicious. Why don't we have stuff like this in Europe? 'Go and explore New York, I guess.'

'I was asking at reception – and there's a guided walking tour which leaves from the hotel at eleven. The concierge highly recommended it.'

'Oh right,' I say, taking a sip of coffee. 'Well, I suppose I could do that . . .'

'Unless you wanted to get any shopping out of the way?' Luke adds, reaching for *The Times*, and I stare at him incredulously. You don't 'get shopping out of the way'. You get *other things* out of the way.

Which, in fact, makes me think. Maybe I should do this tour – and then I've got sightseeing ticked off.

'The guided tour sounds good,' I say. 'In fact, it'll be a great way to get to know my new home city.' I glance around the dining room at all the smart businessmen and groomed women, and waiters bustling discreetly about. 'God, just think, in a few weeks' time, we'll be living here. We'll be real New Yorkers!'

'Becky,' says Luke. He puts down his paper – and all at once he looks rather grave. 'There's something I've been meaning to say to you. Everything's been such a rush, I haven't had a chance – but it's something I really think you need to hear.'

'OK,' I say apprehensively. 'What is it?'

'It's a big step, moving to a new city. Especially a city as extreme as New York. I've been here many times, and even I find it overwhelming at times.'

'Right. So – what are you saying?'

'I'm saying I think you should take it slow. Don't expect to fit in straight away. The sheer pressure and pace of life here is, frankly, on another level from London.'

I stare at him, discomfited.

'Don't you think I'll be able to stand the pace?'

'I'm not saying that,' says Luke. 'I'm just saying – get

to know the city gradually. Get the feel of it; see if you can really see yourself living here. You may hate it! You may decide you can't possibly move here. Of course, I very much hope you don't – but it's worth keeping an open mind.'

'Right,' I say slowly. 'I see.'

'So just see how today goes – and we'll talk some more this evening. OK?'

'OK,' I say, and drain my coffee thoughtfully.

I'll show Luke I can fit into this city. I'll show him I can be a true New Yorker. I'll go to the gym, and then I'll drink some wheatgrassy healthy stuff, and then I'll . . . shoot someone, maybe?

Or maybe just the gym will be enough.

I'm actually quite looking forward to doing a workout, because I bought this fab DKNY exercise outfit in the sales last year, and this is the first time I've had the chance to wear it! I did mean to join a gym, in fact I even went and got a registration pack from Holmes Place in Fulham. But then I read this really interesting article which said you could lose loads of weight just by fidgeting. Just by twitching your fingers and stuff! So I thought I'd go for that method instead, and spend the money I saved on a new dress.

It's not that I don't like exercise or anything – because I do. I love it. And if I'm going to live in New York, I'll have to go to the gym every day, won't I? I mean, it's the law or something. So this is a good way to acclimatize.

As I reach the entrance to the fitness centre I glance at my reflection – and I'm secretly quite impressed. They say people in New York are all pencil thin and fit, don't they? But I reckon I look much fitter than some of these characters. I mean, look at that balding guy over there in the grey T-shirt. He looks like he's never been near a gym in his life!

'Hi there,' says a voice. I look up and see a muscular guy in trendy black Lycra coming towards me. 'I'm Tony. How are you today?'

'I'm fine, thanks,' I say, and casually do a little hamstring stretch. (At least, I think it's my hamstring. The one in your leg.) 'Just here for a workout.'

Nonchalantly I swap legs, clasp my hands and stretch my arms out in front of me. I can see my reflection on the other side of the room – and though I say it myself, I look pretty bloody cool.

'Do you exercise regularly?' asks Tony.

'Not in a gym,' I say, reaching down to touch my toes – then changing my mind halfway down and resting my hands on my knees. 'But I walk a lot.'

'Great!' says Tony. 'On a treadmill? Or cross-country?'

'Round the shops, mostly.'

'OK . . .' he says doubtfully.

'But I'm often holding quite heavy things,' I explain. 'You know, carrier bags and stuff.'

'Right,' says Tony, not looking that convinced. 'Well . . . would you like me to show you how the machines work?'

'It's all right,' I say confidently. 'I'll be fine.'

Honestly, I can't be bothered listening to him explain every single machine and how many settings it has. I mean, I'm not a moron, am I? I take a towel from the pile, drape it around my neck, and head off towards a running machine, which should be fairly simple. I step up onto the treadmill and survey the buttons in front of me. A panel is flashing the word 'Time' at me and after some thought I enter '40 minutes', which sounds about right. I mean, that's how long you'd go on a walk for, isn't it? It flashes 'program' and after a scrolling down the choices I select 'Everest', which sounds much more interesting than 'hill walk'. Then it flashes 'level'. Hmm. Level. I look around for some

155

advice, but Tony is nowhere to be seen.

The balding guy is getting onto the treadmill next to mine, and I lean over.

'Excuse me,' I say politely. 'Which level do you think I should choose?'

'That depends,' says the guy. 'How fit are you?'

'Well,' I say, smiling modestly. 'You know . . .'

'I'm going for level 5, if it's any help,' says the guy, briskly punching at his machine.

'OK,' I say. 'Thanks!'

Well, if he's level 5, I must be at least level 7. I mean, frankly, look at him – and look at me.

I reach up to the machine and punch in '7', then press START. The treadmill starts moving, and I start walking. And this is really pleasant! God, I really should go to the gym more often. Or, in fact, join a gym.

But it just shows, even if you don't work out, you can still have a natural baseline fitness. Because this is causing me absolutely no problems at all. In fact, it's far too easy. I should have chosen level—

Hang on. The machine's tilting upwards. And it's speeding up. I'm having to run to catch up with it.

Which is OK. I mean, this is the point, isn't it? Having a nice healthy jog. Running along, panting a little, but that just means my heart is working. Which is perfect. Just as long as it doesn't get any—

It's tilting again. Oh my God. And it's getting faster. And faster.

I can't do this. My face is red. My chest is hurting. I'm panting frenziedly, and clutching the sides of the machine. I can't run this fast. I have to slow down a bit.

Feverishly I jab at the panel – but the treadmill keeps whirring round – and suddenly cranks up even higher. Oh no. Please, no.

'Time left: 38.00' flashes brightly on a panel in front of me. *38 more minutes*?

I glance to my right, and the balding guy is sprinting

easily along as though he's running down a hill. I want to speak to him, but I can't open my mouth. I can't do anything except keep my legs moving as best I can.

All of a sudden he glances in my direction – and his expression changes.

'Miss? Are you all right?'

Hastily he punches at his machine, which grinds to a halt, then leaps down and jabs at mine.

The treadmill slows down, then comes to a rather abrupt standstill – and I collapse against one of the side bars, gasping for breath.

'Have some water,' says the man, handing me a cup.

'Th-thanks,' I say, and stagger down off the treadmill, still gasping. My lungs feel as if they're about to burst, and when I glimpse my reflection opposite, my face is beetroot.

'Maybe you should leave it for today,' says the man, gazing at me anxiously.

'Yes,' I say. 'Yes, maybe I will.' I take a swig of water, trying to get my breath back. 'I think actually the trouble is, I'm not used to American machines.'

'Could be,' says the man, nodding. 'They can be tricky. Of course, this one – ' he adds, slapping it cheerfully ' – was made in Germany.'

'Right,' I say after a pause. 'Yes. Well, anyway. Thanks for your help.'

'Any time,' says the man – and as he gets back onto his treadmill I can see him smiling.

Oh God, that was really embarrassing. As I make my way, showered and changed, to the foyer of the hotel for the walking tour, I feel a little deflated. Maybe Luke's right. Maybe I won't cope with the pace of New York. Maybe it's a stupid idea, me moving here with him.

A group of sightseers has already assembled – mostly much older than me – and they're all listening to a young, enthusiastic man who's saying something about the Statue of Liberty.

'Hi there!' he says, breaking off as I approach. 'Are you here for the tour?'

'Yes please,' I say.

'And your name?'

'Rebecca Bloomwood,' I say, flushing a little as all the others turn to look at me. 'I paid at the desk, earlier.'

'Well, hi Rebecca!' says the man, ticking something off on his list. 'I'm Christoph. Welcome to our group. Got your walking shoes on?' He looks down at my boots (bright purple, kitten heel, last year's Bertie sale) and his cheery smile falters. 'You realize this is a three-hour tour? All on foot?'

'Absolutely,' I say in surprise. 'That's why I put these boots on.'

'Right,' says Christoph after a pause. 'Well – OK.' He looks around. 'I think that's it, so let's start our tour!'

He leads the way out of the hotel, onto the street, and as everyone else follows him briskly along the pavement, I find myself walking slowly, staring upwards. It's an amazingly clear, fresh day with almost blinding sunlight bouncing off the pavements and buildings. I look around, completely filled with awe. God, this city is an incredible place. I mean, obviously I knew that New York would be full of tall skyscrapers. But it's only when you're actually standing in the street, staring up at them, that you realize how . . . well, how *huge* they are. I gaze up at the tops of the buildings against the sky, until my neck is aching and I'm starting to feel dizzy. Then slowly my eyes wander down, floor by floor to shop-window level. And I find myself staring at two words. 'Prada' and 'Shoes'.

Ooh.

Prada shoes. Right in front of me.

I'll just have a really quick look.

As the others march on, I hurry up to the window and stare at a pair of deep brown pumps. God those are divine. I wonder how much they are? You know, maybe Prada is really cheap over here. Maybe I should just pop in and—

'Rebecca?'

With a start I come to and look round – to see the tour group twenty yards down the street, all staring at me.

'Sorry,' I say, and reluctantly pull myself away from the window. 'I'm coming.'

'There'll be time for shopping later,' says Christoph cheerfully.

'I know,' I say, and give a relaxed laugh. 'Sorry about that.'

'Don't worry about it!'

Of course, he's quite right. There'll be plenty of time to go shopping. Plenty of time.

Right. I'm really going to concentrate on the tour.

'So Rebecca,' says Christoph brightly, as I rejoin the group. 'I was just telling the others that we're heading down East 57th Street to Fifth Avenue, the most famous avenue of New York City.'

'Great!' I say. 'That sounds really good!'

'Fifth Avenue serves as a dividing line between the "East Side" and the "West Side",' continues Christoph. 'Anyone interested in history will like to know that . . .'

I'm nodding intelligently as he speaks, and trying to look interested. But as we walk down the street, my head keeps swivelling from left to right, like someone watching a tennis game. Christian Dior, Hermès, Chanel . . . This street is incredible. If only we could just slow down a bit, and have a proper look – but Christoph is marching on ahead like a hike leader, and everybody else in the group is following him happily, not even glancing at the amazing sights around them. Don't they have eyes in their heads?

'. . . where we're going to take in two well-known landmarks: the Rockefeller Center, which many of you will associate with ice skating . . .'

We swing round a corner – and my heart gives a swoop of excitement. Tiffany's. It's Tiffany's, right in front of me! I *must* just have a quick peek. I mean, this is what New York is all about, isn't it? Little blue boxes, and white ribbon, and those gorgeous silver beans . . . I sidle up to the window and stare longingly at the beautiful display. Wow. That necklace is absolutely stunning. Oh God, and look at that watch. I wonder how much something like that would—

'Hey, everybody, wait up!' rings out Christoph's voice. I look up – and they're all bloody miles ahead again. How come they walk so fast, anyway? 'Are you OK there, Rebecca?' he calls, with a slightly forced cheeriness. 'You're going to have to try to keep up. We have a lot of ground to cover!'

'Sorry,' I say, and scuttle towards the group. 'Just having a quick little look at Tiffany's.' I grin at the woman next to me, expecting her to smile back. But she looks at me blankly and pulls her hood more tightly over her head.

'As I was saying,' he says as we stride off again, 'the grid system of Manhattan means that . . . '

And for a while I really try to concentrate. But it's no good. I can't listen. I mean, come on. This is Fifth Avenue! Everywhere I look, there are fabulous shops. There's Gucci – and that's the hugest Gap I've ever seen in my life . . . and oh God, look at that window display over there! And we're just walking straight past Armani Exchange and no-one's even pausing . . .

I mean, what is *wrong* with these people? Are they complete philistines?

We walk on a bit further, and I'm trying my best to catch a glimpse inside a window full of amazing-looking hats when . . . oh my God. Just . . . just look there. It's Saks Fifth Avenue. Right there, a matter of yards away. One of the most famous department stores in the world. Floors and floors of clothes and shoes and bags . . . And thank God, at *last*, Christoph is coming to his senses, and stopping.

'This is one of New York's most famous landmarks,' he's saying, with a gesture. 'Many New Yorkers regularly visit this magnificent place of worship – once a week or even more often. Some even make it here daily! We don't have time to do more than have a quick look inside – but those that are interested can always make a return trip.'

'Is it very old?' asks a man with a Scandinavian accent.

'The building dates from 1879,' says Christoph, 'and was designed by James Renwick.'

Come on, I think impatiently, as someone else asks a question about the architecture. Come on. Who cares who designed it? Who cares about the stonework? It's what's inside that matters.

'Shall we go in?' says Christoph at last.

'Absolutely!' I say joyfully, and hurry off towards the entrance.

It's only as my hand is actually on the door that I realize no-one else is with me. Where've they all gone? Puzzled, I look back – and the rest of the group is processing into a big stone church, outside which there's a board reading 'St Patrick's Cathedral'.

Oh.

Oh, I see. When he said 'magnificent place of worship' he meant . . .

Right. Of course.

I hesitate, hand on the door, feeling torn. Oh God, maybe I should go into the cathedral. Maybe I should take in some culture and come back to Saks later.

But then – is that going to help me get to know

whether I want to live in New York or not? Looking around some boring old cathedral?

Put it like this: how many millions of cathedrals do we have in England? And how many branches of Saks Fifth Avenue?

'Are you going in?' says an impatient voice behind me.

'Yes!' I say, coming to a decision. 'Absolutely. I'm going in.'

I push my way through the heavy wooden doors and into the store, feeling almost sick with anticipation. I haven't felt this excited since Octagon relaunched their designer floor and I was invited to the cardholders' champagne reception.

I mean, visiting any shop for the first time is exciting. There's always that buzz as you push open the door; that hope; that *belief* – that this is going to be the shop of all shops, which will bring you everything you ever wanted, at magically low prices. But this is a thousand times better. A million times. Because this isn't just any old shop, is it? This is a world-famous shop. I'm actually here. I'm in Saks on Fifth Avenue in New York. As I walk slowly into the store – forcing myself not to rush – I feel as though I'm setting off for a date with a Hollywood movie star.

I wander through the perfumery, gazing around at the elegant art deco panelling; the high, airy ceilings; the foliage everywhere. God, this has to be one of the most beautiful shops I've ever been in. At the back are old-fashioned lifts which make you feel you're in a film with Cary Grant, and on a little table is a pile of store directories. I pick one up, just to get my bearings . . . and I don't quite believe it. There are ten floors to this store.

Ten floors. *Ten.*

I stare at the list, transfixed. I feel like a child trying to choose a sweetie in a chocolate factory. Where am I going to start? How should I do this? Start at the top? Start at the bottom? Oh God, all these names, jumping out at me, calling to me. Anna Sui. Calvin Klein. Kate Spade. Kiehl's. I think I'm going to hyperventilate.

'Excuse me?' A voice interrupts my thoughts and I turn to see a girl with a Saks name badge smiling at me. 'Can I help you?'

'Um . . . yes,' I say, still staring at the directory. 'I'm just trying to work out where to start, really.'

'Were you interested in clothes? Or accessories? Or shoes?'

'Yes,' I say dazedly. 'Both. All. Everything. Erm . . . a bag,' I say randomly. 'I need a new bag!'

Which is true. I mean, I've brought bags with me – but you can always do with a new bag, can't you? Plus, I've been noticing that all the women in Manhattan seem to have very smart designer bags – so this is a very good way of acclimatizing myself to the city.

The girl gives me a friendly smile.

'Bags and accessories are through there,' she says, pointing. 'You might want to start there and work your way up?'

'Yes,' I say. 'That's what I'll do. Thanks!'

God, I adore shopping abroad. I mean, shopping anywhere is always great – but the advantages of doing it abroad are:

1. You can buy things you can't get in Britain.

2. You can name-drop when you get back home. ('Actually, I picked this up in New York.')

3. Foreign money doesn't count, so you can spend as much as you like.

OK, I know that last one isn't entirely true. Somewhere in my head I know that dollars are proper money, with a real value. But I mean, *look* at them. I just can't take them seriously. I've got a whole wodge of them in my purse, and I feel as though I'm carrying around the bank from a Monopoly set. Yesterday I went and bought some magazines from a newsstand, and as I handed over a $20 bill, it was just like playing shop. It's like some weird form of jet-lag – you move into another currency and suddenly feel as though you're spending nothing.

So as I walk around the bag department, trying out gorgeous bag after gorgeous bag, I'm not taking too much notice of the prices. Occasionally I lift a price tag and make a feeble attempt to work out how much that is in real money – but I have to confess, I can't remember the exact exchange rate. And even if I could, I've never been very good at sums.

But the point is, it doesn't matter. I don't need to worry, because this is America, and everyone knows that prices in America are really low. It's common knowledge, isn't it? So basically, I'm working on the principle that everything's a bargain. I mean, look at all these gorgeous designer handbags. They're probably half what they'd cost in England, if not less!

Eventually I choose a beautiful Kate Spade bag in tan leather, and take it up to the counter. It costs $500, which sounds quite a lot – but then, 'a million lire' sounds a lot too, doesn't it? And that's only about 50p.

As the assistant hands me my receipt, she even says something about it being 'a gift' – and I beam in agreement.

'A complete gift! I mean, in London, it would probably cost—'

'Gina, are you going upstairs?' interrupts the woman, turning to a colleague. 'Gina will show you to the seventh floor,' she says, and smiles at me.

'Right,' I say, in slight confusion. 'Well . . . OK.'

Gina beckons me briskly and, after a moment's hesitation, I follow her, wondering what's on the seventh floor. Maybe some complimentary lounge for Kate Spade customers, with free champagne or something!

It's only as we're approaching a department entitled 'Gift Wrapping' that I realize what's going on. When I said 'gift', she must have thought I meant it was an actual—

'Here we are,' says Gina brightly. 'The Saks signature box is complimentary – or choose from a range of quality wrap.'

'Right!' I say. 'Well . . . thanks very much! Although actually, I wasn't really planning to—'

But Gina has already gone, and the two ladies behind the gift wrap counter are smiling encouragingly at me.

Oh God, this is a bit embarrassing. What am I going to do?

'Have you decided which paper you'd like?' says the elder of the two ladies, beaming at me. 'We also have a choice of ribbons and adornments.'

Oh sod it. I'll get it wrapped. I mean, it only costs $7.50 – and it'll be nice to have something to open when I get back to the hotel room, won't it?

'Yes!' I say, and beam back. 'I'd like that silver paper, please, and some purple ribbon . . . and one of those clusters of silver berries.'

The lady reaches for the paper and deftly begins to wrap up my bag – more neatly than I've ever wrapped anything in my life. And you know, this is quite fun! Maybe I should always get my shopping gift-wrapped.

'Who's it to?' says the lady, opening a card and taking out a silver pen.

'Um . . . to Becky,' I say vaguely. Some girls have come into the gift wrap room, and I'm slightly intrigued by their conversation.

'. . . fifty per cent off . . .'

'. . . sample sale . . .'

'. . . Earl jeans . . .'

'And who is it from?' says the gift wrap lady pleasantly.

'Um . . . from Becky,' I say without thinking. The gift wrap lady gives me a rather strange look and I suddenly realize what I've said. 'A . . . a different Becky,' I add awkwardly.

' . . . sample sale . . .'

' . . . Alexander McQueen, pale blue, 80 per cent off . . .'

' . . . sample sale . . .'

' . . . sample sale . . .'

Oh, I can't bear this any longer.

'Excuse me,' I say, turning round. 'I didn't mean to eavesdrop on your conversation – but I just have to know one thing. What is a sample sale?'

The whole gift wrap area goes quiet. Everyone is staring at me, even the lady with the silver pen.

'You don't know what a sample sale is?' says a girl in a leather jacket eventually, as though I've said I don't know my alphabet.

'Erm . . . no,' I say, feeling myself flush red. 'No, I . . . I don't.' The girl raises her eyebrows, reaches in her bag, rummages around, and finally pulls out a card. 'Honey, *this* is a sample sale.'

I take the card from her, and as I read, my skin starts to prickle with excitement.

SAMPLE SALE
Designer clothes, 50–70% off
Ralph Lauren, Comme des Garçons, Gucci
Bags, shoes, hosiery, 40–60% off
Prada, Fendi, Lagerfeld

'Is this for real?' I breathe at last, looking up. 'I mean, could . . . could *I* go to it?'

'Oh yuh,' says the girl. 'It's for real. But it'll only last a day.'

'A day?' My heart starts to thump in panic. 'Just one day?'

'One day,' affirms the girl solemnly. I glance at the other girls, and they're nodding in agreement.

'Sample sales come without much warning,' explains one.

'They can be anywhere. They just appear overnight.'

'Then they're gone. Vanished.'

'And you just have to wait for the next one.'

I look from face to face, utterly mesmerized. I feel like an explorer learning about some mysterious nomadic tribe.

'So you wanna catch this one today,' says the girl in the leather jacket, tapping the card and bringing me back to life, 'you'd better hurry.'

I have never moved as fast as I do out of that shop. Clutching my Saks Fifth Avenue carrier, I hail a taxi, breathlessly read out the address on the card, and sink back into my seat.

I have no idea where we're heading or what famous landmarks we're passing – but I don't care. As long as there are designer clothes on sale, then that's all I need to know.

We come to a stop, and I pay the driver, making sure I tip him about 50 per cent so he doesn't think I'm some stingy English tourist – and, heart thumping, I get out. And I have to admit, on first impressions, things are not promising. I'm in a street full of rather uninspiring shop fronts and office blocks. On the card it said the sample sale was at 405, but when I follow the numbers along the road, 405 turns out to be just another office building. Am I in the wrong place altogether? I walk along the pavement for a little bit, peering up at the buildings – but there are no clues. I don't even know which district I'm in.

Suddenly I feel deflated and rather stupid. I was supposed to be going on a nice organized walking tour today – and what have I done instead? I've gone rushing off to some strange part of the city, where I'll probably get mugged any minute. In fact, the whole thing was probably a scam, I think morosely. I mean, honestly. Designer clothes at 70 per cent discount? I should have realized it was far too good to be—

Hang on. Just . . . hang on a minute.

Another taxi is pulling up, and a girl in a Miu Miu dress is getting out. She consults a piece of paper, walks briskly along the pavement, and disappears inside the door of 405. A moment later, two more girls appear along the street – and as I watch, they go inside, too.

Maybe this *is* the right place.

I push open the glass doors, walk into a shabby foyer furnished with plastic chairs, and nod nervously at the concierge sitting at the desk.

'Erm . . . excuse me,' I say politely. 'I was looking for the—'

'Twelfth floor,' he says in a bored voice. 'Elevators are in the rear.'

I hurry towards the back of the foyer, summon one of the rather elderly lifts and press 12. Slowly and creakily the lift rises – and I begin to hear a kind of faint babble, rising in volume as I get nearer. The lift pings and the doors open and . . . Oh my God. Is this the *queue*?

A line of girls is snaking back from a door at the end of the corridor. They're pressing forwards, and all have the same urgent look in their eyes. Every so often somebody pushes their way out of the door, holding a carrier bag – and about three girls push their way in. Then, just as I join the end of the line, there's a rattling sound, and a woman opens up a door, a few yards behind me.

'Another entrance this way,' she calls. 'Come this way!'

In front of me, a whole line of heads whips round. There's a collective intake of breath – and then it's like a tidal wave of girls, all heading towards me. I find myself running towards the door, just to avoid being knocked down – and suddenly I'm in the middle of the room, slightly shaken, as everybody else peels off and heads for the rails.

I look around, trying to get my bearings. There are rails and rails of clothes, tables covered in bags and shoes and scarves and girls sorting through them. I can spot Ralph Lauren knitwear . . . a rail full of fabulous coats . . . there's a stack of Prada bags . . . I mean, this is like a dream come true!

Conversation is high-pitched and excited, and as I look around, I can hear snippets floating around.

'I have to have it,' a girl is saying, holding up a coat against herself. 'I just *have* to have it.'

'OK, what I'm going to do is, I'm just going to put the $450 I spent today on to my mortgage,' another girl is saying to her friend as they walk out, laden with bags. 'I mean, what's $450 over thirty years?'

'One hundred per cent cashmere!' someone else is exclaiming. 'Did you see this? It's only $50! I'm going to take three.'

I look around the bright, buzzing room, at the girls milling about, grabbing at merchandise, trying on scarves, piling their arms full of glossy new stuff. And I feel a sudden warmth; an overwhelming realization. These are my people. This is where I belong. I've found my homeland.

Several hours later, I arrive back at the Four Seasons on a complete high. I'm laden with carrier bags, and I can't *tell* you what unbelievable bargains I picked up. A fantastic buttermilk leather coat, which is a teeny bit tight but I'm sure I'll soon lose a couple of pounds. (And anyway, leather stretches.) Plus a really gorgeous printed chiffon top, and some silver shoes, and a purse! And the whole lot only came to $500!

Not only that, but I met a really nice girl called Jodie,

who told me all about a website which sends you information on these kind of events every day. Every day! I mean, the possibilities are limitless. You could spend your *whole life* going to sample sales!

You know. In theory.

I go up to our room – and as I open the door I see Luke sitting at the desk, reading through some papers.

'Hi!' I say breathlessly, dumping my bags on the enormous bed. 'Listen, I need to use the laptop.'

'Oh right,' says Luke. 'Sure.' He picks up the laptop from the desk and hands it to me, and I go and sit on the bed. I open the laptop up, consult the piece of paper Jodie gave me, and type in the address.

'So, how was your day?' asks Luke.

'It was great!' I say, tapping the keys impatiently. 'Ooh, and look in that blue bag! I got you some really nice shirts!'

'Did you start to get a feel for the place?'

'Oh, I think so. I mean, obviously it's early days . . .' I frown at the screen. 'Come *on*, already.'

'But you weren't too overwhelmed?'

'Mmm . . . not really,' I say absently. Aha! Suddenly the screen is filling up with images. A row of little sweeties at the top, and logos saying, *It's fun. It's fashion. In New York City.* The Daily Candy home page!

I click on 'Subscribe' and briskly start to type in my e-mail details, as Luke gets up and comes towards me, a concerned look on his face.

'So tell me, Becky,' he says. 'I know it must all seem very strange and daunting to you. I know you couldn't possibly find your feet in just one day. But on first impressions – do you think you could get used to New York? Do you think you could ever see yourself living here?'

I type the last letter with a flourish, press SEND and look at him thoughtfully.

'You know what? I think I probably could.'

HOWSKI AND FORLANO
US IMMIGRATION LAWYERS
568 E 56th St
NEW YORK

Ms Rebecca Bloomwood
Flat 2
4 Burney Rd
London SW6 8FD

Dear Miss Bloomwood

Thank you for your completed US immigration forms, which raised a couple of issues.

Under section B69 referring to special talents, you write 'I'm really good at chemistry, ask anyone at Oxford'. We did in fact contact the Vice-Chancellor of Oxford University, who failed to display any familiarity with your work.

As did the British Olympic long-jump coach.

We enclose fresh forms and request that you fill them out again.

With kind regards

Edgar Forlano

Nine

The next two days are a whirlwind of soaking up the sights and sounds of New York. And you know, some of them are truly awe-inspiring. Like, in Bloomingdale's, they have a chocolate factory! And there's a whole district full of nothing but shoe shops!

It's all so exciting I almost forget why I'm here. But then I wake up on Wednesday morning – and I've got a slight dentisty feeling of dread. It's my first appointment today with a pair of important TV people from HLBC. Oh God. This is actually quite scary.

Luke has to leave early for a breakfast meeting, so I'm left alone in bed, sipping coffee and nibbling at a croissant, and telling myself not to get nervous. The key is not to panic, but to stay calm and cool. As Luke kept reassuring me, this meeting is not an interview as such, it's simply a first stage introduction. A 'getting-to-know-you' lunch, he called it.

Which would be fine – except do I actually *want* them to get to know me? To be honest, I'm not sure it's such a great idea. In fact I'm fairly sure that if they genuinely did get to know me – like if they turned out to be mind-readers or something – my chances of a job would turn out to be about zero.

I spend all morning in our room, trying to read the *Wall Street Journal* and watching CNN – but that only freaks me out even more. I mean, these American television presenters are so slick and immaculate. They never fluff their words, and they never make jokes, and they know everything. Like who's the trade secretary of Iraq, and the implications of global warming for Peru. And here I am, thinking I can do what they do. I must be mad.

My other problem is, I haven't done a proper interview for years. *Morning Coffee* never bothered to interview me, I just kind of fell into it. And for my old job on *Successful Saving*, I just had a cosy chat with Philip, the editor, who already knew me from press conferences. So the idea of having to impress a pair of complete strangers from scratch is terrifying.

'Just be yourself', Luke keeps saying. But frankly, that's a ridiculous idea. Everyone knows the point of an interview is not to demonstrate who you are, but to pretend to be whatever sort of person they want for the job. That's why they call it 'interview technique'.

As I arrive at the restaurant where we're meeting, half of me wants to run away, give up on the idea, and buy myself a nice pair of shoes instead. But I can't. I just have to go through with it.

And that's the worst thing of all. The reason my stomach feels so hollow and my hands feel so damp is that this really matters to me. I can't tell myself I don't care and it's not important, like I do about most things. Because this really does matter. If I don't manage to get a job in New York, then I won't be able to live in New York. If I screw this interview up, and word gets around that I'm hopeless – then it's all over. Oh God. Oh God . . .

OK, calm down, I tell myself firmly. I can do this. I can do it. And afterwards, I'll reward myself with a little treat. The Daily Candy website e-mailed me this morning, and apparently this huge makeup emporium in SoHo called Sephora is running a special promotion today, until four. Every customer gets a goody bag – and if you spend $50, you get a free mascara!

There, you see, I feel better already, just thinking about it. OK, go girl. Go get 'em.

I force myself to push open the door, and suddenly I'm in a very smart restaurant, all black lacquer and white linen and coloured fish swimming in tanks.

'Good afternoon,' says a *maître d'* dressed entirely in black.

'Hello,' I say. 'I'm here to meet—'

Shit, I've completely forgotten the names of the people I'm meeting.

Oh, great start, Becky. This is really professional.

'Could you just . . . hang on?' I say, and turn away, flushing red. I scrabble in my bag for the piece of paper – and here we are. Judd Westbrook and Kent Garland.

Kent? Is that really a name?

'It's Rebecca Bloomwood,' I say to the *maître d'*, hastily shoving the paper back in my bag. 'Meeting Judd Westbrook and Kent Garland of HLBC?' He scans the list, then gives a frosty smile. 'Ah yes. They're already here.'

Taking a deep breath, I follow him to the table – and there they are. A blonde woman in a beige trouser suit, and a chiselled-looking man in an equally immaculate black suit and sage green tie. I fight the urge to run away, and advance with a confident smile, holding out my hand. They both look up at me, and for a moment neither says anything – and I feel a horrible conviction that I've already broken some vital rule of etiquette. I mean, you do shake hands in America, don't you? You're not supposed to kiss? Or bow?

Thankfully the blonde woman is getting up, and clasping my hand warmly.

'Becky!' she says. '*So* thrilled to meet you. I'm Kent Garland.'

'Judd Westbrook,' says the man, gazing at me with deep-set eyes. 'We're very excited to meet you.'

174

'Me too!' I say. 'And thank you so much for your lovely flowers!'

'Not at all,' says Judd, and ushers me into a chair. 'It's a great delight.'

'An enormous pleasure,' says Kent.

There's an expectant silence.

'Well, it's a . . . a fantastic pleasure for me, too,' I say hastily. 'Absolutely . . . phenomenal.'

So far, so good. If we just keep telling each other what a pleasure this is, I should do OK. Carefully I place my bag on the floor, along with my copies of the *FT* and the *Wall Street Journal*. I thought about the *South China Morning Post*, too, but decided that might be a bit much.

'Would you like a drink?' says a waiter, appearing at my side.

'Oh yes!' I say, and glance nervously around the table to see what everyone else is having. Kent and Judd have both got tumblers full of what looks like G&T, so I'd better follow suit. 'A gin and tonic, please.'

To be honest, I think I need it, just to relax. As I open my menu, both Judd and Kent are gazing at me with an alert interest, as though they think I might suddenly burst into blossom or something.

'We've seen your tapes,' says Kent, leaning forwards. 'And we're very impressed.'

'Really?' I say – and then realize I shouldn't sound quite so astonished. 'Really,' I repeat, trying to sound nonchalant. 'Yes well, I'm proud of the show, obviously . . .'

'As you know, Rebecca, we produce a show called *Consumer Today*,' says Kent. 'We don't have a personal finance segment at present, but we'd love to bring in the kind of advisory slot you're doing in Britain.' She glances at Judd, who nods in agreement.

'It's obvious you have a passion for personal finance,' he says.

'Oh,' I say, taken aback. 'Well . . .'

'It shines through your work,' he asserts firmly. 'As does the pincer-like grip you have on your subject.'

Pincer-like grip?

'You know, you're pretty unique, Rebecca,' Kent is saying. 'A young, approachable, charming girl, with such a high level of expertise and conviction in what you're saying . . .'

'You're an inspiration for the financially challenged everywhere,' agrees Judd.

'What we admire the most is the patience you show these people.'

'The empathy you have with them . . .'

'. . . that faux-simplistic style of yours!' says Kent, and looks at me intently. 'How do you keep that up?'

'Erm . . . you know! It just comes, I suppose . . .' The waiter puts a drink in front of me and I grab it thankfully. 'Well, cheers, everyone!' I say, lifting my glass.

'Cheers!' says Kent. 'Are you ready to order, Rebecca?'

'Absolutely!' I reply, quickly scanning the menu. 'The sea bass, please, and a green salad.' I look at the others. 'And shall we share some garlic bread?'

'I'm wheat-free,' says Judd politely.

'Oh right,' I say. 'Well . . . Kent?'

'I don't eat carbohydrate during the week,' she says pleasantly. 'But you go ahead. I'm sure it's delicious!'

'No, it's OK,' I say hastily. 'I'll just have the sea bass.'

God, how could I be so stupid? Of course Manhattanites don't eat garlic bread.

'And to drink?' says the waiter.

'Erm . . .' I look around the table. 'I don't know. A Sauvignon Blanc, maybe? What does everyone else want?'

'Sounds good,' says Kent with a friendly smile, and I

breathe a sigh of relief. 'Just some more Pellegrino for me,' she adds, and gestures to her tumbler.

'And me,' says Judd.

Pellegrino? They're on *Pellegrino*?

'I'll just have water too,' I say quickly. 'I don't need wine! It was just an idea. You know—'

'No!' says Kent. 'You must have whatever you like.' She smiles at the waiter. 'A bottle of the Sauvignon Blanc, please, for our guest.'

'Honestly . . .' I say, flushing red.

'Rebecca,' says Kent, lifting a hand with a smile. 'Whatever makes you comfortable.'

Oh great. Now she thinks I'm a complete alcoholic. She thinks I can't survive one getting-to-know-you lunch without hitting the booze.

Well, never mind. It's done now. And it'll be OK. I'll just drink one glass. One glass, and that's it.

And that is honestly what I mean to do. Drink one glass and leave it at that.

But the trouble is, every time I finish my glass, a waiter comes along and fills it up again, and somehow I find myself drinking it. Besides which, it's occurred to me that it would look rather ungrateful to order a whole bottle of wine and leave it undrunk.

So the upshot is, by the time we've finished our food, I'm feeling quite . . . Well. I suppose one word might be 'drunk'. Another might be 'pissed'. But it's not a problem, because we're having a really good time, and I'm actually being really witty. Probably because I've relaxed a little. I've told them lots of funny stories about behind the scenes at *Morning Coffee*, and they've listened carefully and said it all sounds 'quite fascinating'.

'Of course, you British are very different from us,' says Kent thoughtfully, as I finish telling her about the time Dave the cameraman arrived so pissed he keeled over in the middle of a shot, and got Emma picking her nose. God, that was funny. In fact, I can't stop giggling, just remembering it.

'We just love your British sense of humour,' says Judd, and stares intently at me as though expecting a joke.

OK, quick. Think of something funny. British sense of humour. Erm . . . Monty Python? Victor Meldrew?

'I don't be-*lieve* it!' I hear myself exclaiming. 'Erm . . . thet is an ex-parrot!' I give a snort of laughter, and Judd and Kent exchange puzzled looks.

Just then, the coffee arrives. At least, I'm having coffee, Kent's having English Breakfast tea, and Judd's having some weird tisane thing which he gave to the waiter to make.

'I adore tea,' says Kent, giving me a smile. 'So calming. Now, Rebecca. In England, the custom is that you turn the pot three times clockwise to keep away the devil. Is that right? Or is it anticlockwise?'

Turn the pot? I've never heard of turning the bloody pot.

'Erm . . . let me remember.'

I screw my face up thoughtfully, trying to remember the last time I drank tea from a teapot. But the only image that comes to me is of Suze dunking a teabag in a mug while she tears a KitKat open with her teeth.

'I think it's anticlockwise,' I say at last. 'Because of the old saying, "The devil he creeps around the clock . . . but never backwards he will go." '

What the hell am I talking about? Why have I suddenly put on a Scottish accent?

Oh God, I've drunk too much.

'Fascinating!' says Kent, taking a sip of tea. 'I adore all these quaint old British customs. Do you know any others?'

'Absolutely!' I say brightly. 'I know loads!'

178

Stop it, Becky. Just stop now.

'Like, we have a very old custom of . . . of . . . "turning the tea cake".'

'Really?' says Kent. 'I've never heard of that one.'

'Oh yes,' I say confidently. 'What happens is, you take your tea cake . . .' I grab a bread roll from a passing waiter. 'And you . . . rotate it above your head like so, and you . . . you say a little rhyme . . .'

Crumbs are starting to fall on my head, and I can't think of anything to rhyme with 'teacake', so I put my bread roll down and take a sip of coffee. 'They do it in Cornwall,' I add.

'Really?' says Judd with interest. 'My grandmother comes from Cornwall. I'll have to ask her about it!'

'Only in some bits of Cornwall,' I explain. 'Just in the pointy bits.'

Judd and Kent give each other bewildered looks – then both burst into laughter.

'Your British sense of humour!' says Kent. 'It's so refreshing.'

For a moment I'm not quite sure how to react – then I start laughing too. God, this is great. We're getting on like a house on fire! Then Kent's face lights up.

'Now, Rebecca, I was meaning to say. I have rather a special opportunity for you. I don't know what your plans were for this afternoon. But I have a rather unique ticket . . . to . . .'

She pauses for effect, smiling widely, and I stare at her in sudden excitement. A Gucci invitation sample sale! It has to be!

'. . . the Association of Financiers Annual Conference!' she finishes proudly.

For a few moments I can't speak.

'Really?' I say at last, my voice slightly more high-pitched than usual. 'You're . . . you're joking!'

How am I going to get out of this one? How?

'I know!' says Kent delightedly. 'I thought you'd be

179

pleased. So if you're not doing anything else this afternoon . . .'

I *am* doing something! I want to wail. I'm going to Sephora for my free mascara!

'There are some very high-profile speakers,' puts in Judd. 'Bert Frankel, for one.'

'Really?' I say. 'Bert Frankel!'

I've never even heard of bloody Bert Frankel.

'So . . . I have the pass right here . . .' says Kent, reaching for her bag.

'What a shame!' I hear myself exclaiming. 'Because actually, I was planning to . . . to visit the Guggenheim this afternoon.'

Phew. No-one can argue with culture.

'Really?' says Kent, looking disappointed. 'Couldn't it wait until another day?'

'I'm afraid not,' I say. 'There's a particular exhibit I've been absolutely longing to see since . . . since I was a child of six.'

'Really?' says Kent, eyes wide.

'Yes,' I lean forward earnestly. 'Ever since I saw a photograph of it in my granny's art book, it's been my ambition since childhood to come to New York City and see this piece of art. And now that I'm here . . . I just can't wait any longer. I hope you understand . . .'

'Of course!' says Kent. 'Of course we do. What an inspiring story!' She exchanges impressed looks with Judd, and I smile modestly back. 'So – which piece of art is it?'

I stare at her, still smiling. OK, quick, think. The Guggenheim. Modern paintings? Sculpture?

I'm 50–50 on modern paintings. If only I could phone a friend.

'Actually . . . I'd rather not say,' I say at last. 'I consider artistic preference a very . . . private matter.'

'Oh,' says Kent, looking a little taken aback. 'Well of course, I didn't mean to intrude in any way—'

'Kent,' says Judd, glancing at his watch again. 'We really have to—'

'You're right,' says Kent. She takes another sip of tea, and stands up. 'I'm sorry, Rebecca, we have a meeting at 2.30. But it's been such a pleasure.'

'Of course,' I say. 'No problem!'

I struggle to my feet and follow them out of the restaurant. As I pass the wine bucket I realize with a slight lurch that I've more or less drunk the whole bottle. God, how embarrassing. But I don't think anybody noticed.

We arrive outside the restaurant, and Judd has already hailed a taxi for me.

'Great to meet you, Rebecca,' he says. 'We'll report back to our Vice-President of Production, and we'll . . . be in touch! Enjoy the Guggenheim.'

'Absolutely!' I say, shaking hands with each of them. 'I will. And thank you so much!'

I'm waiting for them to walk away – but they're standing there, waiting for *me* to go – so I get into the taxi, stumbling slightly, lean forward and say clearly, 'The Guggenheim, please.'

The taxi whizzes off, and I wave cheerfully at Judd and Kent until they're out of sight. I think that went really well, actually. Except maybe when I told them the anecdote about Rory and the guide dog. And when I tripped over on my way to the loos. But then, that could happen to anybody.

I wait until we've gone a block or two more, just to be safe – then lean forward again.

'Excuse me,' I say to the driver, 'I've changed my mind. Could we go to SoHo?'

The taxi driver turns and gives me a reproving frown.

'You want to go to SoHo?' he says. 'What about the Guggenheim?'

'Erm . . . I'll go later on.'

181

'Later on?' says the driver. 'You can't rush the Guggenheim. The Guggenheim is a very fine museum. Picasso. Kandinsky. You don't want to miss it.'

'I won't miss it! Honestly, I promise. If we could just go to SoHo now? Please?'

There's silence from the front.

'All right,' says the driver at last, shaking his head. 'All right.' He swings the taxi round in the road and we start to head in the opposite direction. I look at my watch – and it's 2.40. Loads of time. Perfect.

I lean back happily and look out of the window at a glimpse of blue sky. God, this is great, isn't it? Whizzing along in a yellow taxi cab, with the sunlight glinting off skyscrapers and a happy wine-fuelled smile on my face. I really feel as though I'm settling into New York. I mean, I know it's only been three days, but I honestly feel as though I belong here. I'm getting the language and everything. Like, yesterday, I said, 'go figure' without even thinking. And I called a skirt 'cute'! We pull up at a pedestrian crossing and I'm peering interestedly out, wondering which street we're at – when suddenly I freeze in horror.

There are Judd and Kent. Right there, in front of us. They're crossing the road, and Kent is saying something animatedly, and Judd is nodding. Oh God. Oh God. Quick, hide.

My heart thumping, I sink down in my seat and try to hide behind my *Wall Street Journal*. But it's too late. Kent has seen me. Her jaw drops in astonishment and she comes hurrying over. She taps on the window, mouthing something and gesticulating urgently.

'Rebecca! You're going the wrong way!' she exclaims, as I lower the window. 'The Guggenheim is in the other direction!'

'Really?' I say in shocked tones. 'Oh my God! How did that happen?'

'Tell your driver to turn around! These New York

cab drivers! They know nothing!' She knocks on his window. 'The Gugg-en-heim!' she says as though to a very stupid toddler. 'Up on 89th! And hurry! This woman has been waiting to go there since she was six years old!'

'You want me to go to the Guggenheim?' says the driver, looking at me.

'Er . . . yes!' I say, not daring to meet his eye. 'That's what I said, isn't it? The Guggenheim!'

The driver curses under his breath and swings the taxi round, and I wave to Kent, who is making sympathetic gestures of the 'isn't he a brainless idiot?' variety.

We drive off, going north again, and for a few minutes I can't bring myself to say anything. But I can see the streets going by. 34th, 35th . . . It's nearly three, and we're getting further and further away from SoHo and Sephora and my free mascara . . .

'Excuse me,' I say, and clear my throat apologetically. 'Actually . . .'

'What?' says the driver, giving me a menacing look.

'I've . . . I've just remembered I promised to meet my . . . aunt, in . . . in . . .'

'SoHo. You want to go to SoHo.'

He meets my eye in the mirror and I give a tiny, shamefaced nod. As the driver swings the taxi round again, I'm thrown along the seat and bump my head on the window.

'Hey there!' says a disembodied voice, making me jump with fright. 'You be careful! Safety counts, OK? So buckle up!'

'OK,' I say humbly. 'Sorry about that. I'm really sorry. I won't do it again.'

I fasten my seat belt with clumsy fingers, and catch the eye of the driver in the mirror.

'It's a recorded announcement,' he says scornfully. 'You're talking to a tape machine.'

I knew that.

*　　　*　　　*

At last we arrive at Sephora on Broadway, and I thrust wodges of dollars at the driver. (100 per cent tip, which I think is quite reasonable under the circumstances). As I get out of the cab, he looks closely at me.

'Have you been drinking, lady?'

'No,' I say indignantly. 'I mean . . . yes. But it was just a bit of wine at lunch . . .'

The taxi driver shakes his head and drives off, and I head unsteadily into Sephora. To be honest, I am feeling a little giddy. And as I push open the door, I feel even giddier. Oh my God. This is even better than I expected.

There's music pounding, and girls milling everywhere under the spotlights, and trendy guys in black polo necks and headsets handing out goody bags. I turn dazedly around: I've never seen so much makeup in my life. Rows and rows of lipsticks. Rows and rows of nail polishes. In all the colours of the rainbow. And oh look, there are little chairs where you can sit and try it all on, with free cotton buds and everything. This place is . . . I mean, it's heaven.

I take a goody bag and look at it. Something called the 'Sephora promise' is printed on the front: 'All things of beauty bring us together and impart a sweet scent to life'.

God, you know, that is just *so* true. In fact, it's so wise and kind of . . . poignant, it almost brings tears to my eyes.

'Are you all right, miss?' A guy in a headset is peering curiously at me, and I look up, still in a daze.

'I was just reading the Sephora promise. It's . . . it's just so beautiful.'

'Well . . . OK,' says the guy, and gives me a doubtful look. 'You have a good day now.'

I nod at him, then half walk, half lurch to a row of little bottles of nail polish, labelled things like Cosmic

184

Intelligence and Lucid Dream. As I gaze at the display, I feel overcome with emotion. These bottles are speaking to me. They're telling me that if I just paint my nails with the right colour, everything will instantly make sense and my life will fall into place.

Why have I never realized this truth before? Why?

I pick up Lucid Dream and put it in my basket – then make my way towards the back of the shop, where I find a rack labelled 'Treat yourself – you're worth it'.

I *am* worth it, I think hazily. I *deserve* a set of scented candles, and a travel mirror and some 'buffing paste', whatever that is . . . As I stand there, filling up my basket, I'm dimly aware of a ringing, burbling sort of sound – and all of a sudden I realize it's my own mobile phone.

'Hi!' I say, clutching it to my ear. 'Who's this?'

'Hi. It's me,' says Luke. 'I heard your lunch went well.'

'Really?' I say, feeling a jolt of surprise. 'Where did you hear that?'

'I've just been speaking to some people at HLBC. Apparently you were quite a hit. Very entertaining, they said.'

'Wow!' I say, swaying slightly, and clutching at the display for balance. 'Really? Are you sure?'

'Quite sure. They were saying how charming you were, and how cultured . . . I even hear they put you in a taxi to the Guggenheim afterwards.'

'That's right,' I say, reaching for a pot of mandarin lip balm. 'They did.'

'Yes, I was quite intrigued to hear all about your burning childhood dream,' says Luke. 'Kent was very impressed.'

'Really?' I say vaguely. 'Well, that's good.'

'Absolutely.' Luke pauses. 'Slightly strange that you didn't mention the Guggenheim this morning, though,

185

isn't it? Or indeed . . . ever. Bearing in mind you've been longing to go there since you were a child of six.'

I hear the amusement in his voice, and snap to attention. He's bloody well rung up to tease me, hasn't he?

'Have I never mentioned the Guggenheim?' I say innocently, and put the lip balm in my basket. 'How very odd.'

'Isn't it?' says Luke. 'Most peculiar. So, are you there now?'

Bugger.

For a moment, I'm silenced. I simply can't admit to Luke that I've gone shopping again. Not after all that teasing he gave me about my so-called guided tour. I mean OK, I know ten minutes out of a three-hour city tour isn't that much – but I saw a bit, didn't I? I mean, I got as far as Saks, didn't I?

'Yes,' I say defiantly. 'Yes, I am, actually.'

Which is kind of almost true. I mean, I can easily go there after I've finished here.

'Great!' says Luke. 'What particular exhibit are you looking at?'

Oh shut up.

'What's that?' I say, suddenly raising my voice. 'Sorry, I didn't realize! Luke, I have to turn my mobile off. The . . . um . . . curator is complaining. But I'll see you later.'

'Six at the Royalton Bar,' he says. 'You can meet my new associate, Michael. And I'll look forward to hearing all about your afternoon.'

Ten

I put away my phone feeling slightly indignant. Huh. Well, I'll show him. I'll go to the Guggenheim right now. Right this minute. Just as soon as I've bought my makeup and got my free gift.

I stuff my basket full of beauty goodies, hurry up to the checkout, and sign the credit slip without even looking at it, then go out to the crowded street. Right. It's 3.30, which gives me plenty of time to get up there and immerse myself in some culture. Excellent, I'm really looking forward to it, actually.

I'm standing on the edge of the pavement, holding out my hand for a taxi, when I spot a gorgeous, glowing shop called Kate's Paperie. Without quite meaning to, I let my hand drop, and start edging slowly towards the window. Just look at that. Look at that display of marbled wrapping paper. And that decoupage box. And that amazing beaded ribbon.

OK, what I'll do is, I'll just pop in and have a quick look. Just for five minutes. And *then* I'll go to the Guggenheim.

I push the door open and walk slowly around, marvelling at the arrangements of beautiful wrapping paper adorned with dried flowers, raffia and bows, the photograph albums, the boxes of exquisite writing paper . . . And oh God, just look at the greetings cards!

You see, this is it. This is why New York is so great. They don't just have boring old cards saying Happy

187

Birthday. They have handmade creations with twinkly flowers and witty collages, saying things like 'Congratulations on adopting twins!' and 'So sad to hear you broke up!'

I walk up and down, utterly dazzled by the array. I just *have* to have some of these. Like this fantastic pop-up castle, with the flag reading 'I love your remodeled home!' I mean, I don't actually know anyone who's remodelling their home, but I can always keep it until Mum decides to repaper the hall. And this one covered in fake grass, saying 'To a smashing tennis coach with thanks'. Because I'm planning to have some tennis lessons next summer, and I'll want to thank my coach, won't I?

I scoop up a few more, and then move on to the invitation rack. And they're even better! Instead of just saying 'Party' they say things like 'We're meeting at the club for brunch!' and 'Come join us for an informal pizza!'

You know, I think I should buy some of those. It would be short-sighted not to. I mean, Suze and I might easily hold a pizza party, mightn't we? And we'll never find invitations like this in Britain. They're so sweet, with glittery little pizza slices all the way down the sides. I carefully put ten boxes of invitations in my basket, along with all my lovely cards, and a few sheets of candy-striped wrapping paper, which I just can't resist, then head to the checkout. As the assistant scans everything through, I look around the shop again, wondering if I've missed anything – and it's only when she announces the total that I look up in slight shock. That much? Just for a few cards?

For a moment I wonder whether I really do need them all. Like the card saying 'Happy Hanukkah, Boss!'

But then – they're bound to come in useful one day, aren't they? And if I'm to live in New York, I'm going to have to get used to sending expensive cards the whole time, so really, this is a form of acclimatization.

Plus, what's the point of having a nice new credit card limit and not using it? Exactly. And I can put it all down on my budget as 'unavoidable business expenses'.

As I sign my slip, I notice a girl in jeans and a hat hovering behind a display of business cards, who looks strangely familiar. I peer at her curiously – and then realize where I recognize her from.

'Hello,' I say, giving her a friendly smile. 'Didn't I see you at the sample sale yesterday? Did you find any bargains?'

But instead of replying, she quickly turns away. Hurrying out of the shop, she bumps into someone and mutters 'Sorry'. And to my astonishment, she's got a British accent. Well, that's bloody unfriendly, isn't it? Ignoring a compatriot on foreign soil. God, no wonder people say the British are aloof.

Right. I really am going to go to the Guggenheim now. As I come out of Kate's Paperie, I realize I don't know which way I should be facing to catch a cab, and I stand still for a moment, wondering which way is north. Something flashes brightly across the street, and I screw up my face, wondering if it's going to rain. But the sky is clear, and nobody else seems to have noticed it. Maybe it's one of those New York things, like steam coming up from the pavement.

Anyway. Concentrate. Guggenheim.

'Excuse me?' I say to a woman walking past. 'Which way is the Guggenheim?'

'Down the street,' she says, jerking her thumb.

'Right,' I say, confused. 'Thanks.'

That can't be right. I thought the Guggenheim was miles away from here, by Central Park. How can it be down the street? She must be a foreigner. I'll ask somebody else.

Except they all walk so bloody fast, it's hard to get anyone's attention.

'Hey,' I say, practically grabbing the arm of a man in a suit. 'For the Guggenheim—'

'Right there,' he says, nodding his head, and hurries off.

What on earth are they all talking about? I'm sure Kent said that the Guggenheim was right up near the . . . near the . . .

Hang on a minute.

I stop dead in the street, staring in astonishment.

I don't believe it. There it is! There's a sign hanging up ahead of me – and it says GUGGENHEIM, as large as life.

What's going on? Has the Guggenheim *moved*? Are there two Guggenheims?

As I walk towards the doors, I see that this place looks quite small for a museum – so maybe it's not the main Guggenheim. Maybe it's some trendy SoHo offshoot! Yes! I mean, if London can have the Tate Britain and Tate Modern, why can't New York have the Guggenheim and Guggenheim SoHo?

Guggenheim SoHo. That sounds so cool!

Cautiously I push the door open – and sure enough, it's all white and spacious, with modern art on pedestals and places to sit down and people wandering around quietly, whispering to one another.

You know, this is what all museums should be like. Nice and small, for a start, so you don't feel exhausted as soon as you walk in. I mean, you could probably do this lot in about half an hour. Plus, all the things look really interesting. Like, look at those amazing red cubes in that glass cabinet! And this fantastic abstract print, hanging on the wall.

As I'm gazing admiringly at the print, a couple come over and look at it too, and start murmuring to each other about how nice it is. Then the girl says casually,

'How much is it?'

I'm about to turn to her with a friendly smile and say, 'That's what I always want to know, too!' when to my astonishment the man reaches for it, and turns it over. And there's a price label fixed onto the back!

A price label in a museum! This place is perfect! *Finally*, some forward-thinking person has agreed with me that people don't want to just look at art – they want to know how much it is, too. I'm going to write to the people at the Victoria and Albert about this.

You know, now that I look around properly, *all* the exhibits seem to have a price on them. Those red cubes in the cabinet have got a price label, and so has that chair, and so has that . . . that box of pencils.

How weird, having a box of pencils in a museum. Still, maybe it's installation art, like thingummy girl's bed. I walk over to have a closer look – and there's something printed on each pencil. Probably some really meaningful message about art, or life . . . I lean close and find myself reading the words 'Guggenheim Museum Store'.

What?

Is this a—

I lift my head and look around, bewildered.

Am I in a *shop*?

Now I start noticing things I hadn't seen before. Like a pair of cash registers on the other side of the room. And there's somebody walking out with a couple of carrier bags.

Oh God.

Now I feel really stupid. How could I have not recognized a *shop*? But . . . this makes less and less sense. Is it just a shop on its own? With no museum attached?

'Excuse me,' I say, to a fair-haired boy wearing a name-badge. 'Can I just check – this *is* a shop?'

'Yes, ma'am,' says the boy politely. 'This is the Guggenheim Museum Store.'

'And where's the actual Guggenheim Museum?'

'Way up by the park.'

'Right. OK.' I look at him in confusion. 'So let me just get this straight. You can come here and buy loads of stuff – and no-one minds whether you've been to the museum or not? I mean, you don't have to show your ticket or anything?'

'No, ma'am.'

'So you don't have to look at the art *at all*? You can just shop?' My voice rises in delight. 'This city just gets better and better! It's perfect!' I see the boy's shocked expression and quickly add, 'I mean, obviously I *do* want to look at the art. Very much so. I was just . . . you know. Checking.'

'If you're interested in visiting the museum,' says the boy, 'I can call you a cab. Did you want to pay a visit?'

'Erm . . .'

Now, let's just think for a moment. Let's not make any hasty decisions.

'Erm . . . I'm not sure,' I say carefully. 'Could you just give me a minute?'

'Sure,' says the boy, giving me a slightly odd look, and I sit down on a white seat, thinking hard.

OK, here's the thing. I mean, obviously I could go to the Guggenheim. I could get in a cab, and whiz up to wherever it is, and spend all afternoon looking at pieces of art.

Or else . . . I could just buy a book *about* the Guggenheim . . . and spend the rest of the afternoon shopping.

Because the thing is, do you actually need to see a piece of art in the flesh to appreciate it? Of course you don't. And in a way, flicking through a book would be *better* than trekking round lots of galleries – because

I'm bound to cover more ground more quickly and actually learn far more.

Besides, what they have in this shop is art, isn't it? I mean, I've taken in some pretty good culture already. Exactly.

And it's not as if I rush out of the shop. I stay there for at least ten minutes, browsing through the literature and soaking up the cultured atmosphere. In the end I buy a big heavy book which I will give to Luke, plus a really cool mug for Suze, some pencils and a calendar for my mum.

Excellent. Now I can *really* go shopping! As I walk off, I feel all liberated and happy, as though I've been given a surprise day off school. I head down Broadway and turn off on one of the side roads, stepping past stalls selling fake handbags and colourful hair accessories, and a guy playing the guitar not very well. Soon I find myself wandering down a gorgeous little cobbled street, and then down another. On either side there are big old red buildings with fire escapes running up and down them, and trees planted in the pavements, and the atmosphere is suddenly a lot more laid back than it was on Broadway. You know, I could definitely get used to living here. No problem.

And oh God, the shops! Each one is more inviting than the next. One is full of painted velvet dresses hanging on pieces of antique furniture. Another has walls painted to look like clouds, racks of fluffy frou-frou party dresses and bowls of sweets everywhere. Another is all black and white and art deco, like a Fred Astaire movie. And just look at this one!

I stop on the pavement and stare open-mouthed at a mannequin wearing nothing but a transparent plastic shirt, which has a goldfish swimming about in the pocket. That has to be the most amazing piece of clothing I've ever seen.

You know – I've always secretly wanted to wear a piece of real avant-garde fashion. I mean, God, how cool would it be to have some cutting edge piece of clothing and telling everyone you bought it in SoHo. At least . . . Am I still in SoHo? Maybe this is NoLita. Or . . . NoHo? SoLita? To be honest, I'm not sure where I am by now, and I don't want to look at my map in case everyone thinks I'm a tourist.

Anyway, wherever it is, I don't care. I'm going in.

I push open the heavy door and walk into the shop, which is completely empty apart from a smell of incense and some strange, booming music. I walk up to a rail and, trying to look nonchalant, begin to finger the clothes. God, this stuff is way out. There's a pair of trousers about ten feet long, and a plain white shirt with a plastic hood, and a skirt made out of corduroy and newspaper, which is quite nice – but what happens when it rains?

'Hello,' says a guy coming up. He's wearing a black T-shirt and very tight trousers – completely silver apart from the crotch, which is denim, and very . . . Well. Prominent.

'Hi,' I say, trying to sound as cool as possible and *not* look at his crotch.

'How are you today?'

'Fine, thanks!'

I reach for a black skirt – then hastily drop it as I see a shiny red penis appliquéd to the front.

'Would you like to try anything?'

Come on, Becky. Don't be a wimp. Choose something.

'Erm . . .yes. This!' I say, and grab for a purple jumper with a funnel neck which seems quite nice. 'This one, please.' And I follow him to the back, where the fitting cubicle is made out of sheets of zinc.

It's only as I'm taking the jumper off the hanger that I see it has *two* funnel necks. In fact, it looks a bit like the jumper my granny once gave Dad for Christmas.

'Excuse me?' I say, poking my head out of the cubicle. 'This jumper's got . . . it's got two neck-holes.' I give a little laugh, and the guy stares at me blankly, as though I'm subnormal.

'It's supposed to,' he says. 'That's the look.'

'Oh, right!' I say at once. 'Of course.' And I dive back into the cubicle.

I don't dare ask him which neck-hole you're supposed to put your head in, so I struggle into the first one – and that looks terrible. I try the other one – and that looks terrible, too.

'Are you OK?' says the guy from outside the cubicle, and I feel my cheeks flame with colour. I can't admit I don't know how to put it on.

'I'm . . . fine,' I say in a strangled voice.

'Would you like to have a look out here?'

'OK!' I say, my voice a squeak.

Oh God. My cheeks are all flushed, and my hair's standing on end from pushing my head through funnel necks. Hesitantly I push open the door of the cubicle, and look at myself in the big mirror opposite. And I've never looked more stupid in my life.

'It's a fantastic piece of knitwear,' says the guy, folding his arms and staring at me. 'Quite unique.'

'Erm . . . absolutely,' I say after a pause. 'It's very interesting.' I tug awkwardly at my sleeve and try to ignore the fact that I look as though I'm missing a head.

'You look fabulous in it,' says the guy. 'Completely fabulous.'

He sounds so convinced, I peer at my reflection again. And you know – maybe he's right. Maybe I don't look so bad.

'Madonna has it in three colours,' says the guy, and lowers his voice. 'But between you and me, she can't quite pull it off.'

I stare at him, agog.

'*Madonna* has this jumper? This exact one?'

'Oh yuh. But you wear it so much better.' He leans against a mirrored pillar and examines a fingernail. 'So – did you want to take it?'

God, I *love* this city. Where else could you get invitations with twinkly pizza slices, free mascara, and the same jumper that Madonna's got, all in one afternoon? As I arrive at the Royalton, there's a huge, exhilarated grin on my face. I haven't had such a successful shopping trip since . . . well, since yesterday.

I check all my carrier bags in at the cloakroom, then head for the small circular bar where Luke has told me to meet him and his new associate, Michael Ellis.

I've heard quite a lot about this Michael Ellis during the last few days. Apparently he owns a huge advertising agency in Washington and is best friends with the President. Or is it the Vice-President? Something like that, anyway. Basically, he's a big-shot, and crucial to Luke's new deal. So I'd better make sure I impress him.

God this place is trendy, I think as I walk in. All leather and chrome and people in severe black outfits with haircuts to match. I walk into the dim circular bar, and there's Luke, sitting at a table. To my surprise, he's on his own.

'Hi!' I say, and kiss him. 'So – where's your friend?'

'Making a call,' says Luke. He gestures to a waiter. 'Another Gimlet here, please.' He gives me a quizzical look as I sit down. 'So, my darling. How was the Guggenheim?'

'It was good,' I say with a triumphant beam. Ha, ha-di-ha. I've been doing my homework in the cab. 'I particularly enjoyed a fascinating series of acrylic forms based on simple Euclidean shapes.'

'Really?' says Luke, looking a bit surprised.

'Absolutely. The way they absorb and reflect pure

light . . . Riveting. Oh and by the way, I bought you a present.' I plonk on his lap a book entitled *Abstract Art and Artists*, and take a sip of the drink that has been placed in front of me, trying not to look too smug.

'You really went to the Guggenheim!' says Luke, leafing through the book incredulously.

'Erm . . . yes,' I say. 'Of course I did!'

OK, I know you shouldn't lie to your boyfriend. But it's kind of true, isn't it? I mean, I *did* go to the Guggenheim. In the broadest sense of the word.

'This is really interesting,' Luke's saying. 'Did you see that famous sculpture by Brancusi?'

'Erm . . . well . . .' I squint over his shoulder, trying to see what he's talking about. 'Well, I was more concentrating on the . . . um . . . Euclidean shapes, and of course the incomparable . . . um . . .'

'Here comes Michael now,' interrupts Luke. He closes the book and I quickly put it back in its carrier bag. Thank God for that. I look up with interest to see what this famous Michael looks like – and nearly choke on my drink.

I don't believe it. It's him. Michael Ellis is the balding guy from the gym. Last time he saw me, I was dying at his feet.

'Hi!' says Luke, standing up. 'Becky, meet Michael Ellis, my new associate.'

'Hi again,' I say, trying to smile composedly. 'How are you?'

Oh, this shouldn't be allowed. There should be a rule which says that people you've met in the gym should *never* meet you in real life. It's just too embarrassing.

'We've already had the pleasure of meeting,' says Michael Ellis, shaking my hand with a twinkle and sitting down opposite. 'Becky and I worked out together yesterday. Didn't catch you in the gym this morning, though.'

'This morning?' says Luke, giving me a puzzled look as he sits down again. 'I thought you said the gym was closed this morning, Becky.'

Shit.

'Oh. Um, well . . .' I take a deep gulp of my drink and clear my throat. 'When I said it was *closed*, what I really meant was . . . was . . .' I tail away feebly into silence.

Oh God, and I so wanted to make a good impression.

'What am I thinking of?' exclaims Michael suddenly. 'I must be going crazy! It wasn't this morning. The gym *was* closed this morning. Due to vital repair work, I believe. Something of that nature.' He gives me a broad grin and I feel myself blushing.

'So, anyway,' I say, hurriedly changing the subject. 'You're . . . you're doing a deal with Luke. That's great! How's it all going?'

I only really ask to be polite, and steer attention away from my gym activities. I'm expecting them both to start explaining it to me at great length, and I can nod my head at intervals and enjoy my drink. But to my surprise, there's silence between the two men.

'Good question,' says Luke at last, and looks at Michael. 'What did Clark say?'

'We had a long conversation,' says Michael. 'Not entirely satisfactory.'

I look from face to face, feeling disconcerted.

'Is something going wrong?'

'That all depends,' says Michael.

He starts to tell Luke about his phone call with whoever Clark is, and I try to listen intelligently to their conversation. But the trouble is, I'm starting to feel quite giddy. How much have I drunk today? I don't even want to think about it, to be honest. I loll against the leather backrest, my eyes closed, listening to their voices chatting far above my head.

'. . . some sort of paranoia . . .'

'. . . think they can change the goalposts . . .'

'. . . overheads . . . cost reduction . . . with Alicia Billington heading up the London office . . .'

'Alicia?' I struggle to an upright position. '*Alicia's* going to run the London office?'

'Almost definitely,' says Luke, stopping mid-sentence. 'Why?'

'But—'

'But what?' says Michael, looking at me with interest. 'Why shouldn't she run the London office? She's bright, ambitious . . .'

'Oh. Well . . . no reason,' I say feebly.

I can't very well say 'because she's a complete cow'.

'You've heard she's just got engaged, by the way?' says Luke. 'To Ed Collins at Hill Hanson.'

'Really?' I say in surprise. 'I thought she was having an affair with . . . whassisname.'

'With who?' says Michael.

'Erm . . . thingy.' I take a sip of Gimlet to clear my head. 'She was having secret lunches with him, and everything!'

What's his name again? God, I really am pissed.

'Becky likes to keep abreast of the office gossip,' says Luke with an easy laugh. 'Unfortunately one can't always vouch for its accuracy.'

I stare at him crossly. What's he trying to say? That I'm some kind of rumour-monger?

'Nothing wrong with a bit of office gossip,' says Michael with a warm smile. 'Keeps the wheels turning.'

'Absolutely!' I say emphatically. 'I couldn't agree more. I always say to Luke, you should be *interested* in the people who work for you. It's like when I give financial advice on my TV show. You can't just look at the numbers, you have to *talk* to the callers. Like . . . like Enid from Northampton!' I look at Michael expectantly, before remembering that he doesn't know who Enid is. 'On paper she was ready to retire,' I explain. 'Pension and everything. But in real life . . .'

'She wasn't ready?' suggests Michael.

'Exactly! She was really enjoying work and it was only her stupid husband who wanted her to give up. She was only fifty-five!' I gesture randomly with my glass. 'I mean, don't they say, life begins at fifty-five?'

'I'm not sure they do,' says Michael, smiling. 'But maybe they should.' He gives me an interested look. 'I'd like to catch your show one day. Is it shown in the States?'

'No, it isn't,' I say regretfully. 'But I'll be doing the same thing on American TV soon, so you'll be able to watch it then!'

'I look forward to that.' Michael looks at his watch and drains his glass. 'I have to go, I'm afraid. We'll speak later, Luke. And very nice to meet you, Becky. If I ever need financial advice, I'll know where to come.'

As he leaves the bar, I lean back against my squashy seat and turn to look at Luke. His easy demeanour has vanished, and he's staring tensely into space while his fingers methodically tear a match-book into small pieces.

'Michael seems really nice,' I say. 'Really friendly.'

'Yes,' says Luke distantly. 'Yes, he is.'

I take a sip of Gimlet and look at Luke more carefully. He's got exactly the same expression he had last month, when one of his staff cocked up a press release and some confidential figures were released to the press by mistake. My mind spools back over the conversation I was half listening to – and as I watch his face I start to feel a bit worried.

'Luke,' I say at last. 'What's going on? Is there some kind of hitch with your deal?'

'No,' says Luke without moving.

'So what did Michael mean when he said, "that all

depends"? And all that stuff about them changing the goalposts?'

I lean forward and try to take his hand, but Luke doesn't respond. Gazing at him in anxious silence, I gradually become aware of the background chatter and music all around us in the dim bar. At the next table a woman's opening a little box from Tiffany's and gasping – something that would normally have me throwing my napkin onto the floor and sidling over to see what she's got. But this time I'm too concerned with Luke. A waiter comes towards our table and I shake my head at him.

'Luke?' I lean forward. 'Come on, tell me. Is there a problem?'

'No,' says Luke shortly, and tips his glass back into his mouth. 'There's no problem. Things are fine. Come on, let's go.'

Eleven

I wake up the next morning with a pounding head-ache. We went on from the Royalton to some place for dinner, and I drank even more there – and I can't even remember getting back to the hotel. Thank God I don't have an interview today. To be honest, I could quite happily spend the whole day in bed with Luke.

Except that Luke is already up, sitting by the window, talking grimly into the phone.

'OK, Michael. I'll talk to Greg today. God knows. I have no idea.' He listens for a bit. 'That may be the case. But I'm not having a second deal collapse on us.' There's a pause. 'Yes, but that would put us back – what, six months? OK. I hear what you're saying. Yes, I will. Cheers.'

He puts down the receiver and stares tensely out of the window, and I rub my sleepy face, trying to remember if I packed any aspirin.

'Luke, what's wrong?'

'You're awake,' says Luke, turning round, and gives me a quick smile. 'Did you sleep well?'

'What's wrong?' I repeat, ignoring him. 'What's wrong with the deal?'

'Everything's fine,' says Luke shortly, and turns back to the window.

'Everything isn't fine!' I retort. 'Luke, I'm not blind. I'm not deaf. I can tell something's up.'

'A minor blip,' says Luke after a pause. 'You don't need to worry about it.' He reaches for the phone again. 'Shall I order you some breakfast? What would you like?'

'Stop it!' I cry frustratedly. 'Luke, I'm not some . . . some stranger! We're going to live together, for God's sake! I'm on your side. Just tell me what's really going on. Is your deal in trouble?'

There's a silence – and for an awful moment I think Luke's going to tell me to mind my own business. But then he pushes his hands through his hair, exhales sharply, and looks up.

'You're right. The truth is, one of our backers is getting nervous.'

'Oh,' I say, and pull a face. 'Why?'

'Because some *fucking* rumour's going around that we're about to lose Bank of London.'

'Really?' I stare at him, feeling a cold dismay creep down my back. Even I know how important Bank of London is to Brandon Communications. They were one of Luke's first clients – and they still bring in about a quarter of the money the company makes every year. 'Why would people be saying that?'

'Fuck knows.' He pushes his hair back with his hands. 'Bank of London deny it completely, of course. But then, they would. And of course it doesn't help that I'm here, not there . . .'

'So are you going to fly back to London?'

'No.' He looks up. 'That would give out completely the wrong signals. Things are shaky enough here already. If I suddenly disappear . . .' He shakes his head and I stare at him apprehensively.

'So – what happens if your backer pulls out?'

'We find someone else.'

'But what if you can't? Will you have to give up on coming to New York?'

Luke turns to look at me – and he's suddenly got that

blank, scary expression which used to make me want to run away from him at press conferences.

'Not an option.'

'But I mean, you've got a really successful business in London,' I persist. 'I mean, you don't *have* to set up one in New York, do you? You could just . . .'

I tail away at the look on his face.

'Right,' I say nervously. 'Well – I'm sure it'll all be OK. In the end.'

For a while we're both silent – then Luke seems to come to, and looks up.

'I'm afraid I'm going to have to hold a few hands today,' he says abruptly. 'So I won't be able to make this charity lunch with you and my mother.'

Oh shit. Of course, that's today.

'Can't she rearrange?' I suggest. 'So we can both go?'

'Unfortunately not,' says Luke. He gives a quick smile, but I can see true disappointment on his face, and I feel a flash of indignation towards his mother.

'Surely she could find time.'

'She's got a very busy schedule. And as she pointed out, I didn't give her very much warning.' He frowns. 'You know, my mother's not just some . . . society lady of leisure. She has a lot of important commitments. She can't just drop everything, much as she would like to.'

'Of course not,' I say hurriedly. 'Anyway, it'll be fine. I'll just go along to this lunch with her on my own, shall I?' I add, trying to sound as though I'm not at all intimidated by this prospect.

'She has to go to the spa first,' says Luke, 'and she suggested you accompany her.'

'Oh right!' I say cautiously. 'Well, that could be fun . . .'

'It'll be a chance for you two to get to know one another. I really hope you hit it off.'

'Of course we will,' I say firmly. 'It'll be really nice.' I get out of bed and go and put my arms around Luke's neck. His face still looks strained, and I put up my hand to smooth away the creases in his brow. 'Don't worry, Luke. People will be queuing up to back you. Round the block.'

Luke gives a half-smile and kisses my hand.

'Let's hope so.'

As I sit in reception, waiting for Luke's mother to arrive, I feel a combination of nerves and intrigue. To be honest, I find Luke's family set-up just a tad weird. He's got a dad and a step-mum in Britain who brought him up with his two half-sisters, and whom he calls Mum and Dad. And then he's got his real mum, who left his dad when he was little, and married some rich American, and left Luke behind. Then she left the rich American and married another, even richer American and then . . . was there another one?

Anyway, apparently Luke hardly saw his real mother when he was growing up – she just used to send him huge presents to school, and visit about every three years. Which you'd think he'd be a bit resentful about now. But the really strange thing is, he adores her. In fact, he can't find one bad thing to say about her. He's got a huge picture of her in his study at home – much bigger than the one of his dad and step-mum on their wedding day. And I do sometimes wonder what they think about that. But it's not something I really feel I can bring up.

'Rebecca?' A voice interrupts my thoughts and I look up, startled. A tall, elegant woman in a pale suit, with very long legs and crocodile shoes is staring down at me. And she looks just the same as she does in the picture, with high cheekbones and dark, Jackie Kennedy-style hair – except her skin is kind of tighter, and her eyes are unnaturally wide. In fact, it looks as though she might have some difficulty closing them.

'Hello!' I say, getting awkwardly to my feet and holding out my hand. 'How do you do?'

'Elinor Sherman,' she says in a strange half-English, half-American drawl. Her hand is cold and bony, and she's wearing two enormous diamond rings which press into my flesh. 'So pleased to meet you.'

'Luke was very sorry he couldn't make it,' I say, and hand her the present he gave me to give. As she undoes the wrapping, I can't help goggling. A Hermès scarf!

'Nice,' she says dismissively, and puts it back into the box. 'My car is waiting. Shall we go?'

Blimey. A car with a chauffeur. And a crocodile Kelly bag – and are those earrings *real* emeralds?

As we drive away, I can't help surreptitiously staring at Elinor. Now I'm close up I realize she's older than I first thought, probably in her fifties. And although she looks wonderful, it's a bit as though that glamorous photo has been left out in the sun and lost its colour – and then been painted over with makeup. Her lashes are heavy with mascara and her hair is shiny with lacquer and her nails are so heavily varnished they could be red porcelain. She's so completely . . . done. Groomed in a way I know I could never be, however many people went to work on me.

I mean, I'm looking quite nice today, I think. In fact, I'm looking really sharp. There was a spread in American *Vogue* on how black and white is *the* look at the moment, so I've teamed a black pencil skirt with a white shirt I found in the sample sale the other day, and black shoes with fantastic high heels. I was really pleased with myself this morning. But now, as Elinor surveys me, I'm suddenly aware that one of my nails is very slightly chipped, and my shoe has got a tiny smear on the side – and oh God, is that a thread hanging down from my skirt? Should I quickly try to pull it off?

Casually, I put my hand down on my lap to cover up

the loose thread. Maybe she didn't see. It's not that obvious, is it?

But Elinor is silently reaching into her bag, and a moment later she hands me a pair of small silver tortoiseshell-handled scissors.

'Oh . . . er, thanks,' I say awkwardly. I snip the offending thread, and hand back the scissors, feeling like a school child. 'That always happens,' I add, and give a nervous little giggle. 'I look in the mirror in the morning and I think I look fine, but then the minute I get out of the house . . .'

Great, now I'm gabbling. Slow down, Becky.

'The English are incapable of good grooming,' says Elinor. 'Unless it's a horse.'

The corners of her lips move up a couple of millimetres into a smile – although the rest of her face is static – and I burst into sycophantic laughter.

'That's really good! My flat-mate loves horses. But I mean, you're English, aren't you? And you look absolutely . . . immaculate!'

I'm really pleased I've managed to throw in a little compliment, but Elinor's smile abruptly disappears. She gives me a blank stare and suddenly I can see where Luke gets that impassive scary expression from.

'I'm a naturalized American citizen.'

'Oh right,' I say. 'Well, I suppose you've been here for a while. But I mean, in your heart, aren't you still . . . wouldn't you say you're a . . . I mean, Luke's very English . . .'

'I have lived in New York for the majority of my adult life,' says Elinor coldly. 'Any attachment of mine to Britain has long disappeared. The place is twenty years out of date.'

'Right.' I nod fervently, trying to look as though I understand completely. God this is hard work. I feel like I'm being observed under a microscope. Why couldn't Luke have come? Or why couldn't she have

207

rescheduled? I mean, doesn't she *want* to see him?

'Rebecca, who colours your hair?' says Elinor abruptly.

'It's . . . it's my own,' I say, nervously touching a strand.

'Meione,' she echoes suspiciously. 'I don't know the name. At which salon does she work?'

For a moment I'm completely silenced.

'Erm . . . well,' I flounder at last. 'Actually . . . I . . . I'm not sure you'll have heard of it. It's very . . . tiny.'

'Well, I think you should change colourist,' says Elinor. 'It's a very unsubtle shade.'

'Right!' I say hurriedly. 'Absolutely.'

'Guinevere von Landlenburg swears by Julien on Bond Street. Do you know Guinevere von Landlenburg?'

I hesitate thoughtfully, as though going through a mental address book. As though checking all the many, many Guineveres I know.

'Um . . . no,' I say at last. 'I don't think I do.'

'They have a house in South Hampton.' She takes out a compact and checks her reflection. 'We spent some time there last year with the de Bonnevilles.'

I stiffen. The de Bonnevilles. As in Sacha de Bonneville. As in Luke's old girlfriend.

Luke never told me they were friends of the family.

OK, I'm not going to stress. Just because Elinor is tactless enough to mention Sacha's family. It's not as though she's actually mentioned *her*.

'Sacha is such an accomplished girl,' says Elinor, snapping her compact shut. 'Have you ever seen her water-ski?'

'No.'

'Or play polo?'

'No,' I say morosely. 'I haven't.'

Suddenly Elinor is rapping imperiously on the glass panel behind the driver.

'You took that corner too fast!' she says. 'I won't tell you again, I don't wish to be rocked in my seat. So, Rebecca,' she says, sitting back in her seat and giving me a dissatisfied glance. 'What are your own hobbies?'

'Uhm . . .' I open my mouth and close it again. My mind's gone completely blank. Come on, I must have some hobbies. What do I do at the weekends? What do I do to relax?

'Well, I . . .'

This is completely ridiculous. There *must* be things in my life other than shopping.

'Well obviously, I enjoy . . . socializing with friends,' I begin hesitantly. 'And also the . . . the study of fashion through the um . . . medium of magazines . . .'

'Are you a sportswoman?' says Elinor, eyeing me coldly. 'Do you hunt?'

'Erm . . . no. But I've recently taken up fencing!' I add in sudden inspiration. I've got the outfit, haven't I? 'And I've played the piano since I was six.'

Completely true. No need to mention that I gave up when I was nine.

'Indeed,' says Elinor, and gives a wintry smile. 'Sacha is also very musical. She gave a recital of Beethoven piano sonatas in London last year. Did you go to it?'

Bloody Sacha. With her bloody water-skiing and bloody sonatas.

'No,' I say defiantly. 'But I . . . I gave one myself, as it happens. Of . . . of Wagner sonatas.'

'Wagner sonatas?' echoes Elinor suspiciously.

'Erm . . . yes.' I clear my throat, trying to think how to get off the subject of accomplishments. 'So! You must be very proud of Luke!'

I'm hoping this comment will trigger a happy speech from her lasting ten minutes. But Elinor simply looks at me silently, as though I'm speaking nonsense.

'With his . . . his company and everything,' I press on doggedly. 'He's such a success. And he seems very determined to make it in New York. In America.' Elinor gives me a patronizing smile.

'No-one is anything till they make it in America.' She looks out of the window. 'We're here.'

Thank God for that.

To give Elinor her due, the beauty spa is absolutely amazing. The reception area is exactly like a Greek grotto, with pillars and soft music and a lovely scent of essential oils in the air. We go up to the reception desk, where a smart woman in black linen calls Elinor 'Mrs Sherman' very deferentially. They talk for a while in lowered voices, and the woman occasionally gives me a glance and nods her head, and I try to pretend not to be listening, and look at the price list for bath oils. Then abruptly Elinor turns away and ushers me to a seating area where there's a jug of mint tea and a sign asking patrons to respect the tranquillity of the spa and keep their voices down.

We sit in silence for a while – then a girl in a white uniform comes to collect me and takes me to a treatment room, where a robe and slippers are waiting, all wrapped in embossed cellophane. As I get changed, she's busying herself at her counter of goodies, and I wonder pleasurably what I've got in store. Elinor insisted on paying for all my treatments herself, however much I tried to chip in – and apparently she selected the 'top-to-toe grooming' treatment, whatever that is. I'm hoping it'll include a nice relaxing aromatherapy massage – but as I sit down on the couch, I see a pot full of wax heating up.

I feel an unpleasant lurch in my tummy. I've never been that great at having my legs waxed. Which is not because I'm afraid of pain, but because—

Well, OK. It's because I'm afraid of pain.

'So – does my treatment include waxing?' I say, trying to sound light-hearted.

'You're booked in for a full waxing programme,' says the beautician, looking up in surprise. 'The top-to-toe. Legs, arms, eyebrows and Brazilian.'

Arms? Eyebrows? I can feel my throat tightening in fear. I haven't been this scared since I had my jabs for Thailand.

'Brazilian?' I say in a scratchy voice. 'What . . . what's that?'

'It's a form of bikini wax. A total wax.'

I stare at her, my mind working overtime. She can't possibly mean—

'So if you'd like to lie down on the couch—'

'Wait!' I say, trying to keep my voice calm. 'When you say "total", do you mean . . .'

'Uhuh.' The beautician smiles. 'Then, if you wish, I can apply a small crystal tattoo to the . . . area. A love heart is quite popular. Or perhaps the initials of someone special?'

No. This can't be real.

'So, if you could just lay back on the couch and relax—'

Relax? *Relax?*

She turns back to her pot of molten wax – and I feel a surge of pure terror. Suddenly I know exactly how Dustin Hoffman felt in that dentist's chair.

'I'm not doing it,' I hear myself saying, and slither off the couch. 'I'm not having it.'

'The tattoo?'

'Any of it.'

'*Any* of it?'

The beautician comes towards me, the wax pot in hand – and in panic I dodge behind the couch, clasping my robe defensively around me.

'But Mrs Sherman has already pre-paid for the entire treatment—'

'I don't care what she's paid for,' I say, backing away. 'You can wax my legs. But not my arms. And definitely not . . . that other one. The crystal love heart one.'

The beautician looks worried.

'Mrs Sherman is one of our most regular customers. She specifically requested the top-to-toe wax for you.'

'She'll never know!' I say desperately. 'She'll never know! I mean, she's not exactly going to *look*, is she? She's not going to ask her son if his initials are tattooed on his girlfriend's . . .' I can't bring myself to say 'area'. 'I mean, come on. Is she?'

I break off, and there's a tense silence, broken only by the sound of tootling panpipes.

Then suddenly the beautician gives a snort of laughter. I catch her eye – and find myself starting to laugh, too, albeit slightly hysterically.

'You're right,' says the beautician, sitting down and wiping her eyes. 'You're right. She'll never know.'

'How about a compromise?' I say. 'You do my legs and eyebrows and we keep quiet about the rest.'

'I could give you a massage instead,' says the beautician. 'Use up the time.'

'There we are then!' I say in relief. 'Perfect!'

Feeling slightly drained, I lie down on the couch, and the beautician covers me up expertly with a towel.

'So, does Mrs Sherman have a son, then?' she says, smoothing back my hair.

'Yes.' I look up, taken aback. 'Has she never even mentioned him?'

'Not that I recall. And she's been coming here for years . . .' The beautician shrugs. 'I guess I always assumed she didn't have any children.'

'Oh right,' I say, and lie back down, trying not to give away my surprise.

When I emerge an hour and a half later, I feel fantastic. I've got brand new eyebrows, smooth legs, and a glow all over from the most wonderful aromatherapy massage.

Elinor is waiting for me in reception and as I come towards her, she runs her eyes appraisingly up and down my body. For a horrible moment I think she's going to ask me to take off my cardigan to check the smoothness of my arms – but all she says is, 'Your eyebrows look a lot better'. Then she turns and walks out, and I hurry after her.

As we get back into the car, I ask, 'Where are we having lunch?'

'Nina Heywood is holding a small informal charity lunch for famine relief,' she replies, examining one of her immaculate nails. 'Do you know the Heywoods? Or the van Gelders?'

Of course I don't bloody know them.

'No,' I hear myself saying. 'But I know the Websters.'

'The Websters?' She raises her arched eyebrows. 'The Newport Websters?'

'The Oxshott Websters. Janice and Martin.' I give her an innocent look. 'Do you know them?'

'No,' says Elinor, giving me a frosty look. 'I don't believe I do.'

For the rest of the journey we travel in silence. Then suddenly the car is stopping and we're getting out and walking into the grandest, most enormous lobby I've ever seen, with a doorman in uniform and mirrors everywhere. We go up what seems like a zillion floors in a gilded lift with a man in a peaked cap, and into an apartment. And I have *never* seen anything like it.

The place is absolutely huge, with a marble floor and a double staircase and a grand piano on a platform. The pale silk walls are decorated with enormous gold-framed paintings, and on pedestals around the room there are cascading flower arrangements like I've never seen before. Pin-thin women in expensive clothes are talking animatedly to one another, there are waitresses handing out champagne and a girl in a flowing dress is playing the harp.

And this is a *small* charity lunch?

Our hostess Mrs Heywood is a tiny woman in pink, who is about to shake hands with me when she's distracted by the arrival of a woman in a bejewelled turban. Elinor introduces me to a Mrs Parker, a Mr Wunsch, and a Miss Kutomi, then drifts away, and I make conversation as best I can, even though everyone seems to assume I must be a close friend of Prince William.

'Tell me,' says Mrs Parker urgently. 'How is that poor young man bearing up after his . . . great loss?' she whispers.

'That boy has a natural nobility,' says Mr Wunsch fiercely. 'Young people today could learn a lot from him. Tell me, is it the army he's headed for?'

'He . . . he hasn't mentioned it,' I say helplessly. 'Would you excuse me.'

I escape to the bathroom – and that's just as huge and sumptuous as the rest of the apartment, with racks of luxury soaps and bottles of free perfume, and a comfy chair to sit in. I kind of wish I could stay there all day, actually. But I don't dare linger too long in case Elinor comes looking for me. So with a final squirt of Eternity, I force myself to get up and go back into the throng, where waiters are moving quietly around, murmuring 'Lunch will be served now'.

As everyone moves towards a set of grand double doors I look around for Elinor but I can't see her. There's an old lady in black lace sitting on a chair near to me, and she begins to stand up with the aid of a walking stick.

'Let me help,' I say, hurrying forward as her grip falters. 'Shall I hold your champagne glass?'

'Thank you, my dear!' The lady smiles at me as I take her arm, and we walk slowly together into the palatial

214

dining room. People are pulling out chairs and sitting down at circular tables, and waiters are hurrying round with bread rolls.

'Margaret,' says Mrs Heywood, coming forward and holding out her hands to the old lady. 'There you are. Now let me find your seat . . .'

'This young lady was assisting me,' says the old lady as she lowers herself onto a chair, and I smile modestly at Mrs Heywood.

'Thank you dear,' she says absently. 'Now, could you take my glass too, please . . . and bring some water to our table?'

'Of course!' I say with a friendly smile. 'No problem.'

'And I'll have a gin and tonic,' adds an elderly man nearby, swivelling in his chair.

'Coming right up!'

It just shows, what Mum says is right. The way to make a friend is to give a helping hand. I feel quite special, helping out the hostess. It's almost like I'm throwing the party with her!

I'm not sure where the kitchen is, but the waiters are all heading towards one end of the room. I follow them through a set of double doors, and find myself in the kind of kitchen Mum would absolutely die for. Granite and marble everywhere, and a fridge which looks like a space rocket, and a pizza oven set into the wall! There are waiters in white shirts hurrying in and out with trays, and two chefs standing at a central island hob, holding sizzling pans, and someone's yelling 'Where the *fuck* are the napkins?'

I find a bottle of water and a glass, and put them on a tray, then start looking around to see where the gin might be. As I bend down to open a cupboard door, a man with cropped bleached hair taps me on the shoulder.

'Hey. What are you doing?'

'Oh hi!' I say, standing up. 'I'm just looking for

215

the gin, actually. Somebody wanted a gin and tonic.'

'We haven't got time for that!' he barks. 'Do you realize how short-staffed we are? We need food on tables!'

Short-staffed? I stare at him blankly for a moment. Then as my eyes fall on my black skirt and the realization hits me, I give a shocked laugh.

'No! I'm not a . . . I mean, I'm actually one of the . . .'

How do I say this without offending him? I'm sure being a waiter is actually very fulfilling. Anyway, he's probably an actor in his spare time.

But while I'm dithering, he dumps a silver platter full of smoked fish in my arms.

'Get! Now!'

'But I'm not—'

'Now! *Food on tables!*'

With a pang of fright I quickly hurry away. OK. What I'll do is I'll just get away from him, and put this platter down somewhere, and find my place.

Cautiously I walk back into the dining room, and wander about between the tables, looking for a handy surface to leave the platter. But there don't seem to be any side tables or even spare chairs. I can't really leave it on the floor, and it would be a bit too awkward to reach between the guests and dump it on a table.

This is really annoying, actually. The platter's quite heavy, and my arms are starting to ache. I pass by Mr Wunsch's chair and give him a little smile, but he doesn't even notice me. It's as though I'm suddenly invisible.

This is ridiculous. There *must* be somewhere I can put it down.

'Will-you-serve-the-food!' hisses a furious voice behind me, and I feel myself jump.

'OK!' I retort, feeling slightly rattled. 'OK, I will!'

Oh for goodness sake. It's probably easier just to

serve it. Then at least it'll be gone, and I can sit down. Hesitantly I approach the nearest table.

'Erm . . . would anyone like some smoked fish? I think this is salmon . . . and this is trout . . .'

'Rebecca?'

The elegantly coiffured head in front of me swivels round and I give a startled leap. Elinor is staring up at me, her eyes like daggers.

'Hi,' I say nervously. 'Would you like some fish?'

'*What* do you think you're doing?' she says in a low, furious voice.

'Oh!' I swallow. 'Well I was just, you know, helping out . . .'

'I'll have some smoked salmon, thanks,' says a woman in a gold jacket. 'Do you have any non-fat French dressing?'

'Erm . . . well, the thing is, I'm not actually . . .'

'Rebecca!' Elinor's voice comes shooting out of her barely opened mouth. 'Put it down. Just . . . sit down.'

'Right. Of course.' I glance uncertainly at the platter. 'Or should I serve it, since I'm here anyway . . .'

'Put it down. Now!'

'Right.' I look helplessly about for a moment, then see a waiter coming towards me with an empty tray. Before he can protest I deposit the smoked fish platter on his tray, then hurry round with trembling legs to my empty chair, smoothing down my hair.

As I sit down, and spread my thick napkin over my knees, there's silence around the table. I try a friendly little smile, but nobody responds. Then an old lady wearing about six rows of huge pearls and a hearing aid leans towards Elinor and whispers, so audibly we can all hear, 'Your son is dating . . . a *waitress*?'

<u>BECKY BLOOMWOOD'S NEW YORK BUDGET</u>

DAILY BUDGET (PROPOSED)

Food	$50		
Shopping	~~$50~~	$100	
Expenses	~~$50~~	~~$60~~	$100
Total	$250		

DAILY BUDGET (REVISED)

DAY THREE

Food	$50
Shopping	$100
Expenses	$365
Other expenses	$229
Unique sample sale opportunity	$567
Further unique sample sale opportunity	$128
Unavoidable contingency expense	$49
Essential business-linked expense (shoes)	

Twelve

Hmmm. I'm not entirely sure whether Elinor really took to me. She didn't say much in the car back – which could have meant she was quietly impressed. Or . . . not.

When Luke asked me how it all went, I kind of glossed over the fish platter incident. And the beauty spa incident. Instead, I concentrated on how much his mother loved his gift to her.

And OK, maybe I made a few things up. Like the bit about her saying 'my Luke is the best son in the whole world', and dabbing her eyes with a hanky. But I mean, I couldn't tell him what her *real* reaction was, could I? I couldn't tell him she just shoved it back into the box as though it was a pair of socks from Woolworths. And actually I'm glad I did embellish a little, because I've never seen him look so delighted. He even phoned her up to say he was glad she liked it – but she never returned his call.

Personally, I've had more important things to think about over the last couple of days than whether Elinor likes me or not. Suddenly I keep getting phone calls from people who want to meet me! Which Luke says is the 'snowball effect' and he expected it all along. Yesterday I had three meetings with different sets of TV executives – and right now I'm sitting having a breakfast meeting with a Greg Walters from Blue River Productions. He's the one who sent me the basket of fruit and was desperate to see me – and so far, the meeting is going wonderfully! I'm wearing a pair of trousers which I bought yesterday from Banana Republic, and my new designer jumper, and I have to say, Greg seems really impressed.

'You're hot,' he keeps saying, in between bites of croissant. 'You realize that?'

'Erm . . . well . . .'

'No.' He lifts a hand. 'Don't be coy. You are hot. You're all over town. Folks are fighting over you.' He takes a sip of coffee and looks me in the eye. 'I'll be frank – I want to give you your own show.'

I stare at him, almost unable to breathe for excitement.

'Really? My own show? Doing what?'

'Whatever. We'll find you a winning format.' He takes a gulp of coffee. 'You're a political commentator, right?'

'Um . . . not really,' I say awkwardly. 'I do personal finance. You know, mortgages and stuff?'

'Right.' Greg nods. 'Finance. So I'm thinking . . . off the top of my head . . . *Wall Street*. *Wall Street* meets *Ab Fab* meets *Oprah*. You could do that, right?'

'Erm . . . yes! Absolutely!'

I haven't a clue what he's talking about but I beam confidently at him and take a bite of croissant.

'I have to go,' he says as he finishes his coffee. 'But I'm going to call you tomorrow and set up a meeting with our head of development. Is that OK?'

'Fine!' I say, trying to look nonchalant. 'That would be good.'

As he walks off, I can't help a huge grin of delight spreading across my face. My own show! Things are just going better and better. Everyone I speak to seems to want to offer me a job, and they all keep buying me nice meals, and yesterday, someone said I could have a career in Hollywood, no question. Hollywood!

I mean, just imagine if I get my own show in Holly-wood! I'll be able to live in some amazing house in Beverly Hills, and go to parties with all the film stars. And maybe Luke will start a Los Angeles branch of his company, and start representing people like . . . like Minnie Driver. I mean, I know she's not exactly a financial institution, but maybe he'll expand into movies! Yes! And then she'll become my best friend and we'll go shopping together and stuff, and maybe even take our holidays together . . .

'Hello there,' says a cheerful voice, and I look up dazedly to see Michael Ellis pulling out a chair at another table.

'Oh,' I say, wrenching my mind away from a lovely sunlit beach in Malibu. 'Oh, hello. Do join me!' I gesture politely to the chair opposite.

'I'm not disturbing you?' he says, sitting down.

'No. I was having a meeting but it's over.' I look around vaguely. 'Is Luke with you? I've hardly seen him, recently!'

Michael shakes his head.

'He's talking to some people at JD Slade this morning. The big guns.'

A waiter comes and clears away Greg's plate, and Michael orders a cappuccino. When the waiter disappears he eyes the second neck-hole of my jumper quizzically.

'You realize you have a large moth-hole in your sweater? I'd get that seen to.'

Haha, very funny.

'Actually, this is the look at the moment,' I explain kindly. 'Madonna has one just like it.'

'Ah! Madonna.' His cappuccino arrives and he takes a sip.

'So – how are things going?' I ask, lowering my voice slightly. 'Luke told me about one of the backers getting nervous.'

'Right.' Michael nods gravely. 'I don't know what the hell's going on there.'

'But why do you *need* backers?' I ask. 'I mean, Luke's got loads of money . . .'

'Never invest your own money,' says Michael. 'First rule of business. Besides which, Luke has very grand plans, and grand plans tend to need a lot of capital.' He looks up. 'You know, he's very driven, that man of yours. *Very* determined to succeed over here.'

'I know,' I say, rolling my eyes. 'All he ever does is work.'

'Work is good,' says Michael, frowning into his coffee. 'Obsession is . . . not so good.' He's silent for a moment, then looks up with a smile. 'But I gather things are going well for you?'

'They are, actually,' I say, unable to maintain my calm. 'In fact, they're going brilliantly! I've had all these fantastic meetings, and everybody says they want to give me a job. I just had a meeting with Greg Walters from Blue River Productions – and he said he was going to give me my own show. And yesterday, someone was talking about Hollywood!'

'That's great,' says Michael. 'Really great.' He takes a sip of coffee and looks at me thoughtfully. 'If I could just say a word?'

'What?'

'These TV people. You don't necessarily want to believe every single word they say.'

I look at him, a little discomfited.

'What do you mean?'

'These guys like talking big,' says Michael, slowly stirring his coffee. 'It makes them feel good. And they believe everything they say at the time when they're saying it. But when it comes to the cold hard dollar . . .' He stops, and looks up at me. 'I just don't want you to be disappointed.'

'I won't be disappointed!' I retort indignantly.

'Greg Walters said the whole town was fighting over me!'

'I'm sure he did,' says Michael. 'And I very much hope they are. All I'm saying is—'

He stops as a uniformed concierge stops by our table.

'Miss Bloomwood,' he says. 'I have a message for you.'

'Thanks!' I say in surprise.

I open the envelope he gives me, and pull out the sheet of paper – and it's a message from Kent Garland at HLBC.

'Well!' I say, unable to stop a smile of triumph. 'It looks like HLBC weren't just talking big. It looks like they mean business.' I give the piece of paper to Michael Ellis, wanting to add, 'So there!'

' "Please call Kent's assistant to arrange a screen test," ' reads Michael aloud. 'Well. Looks like I'm wrong,' he says, smiling. 'And I'm very glad about it.' He lifts his coffee cup towards me. 'Here's to a successful screen test tomorrow. One piece of advice?'

'What?'

'The sweater.' He pulls a comical face and shakes his head.

OK. What am I going to wear tomorrow? *What am I going to wear?* I mean, this is the most important moment of my life. A screen test for American television. My outfit has to be sharp, flattering, photogenic, immaculate . . . I mean, I've got nothing. Nothing.

I leaf through all my clothes for the millionth time, and flop back down on the bed, exhausted. I can't believe I've come all this way without one single outfit I can wear for a screen test.

Well, there's nothing for it. I'll just have to go shopping.

I pick up my bag and check I've got my purse, and I'm just reaching for my coat when the phone rings.

'Hello?' I say into the receiver, hoping it might be Luke.

'Bex!' comes Suze's voice, all tinny and distant.

'Suze!' I say in delight. 'Hi!'

'How's it going?'

'It's going really well,' I say. 'I've had loads of meetings, and everyone's being really positive. It's just brilliant!'

'Bex! That's great.'

'How about you?' I frown slightly at her voice. 'Is everything OK?'

'Oh yes!' says Suze. 'Everything's fine. Except . . .' She hesitates. 'I just thought you should know, a man phoned up this morning about some money you owe a shop. La Rosa, in Hampstead.'

'Really?' I pull a face. 'Them again?'

'Yes. He asked me when you were going to be out of the artificial limb unit.'

'Oh,' I say after a pause. 'Right. So – what did you say?'

'Bex, why did he think you were in the artificial limb unit?'

'I don't know,' I say evasively. 'Maybe he heard something. Or . . . or I may possibly have written him the odd little letter . . .'

'Bex,' interrupts Suze, and her voice is quivering slightly. 'You told me you'd taken care of all those bills. You promised me!'

'I have taken care of them!' I reach for my hairbrush and begin to brush my hair.

'By telling them your *parachute* didn't open in time?' cries Suze. 'I mean, honestly, Bex—'

'Look, don't stress. I'll sort it all out as soon as I come home.'

'He said he was going to have to take extreme action! He said he was very sorry, but enough allowances had been made, and—'

'They always say that,' I say soothingly. 'Suze, you really don't have to worry. I'm going to earn loads over here. I'll be loaded! And I'll be able to pay everything off, and it will all be fine.'

There's silence, and I imagine Suze on the floor of the sitting room, winding her hair tightly round her fingers.

'Really?' she says at last. 'Is it all going well, then?'

'Yes! I've got a screen test tomorrow, and this guy wants to give me my own show, and they're even talking about Hollywood!'

'Hollywood?' breathes Suze. 'Oh my God! That's amazing.'

'I know.' I beam at my own reflection. 'Isn't it great? I'm hot! That's what the guy from Blue River Productions said.'

'So – what are you going to wear for your screen test?'

'I'm just off to Barney's,' I say happily. 'Choose a new outfit.'

'*Barney's?*' exclaims Suze in horror. 'Bex, you *promised* me you weren't going to go overboard! You completely promised me you were going to stick to a budget.'

'I have! I've completely stuck to it. It's all written out and everything! And anyway, this is a business expense. I'm investing in my career.'

'But—'

'Suze, you can't make money unless you spend it first. Everyone knows that! I mean, you have to spend money on your materials, don't you?'

There's a pause.

'I suppose so,' says Suze doubtfully.

'And anyway, what are credit cards for?'

'Oh Bex . . .' Suze sighs. 'Actually, that's funny – that's just what the council tax girl said.'

'What council tax girl?' I frown at my reflection and reach for an eyeliner.

'The girl who came round this morning,' says Suze vaguely. 'She had a clipboard. And she asked loads of questions about me, and the flat, and how much rent you paid me . . . we had a really nice chat. And I was telling her all about you being in America, and Luke . . . and your TV job . . .'

'Great,' I say, not really listening. 'That sounds really good. Listen, Suze, I've got to run. But honestly, don't worry. If anyone else phones for me, just don't take the call. OK?'

'Well . . . OK,' says Suze. 'And good luck tomorrow!'

'Thanks!' I say, and put down the phone. Hahaha! Off to Barney's!

I've popped into Barney's a few times since we arrived, but I've always been in a bit of a rush. But this time . . . Wow. This is different. I can take my time. I can wander up and down all eight floors of the store, just gazing at the clothes.

And God, the clothes. The *clothes*. They are just the most beautiful things I've ever seen. Everywhere I look, I see shapes and colours and designs I just want to grab and touch and stroke.

But I can't spend all day marvelling. I have to get down to business and decide on an outfit for tomorrow. I'm thinking maybe a jacket, so I look authoritative – but it has to be the right jacket. Not too boxy; not too stiff . . . but I want nice clean lines. And maybe a skirt. Or just look at those trousers. They would look fantastic, if I had the right shoes . . .

I wander slowly round each floor, making mental notes of all the clothes – then go back down to the bottom again, and start collecting all my possibilities. A Calvin Klein jacket . . . and a skirt . . .

'Excuse me?'

A voice interrupts just as I'm reaching for a sleeveless top, and I turn in surprise. A woman in a black trouser suit is smiling at me.

'Would you like any help with your shopping today?'

'Oh, thanks!' I say. 'If you could hold these . . .' I hand her the garments I've already picked out and her smile flickers slightly.

'When I said help . . . we're running a unique promotion of our personal shopping department today. We'd like to introduce the concept to a wider audience. So if you'd like to take up the offer of an introductory session, there are some slots still available.'

'Oh right,' I say interestedly. 'What exactly would that—'

'Our trained, experienced personal shoppers can help you find exactly what you're searching for,' says the woman pleasantly. 'They can help you find your own style, focus in on designs that suit you, and guide you through the daunting fashion maze.' She gives a tight little laugh, and I get the feeling she's gone through this little spiel quite a few times today.

'I see,' I say thoughtfully. 'The thing is . . . I'm not sure I really need guiding. So thanks very much, but—'

'The service is complimentary,' says the woman. 'Today we're also offering tea, coffee, or a glass of champagne.'

Champagne? Free champagne?

'Ooh!' I say. 'Well actually – that sounds really good. Yes please!'

And in fact, I think as I follow her to the third floor, this will probably be really interesting. These trained shoppers must really know their stuff – and they'll have a completely different eye from me. They'll show me a whole side of myself that I've never seen before!

We arrive at a suite of large dressing rooms, and the woman shows me in with a smile.

'Your personal shopper today will be Erin,' she says.

'Erin has only recently joined us from another store, so she will be receiving some occasional guidance from a senior Barney's shopper. Will that be all right?'

'Absolutely!' I say, taking off my coat.

'Would you prefer tea, coffee or champagne?'

'Champagne,' I say quickly. 'Thanks.'

'Very well,' she says with a smile. 'Ah, and here's Erin.'

I look up with interest, to see a long thin girl coming into the dressing room. She's got straight blond hair and a small, kind of squashed-looking mouth. In fact her whole face looks as though she was once squeezed between a pair of lift doors and never quite recovered.

'Hello,' she says, and I watch her mouth in fascination as she smiles. 'I'm Erin – and I'll be helping you find the outfit to best suit your needs.'

'Great!' I say. 'Can't wait!'

I wonder how this Erin got her job. Not by her taste in shoes, certainly.

'So . . .' Erin looks at me thoughtfully. 'What were you looking for today?'

'I have a screen test tomorrow,' I explain. 'I want to look kind of . . . smart and sassy, but approachable, too. Maybe with a little witty twist somewhere.'

'A witty twist,' echoes Erin, scribbling on her pad. 'Right. And were you thinking . . . a suit? A jacket?'

'Well,' I say, and launch into an exact explanation of what I'm looking for. Erin listens carefully, and I notice a dark-haired woman in tortoiseshell glasses occasionally coming to the door of our dressing room and listening, too.

'Right,' says Erin, when at last I've finished. 'Well, you certainly have some ideas there . . .' She taps her teeth for a moment. 'I'm thinking . . . we have a very nice fitted jacket by Moschino, with roses on the collar . . .'

'Oh, I know the one!' I say in delight. 'I was thinking of that, too!'

'Along with . . . there's a new skirt in the Barney's collection . . .'

'The black one?' I say. 'With the buttons just here? Yes, I thought of that, but it's a bit short. I was thinking of the knee-length one. You know, with the ribbon round the hem . . .'

'We'll see,' says Erin, with a pleasant smile. 'Let me line up some clothes for you, and we can have a look.'

As she goes off to gather up clothes, I sit down and sip my champagne. This isn't bad, actually. I mean, it's much less effort than trawling round the shop myself. I can half hear a murmured conversation going on in the dressing room next door – and suddenly a woman's voice rises in distress, saying, 'I just want to show that bastard. I just want to *show* him!'

'And we *will* show him, Marcia,' replies a calm, soothing voice, which I think belongs to the woman in tortoiseshell glasses. 'We will. But not in a cherry-red pant suit.'

'Okaaay!' Erin is back in the dressing room, wheeling in a rack of clothes. I run my eye quickly over them, and notice quite a few of the things I'd already picked out for myself. But what about the knee-length skirt? And what about that amazing aubergine trouser suit with the velvet collar?

'So, here's the jacket for you to try . . . and the skirt . . .'

I take the clothes from her, and look doubtfully at the skirt. I just know it's going to be too short. But then, she's the expert, I suppose . . . Quickly I change into the skirt and jacket, then come and stand in front of the mirror, next to Erin.

'The jacket's fabulous!' I say. 'And it fits me perfectly. I *love* the cut.'

I don't really want to say anything about the skirt. I

mean, I don't want to hurt her feelings – but it looks all wrong.

'Now, let's see,' says Erin. She stands with her head on one side and squints at my reflection. 'I'm thinking a skirt to the knee might look better, after all.'

'Like the one I told you about!' I say in relief. 'It's on the seventh floor, right next to the—'

'Possibly,' she says, and smiles. 'But I have a few other skirts in mind . . .'

'Or the Dolce & Gabbana one on the third floor,' I add. 'I was looking at it earlier. Or the DKNY.'

'DKNY?' says Erin, wrinkling her brow. 'I don't believe . . .'

'They're new in,' I tell her. 'I think they must have come in yesterday. *So* nice. You should have a look at them!' I turn round and look carefully at her outfit. 'You know what? The mauve DKNY would look really good with that turtle-neck you're wearing. And you could team it with a pair of those new Stephane Kélian boots with the spiky heels. You know the ones?'

'I know the ones,' says Erin tightly. 'The crocodile and suede ones.' I look at her in surprise.

'No, not those ones. The *new* range. With the stitching up the back. They're so gorgeous! In fact they'd go well with the knee-length skirt . . .'

'Thank you!' interrupts Erin sharply. 'I'll bear that in mind.'

Honestly. Why's she so stressed out? I'm only giving her a few hints. You'd think she'd be pleased I was so interested in her shop!

Although, I have to say, she doesn't seem to know it very well.

'Hello there!' comes a voice from the door – and the woman in tortoiseshell glasses is leaning against the doorframe, looking at me interestedly. 'Everything all right?'

'Great, thanks!' I say, beaming at her.

'So,' says the woman, looking at Erin. 'You're going to try the knee-length skirt for our customer. Is that right?'

'Yes,' says Erin, and gives a rather forced smile. 'I'll just go get it.'

She disappears, and I can't resist sidling over to the rack of clothes, just to see what else she brought. The woman in glasses watches me for a moment, then comes in and holds out her hand.

'Christina Rowan,' she said. 'I head up the personal shopping department.'

'Well, hello!' I say, looking at a pale blue Jill Stuart shirt. 'I'm Becky Bloomwood.'

'And you're from England, I guess, by your accent?'

'London. But I'm going to move to New York!'

'Are you, indeed.' Christina Rowan gives me a friendly smile. 'Tell me, what do you do, Becky? Do you work in fashion?'

'Oh no. I'm in finance.'

'Finance! Really.' She raises her eyebrows.

'I give financial advice on the telly. You know, pensions and stuff . . .' I reach for a pair of soft cashmere trousers. 'Aren't these beautiful? Much better than the Ralph Lauren ones. *And* they're cheaper.'

'They're great, aren't they?' She gives me a quizzical look. 'Well, it's nice to have such an enthusiastic customer.' She reaches into the pocket of her jacket and pulls out a business card. 'Do come back and visit us when you're here again.'

'I will!' I beam at her. 'And thanks very much.'

It's four o'clock by the time I finally leave Barney's. I hail a cab and travel back to the Four Seasons. As I push open the door to our room and look at my reflection in the silent dressing-table mirror, I'm still on a glittery high; almost a hysterical excitement at what I've just done. What I've just bought.

I know I went out just planning to buy a single outfit

for my screen test. But I ended up . . . Well, I suppose I just got a bit . . . a bit carried away. So my final list of purchases goes like this:

```
1. Moschino jacket
2. Knee-length Barney's skirt
3. Calvin Klein underwear
4. Pair of new tights
   and . . .
5. Vera Wang cocktail dress
```

OK. Just . . . before you say anything, I *know* I wasn't supposed to be buying a cocktail dress. I *know* that when Erin said, 'Are you interested in evening wear at all?' I should simply have said 'no'.

But oh God. Oh *God*. That Vera Wang dress. Inky purple, with a low back and glittering straps. It just looked so completely movie-star perfect. Everyone crowded round to see me in it – and when I drew back the curtain, they all gasped.

I just stared at myself, mesmerized. Entranced by what I could look like; by the person I could be. There was no question. I had to have it. I *had* to. As I signed the credit card slip . . . I wasn't me any more. I was Grace Kelly. I was Gwyneth Paltrow. I was a glittering somebody else who can casually sign a credit card slip for thousands of dollars while smiling and laughing at the assistant, as though this were a nothing-purchase.

Thousands of dollars.

Although, for a designer like Vera Wang, that price is actually quite . . .

Well, it's really very . . .

Oh God, I feel slightly sick. I don't even want to think about how much it cost. I don't want to think about those noughts. The point is, I'll be able to wear it for years. Yes! Years and years. And I *need* designer clothes if I'm going to be a famous television star. I mean I'll have important events to go to – and I can't just turn up in M&S, can I? Exactly.

And I've got a £10,000 credit card limit. That's the real point. I mean, they wouldn't give it to me if they didn't think I could afford it, would they?

I hear a sound at the door, and quickly rise to my feet. Heart thumping, I go to the wardrobe I've been stashing all my shopping in, open the door, and quickly shove my Barney's bags inside – then close the door and turn round with a smile, just as Luke enters the room, talking on his mobile.

'Of course I'm in fucking control,' he's spitting furiously into the phone. 'What the fuck do they think they're—' He breaks off, and is silent for a few moments. 'Yes, I know,' he says in a calmer voice. 'Yes. OK, will do. I'll see you tomorrow, Michael. Thanks.'

He switches off his mobile, puts it away, and looks at me as though he's almost forgotten who I am.

'Hi!' he says, and drops his briefcase onto a chair.

'Hi!' I say brightly, moving away from the wardrobe door. 'Stranger.'

'I know,' says Luke, rubbing his face wearily. 'I'm sorry. Things have been . . . a bit of a nightmare, to be frank. I heard about your screen test, though. Fantastic news.'

He goes to the minibar, pours himself a Scotch and downs it. Then he pours himself another one and takes a slug while I watch anxiously. His face is pale and tense, I notice, and there are shadows under his eyes.

'Is it all . . . going OK?' I ask gingerly.

'It's going,' he replies. 'That's about as much as I can say.' He walks over to the window and stares out, over the glittering Manhattan skyline, and I bite my lip nervously.

'Luke – couldn't someone else go to all these meetings? Couldn't someone else fly out and take some of the load? Like . . . Alicia?'

It nearly kills me even to mention her name – but I honestly am getting a bit worried. Slightly to my relief, Luke shakes his head.

'I can't bring in somebody new at this stage. I've been managing it all until now; I'll have to see it through. I just had no idea they'd be so bloody nervous. I had no idea they'd be so . . .' He sits down in an armchair and takes a slug of his drink. 'I mean, Jesus, they ask a lot of questions. I know Americans are thorough but . . .' He shakes his head disbelievingly. 'They have to know *everything*. About every single client, every single potential client, everybody who's ever worked for the company, every single bloody memo I've ever sent . . . Is there any possibility of litigation here? Who was your receptionist in 1993? What car do you drive? What fucking . . . toothpaste do you use?'

He breaks off and drains his glass, and I stare at him in dismay.

'They sound awful,' I say, and the flicker of a smile passes across Luke's face.

'They're not awful. They're just very conservative, old-school investors – and something's rattling them. I don't know what.' He exhales sharply. 'I just need to keep them steady. I need to keep this thing going.'

His voice is trembling slightly, and when I glance at his hand I see that it's clenched tightly around his glass. I've never seen Luke like this, to be honest. He usually looks so utterly in control, so completely smooth . . .

'Luke, I think you should have an evening off. You haven't got a meeting tonight, have you?'

'No,' says Luke, looking up. 'But I need to go through some paperwork. Big meeting tomorrow, with all the investors. I need to be prepared.'

'You are prepared!' I reply. 'What you need is to be *relaxed*. If you work all night, you'll just be tired and tense and ratty.' I go over to him, take his glass out of his hand and start to massage his shoulders. 'Come on, Luke. You really need a night off. I bet Michael would agree. Wouldn't he?'

'He's been telling me to lighten up,' admits Luke after a long pause.

'Well then, lighten up! Come on, a few hours of fun never did anybody any harm. Let's both dress up and go somewhere really nice, and dance, and drink cocktails.' I kiss him gently on the back of his neck. 'I mean, why on earth come to New York and not enjoy it?'

There's silence – and for an awful moment I think Luke's going to say he hasn't got time. But then suddenly he turns round – and thank God, I can see the faint glimmer of a smile.

'You're right,' he says. 'Come on. Let's do it.'

It turns into the most magical, glamorous, glossy evening of my life. I put on my Vera Wang dress and Luke puts on his smartest suit, and we go to a fabulous restaurant where people are eating lobster and there's an old-fashioned jazz band, just like in the movies. Luke orders Bellinis, and we toast each other, and as he relaxes, he tells me more about his deal. In fact, he confides in me more than he ever has before.

'This city,' he says, shaking his head. 'It's a demanding place. Like . . . skiing down the edge of a precipice. If you make one mistake – that's it. You fall.'

'But if you don't make any mistakes?'

'You win,' says Luke. 'You win it all.'

'You're going to win,' I say confidently. 'You're going to wow them all tomorrow.'

'And you're going to wow them at your screen test,' says Luke, as a waiter appears at our table with our first courses – the most amazing sculptures made out of seafood. He pours out our wine, and Luke lifts his glass in a toast.

'To you, Becky. You're going to be a huge success.'

'No, *you're* going to be a huge success,' I reply, feeling a glow of pleasure all around me. 'We're both going to be huge successes!'

Maybe it's the Bellini, going to my head, but all at once I feel again exactly as I did in Barney's. I'm not the old Becky – I'm someone new and sparkling. Surreptitiously I glance at myself in a nearby mirror, and feel a twinge of delight. I mean, just look at me! All poised and groomed, in a New York restaurant, wearing a thousands-of-dollars dress, with my wonderful, successful boyfriend – and a screen test tomorrow for American television!

I feel intoxicated with happiness. This expensive, glossy world is where I've been heading all along. Limos and flowers; waxed eyebrows and designer clothes from Barney's; a purse stuffed with business cards of TV executives. These are my people; this is where I belong. My old life seems a million, zillion miles away, like a tiny dot on the horizon. Mum and Dad and Suze . . . my untidy room in Fulham . . . *EastEnders* with a pizza . . . I mean, let's face it. That was never really me, was it?

We end up staying out for hours. We dance to the jazz band, eat passion fruit sorbet and talk about everything in the world but work. When we get back to the hotel we're both laughing, and tripping slightly as we walk, and Luke's hand is making its way deftly inside my dress.

'Miss Bloomwood?' says the concierge as we pass the desk. 'There's a message for you to call a Susan Cleath-Stuart, in London. Whatever time you get in. Apparently it's urgent.'

'Oh God,' I say, rolling my eyes. 'She'll just be calling to lecture me about how much I spent on my new dress. "How much? Oh Bex, you *shouldn't* have" . . .'

'It's a fantastic dress,' says Luke, running his hands

appreciatively up and down it. 'Although there's far too much of it. You could lose this bit here . . . and this bit . . .'

'Would you like the number?' says the concierge, holding out a piece of paper.

'No thanks,' I say, waving my hand. 'I'll call her tomorrow.'

'And please,' adds Luke, 'hold off all calls to our room, until further notice.'

'Very well,' says the concierge with a twinkle. 'Goodnight sir. Goodnight, ma'am.'

We travel up in the lift, grinning stupidly at each other in the mirrors, and back in our room I realize that I'm really feeling quite drunk. My only consolation is, Luke looks completely plastered, too.

'That,' I say, as the door closes behind us, 'was the best night of my life. The very best.'

'It isn't over yet,' says Luke, coming towards me with a meaningful gleam in his eye. 'I feel I need to reward you for your most insightful comments, Miss Bloomwood. You *were* right. All work and no play . . .' He starts to pull my Vera Wang straps gently down off my shoulders. 'Makes Jack . . .' he murmurs against my skin. 'A very . . .'

And we're tumbling down onto the bed together, and his mouth is on mine, and my mind is wheeling with alcohol and delight. As he's pulling off his shirt, I catch a glimpse of myself in the mirror. I stare at my intoxicated, happy self for an instant, and hear a voice inside saying: remember this moment for ever. Remember this moment, Becky, because right now, life is perfect.

The rest is a haze of drunken, blurry pleasure, drifting into oblivion. The last thing I remember is Luke kissing me on the eyelids and telling me to sleep well and that he loves me. That's the last thing.

And then, like a car crash, it happens.

ARE THEY WHAT THEY SEEM?

FINANCE GURU IS MONEY MESS!

She sits on the *Morning Coffee* sofa, advising millions of viewers on financial issues. But the *Daily World* can exclusively reveal that hypocritical Becky Bloomwood is herself on the brink of financial disaster. Becky, whose catchphrase is 'Look after your money – and your money will look after you', is being pursued for debts totalling thousands, and her own bank manager has labelled her a 'disgrace'.

SUMMONS

La Rosa clothes boutique has issued a summons against bankrupt Becky, while flatmate Susan Cleath-Stuart (right) admits Becky is often behind in her rent. Meanwhile feckless Becky is unashamedly jetsetting in New York with entrepreneur boyfriend Luke Brandon (below, right). 'Becky quite blatantly uses Luke for his money,' said one inside source at Brandon Communications. Miss Cleath-Stuart meanwhile admits she would like to see Becky gone. 'I could do with more space for my work,' she says. 'Maybe I'll have to hire an office.'

SPENDAHOLIC

Staying in the swanky Four Seasons Hotel, the wayward 26-year-old revealed she had no idea how much her accommodation cost. Our reporter watched as she splurged over £100 on greeting cards alone, then went on a further spree, buying luxury clothes and gifts totalling £1,000 in just a few hours.

SHOCKED

Viewers of *Morning Coffee* were outraged to discover the truth about the self-styled money expert. 'I'm quite appalled,' commented Irene Watson of Sevenoaks. 'I phoned Becky a few weeks ago to ask advice on my banking arrangements. Now I wish I'd never listened to a word, and will be taking further advice.' Mother-of-two Irene added, 'I'm shocked and disgusted that the producers of *Morning Coffee*

turn to page 54

Thirteen

At first, I don't know that anything is wrong. I wake up feeling extremely bleary, to see Luke handing me a cup of tea.

'Why don't you check the messages?' he says, giving me a kiss, and heads towards the shower. After a few sips of tea, I lift the telephone receiver and press the star button.

'You have twenty-three messages,' says the telephone voice – and I gape at it in astonishment. Twenty-three?

Perhaps they're all job offers! is my first thought. Perhaps it's people calling from Hollywood! God yes! In great excitement I press the button to hear the first one. But it's not a job offer – it's Suze, and she's sounding really hassled.

'Bex, please, ring me. As soon as you get this. It's really urgent. Bye.'

The voice asks me if I'd like to hear my remaining messages – and for a moment I hesitate. But Suze did sound pretty desperate – and I remember with a twinge of guilt that she called last night, too. I dial the number, and to my surprise, it clicks on to answermachine.

'Hi! It's me!' I say as soon as Suze's voice has finished speaking. 'Well, you're not in, so I hope whatever it is has sorted itself—'

'Bex!' Suze's voice practically bursts my eardrum. 'Oh my God, Bex, where have you been?'

'Out,' I say, puzzled. 'And then asleep. Suze, is everything—'

'Bex, I never said those things!' she interrupts, sounding distressed. 'You have to believe me. I'd never say *anything* like that. They just twisted everything round. I told your mum, I didn't have any idea—'

'My mum?' I say, bewildered. 'Suze, slow down. What are you talking about?'

There's silence.

'Oh God,' says Suze. 'Bex, haven't you seen it?'

'Seen what?'

'The *Daily World*,' says Suze. 'I . . . I thought you got all the British papers.'

'We do,' I say, rubbing my dry face. 'But they'll still be outside the door. Is there . . . is there something about me?'

'No,' says Suze a little too quickly. 'No. I mean . . . there is this one very tiny thing. But it's not worth looking at. I really wouldn't bother. In fact – throw the *Daily World* away, I would. Just . . . put it in the bin, without even opening it.'

'There's something nasty, isn't there?' I say apprehensively. 'Do my legs look really fat or something?'

'It's really nothing!' says Suze. 'Nothing! So anyway, have you been to the Rockefeller Center yet? It's supposed to be great! Or F.A.O. Schwarz? Or . . .'

'Suze, stop,' I interrupt. 'I'm going to go and get it. I'll call you back.'

'OK, look Bex, just remember,' says Suze in a rush. 'Hardly *anyone* reads the *Daily World*. You know, like about three people. And it's tomorrow's fish and chips. And everyone knows the newspapers make up complete lies . . .'

'Right,' I say, trying to sound relaxed. 'I'll remember that. And don't worry, Suze. These stupid little things don't faze me!'

But as I put the phone down, my hand is trembling

240

slightly. What on earth can they have said about me? I hurry to the door, grab the pile of papers and cart them all back to the bed. I seize hold of the *Daily World* and feverishly start to leaf through it. Page after page . . . but there's nothing there. I go back to the beginning and leaf through more carefully, looking at all the tiny box items – and there really is no mention of me at all. I lean back on my pillows, bemused. What on earth is Suze going on about? Why on earth is she so—

And then I spot the centre double-page spread. A single folded sheet, lying on the bed, which must have fallen out as I grabbed hold of the paper. Very slowly I reach for it. I open it. And it's as though someone's punched me in the stomach.

There's a picture of me. It's a photo I don't recognize – not very flattering. I'm walking along, in some street. A New York street, I realize with a lurch. And I'm holding lots of shopping bags. And there's a picture of Luke, in a circle. And a little picture of Suze. And the headline reads . . .

Oh God. I can't even say it. I can't even tell you what it says. It's . . . it's too awful.

It's a huge article, spanning the whole centre spread. As I read it, my heart is thudding; my head feels hot and cold. It's so nasty. It's so . . . personal. Halfway through I can't stand it any more. I close the paper and stare ahead, feeling as though I might throw up.

Then almost immediately, with trembling hands, I open it again. I have to see exactly what they've said. I have to read every horrible, humiliating line.

When I've finally finished, I feel almost light-headed. I can't quite believe this is really happening. This paper has already been printed millions of times. It's too late to stop it. In Britain, I suddenly realize, this has been out for hours. My parents will have seen it. Everyone I know will have seen it. I'm powerless to do anything.

The telephone gives a shrill ring, and I jump with

fright. After a moment it rings again, and I stare at it in terror. I can't answer. I can't talk to anybody, not even Suze.

The phone rings for the fourth time, and Luke strides out of the bathroom, clad only in a towel with his hair slicked back.

'Aren't you going to get that?' he says shortly, and grabs for the receiver. 'Hello? Yes, Luke Brandon here.'

I feel a swoop of fear, and wrap the duvet more tightly around me.

'Right,' Luke is saying. 'Fine. I'll see you then.' He puts the phone down and scribbles something on a pad of paper.

'Who was that?' I say, trying to keep my voice steady.

'A secretary from JD Slade,' he says, putting his pen down. 'Change of venue.'

He starts to get dressed, and I say nothing. My hand tightens around the *Daily World* page. I want to show him . . . but I don't want to show him. I don't want him to read those horrible things about me. But I can't let him see it from someone else.

Oh God, I can't sit here for ever, saying nothing. I close my eyes — then take a deep breath and say,

'Luke, there's a thing about me in the paper.'

'Good,' says Luke absently, doing up his tie. 'I thought you might get a bit of publicity. Which paper?'

'It's . . . it's not good,' I say, and lick my dry lips. 'It's really awful.'

Luke looks at me properly and sees my expression.

'Oh Becky,' he says. 'It can't be that bad. Come on, show me. What does it say?' He holds out his hand, but I don't move.

'It's just . . . really horrible. And there's a great big picture—'

'Did you have a bad hair day?' says Luke teasingly, and reaches for his jacket. 'Becky, no piece of publicity is ever a hundred per cent perfect. You're always going to find something to fret about, whether it's your hair, or something you said . . .'

'Luke!' I say despairingly. 'It's nothing like that. Just . . . have a look.'

Slowly I unfold the paper and give it to Luke. He takes it cheerfully – but as he gazes at it, his smile slowly disappears.

'What the fuck – Is that *me*?' He glances at me briefly, and I swallow, not daring to say anything. Then he scans the page while I watch nervously.

'Is this true?' he says at last. 'Any of it?'

'N-no!' I stammer. 'At least . . . not . . . not all of it. Some of it is . . .'

'Are you in debt?'

I meet his gaze, feeling my face turn crimson.

'A . . . a little bit. But I mean, not like they say . . . I mean, I don't know anything about a summons . . .'

'Wednesday afternoon!' He hits the paper. 'For Christ's sake. You were at the Guggenheim. Find your ticket, we'll prove you were there, get a retraction—'

'I . . . Actually Luke . . .' He looks up and I feel a lurch of pure fear. 'I didn't go to the Guggenheim. I . . . I went shopping.'

'You went . . .' He stares at me – then silently starts to read again.

When he's finished he stares ahead expressionlessly.

'I don't believe this,' he says, so quietly I can barely hear him.

He looks as grim as I feel – and for the first time this morning I feel tears pricking at my eyes.

'I know,' I say shakily. 'It's awful. They must have been following me. They must have been there all along, watching me, *spying* on me . . .' I look at him for a response, but he's just staring straight ahead. 'Luke, don't you have anything to say? Do you realize—'

'Becky, do *you* realize?' he interrupts. He turns towards me, and at his expression I feel the blood draining from my face. 'Do you realize quite how bad this is for *me*?'

'I'm really sorry,' I gulp. 'I know you hate being in the paper . . .'

'It's not a bloody question of—' He stops himself, and says more calmly, 'Becky, do you realize how this is going to make me look? Today of all fucking days?'

'I . . . I didn't . . .' I whisper.

'I have to go into a meeting in an hour's time and convince a stuffy, conservative New York investment bank that I'm fully in control of every aspect of my business and personal life. They'll all have seen this. I'll be a joke!'

'But of course you're in control!' I say in alarm. 'Luke, surely they'll know . . . surely they won't—'

'Listen,' says Luke, turning round. 'Do you know what the perception of me is in this city? The general perception here – for some inexplicable reason – is that I'm losing my touch.'

'Losing your touch?' I echo in horror.

'That's what I've heard.' Luke takes a deep, controlled breath. 'What I've been doing over the last few days is working my fucking *arse* off to convince these people that their perception is wrong. That I am in control; that I have the media taped. And now . . .' He hits the paper sharply and I wince.

'Maybe . . . maybe they won't have seen it.'

'Becky, everyone sees everything in this town,' says Luke. 'That's their job. That's—'

He breaks off as the phone rings. After a pause, he picks it up.

'Hi. Michael. Ah. You've seen it. Yes, I know. Unfortunate timing. All right. See you in a sec.' He puts down the phone and reaches for his briefcase, without looking at me.

I feel cold and shivery. What have I done? I've wrecked everything. Phrases from the article keep popping into my mind, making me feel sick. *Feckless Becky . . . hypocritical Becky . . .* And they're right. They're all right.

When I look up, Luke's closing his briefcase with a snap.

'I have to go,' he says. 'I'll see you later.' At the door he hesitates, and turns round, looking suddenly confused. 'But I don't understand. If you weren't at the Guggenheim – where did you get the book you gave me?'

'At the museum shop,' I whisper. 'On Broadway. Luke, I'm so sorry . . . I . . .'

I tail away into a hideous silence. I can feel my heart thumping; the blood pulsing in my ears. I don't know what to say; how to redeem myself.

Luke stares at me blankly, then gives a brief nod, turns and reaches for the door handle.

When the door has closed behind him, I sit quite still for a while, staring straight ahead. I can't quite believe all this is really happening. Just a few hours ago we were toasting each other with Bellinis. I was wearing my Vera Wang dress and we were dancing to Cole Porter and I was giddy with happiness. And now . . .

The phone starts to ring, but I don't move. Only on the eighth ring do I stir myself and pick it up.

'Hello?'

'Hello!' says a bright voice. 'Is that Becky Bloomwood?'

'Yes,' I say cautiously.

'Becky, it's Fiona Taggart from the *Daily Herald*. I'm so glad I've tracked you down! Becky, we'd be really interested in running a two-part feature on you and your . . . little problem, shall we call it?'

'I don't want to talk about it,' I mutter.

'Do you deny it, then?'

'No comment,' I say, and thrust the phone down with

a trembling hand. Immediately it rings again, and I pick it up.

'No comment, all right?' I exclaim. 'No comment! No—'

'Becky? Darling?'

'Mum!' At the sound of her voice I feel myself dissolving into tears. 'Oh Mum, I'm so sorry,' I gulp. 'It's so awful. I've messed everything up. I just didn't know . . . I didn't realize . . .'

'Becky!' comes her voice down the line, familiar and reassuring. 'Love! You don't have to be sorry! It's those scumbag reporters who should be sorry. Making up all those stories. Putting words in people's mouths. Poor Suzie phoned us up, very upset. You know, she gave that girl three bourbon biscuits and a KitKat, and this is the thanks she gets. A load of outlandish lies! I mean, pretending to be from the council tax. They should be prosecuted!'

'Mum . . .' I close my eyes, almost unable to say it. 'It's not all lies. They . . . they didn't make everything up.' There's a short silence, and I can hear Mum breathing anxiously down the line. 'I am kind of in a . . . a bit of debt.'

'Well,' says Mum after a pause – and I can hear her gearing herself up to be positive. 'Well. So what? Even if you are, is it any of their business?' She pauses, and I hear a voice in the background. 'Exactly! Dad says, if the American economy can be in debt by billions and still survive, then so can you. And look at the Dome, Dad says.'

God, I love my parents. If I told them I'd committed murder they'd soon find some reason why it was perfectly justified and the victim had it coming to them.

'I suppose so,' I gulp. 'But it's Luke's big meeting today, and all his investors will have seen it.'

'So what? There's no such thing as bad publicity.

Now you keep your chin up, Becky! Best foot forward. Suzie told us you've got a screen test today. Is that right?'

'Yes. I just don't know what time.'

'Well then. You put a brave face on. Run yourself a bath and have a nice cup of tea and put three sugars in it. And a brandy, Dad says. And if any reporters ring up, just tell them to b- off.'

'Have you had any reporters bothering you?' I say in alarm.

'A chap came round asking questions this morning,' says Mum breezily. 'But Dad went for him with the hedge trimmer.'

In spite of myself I give a shaky giggle.

'I'd better go, Mum. But I'll call you later. And . . . thanks.'

When I put down the phone, I feel a million times better. Mum's right. I've just got to be positive and go to my screen test and do as well as I possibly can. And Luke probably did over-react a little bit. He'll probably come back in a much better mood.

I ring up the hotel reception and tell them to hold all calls except from HLBC. Then I run my bath, empty a whole bottle of Uplift bath oil from Sephora into it, and wallow for half an hour in rose, geranium and mallow. As I dry myself I put on MTV and dance around the room to Robbie Williams – and by the time I'm dressed in my knock 'em dead outfit from Barney's I'm feeling pretty positive, if a little shaky. I can do this. I *can*.

They haven't called yet to tell me what time to come in, so I pick up the phone and ring down to reception.

'Hi,' I say. 'Just checking if HLBC have called for me this morning.'

'I don't believe so,' says the girl pleasantly.

'Are you sure? They didn't leave a message?'

'No, ma'am.'

'OK. Thanks.'

I put the phone down and think for a few moments. Well – that's all right, I'll just call them. I mean, I need to know what time the test is, don't I? And Kent told me to call her any time, whatever I needed. She said, don't even hesitate.

I take her business card out of my bag and carefully punch in the number.

'Hello!' says a bright voice. 'Kent Garland's office, this is her assistant Megan, how can I help you?'

'Hello!' I say. 'It's Rebecca Bloomwood here. Could I speak to Kent please?'

'Kent's in a meeting right now,' says Megan pleasantly. 'Could I take a message?'

'Well, I'm just phoning to see what time my screen test is today,' I say. Just saying it gives me a surge of confidence. Who cares about the crappy *Daily World* anyway? I'm going to be on American television. I'm going to be a huge celebrity.

'I see,' says Megan. 'Becky, if you could just hold on a moment . . .'

She puts me on hold, and I find myself listening to a tinny version of 'Heard it through the Grapevine'. It comes to an end, and a voice tells me how important my call is to the HLBC Corporation . . . and then it starts again . . . when suddenly Megan is back.

'Hi, Becky? I'm afraid Kent's going to have to postpone the screen test. She'll give you a call if she wants to rearrange.'

'What?' I say, staring blankly at my made-up face in the mirror. 'Postpone? But . . . why? Do you know when it'll be rescheduled?'

'I'm not sure,' says Megan pleasantly. 'Kent's very busy right now, with the new series of *Consumer Today*.'

'But . . . but that's what the screen test was for! The new series of *Consumer Today*!' I take a deep breath, trying not to sound too anxious. 'Do you know when she'll rearrange it for?'

'I really couldn't say. Her diary's very full at the moment . . . and then she has a two-week vacation . . .'

'Listen,' I say, trying to stay calm. 'I'd really like to talk to Kent, please. It's quite important. Couldn't you get her for me? Just for a second.'

There's a pause – then Megan sighs.

'I'll see if I can fetch her.'

The tinny song begins again – then Kent is on the line.

'Hi, Becky. How are you?'

'Hi!' I say, trying to sound relaxed. 'I'm fine. I just thought I'd see what was happening today. About the screen test?'

'Right,' says Kent thoughtfully. 'Tell the truth, Becky, a couple of issues have come up, which we need to think about. OK? So we'll be passing on the screen test until we're a little more decided about things.'

Issues? What issues is she talking about? What's she—

Suddenly I feel paralysed by fear. Oh God. Oh please no.

She's seen the *Daily World*, hasn't she? That's what she's talking about. I clutch the receiver tightly, my heart thudding, desperately wanting to explain it all; wanting to tell her that it all sounds far worse than it really is. That half of it isn't even true; that it doesn't mean I'm not good at what I do . . .

But I just can't bring myself to. I can't bring myself even to mention it.

'So we'll be in touch,' Kent says. 'Apologies for putting you out today – I was going to have Megan call you later . . .'

'That's all right!' I say, trying to sound bright and easy. 'So when do you think we might reschedule?'

'I'm really not sure . . . Sorry, Becky. I'm going to

have to run. There's a problem on the set. But thanks for calling. And enjoy the rest of your trip!'

The phone goes silent and I slowly put it down.

I'm not having my screen test, after all. They don't want me, after all.

And I bought a new outfit, and everything.

Oh God. Oh God.

I can feel my breath coming quicker and quicker, and for an awful moment I think I might cry.

But then I think of Mum – and force myself to lift my chin. I'm not going to let myself collapse. I'm going to be strong and positive. HLBC aren't the only fish in the sea. There are plenty of other people who want to snap me up. Plenty! I mean, look at . . . look at Greg Walters. He said he wanted me to meet his head of development, didn't he? Well maybe we can fix something up for today. Yes! Perhaps by the end of today, I'll have my own show!

Quickly I find the number and dial it nervously, and to my joy, I get straight through. This is more like it. Straight to the top.

'Hi, Greg? It's Becky Bloomwood here.'

'Becky! Great to hear from you!' says Greg, sounding a little distracted. 'How're you doing?'

'Erm . . . fine! It was really nice to meet you yesterday,' I say, aware that my voice is shrill with nerves. 'And I was very interested in all your ideas.'

'Well, that's great! So – are you enjoying your trip?'

'Yes! Yes I am.' I take a deep breath. 'Greg, you were saying yesterday that I should meet up with your head of development—'

'Absolutely!' says Greg. 'I know Dave would adore to meet you. We both think you have huge potential. Huge.'

Relief floods over me. Thank God. Thank—

'So next time you're in town,' Greg is saying, 'you give me a call, and we'll set something up.'

I stare at the phone, prickly with shock. Next time I'm in town? But that could be months. It could be never. Doesn't he want to—

'Promise you'll do that?'

'Erm . . . OK,' I say, trying to keep the thickening dismay out of my voice. 'That would be great!'

'And maybe we'll meet up when I next come over to London.'

'OK!' I say brightly. 'I hope so. Well . . . see you soon. And good to meet you!'

'Great to meet you too, Becky!'

I'm still smiling my bright fake smile as the phone goes dead. And this time I just can't stop the tears from gathering in my eyes and dripping slowly down my face, taking my makeup with them.

I sit alone in the hotel room for hours. Lunchtime comes and goes, but I can't face any food. The only positive thing I do is listen to the messages on the phone and delete them all except one from Mum, which I listen to over and over again. It's the one she must have left as soon as she got the *Daily World*.

'Now,' she's saying. 'There's a bit of fuss here over a silly article in the paper. Don't take any notice of it, Becky. Just remember, that picture will be going in a million dog baskets tomorrow.'

For some reason that makes me laugh, each time I hear it. So I sit there, half crying, half laughing, letting a pool of wet tears gather on my skirt and not even bothering to wipe it away.

Oh God, I want to go home. For what seems like an eternity I sit on the floor, rocking backwards and forwards, letting my thoughts circle round and round. Going over the same ground over and over again. How could I have been so stupid? What am I going to do now? How can I face anyone, ever again?

I feel as though I've been on a crazy rollercoaster ever

since I got to New York. Like some sort of magical Disney ride – except instead of whizzing through space, I've been whizzing through shops and hotels and interviews and lunches, surrounded by light and glitter and voices telling me I'm the next big thing.

And I had no idea it wasn't real. I believed every moment of it.

When, at long last, I hear the door opening, I feel almost sick with relief. I have a desperate urge to throw myself into Luke's arms, burst into tears and listen to him tell me it's all right. But as he comes in, I feel my whole body contract in fear. His expression is taut and set; he looks as though his face is carved out of stone.

'Hi,' I say at last. 'I . . . I wondered where you were.'

'I had lunch with Michael,' says Luke shortly. 'After the meeting.' He takes off his coat and puts it carefully onto a hanger while I watch fearfully.

'So . . .' I hardly dare ask the question. 'Did it go well?'

'Not particularly well, no.'

My stomach gives a nervous flip. What does that mean? Surely . . . surely it can't be . . .

'Is it . . . off?' I manage at last.

'Good question,' says Luke. 'The people from JD Slade say they need more time.'

'Why do they need time?' I say, licking my dry lips.

'They have a few reservations,' says Luke evenly. 'They didn't specify exactly what those reservations were.'

He pulls off his tie roughly and starts to unbutton his shirt. Oh God, he's not even looking at me. It's as though he can't bring himself to.

'Do you . . .' I swallow. 'Do you think they'd seen the piece?'

'Oh, I think so,' says Luke. There's an edge to his voice which makes me flinch. 'Yes, I'm pretty sure they'd seen it.'

He's fumbling over the last shirt button. Suddenly, in irritation, he rips it off.

'Luke,' I say helplessly. 'I'm . . . I'm so sorry. 'I don't know what I can do.' I take a deep breath. 'I'll do anything I can.'

'There's nothing,' says Luke flatly.

He heads into the bathroom and after a few moments I hear the sound of the shower. I don't move. I can't even think. I feel paralysed, as though I'm crouching on a ledge, trying not to slip.

At last Luke comes out, and without even acknowledging me, pulls on a pair of black jeans and a black turtle neck. He pours himself a drink and there's silence. From the window I can see right across Manhattan. The air is turning dusky and lights are coming on in windows everywhere, right into the distance. But the world has shrunk to this room; these four walls. I haven't been out all day, I abruptly realize.

'I didn't have my screen test, either,' I say at last.

'Really.' Luke's voice is flat and uninterested, and in spite of myself I feel a faint spark of resentment.

'Don't you even want to know why?' I say, tugging at the fringe of a cushion. There's a pause – then Luke says, as though with tremendous effort,

'Why?'

'Because no-one's interested in me any more.' I push my hair back off my head. 'You're not the only one who's had a bad day, Luke. I've wrecked all my chances. No-one wants to know me any more.'

Humiliation creeps over me as I remember all the telephone messages I had to listen to this morning, politely cancelling meetings and calling off lunches.

'And I know it's all my own fault,' I continue. 'I *know* that. But even so . . .' My voice starts to wobble treacherously, and I take a deep breath. 'Things really aren't great for me either.' I look up – but Luke hasn't

253

moved an inch. 'You could . . . you could show a little sympathy.'

'Show a little sympathy,' echoes Luke evenly.

'I know I brought it on myself . . .'

'That's right! You did!' Luke's voice explodes in pent-up frustration, and at last he turns to face me. 'Becky, no-one forced you to go and spend that money! I mean, I know you like shopping. But for Christ's sake. To spend like this . . . It's bloody irresponsible. Couldn't you have stopped yourself?'

'I don't know!' I retort shakily. 'Probably. But I didn't know it was going to become such a . . . a bloody life and death issue, did I? I didn't *know* I was being followed, Luke. I didn't do this on purpose.' To my horror, I feel a tear making its way down my cheek. 'You know, I didn't hurt anybody. I didn't kill anybody. Maybe I was a bit naive . . .'

'A bit naive. That's the understatement of the year.'

'OK, so I was naive! But I didn't commit any crime—'

'You don't think throwing away opportunity is a crime?' says Luke furiously. 'Because as far as I'm concerned . . .' He shakes his head. 'Jesus, Becky! We both had it all. We *had* New York.' His hand clenches into a fist. 'And now, look at us both. All because you're so bloody *obsessed* by shopping—'

'Obsessed?' I cry. I can't stand his accusing gaze any more. '*I'm* obsessed? What about you?'

'What do you mean?' he says dismissively.

'You're obsessed by work! By making it in New York! The first thing you thought of when you saw that piece wasn't me or . . . or how I was feeling, was it? It was how it affected you and your deal.' My voice rises tremulously. 'All you care about is your own success, and I always come second. I mean, you didn't even bother to *tell* me about New York until it was all decided! You just expected me to . . . to fall in line and do exactly what you wanted. No wonder Alicia said I was tagging along!'

'You're not tagging along,' he says impatiently.

'Yes I am! That's the way you see me, isn't it? As some little nobody, who has to be . . . to be slotted into your grand magnificent plan. And I was so stupid, I just went along with it . . .'

'I haven't got time for this,' says Luke, standing up.

'You've never got time!' I say tearfully. 'Suze has got more time for me than you have! You didn't have time to come to Tom's wedding; our holiday turned into a meeting; you didn't have time to visit my parents . . .'

'So I don't have a lot of time!' yells Luke suddenly, shocking me into silence. 'So I can't sit around making mindless tittle-tattle with you and Suze.' He shakes his head in frustration. 'Do you realize how fucking *hard* I work? Do you have any idea how important this deal is?'

'*Why* is it important?' I hear myself shrieking. 'Why is it so bloody important to make it in America? So you can impress your complete cow of a mother? Because if you're trying to impress her, Luke, then I'd give up now! She'll never be impressed. Never! I mean, she hasn't even bothered to *see* you! God, you buy her a Hermès scarf – and she can't even rearrange her schedule to find five minutes for you!'

I break off, panting, into complete silence.

Oh fuck. I shouldn't have said that.

I dart a look at Luke, and he's staring at me, his face ashen with anger.

'What did you call my mother?' he says slowly.

'Look, I . . . I didn't mean it.' I swallow, trying to keep control of my voice. 'I just think . . . there's got to be a sense of proportion in all this. All I did was a bit of shopping . . .'

'A bit of shopping,' echoes Luke scathingly. 'A *bit* of shopping.' He gives me a long look – then, to my horror, heads to the huge cedarwood wardrobe where I've been stashing all my stuff. He opens it silently and we both stare at the bags crammed to the ceiling.

As I see it all, I feel nausea overcoming me. All those things which seemed so vital when I bought them, all those things I got so excited about . . . now just look like a great big pile of rubbish bags. I could barely even tell you what's in any of the packages. It's just . . . stuff. Piles and piles of stuff.

Without saying anything, Luke closes the door again, and I feel shame drenching me like hot water.

'I know,' I say, in a voice barely above a whisper. 'I know. But I'm paying for it. I really am.'

I turn away, unable to meet his eye, and suddenly I just have to get out of this room. I have to get away from Luke, from myself in the mirror; from the whole horrendous day.

'I'll . . . I'll see you later,' I mutter and without looking back, head for the door.

The bar downstairs is dimly lit, soothing and anonymous. I sink into a sumptuous leather chair, feeling weak and shaky, as though I've got the flu. When a waiter comes up, I order an orange juice, then, as he's walking away, change my order to a brandy. It arrives in a huge glass, warm and reviving, and I take a few sips – then look up as a shadow appears on the table in front of me. It's Michael Ellis. My heart sinks. I really don't feel up to talking to him.

'Hello,' he says. 'May I?' He gestures to the chair opposite and I nod weakly. He sits down and gives me a kind look as I drain my glass. For a while, we're both silent.

'I could be polite, and not mention it,' he says at last. 'Or I could tell you the truth – which is that I was very sorry for you this morning. Your British papers are vicious. No-one deserves that kind of treatment.'

'Thank you,' I mumble.

A waiter appears, and Michael orders two more brandies without even asking.

'All I can tell you is, people aren't dumb,' he says as the waiter walks off. 'No-one's going to hold it against you.'

'They already have,' I say, staring at the table. 'My screen test for HLBC was called off.'

'Ah,' says Michael after a pause. 'I'm sorry to hear that.'

'No-one wants to know me any more. They're all saying they've "decided to go another way" or they "feel I don't really suit the American market" and . . . you know. Basically just, "go away".'

I *so* wanted to tell Luke all this. I wanted to pour out all my woes – and for him to give me a huge, uncritical hug. Tell me it was their loss, not mine, like my parents would, or Suze would. But instead, he made me feel even worse about myself. He's right – I've thrown everything away, haven't I? I had opportunities people would kill for, and I wasted them.

Michael is nodding gravely.

'That happens,' he says. 'I'm afraid these idiots are like a pack of sheep. One gets spooked, they all get spooked.'

'I just feel like I've wrecked everything,' I say, feeling my throat tightening. 'I was going to get this amazing job, and Luke was going to be this huge success. It was all going to be perfect. And I've just chucked it in the bin. It's all my fault.'

To my horror, tears are spilling out of my eyes. I can't stop them. And then I give a huge sob. Oh, this is so embarrassing.

'I'm sorry,' I whisper. 'I'm just a complete disaster.'

I bury my hot face in my hands and hope that Michael Ellis will tactfully slip away and leave me alone. Instead, I feel a hand on mine, and a handkerchief being slipped into my fingers. I wipe my face gratefully with the cool cotton and eventually raise my head.

'Thanks,' I gulp. 'Sorry about that.'

'That's quite all right,' says Michael calmly. 'I'd be the same.'

'Yeah right,' I mutter.

'You should see me when I lose a contract. I bawl my eyes out. My secretary has to run out for Kleenex every half-hour.' He sounds so deadpan, I can't help giving a little smile. 'Now, drink your brandy,' he says, 'and let's get a few things straight. Did you invite the *Daily World* to take pictures of you with a long-range lens?'

'No.'

'Did you call them, offering an exclusive on your personal habits and suggesting a choice of offensive headlines?'

'No.' I can't help giving a half-giggle.

'So.' He gives me a quizzical look. 'This would be all your fault because . . .'

'I was naive. I should have realized. I should have . . . seen it coming. I was stupid.'

'You were unlucky.' He shrugs. 'Maybe a little foolish. But you can't heap all the blame on yourself.'

An electronic burble sounds from his pocket, and he reaches for his mobile.

'Excuse me a moment,' he says, and turns away. 'Hi there.'

As he talks quietly into the phone I fold a paper coaster over and over. I want to ask him something – but I'm not sure I want to hear the answer.

'Sorry about that,' says Michael, putting his phone away. He glances at the mangled coaster. 'Feeling better?'

'Michael . . .' I take a deep breath. 'Was it my fault the deal fell through? I mean, did the *Daily World* thing come into it?'

He gives me a sharp look. 'We're being frank here, right?'

'Yes,' I say, feeling a shaft of apprehension. 'We're being frank.'

'Then, to be honest, I can't say it helped proceedings,' says Michael. 'There were various remarks made this morning. Some oh-so-funny jokes. I have to hand it to Luke, he took it all pretty well.'

I stare at him, feeling cold.

'Luke didn't tell me that.' Michael shrugs.

'I wouldn't have thought he particularly wanted to repeat any of the comments.'

'So it *was* my fault.'

'Uh-uh.' Michael shakes his head. 'That's not what I said.' He leans back in his chair. 'Becky, if this deal had been really strong, it would have survived a bit of adverse publicity. My guess is JD Slade used your little . . . embarrassment as an excuse. There's some bigger reason, which they're keeping to themselves.'

'What?'

'Who knows? The rumour about Bank of London? A difference in business ethos? For some reason, they seem to have suffered a general loss of confidence in the whole idea.'

I stare at him, remembering what Luke said.

'Do people really think Luke's losing his touch?'

'Luke is a very talented individual,' says Michael carefully. 'But something's got into him over this deal. He's almost *too* driven. I told him this morning, he needs to prioritize. There's obviously a situation with Bank of London. He should be talking to them. Reassuring them. Frankly, if he loses them, he's in big trouble.' He leans forward. 'If you ask me, he should be on a plane back to London this afternoon.'

'And what does he want to do?'

'He's already setting up meetings with every New York investment bank I've ever heard of.' He shakes his head. 'That boy seems fixated by making it in America.'

'I think he wants to prove something,' I mutter. *To his mother*, I nearly add.

'So Becky,' Michael gives me a kind look. 'What are you going to do? Try to set up some more meetings?'

'No,' I say after a pause. 'To be honest, I don't think there's any point.'

'So will you stay out here with Luke?'

An image of Luke's frozen face flashes through my mind, and I feel a stab of pain.

'I don't think there's much point doing that, either.' I take a deep swig of brandy and try to smile. 'You know what? I think I'm just going to go home.'

Fourteen

I get out of the taxi, hoist my suitcase onto the pavement and look miserably up at the grey English sky. I can't quite believe it's really all over.

Until the very last minute, I had a secret, desperate hope that someone might change their mind and offer me a job. Or that Luke might beg me to stay. Every time the phone rang I felt a spasm of nerves, hoping that a miracle was about to happen. But nothing happened. Of course it didn't.

When I said goodbye to Luke it was as though I was acting a part. I wanted to throw myself on him in tears, slap his face, *something*. But I just couldn't. I had to salvage some kind of dignity. So it was almost businesslike, the way I phoned the airline, packed up my stuff, and ordered a cab. I couldn't bring myself to kiss him on the mouth when I left, so I gave him a brisk peck on each cheek and then turned away before either of us could say anything.

Now, twelve hours later, I feel completely exhausted. I sat awake all through that overnight flight, stiff with misery and disappointment. Only a few days ago I was flying out, thinking I was about to start a fantastic new life in America, and instead, I'm back here with less than I even started with. Not only that – everyone, but *everyone*, knows it. A couple of girls at the airport obviously recognized me, and started whispering and giggling as I was waiting for my bags.

And oh God, I know I'd have been just the same if I'd been them. But right then, I felt so raw with humiliation, I nearly burst into tears.

I lug my bags dejectedly up the steps and let myself into the flat. And for a few moments I just stand there, looking around at the coats and old letters and keys in the bowl. Same old hall. Same old life. Back to square one. I catch sight of my haggard reflection in the mirror and quickly look away.

'Hi!' I call. 'Anyone in? I'm back.'

There's a pause – then Suze appears at her door in a dressing gown. 'Bex?' she exclaims. 'I didn't expect you back so early! Are you all right?' She comes nearer, pulling her dressing gown around her, and peers worriedly at my face. 'Oh Bex.' She bites her lip. 'I don't know what to say.'

'It's fine,' I say. 'I'm fine. Honestly.'

'Bex—'

'Really. I'm fine.' I turn away before the sight of Suze's anxious face reduces me to tears, and scrabble in my bag. 'So anyway . . . I got you that Clinique stuff you asked for, and the special face stuff for your mum . . .' I hand the bottles to her and begin to root roughly around again. 'There's some more stuff for you in here somewhere . . .'

'Bex – don't worry about it. Just come and sit down, or something.' Suze clutches the Clinique bottles to her and peers at me uncertainly. 'Would you like a drink?'

'No!' I make myself smile. 'I'm all right, Suze. I've decided the best thing is just to get on, and not think about what's happened. In fact – I'd rather we didn't talk about it at all.'

'Really?' says Suze. 'Well . . . OK. If you're sure that's what you want.'

'That's what I want.' I take a deep breath. 'Really. I'm fine. So, how are *you*?'

'I'm OK,' says Suze, and gives me another anxious look. 'Bex, you look really pale. Have you eaten anything?'

'Aeroplane food. You know.' I take off my coat with trembling fingers and hang it on a peg.

'Was the . . . the flight OK?' says Suze.

'It was great!' I say with a forced brightness. 'They were showing the new Billy Crystal film.'

'Billy Crystal!' says Suze. She gives me a hesitant glance, as though I'm some psychotic patient who has to be handled carefully. 'Was it a . . . a good film? I love Billy Crystal.'

'Yes it was. It was a good film. I was really enjoying it, actually.' I swallow hard. 'Until my earphones stopped working in the middle.'

'Oh dear!' says Suze.

'It was a really crucial bit. Everyone else on the plane was laughing away – and I couldn't hear anything.' My voice starts to wobble treacherously. 'So I . . . I asked this stewardess if I could have some new earphones. But she didn't understand what I meant, and she got really ratty with me because she was trying to serve drinks . . . And then I didn't want to ask her again. So I don't quite know how the film finished. But apart from that, it was really good . . .' Suddenly I give a huge sob. 'And you know, I can always get it out on video or something . . .'

'Bex!' Suze's face crumples in dismay and she drops the Clinique bottles on the floor. 'Oh God, Bex. Come here.' She envelops me in a hug, and I bury my head in her shoulder.

'Oh, it's all awful,' I weep. 'It was just so humiliating, Suze. Luke was so cross . . . and they cancelled my screen test . . . and suddenly it was like . . . like I had some infectious disease or something. And now nobody wants to know me, and I'm not going to move to New York after all . . .'

I look up, wiping my eyes – and Suze's face is all pink and distressed.

'Bex, I feel so bad,' she exclaims.

'*You* feel bad? Why should you feel bad?'

'It's all my fault. I was such a moron! I let that girl from the paper in here, and she probably poked about when I was making her cup of stupid coffee. I mean, why did I have to offer her coffee? It's all my stupid fault.'

'Of course it's not!'

'Will you ever forgive me?'

'Will I ever forgive *you*?' I stare at her, my face quivering. 'Suze . . . I should be asking you to forgive *me*! You tried to keep tabs on me. You tried to warn me, but I didn't even bother to call you back . . . I was just so . . . stupid, so *thoughtless* . . .'

'No you weren't!'

'I was.' I give another huge sob. 'I just don't know what happened to me in New York. I went mad. Just . . . the shops, all these meetings . . . it was all so exciting . . . I was going to be this huge star and earn loads of money . . . And then it all just disappeared.'

'Oh Bex!' Suze is practically crying herself. 'I feel so terrible!'

'It's not your fault!' I reach for a tissue and blow my nose. 'If it's anyone's fault, it's the *Daily World*'s.'

'I *hate* them!' says Suze savagely. 'They should be strung up and flogged. That's what Tarkie said.'

'Oh right,' I say after a pause. 'So . . . he . . . he saw it, did he?'

'To be honest, Bex – I think most people saw it,' says Suze reluctantly.

I feel a painful lurch as I think about Janice and Martin reading it. About Tom and Lucy reading it. All my old schoolfriends and teachers reading it. All the people I've ever known, reading my most humiliating secrets.

'Look, come on,' says Suze. 'Leave all your stuff. Let's have a nice cup of tea.'

'OK,' I say after a pause. 'That would be really nice.' I follow her into the kitchen and sit down, leaning against the warm radiator for comfort.

'So – how are things going with Luke now?' says Suze cautiously as she puts on the kettle.

'Not great.' I fold my arms tightly round myself. 'In fact, it's not going at all.'

'Really?' Suze gazes at me in dismay. 'God, Bex, what happened?'

'Well, we had this big row . . .'

'About the article?'

'Kind of.' I reach for a tissue and blow my nose. 'He said it messed up his deal, and I was obsessed by shopping. And I said he was obsessed with work, and I said his mother was a . . . a complete cow . . .'

'You called his mother a *cow*?' Suze looks so taken aback, I give a shaky giggle.

'Well, she is! She's awful. And she doesn't even love Luke. But he can't see it . . . all he wants is to land the biggest deal in the world and impress her. He can't think about anything else but that.'

'So what happened then?' says Suze, handing me a mug of tea.

I bite my lip, remembering that last, painful conversation we had, while I was waiting for the taxi to take me to the airport. The polite stilted voices; the way we didn't look each other in the eye.

'Before I left, I said I didn't think he had time for a proper relationship at the moment.'

'Really?' Suze's eyes widen. 'You called it off?'

'I didn't mean to.' My voice is barely above a whisper. 'I wanted him to say he *did* have time. But he didn't say anything. It was . . . awful.'

'Oh Bex.' Suze stares at me over her mug. 'Oh Bex.'

'Still, never mind,' I say, trying to sound upbeat. 'It's

probably all for the best.' I take a sip of tea and close my eyes. 'Oh God, that's good. That's *so* good.' For a while I'm silent, letting the steam warm my face; feeling myself relax. I take a few more sips, then open my eyes. 'They just cannot make tea in America. I went to one place, and they gave me this . . . cup full of hot water, and a teabag in a packet. And the cup was *see-through*.'

'Oooh.' Suze pulls a face. 'Yuck.' She reaches for the tin of biscuits and takes out a couple of Hob-nobs. 'Who needs America, anyway?' she says robustly. 'I mean, everyone knows American TV is rubbish. You're better off here.'

'Maybe I am.' I stare into my mug for a while, then take a deep breath and look up. 'You know, I thought a lot on the plane. I decided I'm going to make this a real turning point in my life. I'm going to concentrate on my career, and finish my book, and be really focused – and just . . .'

'Show them,' finishes Suze.

'Exactly. Just show them.'

It's amazing what a bit of home comfort does for the spirit. Half an hour and three cups of tea later, I'm feeling a million times better. I'm even quite enjoying telling Suze about New York, and all the things I did. When I tell her about going to the spa, and where exactly they wanted to put a crystal tattoo, she starts laughing so hard she almost chokes.

'Hey,' I say, a sudden thought striking me. 'Have you finished the KitKats?'

'No, I haven't,' says Suze, wiping her eyes. 'They seem to go more slowly when you're not around. So, what did Luke's mum say? Did she want to see the results?' And she starts gurgling with laughter again.

'Hang on, I'll just get a couple,' I say, and start to head towards Suze's room, where they're kept.

'Actually – ' says Suze, and her laughter abruptly stops. 'No, don't go in there.'

'Why?' I say, stopping in surprise. 'What's in your . . .' I tail off as Suze's cheeks slowly turn pink. 'Suze!' I say, backing quietly away from the door. 'No. Is there someone in there?'

I stare at her, and she pulls her dressing gown around her defensively, without saying anything.

'I don't believe it!' My voice squeaks incredulously. 'God, I go away for five minutes and you start having a torrid affair!'

This is cheering me up more than anything else. There's nothing like hearing a juicy piece of gossip to raise your spirits.

'It's not a torrid affair!' says Suze at last. 'It's not an affair at all.'

'So, who is it? Do I know them?'

Suze gives me an agonized look.

'OK, just . . . I just have to explain. Before you . . . you jump to the wrong conclusion, or . . .' She closes her eyes. 'God, this is hard.'

'Suze, what's wrong?'

There's the sound of stirring from inside Suze's bedroom, and we stare at each other.

'OK, listen. It was just a one-off,' she says quickly. 'Just a really impetuous, stupid . . . I mean . . .'

'What's wrong, Suze?' I pull a face. 'Oh, God, it's not Nick, is it?'

Nick is Suze's last boyfriend – the one who was constantly depressed and getting drunk and blaming Suze. A complete nightmare, to be honest. But I mean, that was over months ago.

'No, it's not Nick. It's . . . Oh God.'

'Suze—'

'OK! But you have to promise to—'

'To what?'

'To not . . . react.'

267

'Why should I react?' I say, laughing a little. 'I mean, I'm not a prude! All we're talking about is . . .'

I tail off as Suze's door opens – and it's only Tarquin, looking not at all bad, in chinos and the jumper I gave him.

'Oh,' I say in surprise. 'I thought you were going to be Suze's new—'

I break off and look at Suze with a grin.

But she doesn't grin back. She's chewing her nails, avoiding my eyes – and her cheeks are growing redder and redder.

I glance at Tarquin – and *he* looks away, too.

No. *No*.

She can't mean—

No.

But . . .

No.

My brain can't cope with this. Something's about to short-circuit.

'Erm, Tarquin,' says Suze, in a high-pitched voice. 'Could you go and buy some croissants?'

'Oh, ahm . . . OK,' says Tarquin, a little stiltedly. 'Morning, Becky.'

'Morning!' I say. 'Nice to . . . to see you. Nice . . . jumper.'

There's a frozen silence in the kitchen as he walks out, which remains until we hear the front door slam. Then, very slowly, I turn to face Suze.

'Suze . . .'

I don't even know how to begin.

'Suze . . . that was Tarquin.'

'Yes, I know,' she says, studying the kitchen counter intently.

'Suze . . . are you and Tarquin—'

'No!' she exclaims, as though she's been scalded. 'No, of course not! It's just . . . we just . . .' She stops.

'You just . . .' I say encouragingly.

268

'Once or twice . . .'

There's a long pause.

'With Tarquin,' I say, just to make sure.

'Yes,' she says.

'Right,' I say, nodding as though this is a completely reasonable scenario. But my mouth is twitching and I can feel a strange pressure rising inside me – half shock, half hysterical laughter. I mean, Tarquin. *Tarquin!*

A giggle escapes from me and I clamp my hand over my mouth.

'Don't laugh!' wails Suze. 'I knew you'd laugh!'

'I'm not laughing!' I protest, 'I think it's great!' I give another snort of laughter, and try to pretend I'm coughing. 'Sorry! Sorry. So – how did it happen?'

'It was at that party in Scotland!' she wails. 'There was no-one else there except loads of ancient aunts. Tarquin was the only other person under ninety. And somehow . . . he looked all different! He had on this really nice Paul Smith jersey, and his hair looked kind of cool – and it was like, is that really Tarquin? And I got quite pissed – and you know what that does to me. And there he was . . .' She shakes her head helplessly. 'I don't know. He was just . . . transformed. God knows how it happened!'

There's silence. Now I can feel my cheeks growing redder.

'You know what, Suze,' I admit sheepishly at last. 'I think it kind of might have been . . . my fault.'

'*Your* fault?' She raises her head and stares at me. 'How come?'

'I gave him the jumper. And the hairstyle.' I flinch at her expression. 'But I mean, I had no idea it would lead to . . . to this! All I did was give him a look!'

'Well, you've got a lot to answer for!' cries Suze. 'I've been so stressed. I just keep thinking, I must be a complete pervert.'

269

'Why?' I say, my eyes brightening. 'What does he get you to do?'

'No, silly! Because we're cousins.'

'Ooooh.' I pull a face – then realize that isn't exactly tactful. 'But I mean, it's not against the law, or anything, is it?'

'Oh God, Bex!' wails Suze. 'That really makes me feel better.'

She picks up her mug and mine, takes them over to the sink, and starts to run the tap.

'I just can't believe you're having a relationship with Tarquin,' I say.

'We're not having a relationship!' squeals Suze. 'That's the point. Last night was the very last time. We're both completely agreed. It'll never happen again. *Never*. And you mustn't tell anyone.'

'I won't.'

'No, I'm serious, Bex. You mustn't tell anyone. No-one!'

'I won't! I promise. In fact,' I say, having a sudden idea, 'I've got something for you.'

I hurry into the hall, open one of my suitcases and scrabble for the Kate's Paperie carrier bag. I pluck a card from the pile, scribble 'To Suze, love Bex', inside, and return to the kitchen, sticking down the envelope.

'Is this for me?' says Suze in surprise. 'What is it?'

'Open it!'

She tears it open, looks at the picture of a glossy, zipped-up pair of lips, and reads aloud the printed message:

Roomie – your secret's safe with me.

'Wow!' she says, wide-eyed. 'That's so cool! Did you buy it especially? But I mean . . .' She frowns. 'How did you know I'd have a secret?'

'Er . . . just a hunch,' I say. 'Sixth sense.'

270

'You know, Bex, that reminds me,' says Suze, flipping the envelope back and forth in her fingers. 'You got quite a lot of post while you were away.'

'Oh, right.'

In the astonishment of hearing about Suze and Tarquin, I'd kind of forgotten about everything else. But now the hysteria which has been lifting my spirits starts to evaporate. As Suze brings over a pile of unfriendly-looking envelopes, my stomach gives a nasty flip, and I wish I'd never come home. At least while I was away, I didn't have to know about any of this.

'Right,' I say, trying to sound nonchalant and on top of things. I leaf through the letters without really looking at them – then put them down. 'I'll look at them later. When I can give them my full attention.'

'Bex . . .' Suze pulls a face. 'I think you'd better open this one now.' She reaches for the pile and pulls out a brown envelope with the word SUMMONS on the front.

I stare at it, feeling hot and cold. A summons. It was true. I've been summonsed. I take the envelope from Suze, unable to meet her eye, and rip it open with shaking fingers. I scan the letter without saying anything, feeling a coldness growing at the base of my spine. I can't quite believe people would actually take me to court. I mean, court is for criminals. Like drug dealers and murderers. Not for people who just don't pay a couple of bills.

I stuff the letter back into its envelope and put it on the counter, breathing hard.

'Bex . . . what are you going to do?' says Suze, biting her lip. 'You can't just ignore that one.'

'I won't. I'll pay them.'

'But can you afford to pay them?'

'I'll have to.'

There's silence, apart from the drip-drip of the cold water tap in the sink. I look up, to see Suze's face contorted with worry.

271

'Bex – let me give you some money. Or Tarkie will. He can easily afford it.'

'No!' I say, more sharply than I'd intended. 'No, I don't want any help. I'll just . . .' I rub my face. 'I'll go and see the guy at the bank. Today. Right now.'

With a surge of determination I scoop up the pile of letters and head to my room. I'm not going to let all this defeat me. I'm going to wash my face, and put on some makeup, and get my life back in order.

'What will you say?' says Suze, following me down the corridor.

'I'll explain the situation to him honestly, and ask him for a bigger overdraft . . . and take it from there. I'm going to be independent and strong, and stand on my own two feet.'

'Good for you, Bex!' says Suze. 'That's really fantastic. Independent and strong. That's really great!' She watches as I try to open my suitcase with shaking fingers. As I struggle with the clasp for the third time, she comes over and puts a hand on my arm. 'Bex – would you like me to come too?'

'Yes please,' I say in a small voice.

Suze won't let me go anywhere until I've sat down and had a couple of brandies for Dutch courage. Then she tells me how she read an article the other day which said your best negotiating weapon is your appearance – so I must choose my outfit for seeing John Gavin very carefully. We go right through my wardrobe and end up with a plain black skirt and grey cardigan which I reckon shouts 'frugal, sober and steady'. Then she has to choose her own 'sensible, supportive friend' outfit (navy trousers and a white shirt). And we're almost ready to go when Suze decides that if nothing else works, we might have to flirt outrageously with him, so we both change into sexy underwear. Then I look at myself in the mirror and suddenly decide I look too

drab. So I quickly change into a pale pink cardigan –
which means changing my lipstick.

At last we get out of the house and arrive at the
Fulham branch of Endwich Bank. As we go in, Derek
Smeath's old assistant, Erica Parnell, is showing out a
middle-aged couple. Between you and me, she and I
have never exactly got on. I don't think she can be quite
human – she's been wearing exactly the same navy
blue shoes every time I've seen her.

'Oh, hello,' she says, shooting me a look of dislike.
'What do you want?'

'I'd like to see John Gavin, please,' I say, trying to
sound matter-of-fact. 'Is he available?'

'I shouldn't think so,' she says coldly. 'Not without
notice.'

'Well . . . could you possibly just check?'

Erica Parnell rolls her eyes.

'Wait there,' she says and disappears behind a door
marked 'Private'.

'God, they're horrible here!' says Suze, lolling against
a glass partition. 'When I go to see my bank manager he
gives me a glass of sherry and asks me about all the
family. You know, Bex, I really think you should move
to Coutts.'

'Yes well,' I say. 'Maybe.'

I'm feeling slightly jittery as I leaf through a pile
of insurance brochures. I'm remembering what Derek
Smeath said about John Gavin being rigorous and
inflexible. Oh God, I miss old Smeathie.

Oh God, I miss Luke.

The feeling hits me like a hammer blow. Since I got
back from New York I've been trying not to think about
him at all. But as I stand here, all I wish is that I could
talk to him. I wish I could see him looking at me like
he used to before everything went wrong. With that
quizzical little smile on his face, and his arms wrapped
tightly around me.

I wonder what he's doing now. I wonder how his meetings are going.

'Come this way,' says Erica Parnell's voice, and my head jerks up. Feeling sick, I follow her down a blue-carpeted corridor, into a chilly little room furnished with a table and plastic chairs. As the door closes behind her, Suze and I look at each other.

'Shall we run away?' I say, only half joking.

'It's going to be fine,' says Suze. 'He'll probably turn out to be really nice! You know, my parents once had this gardener, and he seemed really grumpy – but then we found out he had a pet rabbit! And it was like, he was a completely different—'

She breaks off as the door swings open and in strides a guy of about thirty. He's got thinning dark hair, is wearing a rather nasty suit and is holding a plastic cup of coffee.

Oh God, he doesn't look as though he's got a friendly bone in his body. Suddenly I wish we hadn't come.

'Right,' he says with a frown. 'I haven't got all day. Which of you is Rebecca Bloomwood?'

The way he says it, it's like he's asking which one of us is the murderer.

'Erm . . . I am,' I say nervously.

'And who's this?'

'Suze is my—'

'People,' says Suze confidently. 'I'm her people.' She looks around the room. 'Do you have any sherry?'

'No,' says John Gavin, looking at her as though she's subnormal. 'I don't have any sherry. Now what's this about?'

'OK, first of all,' I say nervously, 'I've brought you something.' I reach into my bag and hand him another Kate's Paperie envelope.

It was my own idea to bring him a little something to break the ice. After all, it's only good manners. And in Japan, this is how business is done all the time.

'Is this a cheque?' says John Gavin.

'Erm . . . no,' I say, colouring slightly. 'It's a . . . a handmade card.'

John Gavin gives me a look, then rips the envelope open and pulls out a card printed in silver, with pink feathers glued to the corners.

Now I look at it, maybe I should have chosen a less girly one.

Or not brought one at all. But it seemed so perfect for the occasion.

'*Friend – I know I've made mistakes, but can we start over*?' John Gavin reads incredulously. He turns it over, as though suspecting a joke. 'Did you *buy* this?'

'It's nice, isn't it!' says Suze. 'You get them in New York.'

'I see. I'll bear that in mind.' He puts it up on the table and we all look at it. 'Miss Bloomwood, why exactly are you here?'

'Right!' I say. 'Well. As my greetings card states, I'm aware that I have – ' I swallow – 'perhaps not been the perfect . . . ideal customer. However, I'm confident that we can work together as a team, and achieve harmony.'

So far, so good. I learned that bit off by heart.

'Which means?' says John Gavin. I clear my throat.

'Um . . . due to circumstances beyond my control, I have recently found myself in a slight financial . . . situation. So I was wondering whether you could perhaps temporarily . . .'

'Very kindly . . .' puts in Suze.

'Very kindly . . . perhaps extend my overdraft a little further, on a . . . a short-term . . .'

'Goodwill,' interjects Suze.

'Goodwill . . . temporary . . . short-term basis. Obviously to be paid back as soon as is feasibly and humanly possible.' I stop, and draw breath.

'Have you finished?' says John Gavin, folding his arms.

'Erm . . . yes.' I look to Suze for confirmation. 'Yes, we have.'

There's silence while John Gavin drums his biro on the table. Then he looks up and says, 'No.'

'No?' I look at him, puzzled. 'Is that just . . . no?'

'Just no.' He pushes back his chair. 'So if you'll excuse me—'

'What do you mean, no?' says Suze. 'You can't just say no! You have to weigh up the pros and cons.'

'I have weighed up the pros and the cons,' says John Gavin. 'There are no pros.'

'But this is one of your most valued customers!' Suze's voice rises in dismay. 'This is Becky Bloomwood of TV fame, who has a huge, glittering career in front of her!'

'This is Becky Bloomwood who has had her overdraft limit extended six times in the last year,' says John Gavin in a rather nasty voice. 'And who each time has failed to keep within those limits. This is Becky Bloomwood who has consistently lied, who has consistently avoided meetings, who has treated bank staff with little or no respect, and who seems to think we're all here solely to fund her appetite for shoes. I've looked at your file, Miss Bloomwood. I know the picture.'

There's a subdued little silence. I can feel my cheeks getting hotter and hotter and I've got a horrible feeling I might cry.

'I don't think you should be so mean!' says Suze in a burst. 'Becky's just had a really awful time. Would *you* like to be in the tabloids? Would *you* like to have someone stalking you?'

'Oh, I see.' His voice glints with sarcasm. 'You expect me to feel sorry for you!'

'Yes!' I say. 'No. Not exactly. But I think you should give me a chance.'

'You think I should give you another chance. And

what have you done to *merit* another chance?' He shakes his head, and there's silence.

'I just . . . I thought if I explained it all to you . . .' I tail off feebly and shoot Suze a hopeless look to say: Let's just forget it.

'Hey, is it hot in here?' says Suze in a sudden husky voice. She takes off her jacket, shakes back her hair and runs one hand down her cheek. 'I'm feeling really . . . hot. Are you feeling hot, John?'

John Gavin shoots her an irritated look.

'What precisely did you want to explain to me, Miss Bloomwood?'

'Well. Just that I really want to sort things out,' I say, my voice trembling. 'You know, I want to turn things around. I want to stand on my own two feet, and—'

'Stand on your own two feet?' interrupts John Gavin scathingly. 'You call taking handouts from a bank "standing on your own two feet"? If you were really standing on your own two feet, you'd have no overdraft. You'd have a few *assets* by now! You, of all people, shouldn't need telling that.'

'I . . . I know,' I say, my voice barely above a whisper. 'But the fact is, I have got an overdraft. And I just thought—'

'You thought what? That you're special? That you're an exception because you're on the television? That the normal rules don't apply to you? That this bank *owes* you money?'

His voice is like a drill in my head and suddenly I feel myself snap.

'No!' I cry. 'I don't think that. I don't think any of that. I know I've been stupid, and I know I've gone wrong. But I think that everyone goes wrong occasionally.' I take a deep breath. 'You know, if you look at your files, you'll see I *did* pay off my overdraft. And I *did* pay off my store cards. And OK, I'm in debt again. But I'm trying to sort it out – and all you can do is . . .

is sneer. Well, fine. I'll sort myself without your help. Come on, Suze.'

Shaking slightly, I get to my feet. My eyes are hot, but I'm *not* going to cry in front of him. There's a shaft of determination inside me, which strengthens as I turn to face him.

'Endwich – because we care,' I say.

There's a long, tense silence. Then, without saying anything else, I open the door and walk out.

As we walk home, I feel almost high with determination. I'll show him. I'll show that John Gavin. And all of them. The whole world.

I'm going to pay off my debts. I don't know how – but I'm going to do it. I'll take an extra job waitressing, maybe. Or I'll get down to it, and finish my self-help book. I'll just make as much money as I can, as quickly as I can. And then I'll go into that bank with a huge cheque, and plonk it down in front of him, and in a dignified but pointed voice, I'll say—

'Bex?' Suze grabs my arm, and I see that I'm walking straight past our house.

'Are you OK?' says Suze as she lets us in. 'Honestly, what a bastard.'

'I'm fine,' I say, lifting my chin. 'I'm going to show him. I'm going to pay off my overdraft. Just wait. I'm going to show them all.'

'Excellent!' says Suze. She bends down and picks up a letter from the doormat. 'It's for you,' she says. 'From *Morning Coffee*.'

'Oh right!' As I'm opening the envelope, I feel a huge leap of hope. Maybe they're offering me a new job. Something with a huge salary, enough to pay off my debts straight away. Maybe they've sacked Emma and I'm going to take her place as the main presenter! Or maybe . . .

Oh my God. Oh my God, no.

MORNING COFFEE
East-West Television
Corner House
London NW8 4DW

Ms Rebecca Bloomwood
Flat 2
4 Burney Rd
London SW6 8FD

Dear Becky

First of all, bad luck on your recent unfortunate bout of publicity! I really felt for you, and I know I also speak for Rory, Emma and all the rest of the team.

As you know, the Morning Coffee family is a fiercely loyal and supportive one, and it is our policy never to allow adverse publicity to stand in the way of talent. However, completely coincidentally, we have recently been reviewing all our regular contributors. Following some discussion, we have decided to rest you from your slot for a while.

I must emphasize that this is just a temporary measure. However, we would appreciate it if you would return your East-West TV pass in the envelope provided and also sign the enclosed release document.

The work you've done for us has been fabulous (obviously!) We just know that your talents will flourish elsewhere and that this will not prove a set-back to someone as dynamic as yourself!

With very best wishes

Zelda Washington
Assistant Producer

Paradigm Self-help Books Ltd
695 Soho Square
London W1 5AS

Ms Rebecca Bloomwood
Flat 2
4 Burney Rd
London SW6 8FD

Dear Becky

Thank you very much for your first draft of *Manage Money the Bloomwood Way*. We appreciated the care that had gone into your work. Your writing is pacy and fluent, and you certainly made some interesting points.

Unfortunately, 500 words – however excellent they are – is not quite enough for a self-help book. Your suggestion that we could 'pad out the rest with photographs' is unfortunately not really workable.

Sadly, we have therefore decided that this is not a viable project and, as a result, would request that you return our advance forthwith.

With all best wishes

Pippa Brady
Editor

PARADIGM BOOKS: HELPING YOU TO HELP YOURSELF

OUT NOW! *Jungle Survival* by Brig. Roger Flintwood (deceased)

Fifteen

For the next few days, I don't leave the house. I don't answer the phone and I don't talk to anyone. I feel physically raw, as though people's gazes, or their questions, or even the sunlight, might hurt me. I need to be in a dark place, on my own. Suze has gone to Milton Keynes for a big sales and marketing conference with Hadleys, so I'm all alone in the flat. I order takeaway, drink two bottles of white wine, and don't once get out of my pyjamas.

When Suze arrives back, I'm sitting on the floor where she left me, staring blankly at the television, stuffing KitKats into my mouth.

'Oh God,' she says, dropping her bag on the floor. 'Bex, are you OK? I shouldn't have left you on your own.'

'I'm fine!' I say, looking up and forcing my stiff face to twist into a smile. 'How was the sales conference?'

'Well, it was really good, actually,' says Suze, looking abashed. 'People kept congratulating me on the way my frames have been selling. They'd all heard of me! And they did a presentation of my new designs, and everybody loved them . . .'

'That's really great, Suze,' I say, and reach up to squeeze her hand. 'You deserve it.'

'Well. You know.' She bites her lip – then comes into the room, picks up an empty wine bottle from the floor and puts it on the table.

'So, did . . . Luke call?' she says hesitantly.

'No,' I say, after a long silence. 'No, he didn't.' I look at Suze, then look away again.

'What are you watching?' she says, as an ad for Diet Coke comes on.

'I'm watching *Morning Coffee*,' I reply. 'It's the financial advice slot coming up next.'

'What?' Suze's face creases in dismay. 'Bex, let's turn over.' She reaches for the remote control, but I grab it.

'No!' I say, staring rigidly at the screen. 'I want to see it.'

The familiar *Morning Coffee* music blasts out of the screen as the signature graphic of a cup of coffee appears, and then melts away to a studio shot.

'Hello!' says Emma cheerily to camera. 'Welcome back. And it's time for us to introduce our new money expert, Clare Edwards!'

'Who's Clare Edwards?' says Suze, staring at the screen in distaste.

'I used to work with her on *Successful Saving*,' I say without moving my head. 'She used to sit next to me.'

The camera pans away to show Clare sitting on the sofa opposite Emma, staring grimly back.

'She doesn't look much fun,' says Suze.

'She isn't.'

'So Clare,' says Emma brightly. 'What's your basic philosophy of money?'

'Do you have a catchphrase?' interjects Rory cheerfully.

'I don't believe in catchphrases,' says Clare, giving Rory a disapproving look. 'Personal finance isn't a trivial matter.'

'Right!' says Rory. 'Of course not. Erm . . . so – do you have any top tips for savers, Clare?'

'I don't believe in futile and misleading generalizations,' says Clare. 'All savers should choose a spread of investments suitable to their individual requirements and tax status.'

'Absolutely!' says Emma after a pause. 'Right. Well – let's go to the phones, shall we? And it's Mandy from Norwich.'

As the first caller is put through, the phone in our sitting room rings.

'Hello?' says Suze, picking it up and zapping the sound on the television. 'Ooh, hello, Mrs Bloomwood. Do you want to speak to Becky?'

She raises her eyebrows at me and I wince back. I've only spoken to Mum and Dad briefly since my return. They know I'm not going to move to New York any more – but that's all I've said to them so far. I just can't face telling them how badly everything else has turned out too.

'Becky, love, I was just watching *Morning Coffee*!' exclaims Mum. 'What's that girl doing, giving out financial advice?'

'It's . . . it's OK, Mum, don't worry!' I say, feeling my nails dig into my palm. 'They just . . . they got her to cover while I was away.'

'Well. They could have chosen someone better! She's got a miserable face on her, hasn't she?' Her voice goes muffled. 'What's that, Graham? Dad says, at least she shows up how good *you* are! But surely, now you're back, they can let her go?'

'I don't think it's as simple as that,' I say after a pause. 'Contracts and . . . things.'

'So, when will you be back on? Because I know Janice will be asking.'

'I don't know, Mum,' I say desperately. 'Listen, I've got to go, OK? There's someone at the door. But I'll talk to you soon!'

I put down the phone and bury my head in my hands.

'What am I going to do?' I say hopelessly. 'What am I

283

going to do, Suze? I can't tell them I've been fired. I just can't.' To my dismay, I feel tears squeezing out of the sides of my eyes. 'They're so proud of me. And I just keep letting them down.'

'You don't let them down!' retorts Suze hotly. 'It wasn't your fault that stupid *Morning Coffee* completely over-reacted. And I bet they're regretting it now. I mean, *look* at her!'

She turns up the sound, and Clare's voice drones sternly through the room.

'Those who fail to provide for their own retirement are the equivalent of leeches on the rest of us.'

'I say,' says Rory. 'Isn't that a bit harsh?'

'I mean, listen to her,' says Suze. 'She's awful!'

'Maybe she is,' I say after a pause. 'But even if they get rid of her, too, they'll never ask me back. It would be like saying they made a mistake.'

'They have made a mistake!'

The phone rings again and she looks at me. 'Are you in or out?'

'Out. And you don't know when I'll be back.'

'OK . . .' She picks up the phone. 'Hello? Sorry, Becky's out at the moment.'

'Mandy, you've made every mistake possible,' Clare Edwards is saying on the screen. 'Have you never heard of a deposit account? And as for remortgaging your house to buy a boat . . .'

'No, I don't know when she'll be back,' says Suze. 'Would you like me to take a message?' She picks up a pen and starts writing. 'OK . . . fine . . . yes. Yes, I'll tell her. Thanks.'

'So,' I say as she puts the phone down. 'Who was that?'

And I know it's stupid – but as I look up at her, I can't help feeling a hot flicker of hope. Maybe it was a producer from another show. Maybe it was someone wanting to offer me my own column. Maybe it was

John Gavin, ringing to apologize and offer me free, unlimited overdraft facilities. Maybe everything will be all right.

'It was Mel. Luke's assistant.'

'Oh.' I stare at her in apprehension. 'What did she want?'

'Apparently some parcel has arrived at the office, addressed to you. From the States. From Barnes and Noble?'

I stare at her blankly – then, with a pang, suddenly remember that trip to Barnes and Noble I made with Luke. I bought a whole pile of coffee table books, and Luke suggested I send them back on the company courier bill instead of lugging them around. It seems like a million years ago now.

'Oh yes, I know what that is.' I hesitate. 'Did she . . . mention Luke?'

'No,' says Suze apologetically. 'She just said pop in any time you want. And she said she was really sorry about what happened . . . and if you ever want a chat, just call.'

'Right.' I hunch my shoulders, hug my knees, and turn up the television volume. 'OK.'

For the next few days, I tell myself I won't bother going. I don't really want those books any more. And I can't quite cope with the thought of having to go in there – having to face all the curious looks from Luke's staff, and hold my head up and pretend to be OK.

But after a while, I start to think I'd like to see Mel. She's the only one I can talk to who really knows Luke, and it would be nice to have a heart-to-heart with her. Plus, she might have heard something of what's going on in the States. I know Luke and I are effectively over, I know it's really nothing to do with me now. But I still can't help caring about whether he's got his deal or not.

So four days later, at about six o'clock in the evening,

I walk slowly towards the doors of Brandon Communications, my heart thumping. Luckily it's the friendly doorman on duty. He's seen me visit enough times to just wave me in, so I don't have to have any big announcements of my arrival.

I walk out of the lift at the fifth floor, and to my surprise, there's no-one on reception. How weird. I wait for a few seconds – then wander past the desk and down the main corridor. Gradually my steps slow down – and a frown comes to my face. There's something wrong here. Something different.

It's too quiet. The whole place is practically dead. When I look across the open plan space, most of the chairs are empty. There aren't any phones ringing, there aren't any people striding about; there aren't brainstorming sessions going on.

What's going on? What's happened to the buzzy Brandon C atmosphere? What's *happened* to Luke's company?

As I pass the coffee machine, two guys I half recognize are standing, talking by it. One's got a disgruntled expression and the other is agreeing – but I can't quite hear what they're talking about. As I come near, they stop abruptly. They shoot me curious looks, then glance at each other and walk off, before starting to talk again, but in lowered voices.

I can't quite believe this is Brandon Communications. There's a totally different feel about the place. This is like some deadbeat company where no-one cares about what they're doing. I walk to Mel's desk, but, along with everyone else, she's already left for the night. Mel, who normally stays till at least seven, then takes a glass of wine and gets changed in the loos for whatever great night out she's got planned.

I root around behind her chair until I find the parcel addressed to me, and scribble a note to her on a Post-It. Then I stand up, hugging the heavy package to me, and tell myself that I've got what I came for. Now I should leave. There's nothing to keep me.

But instead of walking away, I stand motionless. Staring at Luke's closed office door.

Luke's office. There are probably faxes from him in there. Messages about how things are going in New York. Maybe even messages about me. As I gaze at the smooth blank wood, I feel almost overwhelmed by an urge to go in and find out what I can.

But – what exactly would I do? Look through his files? Listen to his voice-mail? I mean, what if someone caught me?

I'm standing there, torn – knowing I'm not *really* going to go and rifle through his stuff, yet unable just to walk away – when suddenly I stiffen in shock. The handle of his office door is starting to move.

Oh shit. *Shit*. There's someone in there! They're coming out!

In a moment of pure panic, I duck down out of sight, behind Mel's chair. As I curl up into a tiny ball I feel a thrill of terror, like a child playing hide-and-seek. I hear voices murmuring, then the door swings open and someone comes out. From my vantage point, all I can see is that it's a female, and she's wearing those new Chanel shoes which cost an absolute bomb. She's followed by two pairs of male legs, and the three begin to walk down the corridor. I can't resist peeping out from behind the chair – and of course. It's Alicia Bitch Long-legs, with Ben Bridges and a man who looks familiar but whom I can't quite place.

Well, I suppose that's fair enough. She's in charge while Luke is away. But does she have to take over his office? I mean, why can't she just use a meeting room?

'Sorry we had to meet here,' I can hear her saying. 'Obviously, next time, it'll be at 17 King Street.'

They continue talking until they reach the lifts, and I pray desperately that they'll all get inside one and disappear. But as the lift doors ping open, only the familiar-looking man gets in – and a moment later, Alicia and Ben are heading back again.

'I'll just get those files,' says Alicia, and goes back into Luke's office, leaving the door open. Meanwhile, Ben is lolling against the water dispenser, pressing the buttons on his watch and staring intently at the tiny screen.

Oh God, this is horrendous! I'm trapped until they leave. My knees are starting to hurt and I've got an awful feeling that if I move an inch, one of them will crack. What if Ben and Alicia stay here all night? What if they come over to Mel's desk? What if they decide to *make love* on Mel's desk?

'OK,' says Alicia, appearing at the door. 'I think that's it. Good meeting, I thought.'

'I suppose.' Ben looks up from his watch. 'Do you think Frank's right? Do you think he might sue?'

Frank! Of course. That other man was Frank Harper. The publicity guy from Bank of London. I used to see him at press conferences.

'He won't sue,' says Alicia calmly. 'He's got too much face to lose.'

'He's lost a fair amount already,' says Ben, raising his eyebrows. 'He'll be the invisible man before too long.'

'True,' says Alicia, and smirks back at him. She looks at the pile of folders in her arms. 'Have I got everything? I think so. Right, I'm off, Ed will be waiting for me. See you tomorrow.'

They disappear down the corridor and this time, thank God, they get into a lift. When I'm quite sure they've gone, I sit back on my heels with a puzzled frown. What's going on? Why were they talking about suing? Suing who? And how come Bank of London were here?

Are Bank of London going to sue Luke?

For a while I just sit still, trying to work it all out. But

288

I'm not really getting anywhere – and suddenly it occurs to me that I ought to get out while the going's good. I get up, wincing at the cramp in my foot and shake out my legs as the circulation returns to them. Then I pick up my parcel and as nonchalantly as possible walk down the corridor towards the lifts. Just as I'm pressing the button, my mobile phone rings inside my bag, and I give a startled jump. Shit, my phone! Thank *God* that didn't happen while I was hiding behind Mel's desk!

'Hello?' I say, as I get into the lift.

'Bex! It's Suze.'

'Suze,' I say, and give a giggle. 'You have no idea how you nearly just got me in trouble! If you'd rung like, five minutes ago, you would have completely . . .'

'Bex, listen,' says Suze urgently. 'You've just had a call.'

'Oh right?' I press the ground-floor button. 'From who?'

'From Zelda at *Morning Coffee*! She wants to talk to you! She said, do you want to meet for a quick lunch tomorrow?'

That night, I barely get an hour's sleep. Suze and I stay up till late, deciding on what I should wear, and when I've gone to bed, I lie awake, staring at the ceiling, feeling my mind flip around like a fish. Will they offer me my old job back after all? Will they offer me a different job? Maybe they'll upgrade me! Maybe they'll give me my own show!

But by the early hours of the morning, all my wild fantasies have faded away, leaving the simple truth. The truth is, all I really want is my old job back. I want to be able to tell Mum to start watching again, and to start paying off my overdraft . . . and to start my life all over again. Another chance. That's all I want.

'You see?' says Suze the next morning as I'm getting ready. 'You see? I *knew* they'd want you back. That Clare Edwards is crap! Completely and utterly—'

'Suze,' I interrupt. 'How do I look?'

'Very good,' says Suze, looking me up and down approvingly. I'm wearing my black Banana Republic trousers and a pale fitted jacket over a white shirt, and a dark green scarf round my neck.

I would have worn my Denny and George scarf – in fact, I even picked it up from the dressing table. But then, almost immediately, I put it down again. I don't quite know why.

'Very kick-ass,' adds Suze. 'Where are you having lunch?'

'Lorenzo's?'

'*San Lorenzo?*' Her eyes widen impressively.

'No, I don't think so. Just . . . Lorenzo's. I've never been there before.'

'Well, you make sure you order champagne,' says Suze. 'And tell them you're fighting off loads of other offers, so if they want you to come back, they're going to have to pay big bucks. That's the deal, take it or leave it.'

'Right,' I say, unscrewing my mascara.

'If their margins suffer, then so be it,' says Suze emphatically. 'For a quality product you have to pay quality prices. You want to close the deal at *your* price, on *your* terms.'

'Suze . . .' I stop, mascara wand on my lashes. 'Where are you getting all this stuff?'

'What stuff?'

'All this . . . margins and close the deal stuff.'

'Oh, that! From the Hadleys conference. We had a seminar from one of the top sales people in the US. It was great! You know, a product is only as good as the person selling it.'

'If you say so.' I pick up my bag and check I've got

everything – then look up and say firmly, 'Right, I'm going.'

'Good luck!' says Suze. 'Except you know, there is no luck in business. There's only drive, determination, and more drive.'

'OK,' I say dubiously. 'I'll try to remember that.'

The address I've been given for Lorenzo's is a street in Soho, but when I turn into it, I can't see anything that looks obviously like a restaurant. It's mostly just office blocks, with a few little newsagenty-type shops, and a coffee shop, and a . . .

Hang on. I stop still and stare at the sign above the coffee shop. LORENZO'S COFFEE SHOP AND SANDWICH BAR.

But surely . . . this can't be where we're meeting?

'Becky!' My head jerks up, and I see Zelda walking along the street towards me, in jeans and a Puffa. 'You found it all right!'

'Yes,' I say, trying not to look discomfited. 'Yes, I found it.'

'You don't mind just a quick sandwich, do you?' she says, sweeping me inside. 'It's just that this place is quite convenient for me.'

'No! I mean . . . a sandwich would be great.'

'Good. I recommend the Italian chicken.' She eyes me up and down. 'You look very smart. Off somewhere nice?'

I stare at her, feeling a pang of mortification. I can't admit I dressed up specially to see her.

'Erm . . . yes.' I clear my throat. 'A . . . a meeting I've got later.'

'Oh well, I won't keep you long. Just a little proposition we wanted to put to you.' She shoots me a quick smile. 'We thought it would be nicer to do it face to face.'

This isn't exactly what I imagined for our power lunch. But as I watch the sandwich guy smoothing

Italian chicken onto our bread, adding salad and slicing each sandwich into four quarters, I start to feel more positive. OK, maybe this isn't a grand place with tablecloths and champagne. Maybe they aren't pushing the boat out. But then, that's probably good! It shows they still think of me as part of the team, doesn't it? Someone to have a relaxed sandwich with, and thrash out ideas for the forthcoming season.

Maybe they want to take me on board as a features consultant. Or train me to become a producer!

'We all felt for you dreadfully, Becky,' says Zelda as we make our way to a tiny wooden table, balancing our trays of sandwiches and drinks. 'How are things going? Have you got a job lined up in New York?'

'Um . . . not exactly,' I say, and take a sip of my mineral water. 'That's all kind of . . . on hold.' I see her watching me appraisingly, and quickly add, 'but I've been considering lots of offers. You know – various projects, and . . . and ideas in development . . .'

'Oh good! I'm so glad. We all felt very bad that you had to go. And I want you to know, it wasn't my decision.' She puts her hand on mine briefly, then removes it to take a bite of her sandwich. 'So now – to business.' I feel my stomach flutter with nerves. 'You remember our producer, Barry?'

'Of course I do!' I say, slightly taken aback. Are they expecting me to have forgotten the name of the producer, already?

'Well, he's come up with quite an interesting idea.' Zelda beams at me, and I beam back. 'He thinks the *Morning Coffee* viewers would be really interested to hear about your . . . little problem.'

'Right,' I say, feeling my smile freeze on my face. 'Well, it's . . . it's not really a—'

'And he thought perhaps you would be ideal to take part in a discussion and/or phone-in on the subject.' She takes a sip of smoothie. 'What do you think?'

I stare at her in confusion.

'Are you talking about me going back to my regular slot?'

'Oh no! I mean, we could hardly have you giving financial advice, could we?' She gives a little laugh. 'No, this would be more of a one-off, topical piece. "How shopping wrecked my life." That kind of thing.' She takes a bite of sandwich. 'And ideally, it would be quite a . . . how can I put this? An *emotional* piece. Maybe you could bare your soul a little. Talk about your parents, how this has ruined their lives too . . . problems in your childhood . . . relationship trouble . . . these are just ideas, obviously!' She looks up. 'And you know, if you were able to cry . . .'

'To . . . to cry?' I echo disbelievingly.

'It's not compulsory. By *any* means.' Zelda leans earnestly forward. 'We want this to be a good experience for you, too, Becky. We want to help. So we'd have Clare Edwards in the studio too, to offer you advice . . .'

'Clare Edwards?'

'Yes! You used to work with her, didn't you? That was why we thought of approaching her. And you know, she's quite a hit! She really tells the callers off. So we've decided to rename her Scary Clare and give her a whip to crack!'

She beams at me but I can't smile back. My whole face is prickling with shock and humiliation. I've never felt so belittled in my life.

'So what do you think?' she says, slurping at her smoothie.

I put down my sandwich, unable to take another bite. 'I'm afraid my answer's no.'

'Oh! There'd be a fee, of course!' she says. 'I should have mentioned that at the beginning.'

'Even so. I'm not interested.'

'Don't answer yet. Think about it!' Zelda flashes me a

cheery smile, then glances at her watch. 'I must dash, I'm afraid. But it's lovely to see you, Becky. And I'm *so* glad things are going well for you.'

After she's gone I sit still for a while, sipping at my mineral water. I'm outwardly calm – but inside I'm burning with mortified rage. They want me to go on and cry. That's all they want. One article in one crappy tabloid – and suddenly I'm not Becky Bloomwood, financial expert. I'm Becky Bloomwood, failure and flake. I'm Becky Bloomwood, watch her cry and pass the hankies.

Well they can just bloody well stuff their bloody hankies. They can just take their stupid, bloody . . . stupid . . . stupid . . . bloody . . .

'Are you all right?' says the man at the next table, and to my horror I realize I'm muttering aloud.

'I'm fine,' I say. 'Thanks.' I put down my glass and walk out of Lorenzo's, my head high and my chin stiff.

I walk down the road and turn a corner without even noticing where I'm going. I don't know the area and I don't have any place I need to get to – so I just walk, almost hypnotizing myself with the rhythm of my steps, thinking eventually I'll hit a tube station.

My eyes start to smart and I tell myself it's the cold air. It's the wind. I shove my hands in my pockets and tighten my chin and start to walk faster, trying to keep my mind empty. But there's a blank dread inside me; a hollow panic which is getting worse and worse. I haven't got my job back. I haven't even got the prospect of a job. What am I going to say to Suze? What am I going to say to Mum?

What am I going to do with my life?

'Oy! Watch out!' yells someone behind me – and to my horror I find I've stepped off the pavement in front of a cyclist.

'Sorry,' I say in a husky voice as the cyclist swerves

off, shooting me a V-sign. Oh God, this is ridiculous. I've got to pull myself together. I mean, where am I, for a start? I walk more slowly along the pavement, peering up at the glass doors of offices, looking for the name of the road. And I'm just about to ask a traffic warden when suddenly I see a sign. King Street.

For a moment I stare at it blankly, wondering why it's chiming a bell inside my head. Then, with a jolt, I remember. 17 King Street. Alicia.

The number embossed on the glass doors nearest me is 23. Which means . . . I must have just walked past number 17.

Now I'm completely consumed by curiosity. What on earth goes on at 17 King Street? Why was Alicia talking about meeting there? Is it some secret cult, or something? God, it wouldn't surprise me if she was a witch in her spare time.

My whole body is prickling with intrigue as I retrace my steps until I'm standing outside a modest set of double doors marked 17. It's obviously a building with lots of different little companies inside, but as I run my eye down the list, none sounds familiar.

'Hi!' says a bloke in a denim jacket, holding a cup of coffee. He comes up to the doors, presses a code into the keypad and pushes the door open. 'You look lost. Who are you after?'

'I'm not sure actually,' I say hesitantly. 'I thought I knew somebody who worked here, but I can't remember the name of the company.'

'What's her name?'

'It's . . . it's Alicia,' I say – then immediately wish I hadn't. What if this guy knows Alicia? What if she's in there somewhere and he goes and fetches her?

But he's frowning. 'I don't know an Alicia. Mind you, there's a few new faces around at the moment . . . What sort of business is she in?'

'PR,' I say after a pause.

'PR? We're mostly graphic design, here . . .' Suddenly his face clears. 'Hey, but maybe she's with the new company. B and B? BBB? Something like that. They haven't started trading yet, so we haven't met them.' He takes a sip of cappuccino and I stare at him. My mind is starting to twitch.

'A new PR company? Based here?'

'As far as I know, yes. They've taken a big space on the second floor.'

Thoughts are sparking round my head like fireworks.

B and B. Bridges and Billington. Billington and Bridges.

'Do you . . .' I try to keep calm. 'Do you know what sort of PR?'

'Ah! Now, this I *do* know. It's financial. Apparently one of their biggest clients is Bank of London. Or will be. Which must be a nice little earner. But as I say, we haven't met them yet, so . . .' He looks at me and his face changes expression. 'Hey. Are you OK?'

'I'm fine,' I manage. 'I think. I just have to . . . I have to make a phone call.'

I dial the number of the Four Seasons three times – and each time hang up before I can bring myself to ask for Luke Brandon. At last I take a deep breath, dial the number again, and ask to speak to Michael Ellis.

'Michael, it's Becky Bloomwood here,' I say when I'm put through.

'Becky!' he says, sounding genuinely pleased to hear from me. 'How are you doing?'

I close my eyes, trying to keep calm. The sound of his voice has taken me back to the Four Seasons with a whoosh. Back to that dim, expensive lobby. Back to that New York dreamworld.

'I . . .' I take a deep breath. 'I'm fine. You know . . . back to normal life. Busy, busy!'

I'm not going to admit I've lost my job. I'm not going to have everyone feeling sorry for me.

'I'm just on my way to the studio,' I say, crossing my fingers. 'But I wanted a quick word. I think I know why there's a rumour going around that Luke's going to lose Bank of London.'

I tell him exactly what I overheard in the office, how I went to King Street, and what I've discovered.

'I see,' says Michael at intervals, sounding grim. 'I see. You know there's a clause in their contracts forbidding employees to do this? If they poach a client, Luke could sue them.'

'They talked about that. They seem to think he won't sue because he'd lose too much face.'

There's silence. I can almost hear Michael thinking down the line.

'They have a point,' he says at last. 'Becky, I have to talk to Luke. You did a great job finding out what you did.'

'That's not the only thing,' I say. 'Michael, someone's got to talk to Luke. I went into the Brandon Communications office, and it was completely dead. No-one's making any effort, everyone's going home early . . . it's a whole different atmosphere. It's not good.' I bite my lip. 'He needs to come home.'

'Why don't you tell him this yourself?' says Michael gently. 'I'm sure he'd like to hear from you.'

He sounds so kind and concerned, I feel a sudden prickle in my nose.

'I can't. If I ring him up, he'll just think . . . he'll think I'm trying to prove some point, or it's just some more stupid gossip—' I break off, and swallow hard. 'To be honest, Michael, I'd rather you just kept me out of it. Pretend someone else spoke to you. But someone's got to tell him.'

'I'm seeing him in half an hour,' Michael says. 'I'll talk to him then. And Becky . . . well done.'

Sixteen

After a week, I give up on hearing anything from Michael. Whatever he's said to Luke, I'm never going to find out about it. I feel as though that whole part of my life is over. Luke, America, television, everything. Time to start again.

I'm trying to keep positive, and tell myself I've lots of avenues open to me. But what *is* the next career move for an ex-television financial expert? I rang up a television agent, and to my dismay, she sounded exactly like all those TV people in America. She said she was thrilled to hear from me, she'd have absolutely no problem finding me work – if not my own series – and that she'd ring back that day with lots of exciting news. I haven't heard from her since.

So now I'm reduced to looking through the Media *Guardian*, looking for jobs I might just have half a chance of getting. So far, I've ringed a staff writer job on *Investor's Chronicle*, an assistant editorship of *Personal Investment Periodical*, and editor of *Annuities Today*. I don't know much about annuities, but I can always make it up.

'How are you doing?' says Suze, coming into the room with a bowl of Crunchy Nut Cornflakes.

'Fine,' I say, trying to raise a smile. 'I'll get there.' Suze takes a mouthful of cornflakes and eyes me thoughtfully.

'What have you got planned for today?'

'Nothing much,' I say morosely. 'You know – just trying to get a job. Sort out my mess of a life. That kind of thing.'

'Oh right.' Suze pulls a sympathetic face. 'Have you found anything interesting yet?'

I flick my fingers towards a ringed advertisement.

'I thought I'd go for editor of *Annuities Today*. The right candidate may also be considered for editorship of the annual Tax Rebate supplement!'

'Really?' She involuntarily pulls a face, then hastily adds, 'I mean . . . that sounds good! Really interesting!'

'Tax rebates? Suze, please.'

'Well – you know. Relatively speaking.'

I rest my head on my knees and stare at the sitting-room carpet. The sound on the television has been turned down, and there's silence in the room apart from Suze munching.

'Suze . . . what if I can't get a job?' I say in a rush.

'You'll get a job! Don't be silly! You're a TV star!'

'I *was* a TV star. Until I ruined it all. Until my life fell to pieces.'

I close my eyes and slump down further on the floor, until my head's resting on the sofa seat. I feel as though I could stay here for the rest of my life.

'Bex, I'm worried about you,' says Suze. 'You haven't been out for days. What else are you planning to do today?'

I open my eyes briefly and see her peering anxiously down at me.

'Dunno. Watch *Morning Coffee*.'

'You are *not* watching *Morning Coffee*!' says Suze firmly. 'Come on.' She closes the Media *Guardian*. 'I've had a really good idea.'

'What?' I say suspiciously as she drags me to my room. She swings open the door, leads me inside, and spreads her arms around, gesturing to the mess every-where.

'I think you should spend the morning decluttering.'

'What?' I stare at her in horror. 'I don't want to declutter.'

'Yes you do! Honestly, you'll feel great, like I did. It was brilliant! I felt so good afterwards.'

'Yes, and you had no clothes! You had to borrow knickers from me for three weeks.'

'Well, OK,' she concedes. 'Maybe I went a bit too far. But the point is, it completely transforms your life.'

'No it doesn't.'

'It does! It's feng shui. You have to let things *out* of your life to allow the new good things *in*.'

'Yeah right.'

'It's true! The moment I decluttered, I got Hadleys phoning me up with an offer. Come on, Bex. Just a little bit of decluttering would do you the world of good.'

She throws open my wardrobe and begins to leaf through my clothes.

'I mean, look at this,' she says, pulling out a blue fringed suede skirt. 'When did you last wear that?'

'Quite recently,' I say, crossing my fingers behind my back. I bought that skirt off a stall in the Portobello Road without trying it on – and when I got it home it was too small. But you never know, I might lose loads of weight one day.

'And these . . . and these . . .' She gives an incredulous frown. 'Blimey, Bex, how many pairs of black trousers have you got?'

'Only one! Two, maybe.'

'Four . . . five . . . six . . .' She's leafing through the hangers, sternly plucking out pairs of trousers.

'Those ones are just for when I feel fat,' I say defensively as she pulls out my comfy old Benetton boot-cuts. 'And those are jeans!' I exclaim as she starts rooting around at the bottom. 'Jeans don't count as trousers!'

'Says who?'

'Says everybody! It's common knowledge.'

'Ten . . . eleven . . .'

'Yeah . . . and those are for skiing! They're a completely different thing. They're *sportswear*.' Suze turns to look at me.

'Bex, you've never been skiing.'

'I know,' I say after a short silence. 'But . . . you know. Just in case I ever get asked. And they were on sale.'

'And what's this?' She picks up my fencing mask gingerly. 'This could go straight in the bin.'

'I'm taking up fencing,' I say indignantly. 'I'm going to be Catherine Zeta Jones's stunt double.'

'I don't even understand how you can fit all this stuff in here. Don't you *ever* chuck things out?' She picks up a pair of shoes decorated with shells. 'I mean, these. Do you ever wear these any more?'

'Well . . . no.' I see her expression. 'But that's not the point. If I did chuck them out, then shells would come back in the next day and I'd have to buy a new pair. So this is like . . . insurance.'

'Shells are *never* going to come back in.'

'They might! It's like the weather. You just can't tell.'

Suze shakes her head, and picks her way over the piles of stuff on the floor towards the door. 'I'm giving you two hours and when I come back I want to see a transformed room. Transformed room – transformed life. Now start!'

She disappears and I sit on my bed, staring disconsolately around at my room.

Well, OK, maybe she does have a point. Maybe I should have a little tidy-up. But I don't even know where to start. I mean, if I start throwing things out just because I never wear them, where will I stop? I'll end up with nothing.

And it's all so hard. It's all so much *effort*.

301

I pick up a jumper, look at it for a few seconds, then put it down again. Just the thought of trying to decide whether to keep it or not exhausts me.

'How are you doing?' comes Suze's voice from outside the door.

'Fine!' I call back brightly. 'Really good!'

Come on, I've got to do something. OK, maybe I should start in one corner, and work my way round. I pick my way to the corner of my room, where a heap of stuff is teetering on my dressing table, and try to work out what everything is. There's all that office equipment I ordered off the Internet . . . there's that wooden bowl I bought ages ago because it was in *Elle Decoration* (and then saw exactly the same one in Woolworths) . . . a tie-dye kit . . . some sea salt for doing body rubs . . . What *is* all this stuff, anyway? What's this box which I haven't even opened?

I open up the package and stare at a 50 metre roll of turkey foil. Turkey foil? Why would I buy that? Was I once planning to cook a turkey? Baffled, I reach for the letter on top and see the words, 'Welcome to the world of Country Ways. We're so pleased your good friend, Mrs Jane Bloomwood, recommended our catalogue to you . . .'

Oh God, of course. It's that stuff Mum ordered to get her free gift. A casserole dish, some turkey foil . . . some of those plastic bags she was stuffing patio cushions into . . . some weird gadget for putting in the . . .

Hang on.

Just hang on a minute. I drop the gadget and slowly reach for the plastic bags again. A woman with a dodgy blond haircut is staring proudly at me over a shrink-wrapped duvet, and a bubble from her mouth reads 'With up to 75 per cent reduction, I have so much more room in my closet now!'

Cautiously I open my door, and tiptoe along to the broom cupboard. As I pass the sitting room I look in –

and to my astonishment Suze is sitting on the sofa with Tarquin, talking earnestly.

'Tarquin!' I say, and both their heads jerk up guiltily. 'I didn't hear you arrive.'

'Hello Becky,' he says, not meeting my eye.

'We just had to . . . talk about something,' says Suze, giving me an embarrassed look. 'Have you finished?'

'Nearly,' I say. 'I just thought I'd hoover my room. To make it look really good!'

I shut my door behind me, and pull the bags out of their packaging. Right. This should be nice and easy. Just stuff them full, and suck out the air. Ten sweaters per bag, it says – but frankly, who's going to count?

I start to stuff clothes into the first bag, until it's as tightly packed as I can get it. Panting with effort, I close the plastic zip – then attach the hoover nozzle to the hole. And I don't believe this. It works. It works! Before my eyes, my clothes are shrinking away into nothing!

Oh this is fantastic. This is going to revolutionize my life! Why on earth declutter when you can just shrink-wrap?

There are eight bags – and when they're all full, I cram them into my wardrobe and close the door. It's a bit of a tight squash, and I can hear a sort of hissing sound as I force the door shut – but the point is, they're in. They are contained.

And just look at my room now! It's incredible! OK, it's not exactly immaculate – but it's so much better than it was before. I quickly shove a few stray items under my duvet, arrange some cushions on top, and stand back. Looking around, I feel all warm and proud of myself. I've never seen my room look so good before. And Suze is right – I do feel different, somehow.

You know, maybe feng shui's got something to it after all. Maybe this is the turning point. My life will be transformed from now on.

I take one final admiring look at it, then call out, 'I'm done!'

When Suze comes to the door I perch smugly on the bed and beam at her astounded expression.

'Bex, this is fantastic!' she says, peering disbelievingly around the cleared space. 'And you're so quick! It took me ages to sort all my stuff out!'

'Well, you know.' I shrug nonchalantly. 'Once I decide to do something, I do it.'

She takes a few steps in, and looks in astonishment at my dressing table.

'God, I never knew that dressing table had a marble top!'

'I know,' I say proudly. 'It's quite nice, isn't it?'

'But where's all the rubbish? Where are the bin bags?'

'They're . . . I've already got rid of them.'

'So did you chuck loads out?' she says, wandering over to the almost empty mantelpiece. 'You must have done!'

'A . . . a fair amount,' I say evasively. 'You know. I was quite ruthless in the end.'

'I'm so impressed!' She pauses in front of the wardrobe, and I stare at her nervously.

Don't open it, I pray silently. Just *don't* open it.

'Have you got anything left?' she says with a grin, and pulls open the door of the wardrobe. And we both scream.

It's like a nail bomb explosion.

Except, instead of nails, it's clothes.

I don't know what happened. I don't know *what* I did wrong. But one of the bags bursts open, showering jumpers everywhere, and pushing all the other bags out. Then another one bursts open, and another one. It's a clothes storm. Suze is completely covered in stretchy tops. A sequined skirt lands on the light shade. A bra shoots across the room and hits the window.

Suze is half shrieking and half laughing, and I'm flapping my arms madly and yelling 'stop! stop!' like King Canute.

And oh no.

Oh no. Please stop. Please.

But it's too late. Now a cascade of gift-shop carrier bags is tumbling down from their hiding place on the top shelf. One after another, out into the daylight. They're hitting Suze on the head, landing on the floor and spilling open – and revealing the same contents in each. Grey sparkly boxes with a silver S C-S scrawled on the front.

About forty of them.

'What . . .' Suze pulls a T-shirt off her head and stares at them, open-mouthed. 'Where on earth did you . . .' She scrabbles amongst the clothes littering the floor, picks up one of the boxes, pulls it open and stares in silence. There, wrapped in turquoise tissue paper, is a photo frame made out of tan leather.

Oh God. Oh God, *why* did they have to fall down?

Without saying anything, Suze bends down and picks up a Gifts and Goodies carrier bag. She pulls it open and a receipt flutters to the floor. Silently she takes out the two boxes inside – and opens each to reveal a frame made of purple tweed.

I open my mouth to speak – but nothing comes out. For a moment we just stare at each other.

'Bex . . . how many of these have you got?' says Suze at last, in a slightly strangled voice.

'Um . . . not many,' I say, feeling my face grow hot. 'Just . . . you know. A few.'

'There must be about . . . fifty here!'

'No!'

'Yes!' She looks around, cheeks growing pink with distress. 'Bex, these are really expensive.'

'I haven't bought that many!' I give a distracting laugh. 'And I didn't buy them all at once.'

'You shouldn't have bought *any*! I told you, I'd make you one.'

'I know,' I say a little awkwardly. 'I know you did. But I wanted to buy one. I just wanted to . . . to support you.'

There's silence as Suze reaches for another Gifts and Goodies bag, and looks at the two boxes inside.

'It's you, isn't it?' she says suddenly. 'You're the reason I've sold so well.'

'It's not! Honestly, Suze—'

'You've spent all your money on buying my frames.' Her voice starts to wobble. 'All your money. And now you're in debt.'

'I haven't!'

'If it weren't for you, I wouldn't have my deal.'

'You would!' I say in dismay. 'Of course you would. Suze, you make the best frames in the world. I mean . . . look at this one!' I grab for the nearest box and pull out a frame made out of distressed denim. 'I would have bought this even if I hadn't known you. I would have bought all of them!'

'You wouldn't have bought this many,' she gulps. 'You would have bought maybe . . . three.'

'I *would* have bought them all. They'd make a perfect present, or a . . . an ornament for the house . . .'

'You're just saying that,' she says tearfully.

'No I'm not!' I insist, feeling tears coming to my own eyes. 'Suze, everybody loves your frames. I've seen people in shops saying how brilliant they are.'

'No you haven't.'

'I have! There was this woman admiring one in Gifts and Goodies, just the other day, and everyone in the shop was agreeing.'

'Really?' says Suze in a small voice.

'Yes! You're so talented, and successful. . . ' I look around my bomb-site room, and feel a wave of despair. 'And I'm such a mess. John Gavin's right, I should have assets by now. I should be all sorted out. I'm just . . . worthless.'

'You're not!' says Suze in horror. 'You're not worthless.'

'I am!' Miserably, I sink to the carpet of clothes on the floor. 'Suze, just look at me. I'm unemployed, I haven't got any prospects, I'm being taken to court, I owe thousands and thousands of pounds, and I don't know how I'm even going to start paying it all off . . .'

There's an awkward cough at the door. I look up, and Tarquin is standing there holding three mugs of coffee.

'Refreshments?' he says, picking his way across the floor.

'Thanks, Tarquin,' I say, sniffing, and take a mug from him. 'Sorry about all this. It's just . . . not a great time.'

He sits down on the bed and exchanges looks with Suze.

'Bit short of cash?' he says.

'Yes,' I gulp, and wipe my eyes. 'Yes, I am.' Tarquin gives Suze another glance.

'Becky, I'd be only too happy to—'

'No. No, thanks.' I smile at him. 'Really.'

There's silence as we all sip our coffee. A shaft of winter sunlight is coming through the window, and I close my eyes, feeling the soothing warmth on my face.

'Happens to the best of us,' says Tarquin sympathetically. 'Mad Uncle Monty was always going bust, wasn't he, Suze?'

'God, that's right! All the time!' says Suze. 'But he always bounced back, didn't he?'

'Absolutely!' says Tarquin. 'Over and over again.'

'What did he do?' I say, looking up with a spark of interest.

'Usually sold off a Rembrandt,' says Tarquin. 'Or a Stubbs. Something like that.'

Great. What is it about these millionaires? I mean,

307

even Suze, who I love. They just don't get it. They *don't know what it's like to have no money*.

'Right,' I say, trying to smile. 'Well . . . unfortunately, I don't have any spare Rembrandts lying around. All I've got is . . . a zillion pairs of black trousers. And some T-shirts.'

'And a fencing outfit,' puts in Suze.

Next door, the phone starts ringing, but none of us moves.

'And a wooden bowl which I hate.' I give a half-giggle, half-sob. 'And forty photograph frames.'

'And a designer jumper with two necks.'

'And a Vera Wang cocktail dress.' I look around my room, suddenly alert. 'And a brand new Kate Spade bag . . . and . . . and a whole wardrobe full of stuff which I've never even worn . . . Suze . . .' I'm almost too agitated to speak. 'Suze . . .'

'What?'

'Just . . . just think about it. I haven't got nothing. I *have* got assets! I mean, they might have depreciated a little bit . . .'

'What do you mean?' says Suze – then her face lights up. 'Ooh, have you got an ISA that you forgot about?'

'No! Not an ISA!'

'I don't understand!' wails Suze. 'Bex, what are you talking about?'

I'm just opening my mouth to explain, when the answermachine clicks on next door and a gravelly American voice starts speaking which makes me stiffen and turn my head.

'Hello, Becky? It's Michael Ellis here. I've just arrived in London, and I was wondering – could we perhaps meet up for a chat?'

It's so weird to see Michael here in London. In my mind he belongs firmly in New York, in the Four Seasons. But here he is, large as life, in the River

Room at the Savoy, his face creased in a beam. As I sit down at the table he lifts a hand to a waiter.

'A gin and tonic for the lady, please.' He raises his eyebrows at me. 'Am I right?'

'Yes please.' I smile at him gratefully. Even though we talked so much in New York, I'm feeling a bit shy at seeing him again.

'So,' he says, as the waiter brings me my drink. 'Quite a lot has been going on since we last spoke.' He lifts his glass, 'Cheers.'

'Cheers.' I take a sip. 'Like what?'

'Like Alicia Billington and four others have been fired from Brandon Communications.'

'*Four* others?' I gape at him. 'Were they all planning together?'

'Apparently so. It turns out Alicia has been working on this project for some time. This wasn't just some tiny little pie in the sky scheme. This was well organized and thought out. Well backed, too. You know Alicia's future husband is very wealthy?'

'I didn't,' I say, then remember her Chanel shoes. 'But it makes sense.'

'He put together the finance. As you suspected, they were planning to poach Bank of London.'

I take a sip of gin and tonic, relishing the sharp flavour.

'So what happened?'

'Luke swooped in, took them all by surprise, herded them into a meeting room and searched their desks. And he found plenty.'

'Luke did?' I feel a deep thud in my stomach. 'You mean – Luke's in London?'

'Uhuh.'

'How long has he been back?'

'Three days, now.' Michael gives me a quick glance. 'I guess he hasn't called you, then.'

'No,' I say, trying to hide my disappointment. 'No, he

309

hasn't.' I reach for my glass and take a deep swig. Somehow while he was still in New York, I could tell myself that Luke and I weren't speaking because of geography as much as anything else. But now he's in London – and he hasn't even called – it feels different. It feels kind of . . . final.

'So . . . what's he doing now?'

'Damage limitation,' says Michael wryly. 'Upping morale. It turns out as soon as he left for New York, Alicia got busy spreading rumours he was going to close the UK branch down completely. That's why the atmosphere plummeted. Clients have been neglected, the staff have all been on the phone to headhunters . . . frankly, it's a mess.' He shakes his head. 'That girl is trouble.'

'I know.'

'Now, that's something I've been wondering. *How* do you know?' He leans forward and looks interested. 'You picked up on Alicia in a way neither Luke nor I did. Was that based on anything?'

'Not really,' I say honestly. 'Just the fact that she's a complete cow.'

Michael throws his head back and roars with laughter.

'Feminine intuition. Why should there be any other reason?'

He chuckles for a few moments, then puts his glass down and gives me a twinkling smile. 'Speaking of which – I heard the gist of what you said to Luke about his mom.'

'Really?' I look at him in horror. 'He told you?'

'He spoke to me about it, asked if you'd said anything to me.'

'Oh!' I feel a flush creeping across my face. 'Well I was . . . angry. I didn't *mean* to say she was a . . .' I clear my throat. 'I just spoke without thinking.'

'He took it to heart, though.' Michael raises his

eyebrows. 'He called his mom up, said he was damned if he was going to go home without seeing her, and arranged a meeting.'

'Really?' I stare at him, feeling intrigued. 'And what happened?'

'She never showed up. Sent some message about having to go out of town. Luke was pretty disappointed.' Michael shakes his head. 'Between you and me – I think you were right about her.'

'Oh. Well.'

I give an awkward shrug and reach for the menu to hide my embarrassment. I can't *believe* Luke told Michael what I said about his mother. What else did he tell him? My bra size?

For a while I stare at the list of dishes without taking any of them in – then look up, to see Michael gazing seriously at me.

'Becky, I haven't told Luke it was you who tipped me off. The story I've given him is I got an anonymous message and decided to look into it.'

'That sounds fair enough,' I say, gazing at the table-cloth.

'You're basically responsible for saving his company,' says Michael gently. 'He should be very grateful to you. Don't you think he should know?'

'No,' I hunch my shoulders. 'He'd just think . . . he'd think I was . . .' I break off.

I can't believe Luke's been back for three days and hasn't called. I mean – I knew it was over. Of course I did. But secretly, a tiny part of me thought . . .

Anyway. Obviously not.

'What would he think?' probes Michael.

'I dunno,' I mutter gruffly. 'The point is, it's all over between us. So I'd rather just . . . not be involved.'

'Well, I guess I can understand that.' Michael gives me a kind look. 'Shall we order?'

While we eat, we talk about other things. Michael

tells me about his advertising agency in Washington, and makes me laugh with stories of the politicians he knows and all the trouble they get themselves into. I tell him in turn about my family, and Suze, and the way I got my job on *Morning Coffee*.

'It's all going really well, actually,' I say boldly as I dig into a chocolate mousse. 'I've got great prospects, and the producers really like me . . . they're thinking of expanding my slot.'

'Becky,' interrupts Michael gently. 'I heard. I know about your job.'

I stare at him dumbly, my whole face prickling in shame.

'I felt really bad for you,' continued Michael. 'That shouldn't have happened.'

'Does . . . does Luke know?' I say huskily.

'Yes. I believe he does.'

I take a deep swig of my wine. I can't bear the idea of Luke feeling pity for me.

'Well, I've got lots of options open,' I say desperately. 'I mean, maybe not on television . . . but I'm applying for a number of financial journalism posts . . .'

'On the *FT*?'

'On . . . well . . . on *Personal Investment Periodical* . . . and *Annuities Today* . . .'

'*Annuities Today*,' says Michael disbelievingly. At his expression I can't help giving a snort of shaky laughter. 'Becky, do any of these jobs really excite you?'

I'm about to trot out my stock answer – 'Personal finance is more interesting than you'd think, actually!' – when I realize I can't be bothered to pretend any more. Personal finance *isn't* more interesting than you'd think. It's just as boring as you'd think. Even on *Morning Coffee* it was only really when callers started talking about their relationships and family lives that I used to enjoy it.

'What do you think?' I say instead, and take another swig of wine. Michael sits back in his chair and dabs his mouth with a napkin.

'So why are you going for them?'

'I don't know what else to do.' I give a hopeless shrug. 'Personal finance is the only thing I've ever done. I'm kind of . . . pigeonholed.'

'How old are you, Becky? If you don't mind my asking?'

'Twenty-six.'

'Pigeonholed at twenty-six.' Michael shakes his head. 'I don't think so.' He takes a sip of coffee and gives me an appraising look.

'If some opportunity came up for you in America,' he says, 'would you take it?'

'I'd take anything,' I say frankly. 'But what's going to come up for me in America now?'

There's silence. Very slowly, Michael reaches for a chocolate mint, unwraps it and puts it on the edge of his saucer.

'Becky, I have a proposition for you,' he says, looking up. 'We have an opening at the advertising agency for a head of corporate communications.'

I stare at him, cup halfway to my lips. Not daring to hope he's saying what I think he is.

'We want someone with editorial skills, who can coordinate a monthly newsletter. You'd be ideal on those counts. But we also want someone who's good with people. Someone who can pick up on the buzz, make sure people are happy, report to the board on any problems . . .' He shrugs. 'Frankly, I can't think of anyone better suited to it.'

'You're . . . you're offering me a job?' I say disbelievingly, trying to ignore the leaps of hope inside my chest; the little stabs of excitement. 'But . . . but what about the *Daily World*? The . . . shopping?'

'So what?' Michael shrugs. 'So you like to shop. I like

to eat. Nobody's perfect. As long as you're not on some international "most wanted" blacklist . . .'

'No. No,' I say hurriedly. 'In fact, I'm about to sort all that out.'

'And immigration?'

'I've got a lawyer.' I bite my lip. 'I'm not sure he exactly likes me very much.'

'I have contacts in immigration,' says Michael reassuringly. 'I'm sure we can sort something out.' He leans back and takes a sip of coffee. 'Washington isn't New York. But it's a fun place to be, too. Politics is a fascinating arena. I have a feeling you'd take to it. And the salary . . . Well. It won't be what CNN might have offered you. But as a ballpark . . .' He scribbles a figure on a piece of paper and pushes it across the table.

I don't believe it. It's about twice what I'd get for any of those crappy journalism jobs.

Washington. An advertising agency. A whole new career.

America. Without Luke. On my own terms.

I can't quite get my head round all of this.

'Why are you offering this to me?' I manage at last.

'I've been very impressed by you, Becky,' says Michael seriously. 'You're smart. You're intuitive. You get things done.' I stare at him, feeling an embarrassed colour come to my cheeks. 'And maybe I figured you deserve a break,' he adds kindly. 'Now, you don't have to decide at once. I'm over here for a few more days, so if you want to, we can talk again about it. But Becky . . .'

'Yes?'

'I'm serious now. Whether you decide to take up my offer or not, don't fall into anything else.' He shakes his head. 'Don't settle. You're too young to settle. Look into your heart – and go after what you really want.'

314

Seventeen

I don't decide straight away. It takes me about two weeks of pacing around the flat, drinking endless cups of coffee, talking to my parents, Suze, Michael, my old boss Philip, this new television agent Cassandra . . . basically everyone I can think of. But in the end I know. I know in my heart what I really want to do.

Luke hasn't called – and to be honest, I shouldn't think I'll ever speak to him again. Michael says he's working about seventeen hours a day, trying simultaneously to salvage Brandon Communications and keep interest open in the States, and is very stressed indeed. It seems he still hasn't got over the shock of discovering that Alicia was plotting against him – and that Bank of London were considering moving with her. The shock of discovering he wasn't 'immune to shit', as Michael so poetically put it. 'That's the trouble with having the whole world love you,' he said to me the other day. 'One day, you wake up and it's flirting with your best friend instead. And you don't know what to do. You're thrown.'

'So – has Luke been thrown by all this?' I asked, twisting my fingers into a knot.

'Thrown?' exclaimed Michael. 'He's been hurled across the paddock and trampled on by a herd of wild boar.'

Several times I've picked up the phone with a sudden longing to speak to him. But then I've always taken a deep breath and put it down again. That's his life, now. I've got to get on with mine. My whole new life.

There's a sound at the door, and I look round. Suze is standing staring into my empty room.

'Oh Bex,' she says miserably. 'I don't like it. Put it all back. Make it messy again.'

'At least it's all feng shui now,' I say, attempting a smile. 'It'll probably bring you loads of luck.'

She comes in, and walks across the empty carpet to the window, then turns round.

'It seems smaller,' she says slowly. 'It should look bigger without all your clutter, shouldn't it? But somehow . . . it doesn't work like that. It looks like a nasty bare little box.'

There's silence for a while as I watch a tiny spider climbing up the window pane.

'Have you decided what you're going to do with it?' I say at last. 'Are you going to get a new flatmate?'

'I don't think so,' says Suze. 'I mean, there's no rush, is there? Tarkie said why not just have it as my office for a while.'

'Did he?' I turn to look at her with raised eyebrows. 'That reminds me. Did I hear Tarquin here again last night? And creeping out this morning?'

'No,' says Suze, looking flustered. 'I mean – yes.' She catches my eye and blushes. 'But it was completely the last ever time. Ever.'

'You make such a lovely couple,' I say, grinning at her.

'Don't *say* that!' she exclaims in horror. 'We're not a couple.'

'OK,' I say, relenting. 'Whatever.' I look at my watch. 'You know, we ought to be going.'

'Yes. I suppose so. Oh Bex—'

I look at Suze – and her eyes are full of tears.

'I know.' I squeeze her hand tightly and for a moment neither of us says anything. Then I reach for my coat. 'Come on.'

*　　*　　*

We walk along to the King George pub at the end of the road. We make our way through the bar and up a flight of wooden stairs to a large private room furnished with red velvet curtains, a bar and lots of trestle tables at both sides. A makeshift platform has been set up at one end, and there are rows of plastic chairs in the middle.

'Hello!' says Tarquin, spotting us as we enter. 'Come and have a drink.' He lifts his glass. 'The red's not at all bad.'

'Is the tab all set up behind the bar?' says Suze.

'Absolutely,' says Tarquin. 'All organized.'

'Bex – that's on us,' says Suze, putting her hand on me as I reach for my purse. 'A goodbye present.'

'Suze, you don't have to—'

'I wanted to,' she says firmly. 'So did Tarkie.'

'Let me get you some drinks,' says Tarquin, then adds, lowering his voice, 'It's a pretty good turnout, don't you think?'

As he walks off, Suze and I turn to survey the room. At tables set out round the room, people are milling around, looking at neatly folded piles of clothes, shoes, CDs, and assorted bits of bric-à-brac. On one table is a pile of typed, photocopied catalogues, and people are marking them as they wander round.

I can hear a girl in leather jeans saying, 'Look at this coat! Ooh, and these Hobbs boots! I'm definitely going to bid for those!' On the other side of the room, two girls are trying pairs of trousers up against themselves while their boyfriends patiently hold their drinks.

'Who *are* all these people?' I say disbelievingly. 'Did you invite them all?'

'Well, I went down my address book,' says Suze. 'And Tarquin's address book. And Fenny's . . .'

'Oh well,' I say with a laugh. 'That explains it.'

'Hi, Becky!' says a bright voice behind me and I swivel round to see Fenella's friend Milla, with a pair of girls I half recognize. 'I'm going to bid for your purple cardigan! And Tory's going to go for that dress with the fur, and Annabel's seen about six thousand things she wants! We were just wondering, is there an accessories section?'

'Over there,' says Suze, pointing to the corner of the room.

'Thanks!' says Milla. 'See you later!' The three girls trip off into the mêlée, and I hear one of them saying, 'I *really* need a good belt . . .'

'Becky!' says Tarquin, coming up behind me. 'Here's some wine. And let me introduce Caspar, my chum from Christie's.'

'Oh hello!' I say, turning round to see a guy with floppy blond hair, a blue shirt and an enormous gold signet ring. 'Thank you so much for doing this! I'm really grateful.'

'Not at all, not at all,' says Caspar. 'Now, I've been through the catalogue and it all seems fairly straight-forward. Do you have a list of reserve prices?'

'No,' I say without pausing. 'No reserves. Everything must go.'

'Fine.' He smiles at me. 'Well, I'll go and get set up.'

As he walks off I take a sip of my wine. Suze has gone off to look round some of the tables, so I stand alone for a while, watching as the crowd grows. Fenella arrives at the door, and I give her a wave – but she's immediately swallowed up in a group of shrieking friends.

'Hi, Becky,' says a hesitant voice behind me. I wheel round in shock, and find myself staring up at Tom Webster.

'Tom!' I exclaim. 'What are you doing here? How do you know about this?' He takes a sip from his glass and gives a little grin.

'Suze called your mum, and she told me all about it. She and my mum have put in some orders, actually.'

He pulls a list out of his pocket. 'Your mum wants your cappuccino maker. If it's for sale.'

'Oh, it's for sale,' I say. 'I'll tell the auctioneer to make sure you get it.'

'And my mum wants that feathery hat you wore to our wedding.'

'Right. No problem.' At the reminder of his wedding, I feel myself growing slightly warm.

'So – how's married life?' I say, examining one of my nails.

'Oh . . . it's all right,' he says after a pause.

'Is it as blissful as you expected?' I say, trying to sound light-hearted.

'Well, you know . . .' He stares into his glass, a slightly hunted look in his eyes. 'It would be unrealistic to expect everything to be perfect straight off. Wouldn't it?'

'I suppose so.'

There's an awkward silence between us. In the distance I can hear someone saying, 'Kate Spade! Look, brand new!'

'Becky, I'm really sorry,' says Tom in a rush. 'The way we behaved towards you at the wedding.'

'That's all right!' I say, a little too brightly.

'It's not all right.' He shakes his head. 'Your mum was bang on. You're one of my oldest friends. I've been feeling really bad, ever since.'

'Honestly, Tom. It was my fault, too. I mean, I should have just admitted Luke wasn't there.' I smile ruefully. 'It would have been a lot simpler.'

'But if Lucy was giving you a hard time, I can really understand why you felt you just had to . . . to . . .' He breaks off, and takes a deep swig of his drink. 'Anyway, Luke seemed like a nice guy. Is he coming tonight?'

'No,' I say after a pause, and force a smile. 'No, he isn't.'

*　　　*　　　*

After half an hour or so, people begin to take their seats on the rows of plastic chairs. At the back of the room are five or six friends of Tarquin's holding mobile phones, and Caspar explains to me that they're on the line to telephone bidders.

'They're people who heard about it but couldn't come, for whatever reason. We've been circulating the catalogues fairly widely, and a lot of people are interested. The Vera Wang dress alone attracted a great deal of attention.'

'Yes,' I say, feeling a lurch of emotion, 'I expect it did.' I look around the room, at the bright, expectant faces; at the people still taking a last look at the tables. A girl is leafing through a pile of jeans; someone else is trying out the clasp on my dinky little white case. I can't quite believe that after tonight, none of these things will be mine any more. They'll be in other people's wardrobes. Other people's rooms.

'Are you all right?' says Caspar, following my gaze.

'Yes!' I say brightly. 'Why shouldn't I be all right?'

'I've done a lot of house sales,' he says kindly. 'I know what it's like. One gets very attached to one's possessions. Whether it's an eighteenth-century chiffonnier, or . . .' he glances at the catalogue, 'a pink leopard-print coat.'

'Actually – I never much liked that coat.' I give him a resolute smile. 'And anyway, that's not the point. I want to start again and I think – I *know* – this is the best way.' I smile at him. 'Come on. Let's get going, shall we?'

'Absolutely.' He raps on his lectern and raises his voice. 'Ladies and gentlemen! First, on behalf of Becky Bloomwood, I'd like to welcome you all here this evening. We've got quite a lot to get through, so I won't delay you – except to remind you that 25 per cent of everything raised tonight is going to a range of charities, plus any remainder of the proceeds after Becky has paid off all her outstanding accounts.'

320

'I hope they're not holding their breath,' says a dry voice from the back, and everyone laughs. I peer through the crowd to see who it is – and I don't believe it. It's Derek Smeath, standing there with a pint in one hand, a catalogue in the other. He gives me a smile, and I give a shy wave back.

'How did he know about this?' I hiss to Suze, who has come to join me on the platform.

'I told him, of course!' she says. 'He said he thought it was a marvellous idea. He said when you use your brain, no-one comes near you for ingenuity.'

'Really?' I glance at Derek Smeath again and flush slightly.

'So,' says Caspar. 'I present Lot One. A pair of clementine sandals, very good condition, hardly worn.' He lifts them onto the table and Suze squeezes my hand sympathetically. 'Do I have any bids?'

'I bid £15,000,' says Tarquin, sticking up his hand at once.

'Fifteen thousand pounds,' says Caspar, sounding a bit taken aback. 'I have a bid of fifteen thousand—'

'No you don't!' I interrupt. 'Tarquin, you can't bid £15,000!'

'Why not?'

'You have to bid *realistic* prices.' I give him a stern look. 'Otherwise you'll be banned from the bidding.'

'OK . . . £1,000.'

'No! You can bid . . . £10,' I say firmly.

'All right then. Ten pounds.' He puts his hand down meekly.

'Fifteen pounds,' comes a voice from the back.

'Twenty!' cries a girl near the front.

'Twenty-five,' says Tarquin.

'Thirty!'

'Thirt—' Tarquin catches my eye, blushes and stops.

'Thirty pounds. Any further bids on thirty . . .' Caspar looks around the room, his eyes suddenly like a hawk's. 'Going . . . going . . . gone! To the girl in the green velvet coat.' He grins at me, scribbles something on a piece of paper, and hands the shoes to Fenella, who is in charge of distributing sold items.

'Your first £30!' whispers Suze in my ear.

'Lot Two!' says Caspar. 'Three embroidered cardigans from Jigsaw, unworn, with price tags still attached. Can I start the bidding at . . .'

'Twenty pounds!' says a girl in pink.

'Twenty-five!' cries another girl.

'I have a telephone bid of thirty,' says a guy raising his hand at the back.

'Thirty pounds from one of our telephone bidders . . . Any advance on thirty? Remember, ladies and gentlemen, this *will* be raising funds for charity . . .'

'Thirty-five!' cries the girl in pink, and turns to her neighbour. 'I mean, they'd be more than that each in the shop, wouldn't they? And they've never even been worn!'

God, she's right. I mean, thirty-five quid for three cardigans is nothing. Nothing!

'Forty!' I hear myself crying, before I can stop myself. The whole room turns to look at me, and I feel myself furiously blushing. 'I mean . . . does anyone want to bid forty?'

The bidding goes on and on, and I'm amazed how much money is being raised. My shoe collection raises at least £1,000, a set of Dinny Hall jewellery goes for £200 – and Tom Webster bids £600 for my computer.

'Tom,' I say anxiously, as he comes up to the platform to fill in his slip. 'Tom, you shouldn't have bid all that money.'

'For a brand new Apple Mac?' says Tom. 'It's worth it. Besides, Lucy's been saying she wants her own computer for a while.' He gives a half-smile. 'I'm kind of looking forward to telling her she's got your cast-off.'

'Lot 73,' says Caspar beside me. 'And one which I know is going to attract a great deal of interest. A Vera Wang cocktail dress.' Slowly he holds up the inky purple dress, and there's an appreciative gasp from the crowd.

But actually – I don't think I can watch this go. This is too painful; too recent. My beautiful glittering movie-star dress. I can't even look at it without remembering it all, like a slow-motion cine-film. Dancing with Luke in New York; drinking cocktails; that heady, happy excitement. And then waking up and seeing everything crash around me.

'Excuse me,' I murmur, and get to my feet. I head quickly out of the room, down the stairs and into the fresh evening air. I lean against the wall of the pub, listening to the laughter and chatter inside, and try to focus on all the good reasons why I'm doing this.

A few moments later, Suze appears beside me.

'Are you OK?' she says, and hands me a glass of wine. 'Here. Have some of this.'

'Thanks,' I say gratefully, and take a deep gulp. 'I'm fine, really. It's just . . . I suppose it's just hitting me. What I'm doing.'

'Bex . . .' She pauses and rubs her face awkwardly. 'Bex, you could always change your mind. You could always stay. I mean – after tonight, with any luck, all your debts will be paid off. You could get a job, stay in the flat with me . . .'

I look at her for a few silent moments, feeling a temptation so strong, it almost hurts. It would be so easy to agree. Go home with her, have a cup of tea and fall back into my old life.

But then I shake my head.

'No. I'm not going to fall into anything again. I've found something I really want to do, Suze, and I'm going to do it.'

'Rebecca.' A voice interrupts us, and we both look up

to see Derek Smeath coming out of the door of the pub. He's holding the wooden bowl, one of Suze's photograph frames, and a big hard-backed atlas which I remember buying once when I thought I might give up my Western life and go travelling.

'Hi!' I say, and nod at his haul. 'You did well.'

'Very well.' He holds the bowl up. 'This is a very handsome piece.'

'It was in *Elle Decoration* once,' I tell him. 'Very cool.'

'Really? I'll tell my daughter.' He puts it slightly awkwardly under his arm. 'So you're off to America tomorrow.'

'Yes. Tomorrow afternoon. After I've paid a small trip to your friend John Gavin.'

A wry smile passes over Derek Smeath's face.

'I'm sure he'll be pleased to see you.' He extends his hand as best he can to shake mine. 'Well, good luck, Becky. Do let me know how you get on.'

'I will,' I say, smiling warmly. 'And thanks for . . . You know. Everything.'

He nods, and then walks off into the night.

I stay outside with Suze for quite a time. People are leaving now, carrying their loot, and telling each other how much they got it all for. A guy walks by clutching the mini paper shredder and several pots of lavender honey, a girl drags a bin liner full of clothes, someone else has got the invitations with the twinkly pizza slices . . . Just as I'm starting to get cold, a voice hails us from the stairs.

'Hey,' calls Tarquin. 'It's the last lot. D'you want to come and see?'

'Come on,' says Suze, stubbing out her cigarette. 'You've got to see the last thing go. What is it?'

'I don't know,' I say as we mount the stairs. 'The fencing mask, perhaps?'

But as we walk back into the room, I feel a jolt of

324

shock. Caspar's holding up my Denny and George scarf. My precious Denny and George scarf. Shimmering blue, silky velvet, overprinted in a paler blue, and dotted with iridescent beading.

I stand staring at it, with a growing tightness in my throat, remembering with a painful vividness the day I bought it. How desperately I wanted it. How Luke lent me the twenty quid I needed. The way I told him I was buying it for my aunt.

The way he used to look at me whenever I wore it.

My eyes are going blurry, and I blink hard, trying to keep control of myself.

'Bex . . . don't sell your scarf,' says Suze, looking at it in distress. 'Keep one thing, at least.'

'Lot 126,' says Caspar. 'A very attractive silk and velvet scarf.'

'Bex, tell them you've changed your mind!'

'I haven't changed my mind,' I say, staring fixedly ahead. 'There's no point hanging on to it now.'

'What am I bid for this fine designer accessory by Denny and George?'

'Denny and George!' says the girl in pink, looking up. She's got the hugest pile of clothes around her, and I've no idea how she's going to get them all home. 'I collect Denny and George! Thirty pounds!'

'I have a bid at £30,' says Caspar. He looks around the room, but it's swiftly emptying. People are queuing up to collect their items, or buy drinks at the bar, and the very few left sitting on the chairs are mostly chatting.

'Any further bids for this Denny and George scarf?'

'Yes!' says a voice at the back, and I see a girl in black raising a hand. 'I have a telephone bid of £35.'

'Forty pounds,' says the girl in pink promptly.

'Fifty,' says the girl in black.

'Fifty?' says the pink girl, swivelling on her chair. 'Who is it bidding? Is it Miggy Sloane?'

'The bidder wishes to remain anonymous,' says the

girl in black after a pause. She catches my eye and for an instant my heart stops still.

'I bet it's Miggy,' says the girl, turning back. 'Well, she's not going to beat me. Sixty pounds.'

'Sixty pounds?' says the chap next to her, who's been eyeing her pile of stuff with slight alarm. 'For a scarf?'

'A *Denny and George* scarf, stupid!' says the pink girl, and takes a swig of wine. 'It would be at least two hundred in a shop. Seventy! Ooh, silly. It's not my turn, is it?'

The girl in black has been murmuring quietly into the phone. Now she looks up at Caspar.

'A hundred.'

'A hundred?' The pink girl swivels on her chair again. 'Really?'

'The bidding stands at a hundred,' says Caspar calmly. 'I am bid £100 for this Denny and George scarf. Any further bids?'

'A hundred and twenty,' says the pink girl. There are a few moments' silence, and the girl in black talks quietly into the phone again. Then she looks up and says,

'A hundred and fifty.'

There's an interested murmuring around the room, and people who had been chatting at the bar turn towards the auction floor again.

'One hundred and fifty pounds,' says Caspar. 'I am bid £150 for Lot 126, a Denny and George scarf.'

'That's more than I *paid* for it!' I whisper to Suze.

'Bidding rests with the telephone buyer. At £150. One hundred and fifty pounds, ladies and gentlemen.'

There's a tense silence – and suddenly I realize I'm digging my nails into the flesh of my hands.

'Two hundred,' says the girl in pink defiantly, and there's a gasp around the room. 'And tell your so-called anonymous bidder, Miss Miggy Sloane, that whatever *she* bids, *I* can bid.'

Everyone turns to look at the girl in black, who mutters something into the receiver, then nods her head.

'My bidder withdraws,' she says, looking up. I feel an inexplicable pang of disappointment, and quickly smile to cover it.

'Two hundred pounds!' I say to Suze. 'That's pretty good!'

'Going . . . going . . . gone,' says Caspar, and raps his gavel. 'To the lady in pink.'

There's a round of applause, and Caspar beams happily around. He picks up the scarf, and is about to hand it to Fenella, when I stop him.

'Wait,' I say. 'I'd like to give it to her. If that's all right.'

I take the scarf from Caspar and hold it quite still for a few moments, feeling its familiar gossamer texture. I can still smell my scent on it. I can feel Luke tying it round my neck.

The Girl in the Denny and George Scarf.

Then I take a deep breath and walk down, off the platform, towards the girl in pink. I smile at her and hand it over to her.

'Enjoy it,' I say. 'It's quite special.'

'Oh, I know,' she says quietly. 'I know it is.' And just for a moment, as we look at each other, I think she understands completely. Then she turns and lifts it high into the air in triumph, like a trophy. 'Sucks to you, Miggy!'

I turn away and walk back to the platform, where Caspar is sitting down, looking exhausted.

'Well done,' I say, sitting down next to him. 'And thank you so much again. You did a fantastic job.'

'Not at all!' says Caspar. 'I enjoyed it, actually. Bit of a change from early German porcelain.' He gestures to his notes. 'I think we raised a fair bit, too.'

'You did brilliantly!' says Suze, coming to sit down

too, and handing Caspar a beer. 'Honestly Bex, you'll be completely out of the woods now.' She gives an admiring sigh. 'You know, it just shows, you were right all along. Shopping *is* an investment. I mean, like, how much did you make on your Denny and George scarf?'

'Erm . . .' I close my eyes, trying to work it out. 'About . . . 60 per cent?'

'Sixty per cent return! In less than a year! You see? That's better than the crummy old stock market!' She takes out a cigarette and lights it. 'You know, I think I might sell all my stuff, too.'

'You haven't got any stuff,' I point out. 'You decluttered it all.'

'Oh yeah.' Suze's face falls. 'God, why did I do that?'

I lean back on my elbows and close my eyes. Suddenly, for no real reason, I feel absolutely exhausted.

'So you're off tomorrow,' says Caspar, taking a swig of beer.

'I'm off tomorrow,' I echo, staring up at the ceiling. Tomorrow I'm leaving England and flying off to America to live. Leaving everything behind and starting again. Somehow, it just doesn't feel real.

'Not one of these crack of dawn flights, I hope?' he says, glancing at his watch.

'No, thank God. I'm not flying until about five.'

'That's good,' says Caspar nodding. 'Gives you plenty of time.'

'Oh yes.' I sit up and glance at Suze, who grins back. 'Plenty of time for just a couple of little things I've got to do.'

'Becky! We're so glad you changed your mind!' cries Zelda as soon as she sees me. I get up from the sofa where I've been sitting in reception, and give her a quick smile. 'Everyone's so thrilled you're coming on! What made you decide?'

'Oh, I'm not sure,' I say pleasantly. 'Just . . . one of those things.'

'Well, let me take you straight up to makeup . . . we're completely chaotic, as usual, so we've brought your slot forwards slightly . . .'

'No problem,' I say. 'The sooner the better.'

'I have to say, you look very well,' says Zelda, surveying me with a slight air of disappointment. 'Have you lost weight?'

'A little, I suppose.'

'Ah . . . stress,' she says wisely. 'Stress, the silent killer. We're doing a feature on it next week. Now!' she exclaims, bustling me into the makeup room. 'This is Becky . . .'

'Zelda, we know who Becky is,' says Chloe, who's been doing my makeup ever since I first appeared on *Morning Coffee*. She pulls a face at me in the mirror and I stifle a giggle.

'Yes of course you do! Sorry, Becky, I've just got you down in my mind as a guest! Now, Chloe. Don't do too good a job on Becky, today. We don't want her looking too glowing and happy, do we?' She lowers her voice. 'And use waterproof mascara. In fact, everything water-proof. See you later!'

Zelda sweeps out of the room, and Chloe shoots her a scornful glance.

'OK,' she says. 'I'm going to make you look as good as you've ever looked in your life. Extra happy and extra glowing.'

'Thanks, Chloe,' I say, grinning at her, and sit down on a chair.

'Oh, and please don't tell me you're really going to need waterproof mascara,' she adds, tying a cape around me.

'No way,' I say firmly. 'They'll have to shoot me first.'

'Then they probably will,' says a girl from across the room, and we all start giggling helplessly.

'All I can say is, I hope they're paying you well to do this,' says Chloe, as she starts to smooth foundation onto my skin.

'Yes,' I say. 'They are, as it happens. But that's not why I'm doing it.'

Half an hour later, I'm sitting in the green room when Clare Edwards comes walking in. She's wearing a dark green suit which really doesn't do much for her – and is it my imagination, or has someone made her up far too pale? She's going to look really pasty under the lights.

Chloe, I think, and hide a little smile.

'Oh,' says Clare, looking discomfited as she sees me. 'Hello, Becky.'

'Hi, Clare,' I say. 'Long time no see.'

'Yes. Well.' She twists her hands into a knot. 'I was very sorry to read of your troubles.'

'Thanks,' I say lightly. 'Still – it's an ill wind, eh, Clare?'

Clare immediately blushes bright red and looks away, and I feel a bit ashamed of myself. It's not her fault I got sacked.

'Honestly, I'm really pleased you got the job,' I say more kindly. 'And I think you're doing it really well.'

'Right!' says Zelda, hurrying in. 'We're ready for you. Now, Becky.' She puts a hand on my arm as we walk out. 'I know this is going to be very traumatic for you. We're quite prepared for you to take your time . . . again, if you break down completely, start sobbing, whatever . . . don't worry.'

'Thanks, Zelda,' I say, and nod seriously. 'I'll bear that in mind.'

We get to the set, and there are Rory and Emma, sitting on the sofas. I glance at a monitor as I walk past, and see that they've blown up that awful picture of me in New York, tinted it red, and headlined it 'Becky's Tragic Secret'.

330

'Hi, Becky,' says Emma, as I sit down, and pats me sympathetically on the hand. 'Are you all right? Would you like a tissue?'

'Erm . . . no thanks.' I lower my voice. 'But, you know. Perhaps later.'

'Terrifically brave of you to come and do this,' says Rory, and squints at his notes. 'Is it true your parents have disowned you?'

'Ready in five,' calls Zelda from the floor. 'Four . . . three . . .'

'Welcome back,' says Emma sombrely to camera. 'Now, we've got a very special guest with us today. Thousands of you will have followed the story of Becky Bloomwood, our former financial expert. Becky was, of course, revealed by the *Daily World* to be far from financially secure herself.'

The picture of me shopping appears on the monitor, followed by a series of tabloid headlines, accompanied by the song 'Hey Big Spender'.

'So, Becky,' says Emma, as the music dies away. 'Let me begin by saying how *extremely* sorry and sympathetic we are for you in your plight. In a minute, we'll be asking our new financial expert, Clare Edwards, just what you should have done to prevent this catastrophe. But now – just to put our viewers straight . . . could you tell us exactly how much in debt you are?'

'I'd be glad to, Emma,' I say, and take a deep breath. 'At the present moment, my debt amounts to . . .' I pause, and I can feel the whole studio bracing itself for a shock. 'Nothing.'

'Nothing?' Emma looks at Rory as though to check she's heard correctly. '*Nothing?*'

'My overdraft facilities director, John Gavin, will be glad to confirm that this morning, at 9.30, I paid off my overdraft completely. I've paid off every single debt I had.'

I allow myself a tiny smile as I remember John

331

Gavin's face as I handed over wads and wads of cash. I so wanted him to wriggle and squirm and look pissed off. But to give him his due, after the first couple of thousand he started smiling, and beckoning people round to watch. And at the end, he shook my hand really quite warmly – and said now he understood what Derek Smeath meant about me.

I wonder what old Smeathie can have said?

'So you see, I'm not really in a plight at all,' I add. 'In fact, I've never been better.'

'Right,' says Emma. 'I see.' There's a distracted look in her eye – and I know Barry must be yelling something in her earpiece.

'But even if your money situation is temporarily sorted out, your life must still be in ruins.' She leans forward sympathetically again. 'You're unemployed . . . shunned by your friends . . .'

'On the contrary, I'm not unemployed. This afternoon I'm flying to the States, where I have a new career waiting. It's a bit of a gamble for me . . . and it'll certainly be a challenge. But I genuinely think I'll be happy there. And my friends . . .' My voice wobbles a little, and I take a deep breath. 'It was my friends who helped me out. It was my friends who stood by me.'

Oh God, I don't believe it. After all that, I've got bloody tears in my eyes. I blink them back as hard as I can, and smile brightly at Emma.

'So really, my story isn't one of failure. Yes, I got myself into debt; yes, I was fired. But I did something about it.' I turn to the camera. 'And I'd like to say to anyone out there who's got themselves in a mess like I did . . . you can get out of it, too. Take action. Sell all your clothes. Apply for a new job. You can start again, like I'm going to.'

There's silence around the studio. Then suddenly, from behind one of the cameras, there's the sound of clapping. I look over in shock – and see Dave, the cameraman, grinning at me and mouthing 'well done'. Gareth the floor manager joins in . . . and someone else . . . and now the whole studio is applauding, apart from Emma and Rory, who are looking rather nonplussed – and Zelda, who's talking frantically into her mouthpiece.

'Well!' says Emma, over the sound of the applause. 'Um . . . We're taking a short break now – but join us in a few moments to hear more on our lead story today: Becky's . . . Tragic . . . umm . . .' she hesitates, listening to her earpiece '. . . or rather, Becky's . . . um *Triumphant* . . . um . . .'

The signature tune blares out of a loudspeaker and she glances at the producer's box in irritation. 'I wish he'd make up his bloody mind!'

'See you,' I say, and get up. 'I'm off now.'

'Off?' says Emma. 'You can't go yet!'

'Yes I can.' I reach towards my microphone, and Eddie the sound guy rushes forward to unclip it.

'Well said,' he mutters as he unthreads it from my jacket. 'Don't take their shit.' He grins at me. 'Barry's going ballistic up there.'

'Hey Becky!' Zelda's head jerks up in horror. 'Where are you going?'

'I've said what I came to say. Now I've got a plane to catch.'

'You can't leave now! We haven't finished!'

'I've finished,' I say, and reach for my bag.

'But the phone lines are all red!' says Zelda, hurrying towards me. 'The switchboard's jammed! The callers are all saying . . .' She stares at me as though she's never seen me before. 'I mean, we had no idea. Who would ever have thought . . .'

'I've got to go, Zelda.'

'Wait! Becky!' says Zelda as I reach the door of the studio. 'We – Barry and I – we were having a

333

quick little chat just now. And we were wondering whether . . .'

'Zelda,' I interrupt gently. 'It's too late. I'm going.'

It's nearly three by the time I arrive at Heathrow Airport. I'm still flushed from the farewell lunch I had in the pub with Suze, Tarquin and my parents. If I'm honest, there's a small part of me that feels like bursting into tears and running back to them all. But at the same time, I've never felt so confident in my life. I've never been so sure I'm doing the right thing.

There's a promotional stand in the centre of the terminus, giving away free newspapers, and as I pass it, I reach for a *Financial Times*. Just for old times' sake. Plus, if I'm carrying the *FT*, I might get upgraded. I'm just folding it up to place it neatly under my arm, when I notice a name that makes me stop dead.

Brandon in bid to save company. Page 27.

With slightly shaky fingers, I unfold the paper, find the page and read the story.

Financial PR entrepreneur Luke Brandon is fighting to keep his investors on board after severe loss of confidence following the recent defection of several senior employees. Morale is said to be low at the formerly ground-breaking PR agency, with rumours of an uncertain future for the company causing staff to break ranks. In crisis meetings to be held today, Brandon will be seeking to persuade backers to approve his radical restructuring plans, which are said to involve . . .

I read to the end of the piece, and gaze for a few seconds at Luke's picture. He looks as confident as ever – but I remember Michael's remark about him being hurled across the paddock. His world's crashed around him, just like mine did. And the chances are, his mum won't be on the phone telling him not to worry.

For a moment I feel a twinge of pity for Luke. I almost want to call him up and tell him things'll get better. But there's no point. He's busy with his life – and I'm busy with mine. So I fold the paper up again, and resolutely walk forward to the check-in desk.

'Anything to check?' says the check-in girl, smiling at me.

'No,' I say. 'I'm travelling light. Just me and my bag.' I casually lift my *FT* to a more prominent position. 'I don't suppose there's any chance of an upgrade?'

'Not today, sorry.' She pulls a sympathetic face. 'But I can put you by the emergency exit. Plenty of leg-room there. If I could just weigh your bag, please?'

'Sure.'

And just as I'm bending down to put my little case on the belt, a familiar voice behind me exclaims,

'Wait!'

I feel a lurch inside as though I've just dropped twenty feet. I turn disbelievingly – and it's him.

It's Luke, striding across the concourse towards the check-in desk. He's dressed as smartly as ever, but his face is pale and haggard. From the shadows under his eyes he looks as though he's been existing on a diet of late nights and coffee.

'Where the fuck are you going?' he demands as he gets nearer. 'Are you moving to Washington?'

'What are you doing here?' I retort shakily. 'Aren't you at some crisis meeting with your investors?'

'I was. Until Mel came in to hand round tea, and told me she'd seen you on the television this morning.'

'You just *left* your meeting?' I stare at him. 'What, right in the middle?'

'She told me you're leaving the country.' His dark eyes search my face. 'Is that right?'

'Yes,' I say, and clutch my little suitcase more tightly. 'Yes, I am.'

'Just like that? Without even telling me?'

335

'Yes, Just like that,' I say, plonking my case on the belt. 'Just like you came back to Britain without even telling me.' There's an edge to my voice, and Luke flinches.

'Becky—'

'Window or aisle seat?' interrupts the check-in girl.

'Window, please.'

'Becky—'

His mobile phone gives a shrill ring, and he switches it off irritably. 'Becky . . . I want to talk.'

'*Now* you want to talk?' I say disbelievingly. 'Great. Perfect timing. Just as I'm checking in.' I hit the *FT* with the back of my hand. 'And what about this crisis meeting?'

'It can wait.'

'The future of your company can *wait*?' I raise my eyebrows. 'Isn't that a little . . . irresponsible, Luke?'

'My company wouldn't *have* a fucking future if it weren't for you,' he exclaims, almost angrily, and in spite of myself I feel a tingling all over my body. 'Michael told me what you did. How you cottoned on to Alicia. How you warned him, how you sussed the whole thing.' He shakes his head. 'I had no idea. Jesus, if it hadn't been for you, Becky . . .'

'He shouldn't have told you,' I mutter furiously. 'I told him not to. He promised.'

'Well, he did tell me! And now . . .' Luke breaks off. 'And now I don't know what to say,' he says more quietly. ' "Thank you" doesn't even come close.'

We stare at each other in silence for a few moments.

'You don't have to say anything,' I say at last, looking away. 'I only did it because I can't stand Alicia. No other reason.'

'So . . . I've put you on Row 32,' says the check-in girl brightly. 'Boarding should be at 4.30.' She takes one further look at my passport and her expression changes. 'Hey! You're the one off *Morning Coffee*. Aren't you?'

'I used to be,' I say with a polite smile.

'Oh right,' she says, looking confused. As she hands over my passport and boarding card, her eye runs over my *FT*, and stops at Luke's photograph. She looks up at Luke, and down again.

'Hang on. Are you him?' she says, jabbing at the picture.

'I used to be,' says Luke after a pause. 'Come on, Becky. Let me buy you a drink, at least.'

We sit down at a little table with glasses of Pernod. I can see the light on Luke's phone flashing every five seconds, indicating that someone's trying to call him. But he doesn't even seem to notice.

'I wanted to ring you,' he says, staring into his drink. 'Every single day, I wanted to ring. But I knew what you'd think if I called and said I only had ten minutes to talk. What you said, about me not having time for a real relationship, that stuck with me.' He takes a deep gulp of his drink. 'Believe me, I haven't had much more than ten minutes recently. You don't know what it's been like.'

'Michael's given me an idea,' I admit.

'I was waiting until things slowed down.'

'So you chose today.' I can't help a tiny half-smile. 'The day when all your investors have flown in to see you.'

'Not ideal. I'll give you that.' A flicker of amusement passes briefly across his face. 'But how was I to know you were planning to skip the country? Michael's been a secretive bastard.' He frowns. 'And I couldn't just sit there and let you leave.' He pushes his glass around the table abstractedly, as though searching for something, and I stare at him apprehensively. 'You were right,' he says suddenly. 'I was obsessed with making it in New York. It was a kind of . . . madness. I couldn't see anything else. Jesus, I've fucked everything up, haven't I? You . . . us . . . the business . . .'

'Come on, Luke,' I say awkwardly. 'You can't take the

credit for everything. I fucked up a good few things for you.' I stop as Luke shakes his head. He drains his glass and gives me a frank look.

'There's something you need to know. Becky – how do you think the *Daily World* got hold of your financial details?'

I look at him in surprise.

'It . . . it was the council tax girl. The girl who came to the flat and snooped around while Suze was . . .' I tail away as he shakes his head again.

'It was Alicia.'

For a moment I'm too taken aback to speak.

'Alicia?' I manage at last. 'How do you . . . why would she . . .'

'When we searched her office we found bank statements of yours in her desk. Some letters, too. Christ alone knows how she got hold of them.' He exhales sharply. 'This morning, I finally got a guy at the *Daily World* to admit she was the source. They just followed up what she gave them.'

I stare at him, feeling rather cold. Remembering that day I visited his office. The Conran bag with all my letters in it. Alicia standing by Mel's desk, looking like a cat with a mouse.

I *knew* I'd left something behind. Oh God, how could I have been so *stupid*?

'You weren't her real target,' Luke's saying. 'She did it to discredit me and the company – and distract my attention from what she was up to. They won't confirm it, but I'm sure she was also the "inside source" giving all those quotes about me.' He pauses, then goes on: 'The point is, Becky – I got it all wrong. My deal wasn't ruined because of you.' He looks at me matter-of-factly. 'Yours was ruined because of me.'

I sit still for a few moments, unable to speak. It's as though something heavy is slowly lifting from me. I'm not sure what to think or feel.

'I'm just so sorry,' Luke's saying. 'For everything you've been through . . .'

'No.' I take a deep breath. 'Luke, it wasn't your fault. It wasn't even Alicia's fault. Maybe she fed them the details. But I mean, if I hadn't got myself into debt in the first place, and if I hadn't gone crazy shopping in New York, they wouldn't have had anything to write about, would they?' I rub my face. 'It was horrible and humiliating. But in a funny way, seeing that article was a good thing for me. It made me realize a few things about myself, at least.'

I pick up my glass, notice it's empty, and put it down again.

'Do you want another one?' says Luke.

'No. No thanks.'

There's silence between us. In the distance, a voice is telling passengers on flight BA 2340 for San Francisco to please proceed to Gate 29.

'I know Michael offered you a job,' said Luke. He gestures to my case. 'I assume this means you accepted it.' He pauses, and I stare at him, trembling slightly, saying nothing. 'Becky – don't go to Washington. Come and work for me.'

'Work for *you*?' I say, startled.

'Come and work for Brandon Communications.'

'Are you mad?'

He pushes his hair back off his face – and all at once he looks young and vulnerable. Like someone who needs a break.

'I'm not mad. My staff's been decimated. I need someone like you at a senior level. You know about finance. You've been a journalist. You're good with people, you already know the company . . .'

'Luke, you'll easily find someone else like me,' I chip in. 'You'll find someone better! Someone with PR experience, someone who's worked in—'

'OK, I'm lying.' Luke interrupts. 'I'm lying. I don't

339

just need someone like you. I need you.'

He meets my eyes candidly, and with a jolt I realize he's not just talking about Brandon Communications.

'I need you, Becky. I rely on you. I didn't know it until you weren't there any more. Ever since you left, your words have been going round and round in my head. About my ambitions. About our relationship. About my mother, even.'

'Your mother?' I stare at him apprehensively. 'I heard you tried to arrange a meeting with her . . .'

'It wasn't her fault.' He takes a swig of Pernod. 'Something came up, so she couldn't make it. But you're right, I *should* spend more time with her. Really get to know her better, and forge a closer relationship, just like you have with your mother.' He looks up and frowns at my dumbfounded expression. 'That is what you meant, isn't it?'

'Yes!' I say hastily. 'Yes, that's exactly what I meant. Absolutely.'

'That's what I mean. You're the only person who'll tell me the stuff I need to hear, even when I don't want to hear it. I should have confided in you right from the start. I was . . . I don't know. Arrogant. Stupid.'

He sounds so bleak and hard on himself, I feel a twinge of dismay.

'Luke—'

'Becky, I know you've got your own career – and I completely respect that. I wouldn't even ask if I didn't think this could be a good step for you too. But . . . please.' He reaches across the table and puts a warm hand on mine. 'Come back. Let's start again.'

I stare helplessly at him, emotion swelling in me like a balloon.

'Luke, I can't work for you.' I swallow, trying to keep control of my voice. 'I have to go to the States. I have to take this chance.'

'I know it seems like a great opportunity. But what I'm offering could be a great opportunity, too.'

'It's not the same,' I say, clenching my hand tightly round my glass.

'It can be the same. Whatever Michael's offered you, I'll match it.' He leans forward. 'I'll more than match it. I'll—'

'Luke,' I interrupt. 'Luke, I didn't take Michael's job.'

Luke's face jerks in shock.

'You didn't? Then what—'

He looks at my suitcase and back up to my face – and I stare back in resolute silence.

'I understand,' he says at last. 'It's none of my business.'

He looks so defeated, I feel a stab of pain in my chest. I want to tell him – but I just can't. I can't risk talking about it, listening to my own arguments waver; wondering whether I've made the right choice. I can't risk changing my mind.

'Luke, I've got to go,' I say, my throat tight. 'And . . . and you've got to get back to your meeting.'

'Yes,' says Luke after a long pause. 'Yes. You're right. I'll go. I'll go now.' He stands up and reaches into his pocket. 'Just . . . one last thing. You don't want to forget this.'

Very slowly, he pulls out a long, pale blue, silk and velvet scarf, scattered with iridescent beads.

My scarf. My Denny and George scarf.

I feel the blood drain from my face.

'How did you . . .' I swallow. 'The bidder on the phone was you? But . . . but you withdrew. The other bidder got the . . .' I tail off and stare at him in confusion.

'Both the bidders were me.'

He ties the scarf gently round my neck, looks at me for a few seconds, then kisses me on the forehead. Then he turns and walks away, into the airport crowds.

Eighteen

Two months later

'OK. So it's two presentations, one to Saatchis, one to Global Bank. One awards lunch with McKinseys, and dinner with Merrill Lynch.'

'That's it. It's a lot. I know.'

'It'll be fine,' I say reassuringly. 'It'll be fine.'

I scribble something in my notebook and stare at it, thinking hard. This is the moment of my new job I love the most. The initial challenge. Here's the puzzle – find the solution. For a few moments I sit without saying anything, doodling endless small five-pointed stars and letting my mind work it out, while Lalla watches me anxiously.

'OK,' I say at last. 'I have it. Your Helmut Lang pant suit for the meetings, your Jil Sander dress for the lunch – and we'll find you something new for the dinner.' I squint at her. 'Maybe something in a deep green.'

'I can't wear green,' says Lalla.

'You can wear green,' I say firmly. 'You look great in green.'

'Becky,' says Erin, putting her head round my door. 'Sorry to bother you, but Mrs Farlow is on the phone. She loves the jackets you sent over, but is there something lighter she can wear for this evening?'

'OK,' I say. 'I'll call her back.' I look at Lalla. 'So, let's find you an evening dress.'

'What am I going to wear with my pant suit?'

'A shirt,' I say. 'Or a cashmere T. The grey one.'

'The grey one,' repeats Lalla carefully, as though I'm speaking in Arabic.

'You bought it three weeks ago? Armani? Remember?'

'Oh yes! Yes. I think.'

'Or else your blue shell top.'

'Right,' says Lalla, nodding earnestly. 'Right.'

Lalla is high up in some top computer consultancy, with offices all over the world. She has two doctorates and an IQ of about a zillion – and claims she has severe clothes dyslexia. At first I thought she was joking.

'Write it down,' she says, thrusting a leather-bound organizer at me. 'Write down all the combinations.'

'Well, OK . . . but Lalla, I thought we were going to try to let you start putting a few outfits together yourself?'

'I know. I will. One day I will, I promise. Just . . . not this week. I can't deal with that extra pressure.'

'Fine,' I say, hiding a smile, and begin to write in her organizer, screwing up my face as I try to remember all the clothes she's got. I haven't got much time if I'm going to find her an evening dress for tonight, call Mrs Farlow back, and locate that knitwear I promised for Janey van Hassalt.

Every day is completely frenetic; everyone is always in a hurry. But somehow the busier I get and the more challenges are thrown at me – the more I love it here.

'By the way,' says Lalla. 'My sister – the one you said should wear burnt orange . . .'

'Oh yes! She was nice.'

'She said she saw you on the television. In England! Talking about clothes!'

'Oh yes,' I say, feeling a faint flush come to my face. 'I've been doing a little slot for a daytime lifestyle show. Becky from Barney's. It's a kind of New York, fashiony thing . . .'

'Well done!' says Lalla warmly. 'A slot on television! That must be very exciting for you!'

I pause, a beaded jacket in my hand, thinking, a few months ago I was going to have my own show on American network television. And now I have a little slot on a daytime show with half the audience of *Morning Coffee*. But the point is, I'm on the path I want to be.

'Yes it is,' I say, and smile at her. 'It's very exciting.'

It doesn't take too long to sort Lalla out with an outfit for her dinner. As she leaves, clutching a list of possible shoes, Christina, the head of department, comes in and smiles at me.

'How're you doing?'

'Fine,' I say. 'Really good.'

Which is the truth. But even if it wasn't – even if I was having the worst day in the world – I'd never say anything negative to Christina. I'm so grateful to her for remembering who I was. For giving me a chance.

I still can't quite believe how nice she was to me when I hesitantly phoned her up, out of the blue. I reminded her that we'd met, and asked if there was any chance I could come and work at Barney's – and she said she remembered exactly who I was, and how was the Vera Wang dress? So I ended up telling her the whole story, and how I was going to have to sell the dress, and how my TV career was in tatters, and how I'd so love to come and work for her . . . and she was quiet for a bit – and then she said she thought I'd be quite an asset to Barney's. Quite an asset! It was her idea about the TV slot, too.

'Hidden any clothes today?' she says, with a slight twinkle, and I feel myself flush. I'm *never* going to live this down, am I?

It was during that first phone call that Christina also asked me if I had any retail experience. And like a

344

complete moron, I told her all about the time I went to work in Ally Smith, and got the sack when I hid a pair of zebra-print jeans from a customer because I really wanted them myself. When I came to the end of the story there was silence down the phone, and I thought I'd completely scuppered my chances. But then came this bellow of laughter, so loud I almost dropped the phone in fright. She told me last week that that was the moment she decided to hire me.

She's also told the story to all our regular clients, which is a bit embarrassing.

'So.' Christina gives me a long, appraising look. 'Are you ready for your ten o'clock?'

'Yes.' I flush slightly under her gaze. 'Yes, I think so.'

'D'you want to brush your hair?'

'Oh.' My hand flies to my neck. 'Is it untidy?'

'Not really.' There's a slight sparkle to her eye, which I don't understand. 'But you want to look your best for your customer, don't you?'

She goes out of the room, and I quickly pull out a comb. God, I keep forgetting how tidy you have to be in Manhattan. Like, I have my nails done twice a week at a nail bar round the corner from where I live – but sometimes I think I should increase it to every other day. I mean, it's only $9.

Which in real money, is . . . Well, it's $9.

I'm kind of getting used to thinking in dollars. I'm kind of getting used to a lot of things. My studio apartment is tiny and pretty grotty, and for the first few nights I couldn't sleep for the traffic noise. But the point is, I'm here. I'm here in New York, standing on my own two feet, doing something I can honestly say I adore.

Michael's job in Washington sounded wonderful. In many ways it would have been much more sensible to take it – and I know Mum and Dad wanted me to. But what Michael said at that lunch – about not falling into

345

anything else, about going after what I truly wanted – made me think. About my career, about my life, about what I really wanted to do for a living.

And to give my mum her due, as soon as I explained what this job at Barney's would involve, she stared at me, and said, 'But love, why on earth didn't you think of this before?'

'Hi, Becky?' I give a small start, and look up to see Erin at my door. I've got to be quite good friends with Erin, ever since she invited me home to look at her collection of lipsticks and we ended up watching James Bond videos all night. 'I have your ten o'clock here.'

'Who *is* my ten o'clock?' I say as I reach for a Richard Tyler sheath. 'I couldn't see anything in the book.'

'Well . . .uh . . .' Her face is all shiny and excited, for some reason. 'Uh . . . here he is.'

'Thank you very much,' comes a deep male voice.

A deep male British voice.

Oh my God.

I freeze like a rabbit, still holding the Richard Tyler dress, as Luke walks into the room.

'Hello,' he says with a small smile. 'Miss Bloomwood. I've heard you're the best shopper in town.'

I open my mouth and close it again. Thoughts are whizzing round my mind like fireworks. I'm trying to feel surprised, trying to feel as shocked as I know I should. Two months of absolutely nothing – and now here he is. I should be completely thrown.

But somehow – I don't feel thrown at all. Subconsciously, I always knew he would come.

Subconsciously, I realize, I've been waiting for him.

'What are you doing here?' I say, trying to sound as composed as I can.

'As I said, I've heard you're the best shopper in town.' He gives me a quizzical look. 'I thought perhaps you could help me buy a suit. This one is looking rather tired.'

346

He gestures to his immaculate Jermyn Street suit which I happen to know he's only had for three months, and I hide a smile.

'You want a suit.'

'I want a suit.'

'Right.'

Playing for time, I put the dress back on a hanger, turn away, and place it carefully on the rail. Luke's here.

He's here. I want to laugh, or dance, or cry, or something. But instead I reach for my notepad and, without rushing, turn round.

'What I normally do before anything else is ask my clients to tell me a little about themselves.' My voice is a bit jumpy and I pause. 'Perhaps you could . . . do the same?'

'Right. That sounds a good idea.' Luke thinks for a moment. 'I'm a British businessman. I'm based in London.' He meets my eyes. 'But I've recently opened an office in New York. So I'm going to be spending quite a bit of time over here.'

'Really?' I feel a jolt of surprise which I try to conceal. 'You've opened in New York? That's . . . that's very interesting. Because I had the impression that certain British businessmen were finding it tough to do deals with New York investors. Just . . . something I heard.'

'They were.' Luke nods. 'They were finding it tough. But then they downscaled their plans. They decided to open on a much smaller scale.'

'A smaller scale?' I stare at him. 'And they didn't mind that?'

'Perhaps,' says Luke after a pause, 'they realized that they'd been over-ambitious the first time round. Perhaps they realized that they'd become obsessed to the point where they'd let everything else suffer. Perhaps they realized they needed to swallow their pride and put away their grand plans – and slow down a little.'

'That . . . that makes a lot of sense,' I say.

'So they put together a new proposal, found a backer who agreed with them, and this time nothing stood in the way. They're already up and running.'

His face is gleaming with suppressed delight, and I find myself beaming back.

'That's great!' I say. 'I mean . . .' I clear my throat. 'Right. I see.' I scribble some gibberish in my notepad. 'So – how much time are you going to be spending in New York, exactly?' I add in a businesslike manner. 'For my notes, you understand.'

'Absolutely,' says Luke, matching my tone. 'Well, I'll be wanting to keep a significant presence in Britain. So I'll be here for two weeks a month. At least, that's the idea at the moment. It may be more, it may be less.' There's a long pause and his dark eyes meet mine. 'It all depends.'

'On what?' I say, scarcely able to breathe.

'On . . . various things.'

There's a still silence between us.

'You seem very settled, Becky,' says Luke quietly. 'Very together.'

'I'm enjoying it, yes.'

'You look as though you're flourishing.' He looks around with a little smile. 'This environment suits you. Which I suppose comes as no great surprise . . .'

'Do you think I took this job just because I like shopping?' I say, raising my eyebrows. 'Do you think this is just about . . . shoes and nice clothes? Because if that's really what you think, then I'm afraid you're sadly misguided.'

'That's not what I—'

'It's far more than that. *Far* more.' I spread my arms in an emphatic gesture. 'It's about helping people. It's about being creative. It's about—'

A knock at the door interrupts me, and Erin pops her head in.

'Sorry to bother you, Becky. Just to let you know, I've put aside those Donna Karan mules you wanted. In the taupe *and* the black, right?'

'Er . . . yes,' I say hurriedly. 'Yes, that's fine.'

'Oh, and Accounts called, to say that takes you up to your discount limit for this month.'

'Right,' I say, avoiding Luke's amused gaze. 'Right. Thanks. I'll . . . I'll deal with that later.' I wait for Erin to leave, but she's gazing with frank curiosity at Luke.

'So, how are you doing?' she says to him brightly. 'Have you had a chance to look around the store?'

'I don't need to look,' says Luke in a deadpan voice. 'I know what I want.'

My stomach gives a little flip, and I stare straight down at my notebook, pretending to make more notes. Scribbling any old rubbish.

'Oh right!' says Erin. 'And what's that?'

There's a long silence, and eventually I can't bear it any more, I have to look up. When I see Luke's expression, my heart starts to thud.

'I've been reading your literature,' he says, reaching into his pocket and pulling out a leaflet entitled 'The Personal Shopping Service'. ' "For busy people who need some help and can't afford to make mistakes." '

He pauses, and my hand tightens around my pen.

'I've made mistakes,' he says, frowning slightly. 'I want to right those mistakes and not make them again. I want to listen to someone who knows me.'

'Why come to Barney's?' I say in a trembling voice.

'There's only one person whose advice I trust.' His gaze meets mine and I feel a small tremor. 'If she doesn't want to give it, I don't know what I'm going to do.'

'We have Frank Walsh over in menswear,' says Erin helpfully. 'I'm sure he'd—'

'Shut up, Erin,' I say, without moving my head.

'What do you think, Becky?' he says, moving towards me. 'Would you be interested?'

For a few moments I don't answer. I'm trying to gather all the thoughts I've had over the last couple of months. To organize my words into exactly what I want to say.

'I think . . .' I say at last, 'I think the relationship between a shopper and a client is a very close one.'

'That's what I was hoping,' says Luke.

'There has to be respect.' I swallow. 'There can't be cancelled appointments. There can't be sudden business meetings that take priority.'

'I understand,' says Luke. 'If you were to take me on, I can assure you that you would always come first.'

'The client has to realize that sometimes the shopper knows best. And never just dismiss her opinion. Even when he thinks it's just gossip, or . . . or mindless tittle-tattle.'

I catch a glimpse of Erin's confused face, and suddenly want to giggle.

'The client has already realized that,' says Luke. 'The client is humbly prepared to listen and be put right. On most matters.'

'*All* matters,' I retort at once.

'Don't push your luck,' says Luke, his eyes flashing with amusement, and I feel an unwilling grin spread across my face.

'Well . . .' I doodle consideringly on my notepad for a moment. 'I suppose "most" would be acceptable. In the circumstances.'

'So.' His warm eyes meet mine. 'Is that a yes, Becky? Will you be my . . . personal shopper?'

He takes a step forward, and I'm almost touching him. I can smell his familiar scent. Oh God, I've missed him.

'Yes,' I say happily. 'Yes, I will.'

From: Gildenstein, Lalla <L.Gildenstein@anagram.com
To: Bloomwood, Becky <B.Bloomwood@barneys.com
Subject: HELP! URGENT!

Becky.

Help! Help! I lost your list. I have a big formal dinner tonight with some new Japanese clients. My Armani is at the cleaners. What should I wear? Please email back soonest.

Thanks, you are an angel.

Lalla.

PS I heard your news – congratulations!

THE END

I Owe You *One*

'Love means all debts are off.'

Fixie Farr can't help herself. Straightening a crooked object,
removing a barely-there stain, helping out a friend . . .
she just has to put things right. It's how she got her
nickname, after all.

So when a handsome stranger in a coffee shop asks her to
watch his laptop for a moment, she not only agrees, she ends
up saving it from certain disaster. To thank her, the laptop's
owner, Sebastian, scribbles her an IOU – but of course Fixie
never intends to call in the favour.

That is, until her teenage crush, Ryan, comes back into her
life and needs her help – and Fixie turns to Seb.

Soon the pair are caught up in a series of IOUs – from small
favours to life-changing ones – and Fixie is torn between the
past she's used to and the future she deserves.

Does she have the courage to fix things for herself and
fight for the life, and love, she really wants?

Out
7 February
2019 in
hardback, ebook
and audio

Read on for an extract . . .

THREE

And now he's back. The words are thudding through my head like a drumbeat – *he's back, he's back* – while I stand in Anna's Accessories like a starstruck fourteen-year-old, frantically trying out hair clips. As though choosing exactly the right hair decoration will somehow, magically, make Ryan fall in love with me.

I couldn't cope with going straight home from the shop. What if he was there already, lounging on the sofa, ready to catch me out with his irresistible smile? I needed time. I needed to prepare. So at 5 p.m. I told Greg to close up and headed to the High Street. I bought myself a new lipstick. And now I'm standing in front of a display rack, trying to transform my appearance beyond belief with a £3.99 diamanté hair grip. Or maybe I should go for a flower.

Glittery hairband?

I know this is all displacement. I can't even contemplate the momentousness of seeing Ryan again so instead I'm fixating on an irrelevant detail which nobody else will even notice. Story of my life.

In the end I gather up two beaded hair clips, some diamanté hair grips, and a pair of dangling gold earrings for good luck.

I pay for them and head out to the balmy street. Mum will be laying out the table by now. Stacking the paper cups. Wrapping knives and forks in napkins. But even so, I need more time. I need to get my head straight.

On impulse, I duck into Café Allegro, which is our family's favourite local café. I buy a bag of beans for Mum's coffee machine – we're always running out and Café Allegro does the best ones – then order a mint tea and go to sit by the window. I'm trying to think exactly how to greet Ryan. What vibe to give off. *Not* gushy or needy, but self-possessed and alluring.

With a sigh, I retrieve my Anna's Accessories bag, take out the two beaded clips and hold them up against my hair, squinting into my hand mirror. Neither looks remotely alluring. I try the gold earrings against my ears and wince. Oh God. Terrible. I might take them back.

Suddenly I notice a guy opposite me, watching in slight amusement over his laptop, and at once I flush. What am I doing? I would never normally start trying on hair clips in a coffee shop. I've lost all sense of propriety.

As I shove the clips and earrings back in the bag, a drip of water lands on the table and I look up. Now I think about it, there's been a steady stream of drips from the ceiling ever since I sat down, only they've been landing in a bucket on the floor.

A barista is nearby, giving a hot sandwich to a customer, and I attract her attention as she turns to move away.

'Hi, the ceiling's leaking.' I point upwards and she follows my gaze briefly, then shrugs.

'Yeah. We put a bucket down.'

'But it's dripping on the table, too.'

As I study the ceiling, I can see two sources of drips and a patch of damp. That whole area of ceiling looks very unhealthy. I glance at the guy opposite to see if he's noticed, but he's on his mobile phone now and seems totally preoccupied.

'Yes,' he's saying, in a voice which crackles with education and polish. 'I know, Bill, but—'

Nice suit, I notice. Glossy, expensive shoes.

'They're doing building work on the floor above.' The barista seems supremely unconcerned. 'We've called them. You can move seats if you like.'

I should have wondered why this window seat was empty, when the rest of the coffee shop is full. I look around to see if there's another available seat, but there isn't.

Well, I'm not fussy. I can put up with a few drips. I'll be leaving soon, anyway.

'It's OK,' I say. 'Just thought I'd let you know. You might need to get another bucket.'

The barista shrugs again with a look I recognize – it's the famous *I'm going off shift so what do I care?* look – and heads back to the counter.

'Strewth!' the guy opposite suddenly exclaims. His voice has risen and he's making exasperated gestures with his hand.

The word *strewth* makes me smile inside. That's a word Dad used to use. I don't often hear it any more.

'You know what?' he's saying now. 'I'm sick of these intellectual types with their six degrees from Cambridge.' He listens for a bit, then says, 'It should *not* be this hard to fill a junior-level position. It should *not*. But everyone Chloe finds for me . . . I know. You'd think. But all they want to do is tell me their clever theories that they learned at uni. They don't want to *work*.'

He leans forward, takes his cup for a gulp of coffee and meets eyes with me briefly. I can't help smiling, because even though he doesn't know it, I'm hearing my dad again.

'All I want is to hire someone bright and savvy and tough, who knows how the world works,' the guy is saying now, thrusting a hand through his hair. 'Someone who's been *in* the world, hasn't just written a dissertation about it. They don't even need a bloody degree! They need some sense! Sense!'

He's lean and energetic-looking, with an end-of-summer tan. Deep-brown hair, lighter where the sun's caught it. As he reaches for his coffee again, the fronds cast shadows over his face. His cheekbones are two long, strong planes. His eyes are . . . can't quite tell. Mid-brown or hazel, I think, peering surreptitiously at him. Then the light catches them and I see a sudden tinge of green. They're woodland eyes.

It's a thing of mine, classifying eyes. Mine are double espresso. Ryan's are Californian sky. Mum's are deep-sea blue. And this guy's are woodland eyes.

'I know,' he says more calmly, his ire having apparently vanished. 'So I'm having another meeting with Chloe next week. I'm sure she's really looking forward to it.' His mouth curves into a sudden, infectious smile.

'Oh. That.' The guy shifts on his chair. 'Look, I'm sorry.' He passes a hand through his hair again, but this time he doesn't look dynamic, he looks upset. 'I'm just . . . It's not happening. You know Briony, she gets ahead of herself, so . . . no. No home gym, not for now. Tanya's designs were great, she's very talented, but . . . Yeah. I'll pay her for her time, of course . . . No, *not* with dinner,' he adds firmly. 'With a proper invoice. I insist.' He nods a few times. 'OK. I'll see you soon. Cheers.'

The wry blade of humour is back in his voice, but as he puts his phone away he stares out of the window as though trying to rebalance himself. It's weird, but I feel like I know this guy. Like, I *get* him. If we weren't two uptight British people in a London coffee shop, maybe I'd strike up conversation with him.

But we are. And that's just not what you do.

So I do that traditional London thing of pretending I didn't hear a word of his phone call, and staring carefully into mid-air in a way that won't attract his gaze. The guy starts typing at his laptop and I glance at my watch. 5.45 p.m. I should go soon.

My phone buzzes with a text and I reach for it, madly

hoping it's Jake saying 'Ryan's here.' Or even better, Ryan texting me himself. But it's not, of course, it's Hannah, replying to the text I sent her earlier. I quickly scan her words:

Ryan's back? I thought he was in LA.

Unable to stop smiling, I type a quick reply:

He was!!! But he's here and he's unattached and he was asking about me!!!!

I press Send, then instantly realize my error. I've put too many exclamation marks. Hannah will see them as warning signs. She'll be on the phone within half a minute.

I've been friends with Hannah since we were eleven and both elected as class monitors. At once we knew we'd found kindred spirits. We're both organized. We both love lists. We both get things done. Although, to be fair, Hannah gets things done *even more* efficiently than I do. She never procrastinates or finds an excuse. Whatever the task is, she does it straight away, whether it's her tax return or cleaning out her fridge or telling a guy she didn't like the way he kissed, on their very first date. (Fair play to him, he took it on the chin. He said, 'How *do* you like to be kissed, then?' And she showed him. And now they're married.)

She's the most level-headed, straight-talking person I know. She works as an actuary and she starts Christmas shopping in July and . . . here we go. Her name's popping up on my screen. Knew it.

'Hi, Hannah.' I answer my phone casually, as though I don't know why she's calling. 'How are you?'

'Ryan, huh?' she says, ignoring my greeting. 'What happened to that girl in LA?'

'Apparently it's over.' I try to speak calmly, although a voice inside me is singing, *It's over! It's over!*

'Hmm.' She doesn't sound convinced. 'Fixie, I thought you were over him. *Finally*.'

I don't blame her for that emphasis on *finally*. I've been spilling my heart to Hannah about Ryan pretty much since the first day we met. When we were eighteen I used to drag her around endless London pubs, just in the hope of bumping into him. She used to call it the Ryan Route. And it would be fair to say that last spring, after Ryan went back to Hollywood, every other conversation we had was about him.

OK, every conversation.

'I am!' I lower my voice so the whole coffee shop doesn't hear. 'But apparently he was asking after me.' Just the thought of Ryan asking after me makes me feel giddy, but I force myself to sound matter-of-fact. 'So that's interesting. That's all. Just interesting.'

'Hmm,' says Hannah again. 'Has he texted you himself or anything?'

'No. But maybe he wants to surprise me.'

'Hmm,' says Hannah for a third time. 'Fixie, you do remember that he lives in LA?'

'I know,' I say.

'And your whole life is your family shop.'

'I know.'

'So there's no prospect of you actually getting together,' Hannah carries on relentlessly. 'Like having a relationship or anything. It's not going to happen.'

'Stop spelling stuff out!' I hiss crossly, turning towards the window for extra privacy. 'You always have to spell things out!'

Not for the first time, I wish I had a flaky, romantic best friend who would say, 'Oh wow, Ryan's back! You two are *meant* for each other!' and help me choose what outfit to wear.

'I'm spelling things out because I *know* you,' says Hannah.

'And what I worry is that deep down you're still hoping for some sort of miracle.'

There's silence. I'm not going to say, 'Don't be ridiculous,' because there's no point lying to your best friend.

'It's like . . . a ten per cent hope,' I say at last, watching a traffic warden on the prowl. 'It's harmless.'

'It's not harmless,' Hannah contradicts me with energy. 'It means you don't even *look* at any other men. There are nice men out there, you know, Fixie. Good men.'

I know why she's saying that. It's because she tried to set me up with this actuary mate of hers last month, and I wasn't into him. I mean, he was nice. He was just so *earnest*.

'I get it,' Hannah continues. 'Ryan's good-looking and glamorous and whatever. But are you going to give up on finding a proper guy just for ten minutes with Mr Hollywood?'

'No, of course not,' I say after a pause, even though the phrase *ten minutes with Mr Hollywood* has instantly flashed me back to Ryan and me in bed last year, and just the memory is making me damp behind the knees.

'I think you need to draw a line and move on,' says Hannah. I imagine her at her desk, briskly drawing a line under a column of numbers with a ruler, and then turning the page, no problem.

'So what am I supposed to do?' I say, a bit snippily because I know she has a point and I resent it, even though I love her for caring enough to call me up and lecture me. 'What if he's there tonight, and . . .' I break off. I don't want to say it out loud because I'll jinx it.

'You mean, what if he's all hot and sexy and wants to carry on where you left off last year?'

'I guess.'

'Well.' Hannah is silent for a few moments. 'Here's the thing. Can you sleep with him and *not* get upset when he goes back to LA? Be honest.'

'Yes,' I say robustly. 'Of course. Sex is just sex.'

'No, it's not!' says Hannah with an incredulous laugh. 'Not for you. Not with Ryan. He'll mess you up somehow, I know it. You'll end up weeping on my shoulder.'

'Well, maybe I don't care,' I say defiantly.

'You're saying the sex is so good it's worth it even if you *do* end up weeping on my shoulder?' says Hannah, who always likes to analyse everything into equations.

'Pretty much.' I have a sudden memory of Ryan's LA-tanned body entwined with mine. 'Yes.'

'Fine,' says Hannah, and I can hear the rueful eye-roll in her voice. 'Well, I'll buy the tissues.'

'He might not even come tonight,' I point out. 'This whole conversation might have been for nothing.'

'Well, I'll see you later,' says Hannah. 'With or without Ryan.'

I ring off and stare morosely out of the window. Now I've said it, I realize of course that's the most likely scenario. Ryan must have a million more glamorous events to be at tonight than Mum's party. He won't turn up at all. I'll have bought all these hair clips for nothing.

'Hi, Briony.' The guy across the table is answering his phone and I glance round. 'Oh, you've spoken to Tanya. Right. So— No, that's not what—' He seems to be trying to get a word in. 'Listen, Briony—' He breaks off, looking beleaguered. 'Sweetheart, I'm not trying to ruin— No, we did *not* agree anything.'

Ha. Well, at least it's not just me with the messed-up love life.

'Is that what you think?' he's exclaiming now. 'Can I remind you that this is *my* flat, for *me* to—' He lifts his eyes and suddenly seems to become aware that I'm listening. I quickly look away, but even so, he gets to his feet.

'Excuse me,' he says politely to me. 'I'm just stepping out to take a phone call. Could you watch my laptop?'

'Sure.'

I nod and watch him thread his way between the tables,

already back on the phone, saying, 'I never promised anything! It was *your* idea—'

I sip my mint tea and glance at the laptop a couple of times. It's a MacBook. He's left it closed, with a stack of glossy folders next to it. I tilt my head slightly and read the top one. *ESIM: Forward-looking Investment Opportunities*. I've never heard of ESIM – not really my thing – but then investment funds aren't really my thing either.

There's nothing else interesting about the guy's things, so I continue to sip my drink and run my mind over my outfit options for tonight. And I'm just wondering where my blue lace top has got to when something in my mind tweaks. Alarm bells have started to ring. Something's wrong.

Something's happening.

Or something's about to happen.

My brain can't even articulate what it is, properly, but my sixth sense is kicking in. I have to act. Now.

Quick, Fixie. *Go.*

Before I've even thought clearly what's happening, I'm diving across the table like a rugby champion scoring a try, cradling the guy's laptop. A split second later, a whole section of the ceiling crashes down on top of me, in a gush of plaster and water.

'Argh!'

'Oh my God!'

'Help!'

'Is it an *attack*?'

'Help that girl!'

The screams around me are a din in my head. I can feel someone pulling at me, saying, 'Get away from there!' But I'm so worried about the laptop getting wet that I won't move from my rigid protective position until I feel paper towels being thrust at me. The water has finally stopped cascading, but plaster is still falling in bits from above, and as I raise my head at last, I see a freaked-out audience of customers watching me.

'I thought you were dead!' says a teenage girl so tearfully I can't help laughing – and this seems to set off everyone else.

'I saw that water dripping! I knew this would happen.'

'You could have been killed, innit!'

'You need to sue. That's not right, ceilings falling down.'

A moment ago we were all strangers in a coffee shop, studiously ignoring one another. Now it's as though we're best friends. An elderly guy holds out his hand and says, 'I'll hold your computer while you get dry, dear.'

But I don't want to give it up, so I awkwardly mop myself with one hand, thinking, 'Of all the days, of all the days . . .'

'What the *hell* ?'

It's the guy. He's come back inside, and he's staring at me, his mouth open. Gradually the excited comments die down and the coffee shop falls silent. Everyone's watching the pair of us expectantly.

'Oh, hi,' I say, speaking for the first time since I was drenched. 'Here's your laptop. I hope it isn't wet.'

I hold it out – it isn't wet at all – and the guy steps forward to take it. He's looking from me to the ravaged ceiling to the puddles of water and plaster, with increasing disbelief. 'What *happened* ?'

'There was a slight ceiling incident,' I say, trying to downplay it. But like a Greek chorus, all the other customers eagerly start filling him in.

'The ceiling fell in.'

'She dived across the table. Like lightning!'

'She saved your computer. No question. It would have been ruined.'

'Ladies and gentlemen.' A barista raps on the counter to gain our attention. 'Apologies. Due to a health and safety incident, we are closing now. Please come to the counter for a takeaway cup and complimentary cookie.'

There's a surge towards the counter and the most

senior-looking barista of them all comes up to me, her brow crumpled.

'Madam, we would like to apologize for your discomfort,' she says. 'We would like to present you with this fifty-pound voucher and hope that you will not . . .' She clears her throat. 'We will be glad to pay for the dry-cleaning of your clothes.'

'Don't worry,' I say, rolling my eyes. 'I'm not going to *sue*. But I wouldn't mind another mint tea.'

The barista visibly relaxes and hurries off to make it. Meanwhile, the guy in the suit has been scrolling through his laptop. Now he looks up at me with a stricken expression. 'I don't know how to thank you. You've saved my life.'

'Not your *life*.'

'OK, you've saved my bacon. It's not just the computer – that would have been bad enough. But the stuff *on* the computer. Stuff I should have backed up.' He closes his eyes briefly, shaking his head as though in disbelief. 'What a lesson.'

'Well,' I say. 'These things happen. Lucky I was there.'

'Lucky for me,' he says slowly, closing the laptop and surveying me properly. The late sun is full on his face now. His eyes are so green and woodlandy I find myself thinking briefly of deer in dappled forest glades; leafy branches; peaty scents. Then I blink and I'm back in the coffee shop. 'It wasn't lucky for you,' the guy is saying. 'You're a mess and your hair's wet. All on my account. I feel terrible.'

'It wasn't on your account,' I say, embarrassed under his gaze. My T-shirt feels wet, I suddenly register. But how wet? Wet-T-shirt-contest wet? Is *that* why the whole coffee shop was staring at me? Because my T-shirt is, in fact, transparent?

'The ceiling fell in,' I continue, folding my arms casually across my chest. 'I got wet. Nothing to do with you.'

'But would you have dived in that direction if you hadn't promised to look after my laptop?' he counters at once. 'Of course not. You obviously have very quick reactions. You would have dived out of harm's way.'

'Well, whatever.' I shrug it off.

'Not whatever.' He shakes his head firmly. 'I'm indebted to you. Can I . . . I don't know. Buy you a coffee?'

'No, thanks.'

'A muffin?' He squints at the display. 'The double chocolate chip one looks good.'

'No!' I laugh. 'Really.'

'What about . . . Can I buy you dinner?'

'I'm not sure Briony would appreciate it,' I can't resist saying. 'Sorry, I overheard you talking.'

A wry smile comes across his face and he says, '*Touché.*'

'Anyway, it was nice to meet you,' I say, taking my mint tea from the barista. 'But I'd better get going.'

'There must be something I can do to thank you,' he insists.

'No, really, nothing,' I say, equally firmly. 'I'm fine.'

I smile politely, then turn and head towards the door. And I'm nearly there when I hear him shout, 'Wait!' so loudly that I swivel back. 'Don't go,' he adds. 'Please. Just . . . hold on. I have something for you.'

I'm so intrigued, I take a few steps back into the coffee shop. He's standing at the counter with a cardboard coffee sleeve and a pen, and he's writing something.

'I always pay off my debts,' he says at last, coming towards me. 'Always.' He holds out the sleeve and I see that he's written on it:

I owe you one
Redeemable in perpetuity.

As I watch, he signs it underneath – a scribbly signature I can't quite make out, and puts the date.

'If you ever want a favour,' he says, looking up. 'Something I can do for you. Anything at all.' He reaches in his pocket, pulls out a business card and then looks around, frowning. 'I need a paper clip . . . or any kind of clip . . .'

'Here.' I put down my cup, reach into my Anna's Accessories bag and pull out a diamanté hair grip.

'Perfect.' He fixes the business card to the coffee sleeve with the hair grip. 'This is me. Sebastian Marlowe.'

'I'm Fixie Farr,' I reply.

'Fixie.' He nods gravely and extends a hand. 'How do you do?' We shake hands, then Sebastian proffers the coffee sleeve IOU.

'Please take it. I'm serious.'

'I can see.' My mouth can't help twitching. 'Well, if I need any "forward-looking investment opportunities", I'll let you know.'

My tone is a little mocking but he doesn't pick up on it – in fact, his green eyes light up.

'Yes! Please do! If that's the case, we can set up a meeting, I'd be delighted to give you some advice—'

'It's not the case.' I cut him off. 'Far from it. But I appreciate the offer.'

Belatedly he seems to realize I was teasing him, and his face flickers with a smile.

'Something you actually need, then.' He's still holding the coffee sleeve out to me, and at last I take it.

'OK. Thank you.'

To humour him, I put the coffee sleeve into my bag and pat it. 'There we are. Safe and sound. And now I really must be going. I have a family party I need to get back for.'

'You think I'm joking,' he says, watching as I pick up my cup. 'But I'm not. I owe you one, Fixie Farr. Remember that.'

'Oh, I will!' I say, and flash him a last, cheerful smile, not meaning a word of it. 'Absolutely. I really will.'

**Read *I Owe You One* in hardback,
ebook and audio from 7 February**